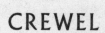

CREWEL

Gennifer Albin holds a master's degree in English Literature from the University of Missouri, and founded the tremendously popular blog theconnectedmom.com. She lives in Lenexa, Kansas, with her husband and two children. Learn more about her at genniferalbin.com.

CREWEL

Gennifer Albin

ff

faber and faber

First published in the US by Farrar Straus Giroux
Books for Young Readers in 2012
First published in the UK in this edition in 2012
by Faber and Faber Limited
Bloomsbury House
74–77 Great Russell Street,
London, WC1B 3DA

The right of Gennifer Albin to be identified as author
of this work has been asserted in accordance with Section 77
of the Copyright, Designs and Patents Act 1988

A CIP record for this book
is available from the British Library

ISBN 978–0–571–28289–0

1 3 5 7 9 10 8 6 4 2

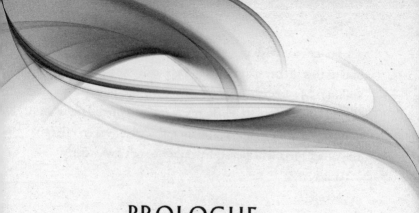

PROLOGUE

They came in the night. Once, families fought them, neighbours coming to their aid. But now that peace has been established, and the looms proven, girls pray to be retrieved. They still come at night, but now it's to avoid the masses with eager hands. It's a blessing to touch a Spinster as she passes. That's what they tell us.

No one knows why some girls have the gift. There are theories, of course. That it's passed down genetically. Or that girls with an open mind can see the weave of life around them at all times. Even that it's a gift only given to the pure-hearted. But I know better. It's a curse.

I've trained at night with my parents ever since they realised I had the calling. They taught me clumsiness, making me fumble until it looked natural when I dropped a bowl or spilled the water jug. Then we practised with time, my parents encouraging me to take the silky strands deftly into

my fingers to twist and tangle them until they were warped and useless in my hands. This was harder than dropping and spilling. My fingers wanted to weave the delicate tendrils seamlessly with matter. By my sixteenth birthday, when it was time for the required testing, the ruse was so effective, the other girls whispered I would be sent away early.

Incapable.

Awkward.

Artless.

Maybe it was their taunts lodging in my back like tiny daggers that poisoned my resolve. Or perhaps it was the way the practice loom sang out, begging to be touched. But today, the last day of testing, I finally slipped – my fingers gracefully winding though the ebbing bands of time.

Tonight they'll come for me.

1

I can count the days until summer draws to a close and autumn seeps into the leaves, painting them ginger and scarlet. Right now, though, the dappled light of mid-afternoon is glorious emerald, and it's hot on my face. With sun soaking into me, everything is possible. When it is inevitably gone – the seasons programmed to begin and end with smooth precision – life will take its predetermined route. Like a machine. Like me.

It's quiet outside my sister's academy. I'm the only one waiting for the girls to be released. When I first began my testing cycle, Amie held her pinkie finger up and made me swear to meet her each day after I got out. It was a hard promise to make, knowing they could call me any time and sweep me away to the Coventry's towers. But I make it, even today. A girl has to have something constant, has to know what to expect. The last bit of chocolate in the

3

monthly rations; the tidy ending to a programme on the Stream. I want my little sister to be able to count on a sweet life, even if the heat of summer tastes bitter now.

A bell tolls and girls pour out in a surge of plaid, their giggles and shouts breaking the perfect stillness of the scene. Amie, who's always had more friends than me, bounces out, surrounded by a handful of other girls in the awkward stages of early adolescence. I wave to her and she dashes towards me, catching my hand and pulling me in the direction of our house. Something about her eager greeting every afternoon makes it okay that I don't have many companions my age.

'Did you do it?' she asks in a breathless voice, skipping ahead of me.

I hesitate for a moment. If anyone will be happy about my mistake, it will be Amie. If I tell her the truth, she'll squeal and clap. She'll hug me, and maybe for a moment I can leach her happiness, fill myself up with it, and believe everything is going to turn out fine.

'No,' I lie, and her face falls.

'It's okay,' she says with a resolved nod. 'At least this way you get to stay in Romen. With me.'

I'd rather pretend she's right, to allow myself to get lost in the twelve-year-old's gossip, than face what's coming. I have my whole life to be a Spinster, and only one more night to be her sister. I ooh and aah at the right times, and she believes I'm listening. I imagine that the attention builds her up and completes her, so that when I'm gone she'll have enough not to waste her life searching for it.

Amie's primary academy lets out at the same time as the metro's day shift, so Mom is waiting when we get home.

4

She's in the kitchen and her head snaps up as we enter, her eyes rushing to meet mine. Taking a deep breath, I shake my head, and her shoulders slump in relief. I let her hug me as long as she wants, her embrace flooding me with love. That's why I don't tell them the truth. I want love — not excitement or worry — to be the lingering imprint they leave on me.

Mom reaches up and brushes a strand of hair from my face, but she doesn't smile. Although she thinks I failed at testing, she also knows my time here is almost up. She's thinking that I'll be assigned a role soon, and married shortly thereafter, even if I won't be taken away. What's the point of telling her she'll lose me tonight? It's not important now, and this moment is what matters.

It's an ordinary evening at our ordinary table, and apart from the overcooked pot roast — Mom's speciality and a rare treat — not much is different, not for my family at least. The grandfather clock ticks in our hall, cicadas perform their summer crescendo, a motopact rumbles down the street, and outside the sky fades into dusky twilight beckoning nightfall. It's a day just like the hundreds that came before it, but tonight I won't tiptoe from my bed to my parents' room. The end of testing also means the end of years of training.

I live with my family in a tiny bungalow outside Romen's metro where my parents have been assigned two children and an appropriately sized house. My mom told me they applied for another child when I was eight — before they discovered my condition — but upon evaluation they were denied. The cost to maintain each individual makes it ne-

cessary for the Guild to regulate population. She explained this matter-of-factly one morning as she pinned her hair up into elaborate curls before work. I had asked her for a brother. She waited until I was older to explain that it would have been impossible anyway, due to segregation, but I was still mortified. Pushing my rations around my plate, I realise how much easier it would be if I had been a boy, or if my sister was a boy. I bet my parents wanted boys, too. Then they wouldn't have to worry about us being taken away.

'Adelice,' my mother says quietly, 'you aren't eating. Testing is over. I would think you'd have an appetite.'

She's very good at projecting a calm demeanour, but I sometimes wonder if the carefully painted cosmetics layered until her face is silken with rouged cheeks and plump lips are a ruse to help her stay balanced. She makes it look effortless – the cosmetics, her perfectly pinned scarlet hair, and her secretary suit. She appears to be exactly what is expected of a woman: beautiful, groomed, obedient. I never knew there was another side to her until I was eleven, the year she and my father began training my fingers towards uselessness.

'I'm fine.' My response is flat and unbelievable, and I wish I had a perfectly painted face to hide under. Girls are expected to remain pure and natural – in body and appearance – until they're officially released from testing. Purity standards ensure that girls with weaving abilities don't lose them by being promiscuous. Some of my classmates look as beautiful in this state as my mother – delicate and fair. I'm *too* pale. My skin is washed out against my strawberry hair.

6

If only it was the brilliant fiery red of my mother's or soft gold like my sister Amie's, but mine is as dull as dirty pennies.

'Your mother made a special dinner,' my dad points out. His voice is kind, but the implication is clear: I'm wasting food. Staring at the potatoes and too-dry slices of roast beef, I feel guilty. This meal probably ate up two nights' rations, and then there's the cake.

It's a large frosted cake from a bakery. My mom has made us small cakes for our birthdays, but nothing like this fancy white cake with sugar flowers and lacy lines of frosting. I know it cost half a week's rations. Most likely they'll resort to eating it for breakfast later in the week while they wait for their next disbursement. The frail white scallops edging the cake make my stomach turn. I'm not used to sweets, and I'm not hungry. As it is, I can barely bring myself to eat a few bites of the overcooked meat.

'This is exactly the cake I want for my birthday,' Amie gushes. She's never had anything like a bakery cake before. When Amie came home from academy today and saw this one, my mom told her she could have one for her next birthday. It's a pretty big deal for a kid who's only had hand-me-downs her whole life, but my mom obviously wants to soften her transition into training.

'It will have to be a bit smaller,' Mom reminds her, 'and you won't be having any of this one if you don't eat your dinner first.'

I can't help smiling as Amie's eyes widen and she begins scooping food into her mouth, gulping it down hard. Mom calls her 'an eater'. I wish I could eat like her when I'm ex-

cited or tense or sad, but nerves kill my appetite, and the fact that this is the last dinner I'll ever share with my family has my stomach in knots.

'Did you get this for Adelice?' Amie asks between bites, revealing bits of chewed food.

'Close your mouth when you eat,' my dad says, but I see the corner of his own curling up a bit.

'Yes, Adelice deserved something special today.' My mother's voice is quiet, but as she speaks her face glows and a faint smile plays at her lips. 'I thought we should celebrate.'

'Marfa Crossix's sister came home from testing last week crying and hasn't left her room yet,' Amie continues after swallowing the meat. 'Marfa said it was like someone died. Everyone is so sad. Her parents are already setting up courtship appointments to cheer her up. She has an appointment with pretty much every boy with an active marriage profile in Romen.'

Amie laughs, but the rest of the table falls silent. I'm studying the scallops in the icing, trying to make out the delicate pattern the baker used. Amie doesn't notice the quiet resistance of my parents to the Guild-approved curriculum and marriage laws, but they haven't exactly been honest with her either. I'm old enough to understand why they don't want me to become a Spinster, even if they've always been careful with what they say to me.

My father clears his throat and looks at my mother for support. 'Some girls really want to go to the Coventry. Marfa's sister must be disappointed.'

'I would be, too,' Amie chirps, shovelling a forkful of pota-

toes into her mouth. 'They showed us pictures at academy. Spinsters are so beautiful, and they have everything.'

'I suppose,' Mom murmurs, slicing small bites of meat with her knife in slow, precise strokes.

'I can't wait for testing.' Amie sighs dreamily, and my mother frowns at her. Amie's in too much of a daze to notice.

'Those girls are very privileged, but if Adelice was called, we would never see her again.' Mom's response is careful. My parents have started trying to plant doubt in Amie's head, although her tendency to rattle on to anyone listening makes it hard to talk to her about important stuff. But I don't mind listening to Amie relate the dramas of every girl in her class or the programmes she saw on the Stream. It's my break before spending every night practising and rehearsing what to say – and not to say. Curling up with my sister before she falls asleep is when I get my only sense of normal.

But a cake can't buy more than a night's happiness. My parents will have a long road ahead of them preparing Amie to fail at her testing. She's never shown an ounce of weaving ability, but they'll prepare her. I wonder if she'll still be eager to go when it's her turn in four years.

'Marfa says when she's a Spinster she'll always get her picture on the front of the *Bulletin* so her parents won't worry. That's what I'd do, too.' Her face is solemn as though she's really thought this through.

Mom smiles but doesn't respond. Amie fawns over the glitzy images in our daily bulletin like most pre-testing girls, but she doesn't truly understand what Spinsters do.

I mean, of course she understands that they maintain and embellish the fabric that makes up our world. Every girl learns that early in academy. But someday my parents will explain what Spinsters really do – that no matter how good their intentions, with absolute power comes corruption. And the Guild has absolute power over us and the Spinsters. But they also feed us and protect us. I listen to my parents, but I don't really understand either. Can a life of providing food and safety for others be that bad? I only know that what's about to happen to me is going to break their hearts, and once I'm gone, I'll never have a chance to tell them I'm okay. I guess I'll have to get my picture on the front of the *Bulletin* like Marfa Crossix.

The meal continues in silence, and everyone's eyes gravitate toward our fluffy white centrepiece. The small oak dining table sits four perfectly; we can pass bowls and plates to one another, but tonight my mother served us because there's room for nothing but the cake. I envy the gleeful sparkle in Amie's eyes as she stares at it, probably imagining how it will taste or building her grand thirteenth birthday cake in her head. My parents, on the other hand, sit in quiet relief: the closest to celebrating they can muster.

'I'm sorry you failed, Ad,' Amie says, looking up at me. Her eyes dart back to the cake, and I see the longing in them.

'Adelice didn't fail,' my father tells her.

'But she wasn't chosen.'

'We didn't want her to be chosen,' my mother says.

'Did you want to be chosen, Ad?' Amie's question is so earnest and innocent.

I barely shake my head.

'But why not?' Amie asks.

'Do you want that life?' Mom asks her quietly.

'Why are you so against the Spinsters? I don't get why we're celebrating.' Amie's eyes stay focused on the cake. She's never been so blunt before.

'We're not against the Spinsterhood,' Mom responds in a rush.

'Or the Guild,' Dad adds.

'Or the Guild,' Mom echoes with a nod. 'But if you pass testing, you can never return here.'

Here – the cramped two-bedroom house in the girls' neighbourhood, where I've been safe from the influence of boys my age. My home, with books stashed in hollowed cubbies behind panels in the walls, along with family heirlooms passed down for almost one hundred years from mother to daughter. I've always loved the radio in particular, even if it doesn't work any more. Mom says that it used to play music and stories and proclaimed the news, like the Stream does now but without the visuals. I asked once why we kept it if it was useless, and she told me that remembering the past is never useless.

'But a Spinster's life is exciting,' Amie argues. 'They have parties and beautiful dresses. Spinsters have control.'

Her last word hangs in the air, and my parents exchange a worried glance. Control? No one granting permission to have children. No predetermined cosmetic routines. No chosen roles. That would be true control.

'If you think they have control—' Mom begins quietly, but my father coughs.

'They have cake,' Amie says with a sigh, slumping against the table.

Dad takes one look at her pitiful face, throws his head back, and laughs. A moment later, my usually stoic mother joins in. Even I feel some giggles bubbling up my throat. Amie does her best to look sad, but her frown twitches until it turns into an impish grin.

'Your cosmetic tokens should arrive next week, Adelice,' my mom says, turning back to me. 'I'll show you how to apply everything.'

'Arras knows, I'd better be able to apply cosmetics. Isn't that a girl's most important job?' The jibe is out of my mouth before I consider what I'm saying. I have a habit of cracking a joke when I'm nervous. But judging from the look of warning on my mom's face, I'm not being very funny.

'And I'll jump right on those courtship appointments,' Dad says with a wink, breaking up the tension between Mom and me.

This actually makes me laugh, despite the numbing dread creeping through my limbs. My parents aren't as eager to get me married and out of the house as most girls' families are, even if I am required to be married by eighteen. But the joke can't elevate my mood for long. Right now the thought of getting married, an inevitability that was always too surreal to consider, is out of the question. Spinsters don't marry.

'And I get to help you choose your cosmetic colours at the co-op, right?' Amie reminds me. She's been studying catalogues and style sets since she could read. Mom doesn't

take us to the metro co-op to shop often, because it's not segregated, and when she has it's been for home supplies, not something exciting like cosmetics.

'I hear they're increasing the number of teachers in the Corps on assignment day,' Dad continues, serious again.

I've always wanted to be a teacher. Secretary, nurse, factory worker – none of the other designated female roles left any room for creativity. Even in a carefully controlled academy curriculum there is more room for expression in teaching than there is in typing notes for businessmen.

'Oh, Ad, you'd be a great teacher,' Amie bursts in. 'Whatever you do, don't get stuck in an office. We just finished our shorthand class, and it was so boring. Besides you have to food-gen coffee all day! Right, Mom?'

Amie looks to her for confirmation, and Mom gives her a quick nod. My sister's too oblivious to see the pain flash across her face, but I'm not.

'I do make a lot of coffee,' Mom says.

My throat is raw from holding back tears, and if I speak . . .

'I'm sure you'll get assigned to be a teacher,' Mom says, eager to change the subject, and then she pats my arm. I must look nervous. I try to imagine what I would be feeling now if assignment day was only a week away for me, but I can't. I was supposed to go to testing for a month, to be dismissed, and then get assigned. It was the first time I'd been on a loom, one of the large automated machines that show us the fabric of Arras. It was the first time any of us Eligibles had even seen a loom. I only had to act as if I couldn't see the weave, like the other girls, and answer the proctor's questions with my practised lies. If I hadn't

slipped, I would have been dismissed, and then assigned based on my strength assessments at academy. For years, I'd dutifully learned shorthand, home economics, and information storage. But now I'd never get the chance to use any of it.

'We need a new teacher.' Amie interrupts my thoughts. 'Mrs Swander left.'

'Is she expecting a baby?' my mother asks in a knowing way. Her eyes dull a bit as she speaks.

'No.' Amie shakes her head. 'Principal Diffet said she had an accident.'

'An accident?' Dad repeats with a frown.

'Yep.' Amie nods, suddenly wide-eyed. 'I've never known anyone who's had an accident before.' Her voice is a mix of awe and solemnity. None of us know anyone who has had an accident, because accidents don't happen in Arras.

'Did Principal Diffet say what happened?' Mom asks so softly that I barely hear her in the quiet dining room.

'No, but he told us not to worry because accidents are very rare and the Guild will be especially careful and investigate and stuff. Is she okay?' she asks, her voice conveying implicit trust. Whatever my father replies, she'll believe it. I long to fall back in time and feel the comfort of knowing my parents have every answer, knowing I am safe.

My father forces a tight-lipped smile and nods at her. Mom's eyes meet mine.

'Do you think it's odd?' She leans in to Dad, so Amie won't hear. It doesn't matter because Amie has returned to worshipping the cake.

'An accident? Of course.'

'No.' Mom shakes her head. 'That the principal told them.'

'It must have been bad,' he whispers.

'Something Manipulation Services couldn't cover up?'

'We haven't heard anything at the station.'

'None of the girls said anything today.'

I wish I had some intelligence to share, because I'm feeling excluded. Outside the dining room night has engulfed our quiet street. I can see the shadowed outline of the oak tree in our yard but little else. It won't be long now, and we're wasting time worrying about Mrs Swander's accident.

'We should eat the cake!' The suggestion bursts from me. My mother, momentarily startled, does a quick inventory of our plates and agrees.

Dad cuts into the cake with an old bread knife, smearing frosting across the blade and blending the vibrant red flowers into dull pink globs. Amie props her body against the table, completely absorbed in the ceremony, while Mom collects the pieces from Dad and passes them around. I'm bringing the first bite to my mouth when Mom stops me.

'Adelice, may your path be blessed. We're proud of you.' There's a break in her voice, and I know how much this moment means to her. She's waited my whole life for this night: my release from testing. I can barely meet her eyes. She motions for us to eat as she wipes a stray tear from her cheek, leaving a smudge of charcoal from her running mascara.

I take a bite and mash it against the roof of my mouth.

The frosting is so sweet that it catches in my throat and makes my nose tingle. I have to wash it down with half a glass of water. Next to me Amie is devouring her piece, but my mother doesn't tell her to slow down. Now that I'm through testing, it's Amie's turn. Tomorrow my parents plan to begin preparing her for her own testing.

'Girls—' my mother begins, but I'll never know what she was going to say.

There's a hammering at the door and the sound of many, many boots on our porch. I drop my fork and feel the blood rush out of my face and pool in my feet, weighting me to my chair.

'Adelice,' my father breathes, but he doesn't ask, because he already knows.

'There isn't time, Benn!' my mother shrieks, her perfectly applied foundation cracking, but just as quickly she regains control and grabs Amie's arm.

A low hum fills the air and suddenly a voice booms through the room: 'Adelice Lewys has been called to serve the Guild of Twelve. Blessings on the Spinsters and Arras!'

Our neighbours will be outside soon; no one in Romen would willingly miss a retrieval. There's nowhere to escape. Everyone here knows me. I rise to my feet to open the door for the retrieval squad, but my father pushes me towards the stairs.

'Daddy!' There's fear in Amie's voice.

I grope forward and find her hand, squeezing it tight. I stumble down behind her as my father herds us to the basement. I have no idea what his plan is. The only thing down here is a dank, meagrely stocked root cellar. Mom rushes

to the basement wall and a moment later she slides a stack of bricks out of place to reveal a narrow tunnel.

Amie and I stand and watch; her wide-eyed horror mirrors the paralysing fear I feel. The scene before us shifts and blurs. I can't wrap my head around what they're doing even as I see it happening. The only constant – the one real thing in this moment – is Amie's fragile hand clutching my own. I hold on to it for life, hers and mine. It anchors me, and when my mother wrenches her away, I shriek, sure I'll vanish into nothing.

'Ad,' Amie cries, stretching out to me through Mom's arms.

It's her fear that spurs me back to this moment, and I call out to her, 'It's okay, Ames. Go with Mommy.'

My mother's hands falter for a moment when I say this. I can't remember when I last called her Mommy. I've been too old and too busy for as long as I can remember. Tears that have been building up wash down her face, and she drops her hold on Amie. My sister jumps into my arms, and I inhale the scent of her soap-clean hair, aware of how fast her small heart beats against my belly. Mom circles us and I soak up the strength of her warm arms. But it's over too quickly, and with a kiss on my forehead, they're gone.

'Adelice, here!' My father shoves me towards another hole as Amie and Mom disappear into the passage, but before I enter he grabs my wrist and presses cold metal near my vein. A second later heat sears the tender skin. When he releases my arm, I draw the spot up to my mouth, trying to blow off the burning.

'What . . .' I search his face for a reason for the tech-

print, and looking back down, I see the pale shape of a flowing hourglass marking the spot. It's barely visible on my fair skin.

'I should have done it a long time ago, but . . .' He shakes off the emotion creeping into his voice and sets his jaw. 'It will help you remember who you are. You have to leave now, honey.'

I look into the tunnel that stretches into nothing. 'Where does it go?' I can't keep the panic out of my voice. There's nowhere to hide in Arras, and this is treason.

Above us a stampede of heavy boots breaks across the wooden floor.

'Go,' he pleads.

They're in the dining room.

'There's food on the table! They can't be far.'

'Search the rest of the house and cordon off the street.'

The feet are in the kitchen now.

'Dad . . .' I throw my arms around him, unsure if he will follow me or go into another tunnel.

'I knew we could never hide how special you are,' he murmurs against my hair. The basement door bangs open.

But before I can say I'm sorry for failing them, or tell him I love him, the boots are on the stairs. I scramble into the hole. He restacks the bricks behind me, shutting out the light. My chest constricts in the darkness. And then he stops. A large crack of light still streams in to the tunnel from the basement. I can't move.

The bricks crash onto the concrete floor and light floods back into the tunnel. Choking down the scream fighting to loose itself, I struggle forward in the dirt, away from the

growing light. I must keep moving forward. I try to forget Dad, and Mom and Amie in the other tunnel, as I crawl through the cold soil.

Keep moving forward.

I repeat it over and over, afraid that if I stop I will be paralysed again. But somehow I do keep moving forward, further and further into darkness, until cold steel clamps down on my leg. I scream as it digs into my skin and begins drawing me back – back to the light and the men in boots, back to the Guild. I tear against the packed dirt of the tunnel, but the claw is stronger and each desperate lunge I make back towards the darkness drives the metal deeper into my calf.

There is no fighting them.

2

As they pull me from the escape tunnel, someone jabs a needle in my wounded leg. I thrash as the liquid burns through my calf, but suddenly I'm calm. When one of the officers helps me stand in the damp basement, I smile at him. I can't remember being happier.

'Patch that up,' barks a tall official coming down the basement stairs. He's not like the others, who are dressed in typical soldier's regalia. He is older and very handsome. His jaw is too smoothly sculpted to be natural, but the slight grey peppering his styled hair gives away his age. His nose, eyes, and teeth are too perfect, and I bet he's been taking advantage of renewal patches. He has the kind of face they put on the Stream to read the news. I blink dreamily at him as a medic begins cleaning the wound from the claw. A group of women scurry down behind the official and begin wiping my face and combing my hair. It feels

so nice I want to fall asleep. The only thing keeping me awake is the cold, gritty concrete under my bare feet. I've lost my shoes in the struggle.

'You gave her too much,' the official grumbles. 'I said get her Stream-ready, not dose her out of her mind.'

'I'm sorry. She was really fighting us,' one of the officers tells him. I can hear the grin in his voice.

'Fix it.'

A moment later another needle pricks my arm, and I stop smiling. I'm still calm, but the euphoria is fading.

'Adelice Lewys?' the official asks, and I nod. 'Do you understand what's going on?'

I try to say yes but nothing comes out, so I bob my head once more.

'There's a Stream crew upstairs and most of your neighbourhood. I'd prefer we didn't have to drag you off looking like a loose thread, but if you try that again I'll have him dose you. Do you understand what I'm saying?' He points to the medic who has finished healing my wound.

I manage to squeak, 'Yes.'

'Good girl. We'll deal with this later,' he says, gesturing to the escape tunnel. 'Your job is to smile and look thrilled to be selected. Can you do that?'

I stare at him.

The official sighs and cocks his head to activate the microscopic complant embedded over his left ear. The device automatically connects you to any other complant user or wall-communication panel. I've seen men in the metro chatting on them, but my father's role as a mechanic doesn't warrant the privilege of having one implanted. A

moment later I'm privy to the man's one-sided conversation.

'Hannox, do you have them? No, hold her.' Turning back to me, he points to the hole my mother and Amie disappeared through. 'Let's pretend my colleague has someone you love very much in his custody, and your performance for the Stream crew decides whether she lives or dies. Can you look thrilled now?'

I muster up the brightest smile I can and flash it at him.

'Not bad, Adelice.' But then he frowns and pushes away the grooming crew. 'Are you idiots? This is a retrieval. She can't wear cosmetics!'

I look away as he continues to berate the aestheticians, and search for signs of my father. He's nowhere, but as my eyes scan the wall I can't make out any other cracks that could hide a passage. Of course, until twenty minutes ago I hadn't known about even the first two passages.

'Are we clear?' the official asks the medic.

'Give her one more minute.'

'I'm fine,' I say with a smile, practising for the Stream crew. But as soon as I speak, my stomach contracts hard and sends my dinner back up my throat. I double over and retch up pot roast and frothy cream.

'Fantastic,' the official bellows. 'Can't I even get a competent squad?'

'She'll be fine now,' the medic says, backing up a few steps.

The official glowers at him and then turns and leads me to the stairs. At the last step, he grabs my arm and leans in close. 'Make it look real. Her life depends on it.'

I don't have the guts to ask him if he means my mother or my sister; his answer will only tell me who is dead. I stagger up the stairs and blink hard against the bright lights of the main floor. Every lamp is on and the kitchen and dining room have been ransacked. As we march through the dining room on our way to the front door, I slip on something dark and sticky. One of the officers catches my arm as I stumble, and I snap my head down to the spot on the floor. It's nearly black and pools out from a large, stiff bag.

I crumple back against the man behind me.

'No time for that now, sweetheart,' he hisses. 'You've got a show to put on or we're going to need more of those bags.'

I can't tear my eyes from the bag, so he leads me away. I try to tell him there's blood on my feet, but he's already barking more orders at his squad.

'Halt,' commands a guard at the door.

The official steps forward, runs his eyes over me, sighs, and steps out onto the porch to thunderous applause. I turn away and focus on the long black bag, but a guard moves over to the table, blocking my view. I glance over to see he's eating the cake.

'Hey,' I call, and everyone looks at me in surprise. 'That's half a week's rations! Leave it for my family.'

The officer's eyes dart to his companion, and I see it on their faces – pity – but he sets down the cake.

'Blessings, Romen! I'm Cormac Patton and . . .' The rude official addresses the crowd from my porch. More applause. He waits a moment for it to calm down.

'He always has time for applause,' an aesthetician notes drily.

'Blessings, Arras. I'm Cormac Patton,' her companion mimics him in a low voice, and they laugh until a guard shushes them.

Cormac Patton. Coventry Ambassador for the Guild of Twelve and the Stream's number-one pretty boy. How could I have not recognised him? They must have really drugged me. Or maybe I'm not used to celebrities hanging out in my basement. Even my mom has a thing for him. But I don't see the appeal. Sure, he's perpetually clad in a black, double-breasted tuxedo, and very handsome, but he has to be at least forty. Or maybe even older, since I can't remember a time in my life when he looked anything but forty.

I can't comprehend that he's standing on my porch right now.

'We are privileged to call to service Adelice Lewys,' Cormac's voice bellows. An officer pushes me out next to him. 'May Arras flourish at her touch.'

The crowd echoes back the blessing and colour floods my cheeks. I paste the bright smile on my face and will it to stick.

'Wave,' Cormac instructs me through gritted teeth, his own smile undiminished as he gives the command.

I wave shyly and keep beaming at the crowd. A moment later, officers surround and flank us, escorting us to a waiting motocarriage. The crowd swarms into a mob and all I see are hands. The officers hold most of them back, and I shrink away from the mob. Everywhere I look, fingers claw at me, grabbing for a bit of my skirt or a caress of my hair.

I'm breathing faster, and beside me Cormac frowns. The drugs must not be as strong as he thought. I think of his threat and force myself to look excited.

The motocarriage is longer than any of the motopacts I've seen in Romen. I've seen ones like this on the Stream. Motopacts are daily cars to drive into the metro, but motocarriages like this have chauffeurs. I fix my eyes on it; I only have to make it that far and then this public charade will be over. An officer ushers me to the rear side door and helps me in. As the door shuts me safely away from the cheering crowd, I scowl.

'That's much more attractive,' Cormac mutters as he slides in next to me. 'At least you're the last retrieval.'

'Had a long day?' I ask harshly.

'No, but I can't imagine dragging your deadweight around much longer,' he snaps back as he pours himself a glass of amber liquid. He doesn't bother to offer me any.

I lapse into silence. Deadweight. The image of the body bag lying casually on my dining-room floor floats into my head and hot tears prick my eyes, threatening to spill over.

I stare out of the window so he won't see me cry. The glass is tinted and the crowd can no longer watch us, but they're still milling around. Neighbours talk animatedly, pointing to our house. Several heads incline, relaying the news to people far away on their complants. We haven't had a retrieval in Romen in ten years. Tomorrow I'll be on Romen's morning Stream. I wonder what they'll say about my parents. My sister.

Cormac is downing the last drops of his cocktail when his head cocks to the side to take a call. 'Here,' he grunts.

He's quiet but soon indifference turns to mild annoyance.

'Clean it,' he says. 'No, clean all of it.'

His head shifts back down, disconnecting from the call, and he looks at me. 'Lucky girl.'

I shrug, not willing to betray my feelings at the moment. I'm not sure what cleaning is, and from the way he growled the order, I'm not sure I want to know.

'Oh, you have no idea,' he says. 'How's your leg?'

I glance down to the gashes the claw left and find they're gone.

'Fine, I guess.' I try to keep the surprise out of my voice but can't.

'Renewal patch,' he informs me. 'One of the many perks you'll have as a Spinster.'

I don't respond, and he returns to the crystal bottle for another drink. My eyes wander back to the window. We're nearly out of Romen, and it's hard to believe I'll never come back here. The view grows hazy and my eyelids droop; the drugs they administered earlier are making me sleepy. But right before my eyes close, the street disappears behind us, shimmering and fading into nothing.

An officer shakes me awake when we get to the Nilus Station and hands me a pair of shoes. Another escorts me to the toilet and stands guard. Afterwards, I'm taken to a small private powder room and given a simple white shift to change into. They take away everything I was wearing before. I dress as slowly as possible, trying to sift through the fog in my head.

I can't put off going out into the station for long. The

26

Nilus Station is situated in the capital of the Western Sector and it rebounds travellers to the other three capital cities in Arras. It's also strictly policed. Only the most important businessmen can travel between the four sectors; someone like my dad wouldn't qualify. I've never been out of Romen's city limits before today. I should be excited, but all I feel is a dull twinge at the thought.

Cormac is lounging in a turquoise chair outside the powder room.

'Ever been to a rebound station, Adelice?' Cormac asks conversationally as he stands to greet me when I step back into the station lobby.

I shake my head. I'm not eager to act like we're friends.

'Didn't think so. It's pretty rare these days for some citizens to get border passes.' He smiles, and for the first time I notice a crease in his flawless skin. By 'some citizens' he means women and service workers.

Cormac sets the pace, and I stroll with him along the periphery of the station. There's a small booth offering shoe shines, a coat-check stand, and a little café. He gestures for me to follow him into the restaurant, and we're led up to the second-floor mezzanine by a waiter. From here we can watch the travellers waiting for their rebound appointments in the great marble hall. Even though it's busy, the sounds of travel – shoes clicking, complant conversations, rustling *Bulletins* – fill the space and bounce back across it. The roar of energy is nearly deafening.

'Miss, I'll need to see your privilege card,' the waiter says, sneering at me.

I glance down at my simple dress and realise I don't even

have my citizen ID with me, but Cormac speaks before I can make excuses.

'She's my guest. Do you need to see my PC?' It's more a challenge than a question.

The waiter glances at him and the haughty smile evaporates. 'Ambassador Patton, I apologise. I didn't recognise you. I only saw the girl.'

Something about the way he says *the girl* makes me feel dirty.

'No need to apologise. You don't get many girls in here, I imagine.' He laughs, and the waiter joins him.

'We weren't informed there would be a retrieval squad travelling through, or we would have been prepared,' the young man assures him.

'It was a last-minute retrieval, so the usual call-aheads weren't possible.'

'So she's a . . .' He eyes me admiringly.

'She is an Eligible. Treat her as you would a Spinster.' There's an edge of warning to Cormac's voice, and the young man nods solemnly.

He waits on me hand and foot, although I'm not allowed to order for myself. And as if a hovering waiter isn't annoying enough, every man in the place stares at me. It's the shameless gaze of the patrons that provokes a startling realisation. Glancing back at the bustling travellers, I see the outline of suits and fedoras. The only other woman in the station takes coats at the stand I noticed earlier. Apparently only men are allowed to eat here. I knew rebounding was reserved for important businessmen, but I never realised that even the station was segregated. I rub

my hands on the hem of my shift, aware of how warm it is here.

'Lecherous lot,' Cormac says, and chuckles. 'Actually, you don't see many women out from behind the desk these days. Not without their husbands.'

It takes a minute for me to realise he means me. I'm the woman out and about.

'I'd suggest eating. I know you can't have much left in you after that stupid medic screwed up. You would think they would know how much juice to give a 52 kg girl, and yet it's always too much or too little. You're lucky though – the Nilus Station has a great café.' He tips his head back toward the kitchen door. 'It might be a while before you eat again.'

'I'm not very hungry,' I say. My lamb chop sits untouched on the plate in front of me. Cormac's meal is similarly neglected, for all his advice to eat, but only because he's nursing a bourbon.

Cormac leans against the table and looks at me. 'I figured as much. Take my advice though, and eat something.'

I think of the dining-room table and white cake sitting on it, the puddle of black blood under its legs, and shake my head. The only thing I'm hungry for is answers.

'Eat, and I'll tell you what you want to know.'

I take a couple of bites, knowing I won't be able to eat if he answers me first anyway, but as soon as I swallow, I turn my attention back to him. 'Are they dead?' The words come out flat, and in that moment I know I've lost hope.

'Your father is,' Cormac admits in a low voice. There's no remorse in his face. It's a fact.

I look down and take a deep breath. 'And my mother and sister?'

'Your sister is in custody, but I have no news on your mother.'

'Then she got away?' I ask breathlessly, wondering how they managed to catch Amie. Despite the news about my father, I feel a tug of hope.

'She got away for now. You'll be more upset later when the Valpron wears off.'

'Maybe I'm stronger than you think,' I challenge, although I'm all too aware of the numbness throughout my body.

'That would be a surprise. Valpron is a calming agent.' Cormac's eyes narrow, and he sets down his fork. 'What was your plan anyway?'

'Plan?'

'Don't be stupid, Adelice,' he snarls. 'They found four tunnels under your house that lead to places around your neighbourhood. Where were you going to go?'

'I have no idea. I didn't know about them.' It's the truth. I'm not sure I could lie right now if I wanted to, but I'd never guessed exactly how far my parents were willing to go to keep me from the Guild. How long ago had they dug those four tunnels, and how had they got away with it? From the way Cormac is staring at me, I'm sure he believes I know more than I'm telling.

Cormac snorts, but resumes eating. Or rather, drinking. 'Sure you didn't. Just like you didn't try to fail at the testing.'

My eyes snap up to his, and I wonder how much he knows about this, but I don't say anything else.

'I've seen the surveillance Stream on your testing. The moment you wove was an accident,' he continues.

'I had no idea what I was doing,' I say, and in truth, I didn't. I'd never used a loom to weave before and something about seeing the fabric of life – the very raw materials that composed the space around me – laid out before me, rattled me. We'd been measured and questioned, and had practised basic tasks like weaving actual fabric, but none of my classmates had much success with it. It took a certain talent they didn't seem to possess, and I'd spent my whole childhood learning to ignore mine.

'I doubt that,' Cormac says, setting down his glass. 'I know it was an accident because the loom wasn't on. A girl who can weave through time without a loom is a rare thing. It takes a very special girl to do that. We almost retrieved you right there.'

I want to sink under the table. I'd known I'd given myself away, but not how much I'd revealed. This is my fault.

'Fine. Don't say anything. There's no way your mother got out,' he tells me coldly. 'We had to clean the area after the Stream crew left.'

'Clean?' I think back to the complant conversation I overheard in the motocarriage. It was short and he was mad, but the rest is lost in a haze. As I sift back further, the evening comes in bursts of images. Eating with my family. A white cake. Cold, dark dirt.

'I love how innocent you are. It's really just . . . delightful.' He smirks, and this time I see tiny crinkles around his eyes. 'The section has been cleaned and rewoven. No use trying to explain why a whole family went missing, espe-

cially not with the recent accident.'

'My sister's teacher,' I murmur.

'Mrs Swander,' he confirms. 'What a mess, but not significant enough to justify a full cleaning.'

I try to wrap my mind around what he's saying. The Guild transports food, assigns roles and houses, and oversees the addition of new babies to the population. But Arras hasn't had an accident or crime in years. At least not that I know of. 'Wait, are you saying you removed the memories of all the people in Romen?'

'Not exactly,' he says, downing the last of his bourbon. 'We adjusted them a bit. When people try to remember your family, it will be a bit blurry. Your history now indicates you were an only child and your parents have been given clearance to move closer to the Coventry – that's if anyone bothers to check up on you, but they won't.'

'You made it all disappear,' I whisper.

'It's easy to adjust at night thanks to the curfew,' he says, taking a bite of steak. 'I'm sure it sounds horrible to you, but there's no need to cause massive panic.'

'You mean' – I lean in and keep my voice low – 'there's no need to let people know you murdered their neighbours.'

The wicked grin fades from his face. 'Some day you'll understand, Adelice, that everything I do ensures people are safe. Cleaning a whole town isn't something I take lightly, and it's not easy. Most Spinsters don't have the talent for it. You'd be wise to remember you're the reason I had to order it.'

'I thought Arras didn't have to worry about safety. Isn't

32

that why you need girls like me?' I challenge, gripping the butter knife next to my plate.

'Like I said, your ignorance is truly delightful.' But he doesn't seem amused any more. Instead his black eyes blaze with repressed fury. 'Spinsters do ensure safety, by following my orders. It's not all parties and loom work. The Guild demands loyalty. Never forget that.'

I can hear the warning in his voice not to push this further, so I relax my hand and the knife clatters back to the table.

'I hope you had enough to eat,' he snaps, rising from his seat. Apparently two bites of food is enough to appease him.

I follow. I don't have any other choice.

A girl from our neighbourhood was labelled a deviant a few years back. It's a very rare thing, since everyone in Arras lives by a zero-tolerance policy for misbehaviour. But my dad told me that occasionally a child is brought up on charges and taken away. He said sometimes they come back, but most don't. The little girl came back, but she was always in a daze, never quite in the moment with the rest of us. That's how my neighbours will be when they think of me. It's as though I don't exist, and even the meds still coursing through my body can't block the tingle of pain that runs down to my fingertips when I think of it.

The meal was a courtesy, it turns out, because we don't have rebound appointments. We don't need them. I'm torn between feeling guilty that he was being nice to me and wondering what his motives were. I trail Cormac as he strides past the line of men waiting on deck for their sched-

uled departures. A few grumble as we pass but the others shush them.

'I need to bump two spots,' Cormac tells the man at the counter, flashing him his PC.

I have no doubt this man knows who he is, but he takes the card and studies it for a moment before keying in a code on the companel, a communications system built into the wall behind him. A moment later, a young woman dressed in a snug sky-blue suit steps out from the corridor behind the desk and leads us past the counter.

'Ambassador Patton, will you require a refreshment while you rebound?' She's all bubbles and pink lipstick.

'I ate. Thank you,' he tells her with a wink.

She doesn't ask me.

Cormac's rebound compartment is before my own, and I half expect him to disappear through the door without another word to me, but he turns and sizes me up one last time. 'Adelice, I suggest you get some rest during your rebound.'

I keep my eyes focused on the end of the corridor. He's acting like my dad. Telling me when to eat, when to sleep. But he's the reason I need a surrogate father in the first place.

'You know you don't deserve the way they're going to treat you.' His voice sounds concerned but the Valpron must be wearing off, because I can barely keep myself from spitting at him. I don't need his kindness.

'You have no idea what you're getting yourself into,' he says, reading my face. He sighs and opens the chamber door. 'I hope you learn to listen before it's too late.'

I don't bother to respond. I don't want his arrogant ad-

vice. I watch him fixedly until the door shuts behind him. My guide shepherds me to the next compartment and follows me in.

'This is the first time you've rebounded,' she says matter-of-factly as she ushers me to a single chair on a small platform in the centre of the room. 'You're likely to experience some nausea or vomiting.'

I sit down awkwardly and take in the sparse room.

'Here.' She reaches around me and buckles a strap against my waist.

'What's that for?'

'We need to keep your movement confined to a minimal space during the rebounding process. Usually you can read or eat or drink,' she tells me, unfolding a small tray from the arm of the chair. 'But no getting up.'

I glance down at the straps, and raise an eyebrow.

'I'm sorry.' She lifts her heavily lined eyes, and I can see she means it. 'I'm not authorised to give you anything.'

'It's okay,' I say with a shrug. 'I get the impression girls are rare around here.'

The girl adjusts my straps and checks the buckle before she steps back. She hesitates and checks the countdown on the wall: I have two minutes until the rebound will begin.

'That's it though.' She pauses and glances around the room. 'I probably should shut up.'

'What?' The medication is definitely wearing off, because now I'm holding back panic.

'Yes, women very rarely rebound, only Spinsters and Ministers' wives. But they are given anything they want,' she whispers.

'I don't understand,' I admit slowly.

She leans forward and pretends to adjust the tray. 'They come in dressed up and we are supposed to give them bulletins and fashion catalogues to peruse. But you . . .'

I stare at her, trying to get what she's telling me.

'My directions were to keep you buckled and locked down.'

'Locked down?'

'Yes.' She sighs and gives me a sympathetic pat. 'I'm sorry.'

She reaches behind my back, and a second later, a large helmet woven of thick steel chains clamps down over my head. I cry out, but the sound is muffled. She squeezes my hand once, and I calm a little. Then more metal locks down, binding my wrists.

'Your rebound will only take an hour,' she reassures me, although I can barely hear her through the twisted metal. 'Good luck, Adelice.'

I wish I'd asked her name.

The helmet blocks most of the room around me, but I can see through the gaps. It's an inconsequential room with bare white walls, except for the clock counting down in the corner.

The nausea hits first. The floor drops from under me and my stomach turns over, but I don't fall. The helmet keeps my head perfectly straight and my neck stretched, so I don't throw up, but I want to. Closing my eyes, I breathe evenly, trying to keep the sickness at bay. When I open them and peer through the steel wires, the room around me is gone, and I'm surrounded by a shimmering

array of lights. The sight calms me and I focus on studying the gleaming strands that comprise the rebound compartment. Glowing beams twist across the room and then long threads of grey knit up through them, crisscrossing over the light into a luminous fabric of gold and silver. Somewhere a girl sits, replacing the weave of the rebound chamber with that of a chamber in a coventry, effectively moving me from one location to the other. I'm travelling hundreds of miles without moving a muscle. It's a delicate procedure, which is why it's reserved for the most important people in Arras. The Stream ran a special story vlip about the process a few years ago.

Gradually the light disappears and slowly – too slowly – grey walls form in patches around me, and the radiant canvas of the rebound process fades into a concrete room. It takes an eternity before the beams are gone, but when the last flickers into wall, I'm happy to feel the helmet being lifted from my head.

A group of sombrely clad officers surrounds me. The one who removed the helmet hesitates at the cuffs on my arms. They ache from being shackled during the trip, and I'm about to tell him so when a young blond in an expensive suit steps forward and holds his hand up. His head is cocked to the side, and I realise he's on his complant. Despite his obvious youth, he seems to be in charge. He's the kind of boy my classmates would zero in on in the daily *Bulletin* and giggle over as they passed his image around. But even this close to him, I only feel curiosity.

'Sedate her.'

'Sir?' the officer asks in surprise.

'She wants her sedated,' the blond boy orders. 'You want to ask her why?'

The officer shakes his head, but as a medic rushes forward with a syringe I can see the apology in the boy's blindingly blue eyes.

3

When I was eight, the girl next door, Beth, found a bird's nest that had fallen on the line marking her yard from ours. I was not allowed to enter her yard, and she never came into mine. She applied that line to all of our interactions, keeping a firm boundary between us at home, at academy, and at the commons where we played with the rest of the neighbourhood girls. Beth made sure the other girls didn't talk to me either, so I kept to myself. Her bullying made me timid in her presence – always drawing back instead of coming forward – so I watched as she batted the nest along the property marker with a stick. I didn't say anything until I saw the speckle of blue as it tumbled over.

'Stop.' My command was so low she shouldn't have heard it, but our street was as quiet as usual, and her head perked up to stare at me, the stick frozen in place.

'What did you say?' she asked in a voice that wanted me to remember my place, not answer her.

Whatever that glimpse of blue had stirred in my chest, I grabbed on to it and pushed the demand out louder.

Beth edged closer to the line, but didn't cross it. Instead, she hoisted the nest on her stick and tossed it over to my yard. 'There,' she mocked. 'Take your precious nest. It doesn't matter, the mama bird isn't coming back for it now. They don't want their eggs after someone else has touched them.'

Hatred seethed inside me, but I stood on my side and watched her walk into her house without saying another word. She glanced at me just once as she opened her front door, and her eyes were full of scorn. I stared at the nest for a long time: two eggs peeked out of the grass next to it. I thought of myself and my sister when I looked at them: two sister sparrows. Gathering up some fallen leaves from our yard, I covered my bare hands before placing the eggs into their spots in the nest, and then lifted it back to the tree in our yard. But the small gesture did nothing to soothe the aching rage building in my chest.

As I watched the nest, growing increasingly frustrated with my inability to protect the tiny lives inside, the strands of the weave glimmered to life around me. The tree and the nest blurred like a delicate tapestry before my eyes, strands that called out to be touched, and I reached and slipped my fingers around them. Although I'd been aware of the fabric of life woven around us before, for the first time I noticed how bands of gold stretched across it horizontally, and how coloured threads wove up through them to create

the objects around me. As I watched, the golden strands of light flickered slightly, and I realised they were slowly moving forwards, away from the moment in front of me. They weren't simply fibres in Arras's tapestry – they were lines of time. Tentatively, I reached for one of the golden fibres. Encouraged by its silky texture, I took it and yanked it hard, trying to force the time bands back to a moment when the mama bird was guarding her precious babies. But the strands resisted. No matter what I did, they kept on creeping forward. There was no going back.

The mama bird never returned. I checked on the little blue eggs every morning until one day my dad relieved me from my vigilance and the whole nest vanished. I didn't touch those eggs, but I guess the mama bird didn't know where to look; that's why she didn't come back.

There is only darkness. It is damp, and with the palms of my hands I can feel that the floor of my cell alternates between smooth and jagged, but one thing is constant: it is always cold. My parents' suspicions about the Guild were well-founded. I wonder if my mother knows where I am. I picture her circling our house, searching for me in her own empty nest.

If she's still alive. My heart flutters in response to some new emotion. It sits like a big lump in my throat as I re-member the body bag leaking onto the floor. And now they have Amie. The idea that she's at their mercy claws at my stomach. Never in the years my parents were training me did I understand why they were doing it. They told me that they didn't want to lose me. My father spoke of the dangers

of too much power, but in vague, noncommittal terms, and my mother always shushed him when he became too impassioned. The Guild gave us food and perfectly controlled weather and health patches. I have to believe those people – the humane government of my memory – have Amie now. Whatever my crimes, those officials wouldn't hold her accountable. But I can't ignore how wrong I was about the Guild or my parents. And it's my fault she was taken. It was my hands that gave me away at testing. I run them along the rough cracks in the patches of stone until my fingertips are torn and bloody.

The facts are inescapable. I'd been taught to hide my gift by my parents. All I had to do was pretend for a month while I performed the Guild's testing and I would have been released from service. And if I hadn't been so selfish, so scared of disappointing my mom and dad on the night of my retrieval, none of this would have happened. But I'm not sure I know how things might be different now. Even if I had told them I'd slipped during testing, would we have escaped? Sifting through flashes of my childhood for clues, I remember my parents being strong, but isolated from the rest of our community. They genuinely loved each other. Dad would leave Mom little love notes around the house, which I found both revolting and oddly reassuring when I stumbled across one. He treated her with a respect that few of the other grown men I encountered in Romen showed women or girls. I'd believed this was why they didn't want me to become a Spinster, because it would tear our family apart – and our family was all we had. But beneath the happy veneer of our home, there were always secrets, par-

ticularly my training, which was kept from Amie. They told me she wouldn't understand, and the tone they used when they explained this was the same one they used when discussing my 'condition' with each other.

In the dark, I can't hide from the only thing I can finally see. I didn't want to see the treason in their actions. I ignored the implication of their words and heard what I needed to hear to feel safe, not what they were actually telling me. And now I've lost my chance to know my parents. All I can do is fit together the pieces they left behind in my memory.

No one comes to visit me. There's no food and no water. And no light. This can't be how they treat the Spinsters. I must be being punished for my family's treason. I was taught about the coventries in academy and shown pictures of the formidable towered compounds, one of which I think I'm in now. But the walls and buttresses of those compounds housed sumptuous rooms and art and plumbing. There's not even a toilet in this cell. I'm forced to go in the corner. The mustiness of the stone overpowers the smell at first, but even the muck of the cell can't control it forever and now the acrid odour of bile prickles my nostrils. In the dark, the smells are becoming more acute, burning my throat.

I lie on the floor and try to picture my location. I imagine there is a window in the room and light streams in from the sun. Cormac told me I was being taken to the Western Compound, which houses the largest coventry of Spinsters in Arras and sits on the edge of the Endless Sea, so if I looked out I might see pine trees or maybe the ocean. Even

though my hometown of Romen is only a few hours from the ocean, I've never travelled outside metro limits. The population of each metro is strictly regulated to ensure the local weave isn't damaged by excessive change to its structure. That's why the boundaries of each metro are carefully guarded – for our safety.

Each of the four sectors has these special compounds, built on the edge of the Endless Sea, that are responsible for keeping Arras functioning. In academy, we were permitted to study a very simple map that outlined the sectors and their capitals. Four perfect triangles of land, surrounded by an ocean that never ceases, and their coventries arranged in perfect symmetry like the points of a cross. But that's all we were shown. The Guild didn't want to tempt students to try to travel outside their hometowns. We were taught that if too many people travelled at a time, it could undermine the structural integrity of Arras. So all travelling arrangements have to be pre-approved through proper channels or it wouldn't be safe, but Spinsters have special border privileges, making them almost as important as businessmen and politicians. It was the one thing that ever appealed to me about becoming a Spinster – being able to see the world – but the idea that I could never return home outweighed the travel perks.

And there're not many other perks to being a Spinster, as it turns out. I can't force myself to pretend there is a window in the cell. Because there is no sun. No clock. No hum of insects. I have no idea how long I've been here. I'm starting to wonder if I'm dead. I decide to sleep and not wake up. If this is the afterlife, I should be free from dreams. But

no such luck – nightmares continually interrupt my sleep. I lie here, eyes burning in the dark, still trying to adjust, hopelessly, and my mind rages with the injustice.

And then the door opens and light streams in, blinding me, until my eyes begin to see the dark outlines of the tiny chamber.

'Adelice?'

Is that my name? I can't remember.

'Adelice!' Less timid this time, but still a squeaky yap.

'Take her up to the clinic and rehydrate her. I want her in the salon in an hour.' The squeaky voice instructs someone I don't care to see. The voiceless one crosses over to me, boots clicking against the stones, and lifts me casually over his shoulder.

'What a stink. Never thought something so foul could come out of such a tiny thing.' He laughs. Maybe later he can buy himself a drink to celebrate his cleverness. 'At least you're light.'

I consider reminding him that starving a person has an influence on her weight, but I don't want to encourage his feeble sense of humour. And I'm too weak to think of something smart to defend myself.

'Are you even old enough to be chosen?'

I say nothing.

'I know they found you during testing,' he continues. I begin to count each of his tangled curls. They're so dark they are almost black, but looking closer I realise his hair is actually brown. He's not like metro men, who are polished and groomed and chiselled until their jawlines are angular and smooth without a trace of facial hair. Even my father

45

scrubbed his nails and shaved each night. He smells of hops and sweat and work. He must do more physical labour than most men in Arras, because he carries me like I'm nothing, and I can feel how taut the muscles of his arms and chest are against my thin gown.

'Not much to say, huh,' he mocks. 'Well, good. It'll be a nice change not to have another over-privileged brat bossing us around. I wish they were all mute like you.'

'I suppose even a mute girl,' I snarl, 'has more privileges than the scum that has to drag her stinking body upstairs.'

He drops me, and it's a testament to how long I was imprisoned that being dropped on a hard stone floor doesn't hurt. I'm so used to it that I sit and stare up at him. I'm surprised to find that my eyes have adjusted enough to see the look of loathing on his face. He's as dirty as he smells, a coat of grime almost theatrically applied to his face and neck, but underneath it, he's striking. His cobalt-blue eyes, accented by the dirt, radiate out against the filth all over him and for a moment something stirs in my stomach, and I'm rendered speechless again.

'You can walk on your own. I was doing you a favour,' he growls. 'I thought maybe you were different. But don't worry, you'll fit right in with the rest of them.'

I swallow hard and stumble to my feet. I almost lose my balance, but I'm too proud to apologise or to ask for the strange boy's help. And I can't deny that now that I've really looked at him, I feel funny about letting him touch me again. Girls don't talk to boys back home, and they certainly don't let boys carry them. Most parents, like my own, bring their daughters into the metro rarely, to avoid

46

any pre-dismissal contact with the opposite sex. But I'm guessing the electric pulse racing through me where his arms and hands held me up wasn't caused by the modesty the academy tried to instil in me for years. I find myself wanting to say something clever to him, but the words won't come, so I concentrate on trying to walk. Something that's definitely harder than it used to be.

'You can tattle on me when you've been processed. Maybe they'll rip me for mistreating a new Eligible.' His tone is cruel, and I'm surprised at how much it stings. I lumped him in with all my other captors, and now he's lumping me in with the Guild, too.

He walks briskly, and I can barely keep up. My feet prickle, shooting needles up my legs, but I follow behind him and eventually catch up. He glances down, obviously surprised to see me walking beside him.

'Probably dying to get your hands on some fancy cosmetics,' he chides, and I'm tempted to call him scum again.

'The Spinsters have the best aestheticians,' he continues. 'It's one of the perks. All you poor, new Eligibles are so eager to get beautified. It must be such a burden to wait sixteen years to wear lipstick.'

I hate being treated like I'm some stupid metro girl eager to paint her face, curl her hair, and step into the working world. I've seen pictures of the Spinsters made up until they look like moulded plastic, but I'm not about to talk to him about it. He can think whatever he wants; he's a nobody anyway. I repeat the words in my head – he's a nobody – but I can't seem to believe it myself.

''Course, you were in the cells,' he continues, clearly

not needing me to participate in this conversation, 'which means you tried to run.' Our eyes meet for the first time and the brilliant blue seems to warm a little. 'Guess you have some fire in you, girl.'

That does it. 'Do you always call women a few years younger than you "girl"?'

'Only ones that look like they're *girls*,' he says, purposefully emphasising the offending term.

'Oh, right. And what are you? Eighteen?' I point out. Does he think the dirt covers his age?

He taps his grimy forehead. 'I'm older up here than most men twice my age.'

I don't ask him why. I don't want to get too cosy with him. There's no point. We continue to walk, but his eyes stay locked on me. He must have passed this way many times before, because he doesn't need to look ahead to see where he's going.

'Let me carry you.' He sounds resigned but there's a note of kindness to his offer.

'I'm fine,' I insist too harshly, and I try to hide the blush that's creeping onto my neck at the thought of his arms around me again.

He grunts and stops staring at me. 'So you ran?'

I keep my eyes on the door at the end of the stone hall.

'Let me guess, you think I'm going to tattle on you?' He grabs my arm to halt our progression, leaning in to keep his voice from echoing. 'If you ran, it doesn't matter why. It doesn't matter if you admit it. They've marked you and they'll watch you. So take my advice and play dumb.'

His eyes flicker like the tip of a flame, accentuating his

warning, and I know he means it.

'Why do you even care?'

'Because they'll kill you,' he says without hesitation. 'And a girl with enough smarts to run is hard to come by these days.'

'Then they could kill you for talking to me like this,' I whisper, and it comes out as desperation, fear, everything I've been feeling in the cell. He seems to respond to the emotion in my voice, as though I'm putting words to the unspoken tension in the air, and for just a moment, he leans down closer to me, and I wait for what he'll tell me next, with my breath caught in my throat.

He shrugs. 'If you tell. And you won't.'

I try to hide my disappointment, but he's right. I won't tell on him, but I'm not sure if it's because he said I was smart or if it's because I feel like we share a secret. Neither of us is what we appear to be.

He opens the door to reveal a sterile staircase with bright white walls that feel out of step with the old, musty cell block. My guide flourishes his arm, but as I cross the threshold, he whispers, so softly I barely hear: 'Besides, there are worse things than death here.'

The clucking disapproval of the Coventry cosmeticians is beginning to wear me out. The boy left me at the top of the steps, and a girl herded me to a shower. The water was painfully cold, reinforcing my belief that I'll never be warm again unless I start to play along. So here I sit, eyes cast down, quiet, completely malleable to their designs. It isn't bad. They've given me a downy white robe, and despite

49

my fervent desire to hate this, the feeling of having my hair combed and shampooed is relaxing. Maybe I've just missed human contact.

A woman snips furiously at my hair, while another smooths cream over my face. They shape my eyebrows into trim arches and line them for emphasis. Then they spread a milky white paint across my face and set it with powder. I remember my mother carefully doing the same, explaining step-by-step what each item was, and stopping to tell me how few cosmetics I would need when my time came – how flawless my skin was. She would cringe to see them paint my face now, and I keep imagining she'll burst through the door and save me from the powders and rough pots of colour and long pricking pens for my eyes.

'She's horribly gaunt,' the scissor woman notes, now applying thick globs of gel with a brush to my still-wet hair.

'She was in the cells . . . ?' Her companion's voice trails into a question. I look up to see the face I know she's making – the one that is suggestive and haughty – but instead find a plaster mould of serenity. Only the lingering peak in her voice betrays her curiosity, but it's not my own interest in what she's saying that keeps me riveted to her face. It's her beauty, one rivalled only by that of the woman cutting my hair. Skin as pure as fresh honey, and deep, black eyes painted into exaggerated almonds. The other has silvery skin and corn-silk hair, woven delicately into braids around her head. Her lips are as red as fresh blood. Looking away, I imagine what they think of my dull copper hair and pasty skin. I don't look back up as they buff and remake me. I don't bother to speak. They finish, and continue their

idle gossip, never once addressing me, and I'm not sure if it is because I am beneath them or above them. When they're done, they leave me in the chair, and I finally brave a look at the mirrored walls around me. My image confronts me on every side, some staring back and others turning away like a stranger. In my simple robe, I look like my mother — older and more beautiful. I look like a woman.

Standing, I take a few steps forward to touch the cool glass. I've never spent much time at the mirror, but it's comforting to stand here now. A hundred images of me gazing back, proving my existence. I turn my name over in my head and try to attach it to this woman with scarlet hair that drapes down against her snowy robe, and emerald eyes set by dark gold lines against a smooth, sculpted face. This stranger. Myself. Adelice.

As I stare, unable to turn away, one of the mirrors cracks cleanly down the side and for a moment, startled, I back away, unsure how I've broken it. The crack grows to reveal a panel in the glass. A woman steps through, and it seals seamlessly behind her. She's wearing a tailored suit, and her raven hair is perfectly pinned into a twist. Her age doesn't show in her made-up face, but the angles of her cheekbones and the arch of her eyebrows set over her luminous but clearly artificial violet eyes make her look older to me. But it's the way she carries herself — it's the aura of control and authority reflected in her refined face and smart suit — that tells me this is no ordinary Spinster.

She doesn't speak at first. Instead she runs her eyes down me, and I wonder if it's permissible to speak to a Spinster. I think of the boy who carried me in the cells. *Play dumb.* I

can't imagine keeping my tongue still and dry in my mouth day after day.

'Congratulations on your achievement,' she whispers, and even in the empty room I strain to hear her. I catch my breath, afraid an inhale or exhale will overwhelm her small voice.

'Not many make it to this point, Adelice. You should be proud.' Her smile doesn't reach her false eyes. 'My name is Maela, and it's my job to welcome and train Eligibles. We've been processing the other girls. Orientation begins tomorrow. You almost missed it.'

'I'm sorry,' I mumble, as shame washes over me, forcing me to cast my eyes down to my bare feet.

'Sit,' Maela commands, pointing to the prep chair. 'The life of the Spinster is full of honour. You can do that which few can. You have power.' Her whisper-quiet voice is feverish. 'But, Adelice,' Maela purrs into my ear, 'you must not presume you are in control.'

My heart is a war drum, pounding too loudly. She has been sent to break me or at least to begin the process, but it won't work. I rub my thumb over the hourglass scar on my wrist and remember my father's final words. I won't let this woman scare me. But the memory of him burned into my skin sends a surge of renewed hatred seething through me. It burns through my chest and out into my arms, and I have to suppress the urge to attack this sly woman.

Maela towers behind me and strokes my hair. I breathe carefully – in and out – aware of each breath. I watch these strangers in the mirror as she smiles, showing rows of perfect teeth against her lipsticked mouth.

'We are set above those in Arras.' Her voice is steady now, and she speaks in a normal, conversational tone as she flicks stray bits of cut hair from my shoulders. 'But you belong to the Guild.'

Belong. I swallow hard on the word and try to shove its bitterness down my throat.

'You will have everything.' She leans down and tucks her chin against my shoulder, taking my strange face into her cold, slick hand. 'You will be beautiful and young.' She squeezes my face and looses a quiet, bell-like laugh as though we're old friends or sisters confiding in one another. 'Oh, Adelice, the life that awaits you . . .' With a sigh, Maela draws back up and studies us in the mirror. In one swift motion she raises a long, thin wand and I cringe back. She laughs again and strikes a match. A moment later the spark from her cigarette is flickering back at me in a thousand reflections.

'I'm almost jealous,' Maela says.

'I'm very honoured.' I manage to push the words out of my mouth.

Her smile widens as I play her game. 'Of course you are. Only someone very stupid would not want this life.'

She whirls around and somehow she doesn't look foolish, but even more stunning, even more controlling. 'Here, you are beautiful, Adelice. Here, you have a chance at something other than serving the ridiculous demands of men. Here,' Maela adds thoughtfully, 'you are more than a secretary.'

I know from the way she watches my face that she's mocking my mother, but I keep my gaze level with hers.

'But there's just one thing you have to remember.' She

53

breathes down on me, and the stench of her cigarette stings my nostrils. 'There is no running away from here, Adelice Lewys.'

I feel the cosmetics hiding me now, and I see my mother reflected back at me in the mirror.

Do not let her see you worry. Give nothing away.

'There is no hiding.' Her sweet whisper sounds strangely like a hiss. 'There is not even death. So choose now what side you are on.'

I stare back. I hear the boy's final words to me, and I wonder what could possibly be worse than death. But I know the answer: cold stone and burning darkness.

'Of course.' My response is simple and I dare not test myself by speaking more.

Maela's smile fades into a self-satisfied smirk, and I'm sure this is the only genuine emotion she's displayed thus far.

'Well, then.' She pats my shoulder, dropping ash onto my robe. 'Your room is waiting for you.'

'Maela,' I say, my voice timid but steady, 'do you know what happened to my mother and sister?' I have to ask even though I'm terrified of showing her my weakness. I try to look strong.

'I can imagine,' she says, but instead of telling me what she thinks, she leaves me to my own desperate fantasies and calls for her assistant to join us. I'm surprised to see it's a boy, but I suppose the girls here are busy with more important tasks. I watch as she whispers orders to him, throwing meaningful glances over her shoulder at me.

Her personal assistant escorts me to my new quarters.

The sterile halls of the compound shift slowly as we enter the housing unit. First, the concrete changes to smooth wood. Then the white walls blossom: vermilion, garnet. We pass velvet divans and marble pillars and enter a bronze-gated lift. It reminds me of Romen's metro hall, and I shudder, remembering the grotesque figures perched on the exterior corners of the hall of records there. Monsters carved from stone that leered down at the citizens, beautiful and terrifying.

Everything here throbs with brilliant energy, and yet there's an absence of real life. The lift is silent, and my guide doesn't speak as we ride further and further up into the tower. I stand behind him and study how his gold hair glistens and waves against his shoulders. It's not typical Guild-approved grooming, but I suppose it's a perk of being an errand boy for such a powerful Spinster.

My room sits at the end of the hall behind a plum-lacquered door on the fifteenth floor. It's a beautiful apartment trimmed with carved woodwork painted in rich cream and subtle gold. At the far end, a fire blazes in a brick-and-wrought-iron hearth. Above it hangs a portrait of a woman who looks strangely like the new me. Intricate patterns decorate the woven rugs that stretch across the large room, and silk pillows in emerald and garnet and champagne lie scattered around small mahogany tables.

'I'll see that they deliver some supper to you. You missed the evening meal,' my guide informs me. He watches as I wander around the room, and when I turn back, he's grinning.

'Th-th-thank you,' I stammer.

'It's a bit of an upgrade from the cell, I imagine,' he says, and I turn to look at him more carefully: it's the same boy who gave the order to sedate me in the rebound chamber. He's taller than I am, and his suit hugs his broad shoulders and rigid arms enough to show he has the strength necessary to be a bodyguard. But despite his powerful body, his face is fair and framed by delicate hair. It's the hair that perks my fuzzy memory of my retrieval night.

'You—' I stop short of accusing him.

'I'm sorry about that,' he says, the cocky grin fading from his face. 'Orders are orders. If it makes you feel better, you got off easy. Name's Erik.'

I stare coldly at the hand he stretches out in greeting. *Sure, let's be friends. You only left me in the cold with no food.*

The thought twists my stomach with hunger, reminding me that I've still not eaten since the few bites at the café in Nilus. 'It doesn't actually.'

Erik laughs and shakes his head, proving he's a first-class jerk. 'I'll make sure they send you up plenty of food. You'll begin training in the morning.'

I want to refuse the food and the fancy room with its luxurious furnishings. I want to crawl into a hole and starve slowly, but if I do I won't be in a position to protect Amie or find out where my mother is, so I turn away from him instead. The door locks behind him, and I'm alone in this strange, new world.

4

As dawn arrives I rest on soft satin and cotton. My bed is a long cushion that runs the entire length of one wall, butting against floor-to-ceiling windows that look out over the Endless Sea. I imagine slipping my toes into the water, wondering if it is cold and if the salt would sting my feet as the sun creeps up and paints the water dusty pink and orange.

I've never been so comfortable in my whole life. A tray of half-eaten delicacies sits at my feet. My mom was an adequate cook, and she did the best she could with the rationed food available in our metro. But last night I ate duck in butter sauce. Rice with saffron and apricots. *Torta di cioccolato.* I only know the names of the foods because they're written on the small menu card tucked under the etched silver plate they came piled on.

Outside, a storm lingers on the periphery of my view,

tainting the rose-coloured morning. It's woven in for entertainment or local crops. The clouds build and swell with the coming rain. As I watch, the texture of the weave comes into focus, and I can see the additions of rain and lightning slowly snaking across the sky. I reach out to open the window and am surprised when my fingers make direct contact with the fibres, drawing the darkness towards me. There's no glass between me and the weave outside. But how can that be? I struggle to understand how I'm able to expand the thunderstorm from the confines of my quarters. Unless it's not a window I'm looking through. Looking closer I see that the weave of the window and the scene outside it are artificial, layered on top of the real weave of the room, like a painting done on top of a masterpiece. The original weave of the room is still visible when I strain to see it, but the artificial top layer only mimics that of the genuine article. I know because the golden bands that should be present are stagnant. Time isn't moving forward in this window, because it's not a real piece of Arras. It must be some type of programme created to look like a real window with real scenery. As I consider that possibility, I lose track of my work. The storm swells in the clouds until they are ripe with moisture. It looks so real that I almost believe the rain strands leave my fingers wet. My hands become heavy with the material knitted through my fingers, and I drop the weave, shocked to discover how much is pooled across my lap. It dissipates as thunder crescendos and cracks along the false windowpanes. The rain pours down, a dam bursting the skyline. I wish I could weave tears into my eyes, loosing the constant ache from

my chest. But they won't come, so I stare at the rain, which I've freed to fall from the bloated clouds.

I don't even notice she's watching me, wide-eyed and curious, until she clears her throat. I spin around awkwardly. She isn't much older than I am, but in typical Spinster fashion her honey-gold hair is piled in curls on top of her head and her black suit hugs her willowy figure, precisely tailored to fit her. She looks softer than most of the women I've met here so far and her cosmetics are applied to highlight her graceful features rather than to draw unnecessary attention to her. Everything about her feels approachable and welcoming. And here I am lying around with last night's cosmetics smeared across my face, and a pile of half-eaten food at my feet.

She raises her hand as if to stop me from getting up. 'I didn't mean to startle you. I thought you might be sleeping. I'm here to serve as your mentor. Call me Enora.'

'Am I expected to be somewhere?' The words tumble out in a rush of speech that even I barely comprehend. 'I can get dressed!'

But the word *dressed* stops me cold. I'm still wearing the robe from yesterday, and I don't own a stitch of clothing. I've spent an entire night in bed watching the waves, and I don't even know if I have a wardrobe.

'Adelice.' Enora says my name in a forceful but gentle tone. 'Sit down and relax. Breakfast will be delivered soon. I'm here to discuss everything with you.'

I'm rooted to the spot, still embarrassed at my total ignorance.

'Including your clothes,' she assures me, as though she

knows exactly what I'm thinking. I sit down, as instructed, on a large cushion in the middle of the room. Moments later heaped trays of food appear, wafting buttery, salty smells around us. The server lays out the food and plates on the small tables dotting the large space around the fireplace. My guest smiles and takes a seat in one of the few actual chairs the room offers while the server stokes the dying embers in my hearth and adds fresh wood.

'You must have a million questions,' Enora begins warmly.

I nod, painfully aware of the gnawing growl of my stomach. Nerves and hunger – not a good combination.

'You're hungry,' she points out, obviously attuned to the slight shake of my hands. 'You eat, and I'll talk. You can ask questions when you're done.'

There is something easy and genuine about her. I get the sense that she, unlike Maela, can be trusted. I feel comfortable enough to slowly, and as politely as possible, begin shoving food in my mouth.

'I will be your mentor while you train to spin. I am a Guild-appointed Spinster and I assist the Creweler. I'm here to answer questions, provide advice, and offer moral support. Your first few years in the Coventry may require some . . . transition.' I can hear how carefully she chooses this word, but unlike the other Spinster, whose saccharine speech belied venom, this woman's intentions are clear. She's trying not to frighten me.

'What's a Creweler?' The question is out of my mouth before I swallow, and despite her kind smile I'm ashamed of my crass behaviour.

'In a moment. We have more pressing issues to discuss.'

As if on cue the door to my apartment swings open and several plainly dressed young girls roll large racks of wildly coloured textiles into the entryway.

'Thank you.' Enora holds out a small card and one of the girls swiftly retrieves it with a curtsy. They are gone as quickly as they appeared.

'Your aestheticians sent your measurements to the mill last night and this is the start of your wardrobe,' she tells me, busily plucking through the hangers and pulling out a brilliant green dress and a charcoal suit. I hear her murmur something like 'lovely' to herself.

'I know we have a dress code, but is there a reason I have to get so decked out?' I ask as she pulls another satin evening gown from the rack.

'Aren't they beautiful?' she asks with her back to me.

'Yes.' And it's the truth. 'But where am I going to wear this?' I hold up a slinky grey dress. I've always understood why career women need to dress neatly for their bosses – my mother sported suits with gold buttons and pressed lapels to the office daily – but I can't imagine weaving in an evening gown.

'It's one of the perks. Every girl attends her share of Guild dinner parties and then of course there're the *Bulletin* reports. You'll have occasion to wear them, but nothing this extravagant for everyday weaving,' Enora assures me. 'Sometimes the Guild calls girls who are very talented but lack the finesse necessary to work on the looms. It would be wasteful to put them to work in the quarters or in the kitchen, so they go to work as our seamstresses.'

'What if I don't want to wear things like this?' I try to keep the challenge out of my voice, but it slips through anyway.

Enora stares at me, not blinking, before she answers, 'Would you waste these girls' talents?'

'Why not send them home?' I immediately wish I could take the question back as her eyes flash to me and then to the garment rack.

'No one goes home,' she responds evenly, but there's an edge to her voice and her fingers tremble as they weed through my new wardrobe.

'I guess I knew that.'

'That won't be an issue for you,' she chirps, clearly trying to lighten the mood. 'You should know that whatever you say to me stays between us.'

This strikes me as exactly the kind of thing you say when you're a spy, but my gut wants to believe her, so I merely nod.

'Good.' Enora saunters over to sit on the cushion next to mine and lowers her voice. 'What I saw you doing, Adelice — weaving without a loom. Have you done that before?'

It takes a moment to realise she is referring to the storm earlier. 'Yes. Not often, though.'

'And you don't need any instruments?' she presses, her voice the hint of a whisper.

'No.' I'm confused, but I whisper along with her. 'I've always been able to do it that way. But the windows aren't real . . .'

She nods conspiratorially.

'Of course not. Glass is breakable, and the Guild wants

62

the Spinsters kept secure. It's basically a large screen created to look like a window. There's a special programme coded to run scenic views throughout the compound. There are no real windows. Nearly every wall here is a giant screen programmed to specific images. We have seasons and everything. Most girls never notice it's a programme.'

'It looks so real, but I wondered why I could touch it,' I murmur.

Fear flashes through her chocolate-brown eyes.

'I need you to trust me. You must never tell anyone else you can do that. Always use a loom to weave – try not to do it without one, even when you are alone.'

I raise my eyebrows. Her words remind me of the boy from the prison and his admonition to play dumb. They are keeping me alive, these kind tips from mysterious strangers. I consider telling her about my slip at testing, and that I'm sure Cormac already knows, but I'm not sure what good it would do.

'So they're like vlip screens then?' I clarify.

'Almost exactly, but much higher-tech than the ones available for home use. The images are more realistic.'

She's right. I had thought it was a real window before I touched it and found it was so easy to manipulate. Something's bothering me though about how I changed the rainstorm. 'If someone else were to touch it, would they be able to change it?'

'I've never seen anyone do that before,' she admits. 'Every Spinster here works the weave on looms. That's why you can't tell anyone about what I saw you do. Do you understand?'

I'm not certain how my weaving skills could possibly be dangerous to me now that I'm already locked away in the Coventry, but I nod that I will keep quiet about it.

'Smart girl,' she breathes and then pops back onto her heels – back to business. 'Your stylists can be expected to arrive at seven-thirty. Please be bathed by then. That isn't their job. Should you require someone to wash you, I will appoint a hand servant.'

'To wash me?' I repeat in disbelief. 'In case I don't know how?'

My incredulity is rewarded by a short, amused laugh. 'Some Spinsters prefer that someone else . . .'

'Do their dirty work?'

'Something like that.' Enora grins, and I feel trust growing roots in my belly. Despite my best attempts to remain wary and detached, I like Enora. Maybe this is how they'll break me – by giving me a friend.

'Valery is your primary aesthetician,' she says. 'She's kind and she won't make you look ridiculous.'

I study Enora's delicate face and hair. 'Is she your stylist?'

'She was . . .' She hesitates as though this subject is painful. Or maybe just off-limits. 'You will be in training for the next month,' she continues.

'It takes that long?' I ask, picking apart small cakes to remove dried fruits and nuts.

'For some,' she says with a shrug. 'Others are cleared more quickly, but everyone gets at least a month to prove herself.'

'And if I don't prove myself?'

Enora bites her lip and pretends to inspect the shoes lin-

ing the carts displaying my new wardrobe.

'Will I go to work making clothes for the other Spinsters?' I ask, sounding too hopeful.

'Yes, some do, but others become servants here at the Coventry.'

'They get to do the literal dirty work,' I murmur. The hierarchy is clearer now, and I understand why it's important to fall into place.

'Yes, it happens. Many Eligibles find the amount of stress that naturally comes with weaving to be too much. Their work lacks the focus and precision necessary in a Spinster.'

I hate to admit it, but this makes sense. You don't want someone with shaky hands working with the weave. It's so delicate that it could be disastrous. 'But how do we learn?'

'To weave?' she asks.

'Yes.' I bite my lip. 'What if I make a mistake?'

'Well, I'm not terribly worried about your ability, but you will be monitored. Spinsters follow close patterns established by the Creweler. Once you've spent some time on the practice sections and learned the various patterns, the work is fairly simple. It will be a while before you advance to ripping and altering.'

'Ripping?' The word scratches across my tongue. I'm not sure I want to know what it means.

'It's not as bad as it sounds,' Enora says, but her voice is unconvincing. 'It merely refers to removing weak or brittle threads.'

'By "threads", you mean people?'

There's a slight pause before she says, 'Yes.'

'So when you rip, you're killing someone?' I remember

my mother crying outside my grandmother's hospital room after a stern nurse sent us away for a moment; we never saw my grandmother again.

'It's much more humane than what used to happen,' Enora continues, her warm chocolate eyes misting over a little. 'In the past, people watched their loved ones die, and then buried their bodies.'

'What happens to people when they're ripped?' I whisper, recalling my grandmother's fragile hand squeezing mine tightly before we were sent to the hallway, still so strong.

'Honestly, I don't know,' she says. 'I'm sorry, it's just not my department.'

It's obvious from the tone of her voice. This conversation is over.

'You've mentioned the Creweler twice,' I say, shifting topics and hoping she's game to answer a few more questions. 'What exactly does she do?'

Enora smiles and something about the way her eyes dull tells me this is going to be a rehearsed answer. 'The Creweler helps the Guild harvest raw materials for the weave of Arras, and she guides our own work.'

'So I'll be working under her then?' For one brief moment, I want to ask if Maela is the Creweler, but if she is, I'd rather not know.

'No,' Enora says in a heavy voice. 'Her work is delicate and time-consuming. She rarely interacts with anyone but the officials and highest-ranked Spinsters. There's a lot you'll have to learn about how things work here, Adelice.'

Somehow this doesn't surprise me, but I hold back the comment I want to make.

'I'm sorry, I have a lot of questions,' I say instead. I want her to like me. I need allies here, but her dismissal leaves a bitter taste in my mouth.

'I can't blame you. It's been a difficult transition for you.' She stumbles on 'transition', and I realise how inadequate it sounds. With a full belly and a warm fire, it's been easy to forget my initial imprisonment, but now doubt creeps back up my spine and down through my limbs, shooting a chill along my nerves. I hate myself for forgetting what they did to me – to my whole family – after two hot meals and a night of luxury.

Enora glides over and waves me to my feet. Moments later she's fussily holding up ensembles, one after another, and muttering and sighing her disapproval. I see silk and satin, and each outfit looks skimpier than the last. I was never allowed to wear anything so revealing back home. It wouldn't have been proper for me to show my arms, let alone my flat chest. Between my guilt and my complete fear of anything without sleeves, I begin cracking my knuckles. Enora notices and leads me to the bathroom. My mom used to do the same thing – distract me when I was upset. Now that the Valpron has long worn off, I feel a constant throbbing ache when I think of my family. With the clutching pain of hunger loosened, it's become more acute. Almost unbearable.

'Enora,' I whisper, as she waves her hand over the switch scan, 'do you know what happened to my family?'

Enora gives me a slight shake of the head, but I can see the understanding in her eyes. 'I'll see what I can find out, but, for now, you need to get ready for orientation.'

The bathroom is every bit as oversized and decadent as my sleeping chamber. At one end, a small station with an aesthetician's chair waits ominously. I can only imagine how many hours I'll waste being fussed over there. The rest of the room is tiled in marble and porcelain. In the centre sits a large bath with small marble steps and benches carved along its edges. I could easily swim in it. It's already full and I wonder how this has been taken care of without my knowledge, like so many things here at the Coventry. I'm not sure I want to know the answer. There are no taps or spouts easily accessible, but I dip my toe gingerly at the edge and discover it's hot. The thought of heat soaking into my skin is so tempting. I'm pretty sure I would sell my soul for a bath after the nights in the cell.

'Your profile indicated that you liked water, so this was created for you.' Enora points to the extravagant pool. 'And you were appointed an ocean view.'

'I would have been fine with a shower stall,' I mutter.

'We could arrange to have it changed . . .' she says, a smirk playing on her lips, but I quickly shake my head, recalling the cramped old tub in my family's one bathroom.

'It'll be fine,' I say.

'I thought it would be.' She chuckles and takes my arm, shepherding me to the chair at the far end. 'Valery is here to work on you.'

I sigh and flop down in the chair, resigned to my fate. Valery is almost as beautiful as Enora or Maela. But her features are Eastern in origin, her eyes sloping elegantly around toffee irises. Even in her heels, she's much smaller than the rest of us. I'm beginning to understand why Spin-

sters are so finely polished. They could never allow other, inferior women to be more beautiful than they are. Staring at the number of prep tools on the cart next to me, I can't help wondering how much time they waste in pursuit of perfection.

After an hour of lining and curling and spraying, Enora brings in her final choice for today's outfit – a peacock-green suit that puffs at the sleeves and tapers to my knees. It is at once perfectly understated and completely unmissable. I slip into it and then grip the post of my bed while Enora hands me a pump.

'Wrong foot,' I say, passing it back to her. 'Left first, please.'

She gives it to me with a raised eyebrow. 'Superstitious? I've never heard that before.'

'Not superstitious.' I shake my head. 'My grandmother always told me to put my left shoe on first, because my left leg's stronger than my right. Easier to stand on one heel.' I slide on the shoe and demonstrate my perfect balance.

'Are you left-handed as well?' she asks.

'Yes, my grandmother was, too.' The memory of her tugs at me; it's an old sadness, more of a ghost than an ache, although it pulls harder on me here than it has for years. It's different from the hot, panicked grief I feel for the rest of my family.

Enora hands me my other shoe, and Valery pushes me towards the mirror. The image is not the shock it was yesterday, but this girl with the brilliant hair and bright eyes is not me. I'm simply dressed in someone else's skin.

Valery and Enora stand behind me like proud parents.

My new mentor places a hand gently on my shoulder.
'You're stunning, Adelice.'

'This isn't me,' I say, watching the strange scarlet lips
move.

'It is now,' Enora whispers firmly. I can hear in her voice
the same tone I use with Amie when I know what's best
for her, even when it's something she hates, like brussel
sprouts. I wonder if she has anyone watching over her now.
I feel the panic creeping from my belly into my throat, but
my reflection doesn't change.

Now that I'm dressed, Enora escorts me to my first
training class. I try to memorise the route — what my
hall looks like, which floor to choose on the lift — on
the off-chance that I'm ever allowed to move around the
compound alone. We don't pass through the same sterile
hallway we used yesterday. Instead she guides me out into
a beautiful garden surrounded by the high towered walls of
the Coventry. Sunlight radiates down on us directly, creating a bright spot in the centre of a concrete fortress. Palm
trees shade small, prickly pines. Animals scamper peace-
fully at my feet. It is the most wild — but tame — place I've
ever been. Just when I'm sure it's all screens like the ones
in my room, reflecting a pre-programmed code, I spy him
and a thrill sends my heart into my throat.

Crouched next to a wheelbarrow and wiping his forehead with a simple rag, there he is: the boy from the cells.
A gardener, an escort? What other jobs does he occupy
here and why? He glances up as we pass, and then he
looks more closely, and I feel a tense energy fill the space
between us — the force of it almost palpable. He's taking in

my vibrant tailored suit and new face. He looks puzzled for a moment, then something darker flickers across his face. It's not anger or hatred. It's not even lust.

It's disappointment.

5

Enora pushes past the young man and hurries me along to another tower door on the far side of the garden. I fight the urge to turn back to him. What would I do? Apologise? Explain myself? What did he expect? Did he think I was going to set fire to the compound and run away, hungry and cold?

'Adelice.' Enora's voice breaks into my thoughts.

'Sorry?'

'Try to pay closer attention during your orientation,' she says with a sigh, ushering me inside the other wing of the compound.

'It's just . . .' I struggle with exactly how to express my confused feelings about the boy in the garden. 'Why are there boys here?'

'There are a lot of tasks we can't do for ourselves,' she says matter-of-factly.

I give a slight nod, but I can't quite hide the fact that I don't buy it.

'Spinsters have important work to do,' Enora says, lowering her voice. 'The men make sure everything around here functions, and . . .' Her voice trails off and I can see she's making a choice.

'And?' I prompt.

'They're security,' she finishes.

'Are we in danger?' I ask in surprise.

'Us? No,' she says, and there's bitter edge to her voice. 'The Guild isn't keen on a compound made up entirely of women.'

Enora wasn't lying when she said she'd answer my questions, but I'm taken back by the trust she's shown me already. Considering she knows my biggest secret, I suppose it makes sense.

'You'll be with the rest of the Eligibles today. Make friends,' she says, changing the subject to the task at hand.

'It's the first day of academy all over again,' I mutter, eyeing the gaggle of women gathered around a large oak door.

'Yes,' she says, taking my shoulders in her tiny hands and directing my eyes back to hers. 'But you'll live with these girls for the rest of your life.'

I swallow hard. Academy doesn't seem so long ago, and yet the faces of the girls in my class are slipping away. It was one long beauty contest, each girl treading a fine line, maintaining the purity standards expected of Eligibles, while doing everything in her power to outshine the rest. Every week, someone had discovered something close to,

73

but not quite, a cosmetic. I hadn't been very good at gushing and primping. Pinch my cheeks? No thanks. Cosmetics and beauty treatments might be a reward for good behaviour growing up, and necessary when finally stepping into the less segregated work world, but here they feel like an even bigger joke than purity standards. As though we'll be happy to waste away behind locked doors if we can look pretty.

Making my way to join the group, I try to maintain a neutral expression. We're crowded in a plain hallway, waiting for the door in front of us to open. But the other girls, having broken into several smaller groups, maintain a steady stream of chatter with one another. It's a motley group – a lithe girl with delicately braided oil-black hair; another with skin the colour of rich coffee, her hair short and waved close to her scalp; girls with platinum hair and tailored blouses. I wonder if they are excited or nervous. If they have sold their souls for large bathtubs and fireplaces. If they'll do anything the Guild asks of them.

Two young officers usher us into a vast, open space filled with rows and rows of carefully placed chairs pointed towards a blank white wall. We file in and take our seats. The other girls sit together, giggling and chattering. I watch as a blonde girl reaches to touch the hair of the girl next to her. They're so familiar with one another. These girls weren't kept in cells, and they've obviously spent time together before now. I've missed a lot in the last few days.

The girl with oil-black hair drops into the chair next to mine. I can smell a rich hint of coconut drifting from her. Up close her skin is tawny, and her long legs stream past

her pencil skirt. She must be half a foot taller than me at least – without heels. I can't help but feel a little jealous of her exotic beauty as well as how relaxed she is in her new role. To my surprise she turns to speak to me. 'They've broken us into two groups. You're in mine.'

'Do I look lost?' I ask with a sheepish grin.

'No, you look overwhelmed,' she responds. 'It's easy to tell you're new, because most of us room together.'

I lower my voice to match hers: 'Together?'

'Not everyone gets her own room.' She grins, displaying a dazzling white smile set against chocolate lips.

'I'm sorry, you seem to have me at an advantage,' I say, curious as to how this girl knows me or my situation. 'I'm Adelice.'

'I know,' she says. 'My name is Pryana, and my mother was a maid in a small hotel for businessmen. She taught me that if you want to know the best gossip, you should get to know your maids. And right now, the best gossip around involves you.'

I think of the girls and boys bringing me food, stoking my fire, delivering my clothes, and feel like an elitist snob. I'm sure that's how I come off to them – an eager young Eligible hungry for power. It never occurred to me that they could be sources of information. Or that they were watching me.

'I'll keep that in mind.'

'Well, be careful,' Pryana says, dropping her voice even further so that our conversation is lost among the flurry of gossip. 'At your level, they pay more attention to who they have attending you. And with your history—'

'My level?'

'Girl, do you think we are all living in the lap of luxury? Do not get me wrong, I am very pleased with my current situation. But everyone in the Coventry wonders what landed a simple Eligible in the high tower.'

'I clearly need to befriend a maid,' I mutter. My mind is swimming with this new information. I have a pretty good idea why I'm getting special treatment, and it has nothing to do with favouritism.

Pryana gives me a sceptical look, unconvinced I'm the innocent I claim to be. But if she's going to press the matter, she doesn't get the chance because a brilliant display of colour lights up the blank wall we face. It fades in along the edges and gradually forms into the shape of a woman. The vlip is holographic, giving it the appearance of three dimensions. As though the woman were in the room with us, and not a mere recording.

'Welcome to training,' the holograph says with a smile. 'Being called to serve the Guild of Twelve is an honour and with honour comes privilege. The Western Coventry wants to ensure your transition into your new life as a Spinster is smooth and joyful. Each of you will be assigned a mentor during the training process. She will answer your questions and provide guidance on appropriate behaviour and dress.'

I look around the aisles. The other girls' eyes are glued to the vlip. Pryana catches my eye and grins.

'Arras depends on girls like you,' the actress in the vlip continues. 'The Guild is a complex organisation charged with the care of our entire world, and you are a vital piece of our oligarchy. During training you will be observed as

you complete a variety of tasks designed to test your skill, precision, and dedication to preserving the integrity of Arras. Your work will be carefully supervised as you learn how to read the specific patterns of our world, and your behaviour will be monitored by security personnel and audio surveillance to ensure the safety of everyone in the compound. This is precious information given to you in confidence of your allegiance to the Guild of Twelve. Each of you was brought here because you exhibited the potential to become a Spinster, but your placement and position within the Coventry will be made based on the observations of our specially appointed training panel.'

A few of the girls murmur in surprise at this news. They must not have been appointed mentors yet. I almost feel sorry that some of them have left everything they know and love behind to wind up as servants. Almost.

'Rest assured that once you have been called by the Guild, you have a place here. There are opportunities for every girl's skills in the Western Coventry, and regardless of where in Manipulation Services you are ultimately placed, you will enjoy many of the privileges allotted to Spinsters. Due to the sensitive nature of your training, it is impossible for you to return to civilian lives, but you will each have a home and job here from this day forward.'

'What exactly does that mean?' Pryana hisses beside me.

'It means'— I lean in so only she can hear — 'that some of us might wind up scrubbing kitchen floors.'

Her eyes widen, but she shakes her head in disbelief.

'Ever ask your maid how she landed a job cleaning your toilet?' I ask.

'I will now.'

I can't imagine anyone could be charming enough to prompt a former Eligible to reveal her rejection. It's one thing to be catty about others' misfortunes but harder to admit your own.

'Your duties will be assigned based on skill level. There are always opportunities for advancement for loyal Spinsters of the Guild,' the holographic woman continues. Behind her an enormous machine flickers into view on the screen. It's a loom, like the one they presented me with in testing, only bigger. Gears and wheels grind together silently, connected to a series of intricate silver tubes. As she speaks, sparkling strands weave across it in a mixture of gold and other colours. I know from experience that the gold is time, and when I focus hard enough to see the weave around me, these strands flow across, forming bands. The other strands weave through the bands, forming a tight, colourful tapestry.

Before this moment, I've only seen looms during testing, and then I spent so much time ignoring my compulsion to touch the weave that its subtlety was lost on me. Now it shimmers with life. But as I watch, the image on the screen changes. The gears of the loom adjust, zooming in on a portion of the weave on the loom. First, the fibres suggest an aerial view of a neighbourhood. Then the weave is focused more closely until it reveals the image of a street. And finally, the weave reveals a family sitting inside their home. The vlip then winds the image back to the complex weave it first showed us.

'Spinsters work hand in hand with the men who oversee

the Guild of Twelve. In the Western Coventry compound, your work will be focused on basic weaving, maintenance, and Crewel work. Our compound is responsible for food and weather, and our most advanced Spinsters handle special issues specific to our sector. You were each transported to this facility based on your aptitude tests. Should you develop skills in other areas, the Guild may issue a transfer of assignment at any time. All four coventries work together to maintain the physical integrity of Arras's weave and to ensure our world is bound together in safety and prosperity. Each coventry is carefully located to provide optimum control over the weave, and while each has specific tasks assigned to the women working its looms, all are of equal importance. Advanced Spinsters may perform Crewel work, a form of manipulation that adds to Arras and controls elements crucial to our survival.

'The peace and prosperity of Arras are enabled through your work on the looms. Following patterns strictly to ensure the metros function smoothly, and monitoring the weave for evidence of deterioration, allow us to catch dangerous behaviour and conditions before they can affect the safety of our citizens. Special techniques have been designed to clean and renew threads damaged by aberrant tendencies. We work closely with academies across the world to catch deviants at a young age. This ensures a crime- and accident-free population. We rely on you to report any irregularities found in the weave in a timely manner.'

So that's what Cormac meant when he laughed at me in the café. Arras isn't as peaceful as the Stream and officials

would have us believe, at least not naturally. Whatever this procedure is that cleans strands, I'm sure it's what they used in Romen after my disastrous retrieval. Would citizens feel as safe knowing deviant behaviour exists but is merely wiped away from recollection? Or that their children's threads can be cleaned at any time if a teacher expresses concern? For the first time, I'm glad I'm not a teacher put in that impossible situation. And I understand the gilded cage of false windows and concrete they keep us in. We can never go home with this knowledge.

The vlip fades from the holographic message to a slideshow of images from across Arras, drawing my attention away from this revelation. I'm glued to the images now, but to my disappointment, the metros on the vlip look the same as Romen – concrete, sky towers with thousands of windows spiking up from the metro centre, and small houses and stores dotting the perimeter in perfect spirals. The plants are the only parts of the landscapes that seem to vary. In Romen, we had grass and looming elm trees, bushes, and carefully preened flowers in yellow and white. But these metros have palm trees, pines, ferns, and tall yellow grass; these are plants I've only seen on screens during academy lessons. The differences are minute, but seeing all of Arras before me is exciting.

'Welcome to the Western Coventry and may your hands be blessed,' the woman's voice concludes.

The final image is one of a towering complex that I've seen dozens of times in academy. It's where I sit now: the Western Coventry. Several girls squeal with delight but I feel the weight of the concrete and brick pressing down

on me. There's nothing exciting about the compound. It's walled. Industrial. It's what it stands for – the promise of power and privilege – that thrills the others. But all I see is the lack of windows and how it rises like an endless cage into the cloudless sky. No one can ever escape it.

'You don't look so good,' Pryana whispers to me as the vlip fades away. 'Did the images give you motion sickness?'

I shake my head, genuinely pleased by her concern. 'I'm fine. It's just been a long few days.'

'Well, I for one am ready to get on those looms. I've been dying to since testing,' she says, her coffee-black eyes sparkling at the prospect.

'You haven't got to try them out yet?' I ask, more than a little surprised.

'No,' Pryana confirms. 'So far it's been measurements, etiquette lessons, and small-group vlips. Let's see. We've been reminded at least a hundred times about the import-ance of chastity to maintain our skills.'

'Not much of a chance that will be an issue here.' I laugh at her annoyed look.

'Are you kidding me?' she says, rolling her eyes. 'Have you seen him?'

She points to the door, and I look over to see Erik wait-ing to usher us to our next session. Enora is nowhere in sight, but I guess most of the Spinsters are working.

'Him?' I ask nonchalantly.

'Come on, he's gorgeous,' she gushes. 'If half the officers look half as good as him, they'll need to show me that stu-pid purity-standards vlip every day.'

I have to admit she's right. Today his wild blond hair is

smoothed back and it neatly brushes the shoulders of his dark pinstriped suit. I wonder if it was his skills or his looks that got him the job assisting Maela. But Pryana's blatant attention is a bit much. I can't help but notice now the reactions of the girls in the room to his entrance. Several glance over shyly, others sit up and thrust their chests forward, but every girl is aware of him. I suppose it's not so surprising given segregation. Someone like Erik, or any of the many officers, is the first contact most of us have had with boys close to our own age. I don't want to shrink down like some of other Eligibles, as though I'm embarrassed by my femininity. But maybe that explains my sharp tongue when I'm around men, or the way the strange boy made my heart race as he led me from the cells.

'Yeah, he's cute,' I say, trying to be friendly. 'His hair is awfully long though. I'm surprised they let him wear it that way.'

'I guess they're not going to have any problems with you and purity standards,' Pryana teases. 'Besides, I hear long hair is common in coastal villages like Saxun. Oh, it's time to go!'

Most of the girls are already in the hallway, and Erik takes the lead, while several other officers trail behind us.

'Ladies, today I'll be leading you on a tour of the compound. As you may know, I assist Maela, the Spinster in charge of training, but her duties require her on the loom today. We'll be visiting the studios and departments housed in the Western Coventry,' Erik says loudly, so the whole group can hear. 'Rest assured that I've been well trained to guide you.'

'Drat,' Pryana mutters. 'No looms, but at least we get to follow him around today.'

Instead of agreeing with her, I grab her arm and drag her to the front of the group. I'm not missing a minute of this tour. Erik raises one eyebrow as I push to the front, but he doesn't say anything.

'Girl,' Pryana whispers, 'he's looking at you.'

'Yeah, because I knocked over half the group to get up here,' I whisper back.

'About that – I like your style.'

I give her an appreciative grin, and then turn my attention back to Erik, who has continued his spiel. At the end of the hallway, three corridors split off, and he leads us into the leftmost hallway.

'Most of you will be working in entry-level positions,' he says as he opens a door into a large room. Inside, rows of small looms form perfect lines and each is occupied by a Spinster busily working with her piece of Arras. On the far wall, a couple of square windows allow light to stream through, but the packed atmosphere of the studio is claustrophobic.

'You'd think they could give us more light,' Pryana says.

'Especially since those aren't real windows,' I mutter back. Out of the corner of my eye, I see Erik frown.

'Not real windows?' Pryana repeats.

Between her surprise and Erik's annoyed look, I realise I'm not supposed to know that the walls and windows of the compound are programmed screens. Wild creatures are happy enough if they don't know they're being kept in a cage.

83

'Yeah, the windows in my room are huge,' I lie. 'They could put bigger windows in the studios.'

Pryana relaxes, happy to believe my explanation, but Erik tilts his head and stares me down before he motions for the group to move on.

'At the entry level, you will handle rationing – weaving food from the farm cities into cities across Arras. You may also watch for loose threads or any other signs of decay,' he tells us as we pass room after room like the first one. There must be hundreds of Spinsters focused on these simple tasks.

'From there,' he continues, leading us into a new passage, 'you may progress to studios that focus on weather, ensuring the right amount of precipitation falls throughout each sector. In others, you may perform standard removals and alterations like rebounds.'

The weather studios are roomier and only a dozen or so girls work in each. The looms they occupy are larger, and none of them seem to notice the new girls watching them. Or maybe they don't care.

'I think I'd rather work here,' Pryana says to me.

I have to agree with her. I'm not sure I could handle the stuffiness of the earlier rooms, or the menial tasks expected of entry-level Spinsters.

'The most gifted Spinsters will work in the next wing, though,' Erik calls to the crowd.

We follow him out of the passage and into a circular room. The heavy door to these studios is guarded and requires security clearance.

'Unfortunately, the work done in these studios is so

sensitive that we can't risk interrupting the Spinsters work-ing there,' he says.

The girls around me groan and hiss, but he raises a hand to indicate he wants to finish his lecture.

'I understand that it's disappointing, but it's also neces-sary. The upper studios house the Emergency Department, which ensures no accidents occur in the Western Sector. They also house our Western Department of Origins. The Spinsters there oversee the delivery of babies into Arras.'

'Say what?' Pryana asks loudly, and a few girls around us chuckle. 'There's babies up there?'

Erik shakes his head, but I spy a smile tugging at his lips.

'No,' he reassures her. 'The process of bringing new life into Arras is very precise. Once a pregnancy has been approved through local Guild clinics, the department of origins in that sector works in tandem with the local doc-tors and hospitals to bring the new life into Arras smoothly. To accomplish this, Spinsters schedule births, so the new thread can be woven in as the baby is delivered by the doc-tor and surgical team. It's a routine procedure here at the Coventry, but it requires a delicate touch.'

'I want to deliver babies,' a short girl with light brown hair says. 'Wouldn't that be so nice?'

I nod my head automatically, but my mind is on my mother and the scar that marred her perfect figure, right across her belly. My parents made sure I knew how babies were made, insisting it was unfair to expect me to meet purity standards without knowing what I had to stay away from, but they never explained how babies actually came into the world. Now I understood why it was impossible

for her to have another child without permission. And all those years I had pleaded with her to have a baby and talked back when she said it was impossible. Why couldn't she have opened up more to me about the expectations and rules? Maybe then I would have known to run from retrieval instead of waiting in my chair for them to come.

'What else is up there?' Pryana asks Erik, edging a little too close to him.

I watch as she ventures from the safety of our group. She's so at ease, clearly secure in her tight dress suit that shows off her long, amber legs. I can't help marvelling at the way confidence rolls off her, and if I'm being honest, I'm a bit jealous, too. Erik barely notices her, though, which means he's either very good at his job or my suspicion that he's more than Maela's personal assistant is correct.

'Everything else is classified information,' he says, stepping away from Pryana and beckoning to the group to show that it's time to go.

'Maybe he doesn't like girls,' Pryana mutters as she drifts back over to me.

'He's trained to keep us at a distance,' I say. 'I doubt he'd last long here if all the new Spinsters couldn't keep their purity standards around him.'

'You're probably right,' she says with a sigh. 'I can keep looking at him though.'

We continue on our tour, and I struggle between wanting to ask Pryana about everything I missed and trying to play it cool. Thankfully, she seems eager to fill me in on all the gossip.

'We had ten retrievals in Cypress,' she says as we walk with the group. 'I think it broke some kind of record.'

I hear pride in her voice.

'And they found you all at testing?' I ask, wondering if girls from Romen are particularly untalented.

'Of course,' Pryana says. 'They're up there mostly.'

She points to the girls who had trailed at the back of the original group and now led it. They have the same shiny black hair and tawny skin as she does.

'Were you friends with any of them?' I ask.

Pryana shakes her head in disgust.

'No, girls in that town only care about getting their courtship appointments. Northern cities are like that. I hear they're more ambitious in the east.'

I wonder for a moment what they say about us westerners, but I don't ask. I'm more interested in why Pryana wants to be here. 'What about you?' I ask. 'What about your family? Were they happy you were called?'

'Sure,' she says, looking at me like I'm crazy. 'My mom's a maid. She always dreamed I'd move up, and my kid sister can't wait to get called in a few years.'

My heart aches at the thought of Pryana possibly getting to see her sister in a few years. After my parents' struggle, the Guild will probably ensure that Amie never winds up here, even if she is called. And I'm more than a little jealous of how easily Pryana is adjusting to her new life.

To my surprise, when we reach the entrance to this wing of the compound, we're stopped. Erik whispers with another guard and disappears into the next room. Instead of leading us forward, the guard motions that we should wait

here. A few moments later, more guards appear, and my stomach twists. We're asked to return to the hallway, and then we're herded to a long, winding staircase. We climb up the towers like the tragic princesses in the family story-books secreted away in my parents' cubby-holes.

The staircase opens into a grand stone room with oddly shaped windows speckling the walls, too small to fit through but easy to see out of – the kind of room you hide a girl away in. Everywhere there are large, steel looms like the ones from the vlip, but these are cold and slick and empty. Each connects to the others through a series of gears and wheels. Tubes run along the walls, curving and wrapping around the great steel beasts. Evenly spaced around the room are short padded stools. I wonder if they've dismissed the Spinsters who work here so we can use the machines.

The other girls point and whisper, with wide eyes, and I feel left out again.

Maela, looking as stunning as she did in the room of mirrors, sweeps into the room followed by Erik and another bodyguard. The other guard's hair is cropped close to his scalp, but both men are perfectly angular, striking, and clearly dangerous. Maela towers in front of us, her crimson dress a splash of blood against the dark backdrop of the men. I know she wants to intimidate us, but I straighten up and raise my jaw ever so slightly to show it's not working.

'Good afternoon,' she trills, flourishing her arms. 'Today we begin your journey to becoming Spinsters, and you will have your first test. It will measure your natural ability to read the weave and your control over your ability.

It will also provide immeasurable benefit to the cities you see before you now.'

Several girls applaud this announcement, but I stare straight ahead.

'We have an unexpected treat for you. Normally you wouldn't have access to a real loom until your talent has been confirmed and honed, but we have occasion to do a little pre-emptive pruning this year. I know how excited you are to have this opportunity.' Her eyes flick over to me as she speaks. 'But as the orientation vlip told you, not all of you will become Spinsters.'

The group around me shifts and fidgets. The buzz of delight that filled the group an hour ago has faded into quiet panic.

'Rest assured that when you were invited—'

I laugh before I can stop myself.

'Adelice, is something humorous?' Maela asks sharply, and every head swivels around to stare at me.

'You reminded me of something that happened earlier.' I smile, forcing myself to meet her gaze. 'But please continue.'

If looks could kill.

'As I was saying . . .' Maela only misses a beat, but I'm sure I've drawn unnecessary attention to myself. 'You will all remain here in service to the Coventry. Many of those dismissed from Spinning or Crewel work are quite happy working in our mill or in various other necessary positions.'

As maids and servants.

'There will always be a place for you here.' Maela gives a precise sort of smile.

Many of the girls look pacified, although a few seem to be considering what they've just been told.

'One of the most important aspects of Spinning is the removal of weak strands. Each person, object, and place within Arras has its own thread – or in the case of a place, a woven section. We maintain Arras by redistributing, adding, and removing these strands and sections of the whole. If one thread is weak, it jeopardises the others around it. The weave is pliable, allowing for some flexibility within the cities, and for our work, of course. But put simply, some threads are more resilient than others. We must be careful to repair and replace when necessary, but we must also remove at times.'

She is speaking directly to me now. 'If too many strands are weak, it compromises large sections, and as you can imagine, this puts everyone at risk.' She breaks eye contact with me to seek affirmation from her silent audience.

The other Eligibles nod earnestly. I don't. Next to me Pryana bumps my arm as though she's urging me to join in and agree.

No one asks any questions. They bob their heads in synchronised conformity as though *why* we are being asked to do these things is trivial. All that matters is doing what the Guild asks us, because they say it's important. Doesn't the gradual ebbing of the time bands spark curiosity? Don't they want to know how the machines help us work? I'm not in a position, as Maela's least favourite student, to ask these questions, and no one else seems to care.

'Today you will each be completing your first removal,' Maela tells us.

'You mean ripping?' Pryana asks. For a brief moment the muscles of Maela's jaw visibly tense, but she remains composed.

I think I like Pryana enough to make friends, like Enora instructed.

'Yes, some people refer to it as such. I find the term vulgar,' Maela answers smoothly, but her jaw is still tensed.

I find the whole thing vulgar, but I bite my tongue so as not to attract her wrath or more attention from her rapt disciples.

Maela nods to Erik, who steps towards the far wall and presses a series of buttons. The other girls watch him. Even Pryana's gaze is greedy as he strides by. As soon as he enters the code, glistening, nearly transparent tapestries appear on the strange steel looms dotting the room. The appearance of the weave is the only thing that can tear their attention from him. Many of the girls gasp, and one even shrinks back as if the mere sight scares her. For girls who've only touched a practice loom at testing, the sight of Arras laid before them must be overwhelming. Even though I've always been able to visualise the weave, seeing it like this, called up for our use, makes my stomach knot.

'Can you see the weave without a loom?' The question is out of my mouth before I can swallow it back, but I need to know how big a freak I am.

Erik stares at me curiously, but Maela looks annoyed at the interruption.

'No, that's ridiculous. The weave is the very time and matter that we occupy. Of course you can't just see it,' she snaps.

Except, *of course* I can. But apparently she can't, and judging from the looks on the others' faces, neither can they. I'm alone in this ability.

'This,' she continues, gesturing to a large ornate piece woven with vibrant greens, pinks, and reds, 'is you.'

The girls crowd closer together and press forward to see the brilliant weave.

'We're beautiful,' a petite girl notes with awe.

'Of course you are,' Maela coos. 'The rest of these pieces are from various cities within the Western Sector. The looms allow us to call up and view the actual fabric of Arras, and each day the Spinsters prune the parts of the weave that are our responsibility. They check for brittle threads, and they handle any removal requests we receive through proper authorities.'

She demonstrates how to adjust the settings on the loom to pull the weave's image into more detailed focus. As we watch, the piece of Arras on the loom zooms from a swirling array of colours and light into the subtle image of a house.

'You can request removal?'

'Yes, certainly. Individuals may request removal as well as law enforcement officials. Hospital staff submit removal requests for individuals in poor health and for the elderly.'

I think of my grandmother and wonder who put in her request – certainly not her or my mother. She wasn't weak enough to need removal. My eyes smart at the idea of some doctor deciding it was her time to go.

'These looms feature areas where maintenance is needed. We will visit each, and you will be given a chance

to identify the weak point and remove it. Although the looms are equipped to allow you to zoom in and out of the piece as necessary and even to locate very specific strands, there's a certain skill to being able to find the weakness without using the magnifiers and locators.'

I shift uncomfortably in my heels and notice several other Eligibles doing the same. It's a lot to ask considering we're so new.

'No need to be frightened,' Maela says reassuringly, obviously sensing the apprehension around her. 'You simply use your fingers to read the weave. Watch.'

Moving to the nearest loom, Maela traces a long, polished finger over the surface, from left to right, moving in lines down the piece until her hand stops. Closing her eyes briefly, Maela lets her hand rest there.

'Here,' she says, and the group goes utterly still. 'It is thinner than the rest. Worn and tired. I can feel the stress it is placing on the other threads nearby. They are doing more than their fair share to keep everything together.'

No one breathes as Maela takes a long silver instrument from the caddy at the edge of the loom. 'Simply hook this end,' she says as she gently threads the crook between the strands and with a swift motion rends the piece. A shimmering thread hangs from the end of the hook and she holds it out for us to inspect. 'Simple.'

My stomach flips over. What does it feel like to be removed? The piece still exists, but where is that person now?

'Now, who is ready for her turn?' asks Maela.

A dozen girls crowd forward, eager to prove themselves.

Pryana meets my eye, and I see horror reflecting back in her almond eyes. At least I'm not the only one sickened by this test.

Girl after girl steps up and attempts the test. One girl nearly takes out an entire section, but Maela swiftly stops her. I wonder if her mistake will doom her to a life slaving away at the mercy of the Coventry. Soon only Pryana and I are left. I see how unnerved she is, and I step forward, not only to give her a few more moments to compose herself, but also to get it over with.

Maela leads me to a new piece. It is more intricately woven than the other pieces we've seen so far; thousands of glinting threads lace and wind together in a rainbow canvas of light. A few girls eye it apprehensively. It is much more complex than the rest, but it's not what scares me.

'Let's see what you can do,' she says encouragingly.

I reach forward and softly touch my fingertips to the piece. The sensation is shocking. I've touched pieces of a weave before, but never sections that contained people. There's a charge running through the piece, and I realise that what I'm feeling is the energy of the thousands of lives that rest under my fingers. Despite the complexity, my hand immediately senses the weakness. It's so minuscule I can't imagine trying to remove it without damaging all the other strands around it. I also can't imagine that this tiny weakness could be a real threat to such a large, tightly woven piece.

'It's here,' I murmur, and I hear an impressed buzz from the others around me.

'Very good,' Maela replies simply. She brandishes the

hook like a weapon, and I see the dare in her eyes. She must know this ripping is unnecessary – possibly dangerous – but it's clear I'm being tested at a more advanced level.

'No need.' I remove my hand from the spot. 'It's no danger to such a beautifully woven piece.'

'That's not really a determination for you to make, Adelice,' she hisses, and she holds the hook out further.

'Removing it would risk all the surrounding threads. It's not necessary.' I lift my chin and meet her eyes, daring her to defy my proclamation.

'Adelice, I won't tell you again. You put us all in danger when you don't do your part,' she says, as though she's instructing me on simple addition and subtraction.

'And I'm telling you there is no risk,' I reiterate, my heart beginning to race. 'In fact, it would be more dangerous to remove it.'

'Is that so?' She seems genuinely interested in my opinion, but I know it's just a show. 'In that case . . .'

Her motion is so swift, I don't see it coming. She wields the hook like a razor, slashing across the piece and brashly ripping an entire section out. Hundreds of shimmering threads hang off the hook, and she beckons for the burly officer.

'Take these – and the others – to storage, and inform the Spinster on duty that we need an emergency patch.' She hands the hook to him nonchalantly. No one else speaks; we only stare.

I try to bite my tongue, but the flood of hot anger rising up my body and into my cheeks prevents it. 'That was unnecessary.'

'I told you that even one weak thread was a danger.' Maela frowns and shakes her head in a gesture meant to convey sympathy. Or perhaps remorse. Neither is believable.

'Do you want to be responsible for a tragedy?' she asks me, her gaze travelling around the room. The question is rhetorical, but several of the girls shake their heads.

'If we fail to do our job, we compromise everything that's been built,' she continues, and as she stares me down, she turns a tiny knob on the side of the loom. The weave before us, mangled and torn open, begins to shift into clearer focus. At first it looks like a piece of cloth, intricately woven, stretching across the machine, but as she zooms in and adjusts the visual it becomes a town. It's as though I'm looking at a map with a hole in it, and then she clicks the wheel another notch and it becomes a street view. A perfect tree-lined lane, much like the one at home, leading up to a building, an academy. There is the arch of a doorway and the brick façade of the entrance and then nothing. The rest of the building is gone, simply ripped away, leaving bits of bricks tumbling and disappearing into an abyss. It just isn't there any more.

I haven't been able to grasp what she's done until now. Seeing the weave in tapestry form couldn't call up the anger this image did. This for a lesson? And what have we learned? That Maela is a psycho. Sure, I could have guessed that. Is this why they need cleaning technology, to sweep away the actions of people like her? Is she who we need to forget?

She keeps her violet eyes on me, until the hint of a smile flits across her face. She doesn't allow it to settle there long

96

enough for anyone but me to notice. 'I think we're done for today.'

I glance back at Pryana, who may be my friend now. I've saved *her* at least, if only for the moment. Her face says it all – she's not ready for this. As eager as she was to become a Spinster, it's clear she didn't expect this. But if I'm being honest, I didn't either.

'Pryana, you are excused,' Maela says. 'In light of the situation, it wouldn't be fair.'

Pryana's coffee eyes echo the alarm I feel.

'I'm so sorry for your loss,' Maela simpers, squeezing Pryana's shoulder.

'What loss?' The girl's voice is so low, Maela looks at her like she can't hear.

I speak up instead, my mouth dry. 'She asked, what loss?'

'Unfortunately –'Maela lingers on the word – 'this piece is from the academy in Cypress.'

Pryana gasps as her eyes dart to the spot, trying to read the brilliant web.

'I can't imagine much of it is left.' Maela offers an apologetic look and then turns to whisper to Erik.

'My sister attends the academy in Cypress,' Pryana says quietly.

Everyone is watching her now, but her eyes stay fixed on the mutilated piece. A few of the other girls glance over at me. When Pryana lifts her eyes, she looks directly at me.

'You killed her.'

I'm fairly positive Maela expects *her* to kill *me*. I'm certainly bracing for it when a pair of firm hands grip my arms. Erik is pulling me away to safety.

6

We walk swiftly until we reach the stone hallway I was led from only yesterday. There Erik slows and loosens his grip on me. I look up to catch him grinning at me. He's all business in his dark, trim suit, carefully shaved and groomed. Only his wild blond hair and lopsided smirk belie his professionalism. He's younger than I thought. In total fairness, I've been half-drugged or half-starved during our previous meetings. Still, I can't help wondering if he's as dangerous as his boss.

'Did I miss a joke?' I ask.

'Oh, you were there,' Erik assures me, still grinning. 'You sure know how to get under Maela's skin. I've never seen her lose it like that.'

'You have a strange sense of humour.' I think back to Maela's perfect calm, broken by a single, disastrous moment of fury. But perhaps even then she was in control, her

anger precise in its purpose, turning Pryana against me.

'Why didn't you do it?' he asks.

'It wasn't necessary. That thread was strong,' I answer without hesitation.

'But the Guild has a purpose in asking for its removal,' Erik argues, dropping my arm altogether.

'Do they?' I ask, and then wish I hadn't. I'm sure that everything I say to him will be reported straight back to Maela, especially if it sounds like I'm questioning things. But if he's got a response to my scepticism, he doesn't share it.

We stop at a towering oak door, and he jostles it open.

'Do you want the penny tour?' he offers, his blue eyes twinkling a bit.

I take a look around the empty stone cell and shake my head. 'I've been here before, but thanks anyway.'

'Well, I'll check on you later,' he says, stepping back into the hall.

'I can't wait.'

'I know.' Erik shoots me a wink as he pulls the large door closed.

The first thing I notice is the toilet. I must have done something to deserve this slight improvement in my imprisonment, but I'm not sure what. Regardless, it's small comfort. I know now I'll die here. Maybe not in this cell, but somewhere in the Coventry. It should bother me more than it does. But rather than focus on my own fate, here in the dark, I think of my mother and Amie. Here in this cell without the blinding lamps and overbearing colour of the compound, I can sketch them in my mind. The way my

mother chewed her lipstick off when she was concentrating. Or how Amie would tell me, down to the colour of their socks, what every girl in her class wore to academy and who got in trouble for talking during quiet hour. The blackness lets me imagine we're back in my room, giggling at how Yuna Landew got called out of class to be interrogated about her purity. Of course, that part doesn't seem so funny to me any more.

Now that I know how far the Guild will go to prove a point, I wonder what really happened to Yuna. Maybe she played dumb better than I can. I should have known Maela's little test wasn't aimed at weeding out the weak girls so much as testing my loyalty. Hundreds are dead because of me. And who have I 'saved'? An elderly teacher or a terminally ill child?

Just as I'm sinking into total hopelessness, the door to my cell creaks open. I start when I realise that it's the strange boy with the disappointed eyes, bringing my meal.

'Miss me that much?' he teases, setting the tray down near me. I've been huddling in a corner that feels warmer than the rest of the cell.

'Don't flatter yourself. I have a fetish for cold prison floors.'

'Fetish? Big word.' He raises one eyebrow at me, challenging me to explain how a pure Eligible knows a word like that.

I want to tell him that unlike the other simpering idiots here I've actually read a book or two in my life, but no matter how much it might impress him, I keep the information locked in my head and glare up at him. It's not a very

impressive glare, because something about the smirk he's trying to hide at my wounded expression makes me feel silly and excited and happy all at the same time.

To my surprise, he crosses the cell and drops down beside me.

'Thought I warned you to play dumb,' he says with a lowered voice.

'Guess I didn't listen,' I retort with a shrug.

'You'll get yourself killed.' He sounds resigned as though he knows I don't care any more.

'I'm dead already. We all are.'

'Death is peaceful,' he growls. 'This half-life is worse.'

He's less grimy than before but still unshaved and rough, and he hasn't bothered to tie back his curly brown hair. He's nothing like my dad or my friends' fathers or even the guards here at the compound. It's this coarseness that sets him apart from the well-groomed men of Arras I know. But it's the penetrating way he watches me that makes me catch my breath when our eyes meet.

'You're a lot cleaner than the last time I saw you,' I point out, and immediately wish I could take it back.

'I don't waste my time on manicures like some men,' he says lightly.

I assume he's taking a shot at Erik, but then again my dad kept his nails clean, too.

'So you don't shave. You don't get manicures. What do you do?'

'I keep this place running,' he says, as though that's enough of an answer.

'And?' I push.

'Technically I'm the head valet, which means I communicate between the staff and the Spinsters. I make sure things run smoothly. I got the call that you were to be taken to the salons and thought I'd check you out.'

I bite my lip and nod.

'What?' he asks. 'Oh, I guess I was pretty unkempt when we met, even for me. I had been gardening. It's the one thing I do just for me. I like the feeling of soil. It's honest labour.'

'My grandmother gardened,' I say. 'A long time ago, before you had to have a permit. She said the same thing.'

'Stupid Guild,' he says. 'I bet she missed it. I'm lucky I can bend the rules here. Everyone is too busy controlling the outside world to care.'

'How come you aren't dead?' I ask. 'Or at least stuck in a cell? I haven't heard a word from you yet that isn't treasonous.'

'Unlike you, I pay attention to who I'm talking to. I have a special traitor filter I use around others.' He gives me a tired smile that belongs to someone much older.

'So why me?'

''Cause you ran,' he responds simply.

'I can't be the first Eligible who ever ran.' I shake my head at the impossibility that no one else has ever tried to escape the Coventry.

'No, but you're special.'

'Yeah, what makes me different? Or do you talk treason with all the flighty girls?' I realise that I'm flirting with him, and I'm surprised at how comfortable it feels.

'They didn't kill you.' The playful mood dissipates immediately. It's clear that he's not joking.

'Well, I guess it's good to be different,' I mutter.

Neither of us laughs.

'Why?' I ask after a moment.

'I'm sorry?'

'Why not kill me? I ran. My parents tried to hide me. Why leave me alive?' I ask earnestly, and he turns away.

'I have my theories.'

'And they are?' I press.

'I'm not sure you're ready to hear them yet.'

'That's sort of condescending. Telling me only what you think I'm ready to hear,' I point out, annoyed as much by it as by his lack of transparency.

'I thought it was endearing, me looking out for you.' He grins, and the mood in the dark cell lightens again.

'Are you trying to endear yourself to me?'

'I have a thing for traitors.'

'How do you know I'm a traitor anyway?' I ask. 'Maybe everyone is wasting their time worrying about me.'

'You're in the cells for the second time in a week and you're still alive.' He squints against the dark as if to get a clearer look at my face. 'Either Maela is breaking in her new pet, or you've got something they want.'

'Like an attitude?'

'Maela is all stocked up on that.' He snorts. 'If you could lie low and not draw so much attention to yourself, we might actually be able to find out, Adelice.'

'See, that's our problem,' I point out.

'What? Your inability to keep a low profile?' he asks.

'No, the fact that I don't even know your name. How am I supposed to trust you?'

'Josten.' He smiles all the way up through his eyes. 'But traitors call me Jost.'

'Nice to meet you, Jost.' I stretch out a hand and immediately regret it because the change in position makes me shiver.

'Here.' He shrugs off a simple, threadbare jacket and wraps it around me. 'Unfortunately, I'll have to take that when I go. It wouldn't do for anyone to see me giving gifts to the prisoners. It might detract from *my* low profile.'

The jacket is soft and smells like woodsmoke and cut lavender. I nod, grateful for its warmth if only for a few moments.

'You shouldn't be here,' I say. 'They're probably watching me.'

'The good news is that they don't bother to keep an eye on the cells. Poor light, stone walls — what's the point?' He gestures around us. 'The bad news is that you're right. They're definitely keeping tabs on you.'

'So why are you here then? What help can I be to you if I'm already under suspicion?'

'That's true, but no one comes down here, so it's easy enough for us to chat if you keep getting thrown in the cell,' he points out.

'Of course,' I agree. 'But that won't really help me lie low now, will it?'

'Yep, it's a no-win situation,' he says. 'I'm actually only here today because Erik had lapdog duties.'

'Erik sent you?'

'The pretty blond that just threw you in here.'

'I know who he is, and he is pretty, but why send you now?'

'It's my job to keep the Spinsters happy and fed, so pretty boy sent me. Sorry to disappoint you, but please tell me you have better taste than him.'

'I'm not marrying him. He's just well-groomed,' I assure Jost. 'But lapdogs usually are.'

'Case in point.' Jost fingers the hem of my tailored skirt.

'I think I'm failing at being a lapdog.'

'Yes, you are,' he says. 'So I'll remind you of my earlier advice: play dumb.'

'That's easier said than done.'

'Ob-vi-ous-ly.' He stretches out the word. 'But it's important if you want to live. Maela may have a use for you, but she's not sentimental enough to keep you around indefinitely.'

'Why?'

'You're going to have to trust me for a bit on that.'

'Just so long as your reasons are as vague and menacing as theirs are,' I mutter.

'Ouch.' Jost frowns. 'I may not tell you everything, but my interests are in line with your own.'

He straightens back up, and I shrug the jacket off and hand it to him. 'Thank you.'

'It was nothing.' He waves my thanks away as he puts his jacket on.

'Not for the jacket.' I struggle to put into words how I feel. 'For the company.'

'Also nothing. Take my advice, Ad.' This time the cockiness is gone and the nickname wraps around me like his jacket – soft and comfortable. I feel warmer. 'They'll let you go soon. Try to stay out of trouble.'

Jost leaves me in the darkness, and I continue to wait, turning over his words in my mind. He's being too honest with me. Either he knows something that makes him trust me more than he should, or . . . I stop myself there. I don't want to consider his other possible motive.

Knowing they aren't watching me here relaxes me. I fiddle with the time around me. If only there was a spot of heat in this room, I could weave warmth, or maybe even light.

The food at my feet is stale and cold. A tough bit of bread and thin soup. It's food to keep me alive and not much more. I could weave and stretch it, but I have to work with the materials I have, and more of this food wouldn't be much of an upgrade. Then I remember promising my parents that I would never stretch food again, and I falter.

It wasn't like I did anything wrong. I was only nine years old, and I didn't know what I was doing. I guess I thought I was helping. Each month my mother allotted a small portion of our rations to sweets. It never went very far, and then one month, the co-op had no sweets available. Mom explained that there was a shortage of sugar supplies and put the few bits of chocolate from the previous month in the highest cabinet, with the admonishment that we'd save them for my father's birthday. It's not that I didn't want to save the chocolate for Dad. It was that I couldn't let Amie get in trouble.

Ever since I'd discovered I could touch the weave in our yard, I'd studied it, although I'd rarely touched it. But when Amie came home from academy crying because she'd taken

some of the chocolate to class and been caught with it, I decided I had to do something.

Most days Amie and I walked home from academy together, but that day I had been kept behind after class was dismissed. I'd been daydreaming, which my teacher said was pointless.

'What will your boss think if he catches you staring at the sky instead of doing your work?' she had asked in a cold voice.

I kept my eyes trained on the floor as she berated me, and by the time it was over, anger and humiliation burned in my chest. And then to make it even worse, Amie hadn't waited for me to walk home.

By the time I got to our house, I'd focused my rage on Amie for leaving me behind. I was so mad that I didn't notice how her lower lip trembled at first. But when she saw me she burst into tears, and my anger dissipated.

'What happened?' I asked her quietly.

Amie shook her head.

'You can tell me anything,' I pushed.

Amie hesitated for a moment, but then began telling me about her day. Between her sobs, I pieced together what had happened. One of her friends had demanded that they each bring a piece of chocolate to academy that day. It was a game to see who would have the biggest piece, and poor Amie knew Mom wouldn't give her any. So she took it instead.

'I wasn't going to eat it,' Amie told me. 'I was going to show it to them, and bring it home. I didn't want to be left out.'

'It's okay, Ames,' I said, giving her a hug. 'Go wash your face, and I'll see if I can find some.'

She turned the full force of her pale green eyes on me then, and I saw the tears glistening.

'But I looked. There's only a tiny piece left,' she whispered.

'Don't worry about that,' I said with a shrug. 'I know a secret. Go wash up.'

Amie looked at me doubtfully, but she did as she was told.

When I was sure she was in the bathroom, I climbed onto the slick wooden counter in our kitchen and pulled down the last bit of chocolate. I didn't want her to *see* me trying to touch the chocolate's weave. I was still stretching out the strands of the chocolate to make more of it when my mom walked in from work.

'What are you doing on my kitchen counter?' she demanded. 'And you're filthy, too. Were you . . .' The words dropped off her tongue when she saw what was in my hand.

'That's your father's chocolate,' she said softly.

'I didn't waste any of it,' I said, showing her the pieces. There was at least twice as much chocolate as there had been earlier.

'Go to your room,' she ordered.

I left the pieces on the counter and stalked away. I didn't tell them what Amie had done. Instead I let them believe I had eaten the chocolate. And as punishment, I was sent to my room, where I waited until my parents came in later that evening. Amie was probably still too scared to talk to them, so she stayed in the living room watching the Stream.

'Do you understand why what you did was wrong?' my father asked as he sat down next to me on the edge of the bed. My mother stayed by the door.

I nodded my head but wouldn't meet his eyes.

'Why was it wrong?' he asked.

I gritted my teeth for a moment before I answered. I knew the answer. I'd learned it at academy for years. 'Because it wouldn't be fair for us to have more.'

I heard a strange gasp from my mom, as if someone had physically hurt her, and I looked up to see her regarding me with tired eyes. She turned away from me to look at Amie in the next room.

'Yes, that's part of it,' he said slowly. 'But, Adelice, it's also dangerous.'

'To eat too much chocolate?' I asked, confused.

He smiled a little at my answer, but it was my mother who spoke.

'It's dangerous to use your gift,' she said. 'Promise us that you'll never do that again.'

There was a raspy quality to her words, and I realised she'd been crying.

'I promise,' I whispered.

'Good,' she said. 'Because I swear I'll cut off your hands before I let you do it again.'

Even now, as I nibble at the stale bread, the threat echoes in my ears, warning me to keep my skills hidden. So what if the Guild already knows what I can do? I can't betray my parents again.

The next day, when someone finally comes to see me, it's not Erik or Josten, but Maela herself. She saunters

into my cell in a long black gown, holding a lit cigarette. Light streams in from the hallway and outlines her sculpted silhouette. It's how I imagine death will come to me: overdressed and smoking.

'Adelice, I trust you find your accommodations lacking,' she purrs.

'I've definitely seen better,' I say.

'Two nights ago,' she reminds me, puffing thoughtfully on the brass cigarette holder. 'You are a peculiar case.'

I remember what Jost said about them killing the other girls. I'm a *peculiar* case because I'm breathing.

'I thought you might like to see this,' she says, showing me a small digifile. Maela sweeps her fingers along it and the screen glows, displaying a series of numbers and charts.

'This is what insubordination causes,' she murmurs, sounding amused with her little toy, and I realise with horror that she's showing me the number of people killed during the test.

'Insubordination,' I say softly, 'had nothing to do with it.'

'When I tell you to remove a weak thread, you do it,' she snarls, dropping her charade of calm amusement.

'Or you'll murder people?' I don't disguise the hate in my voice.

'Examples,' she starts slowly, evidently intent on keeping her composure, 'are necessary to show the importance of our work. You can play the victim, Adelice, but you are as culpable as I am. When you cannot make the difficult decision for the good of others, you jeopardise everyone.'

'It wasn't a coincidence that Pryana's sister was in that

piece,' I accuse her, but she ignores me.

'It seems you won't learn your lesson,' she says between drags.

'Maybe I'm not the only one.'

Maela smiles, and it's a real smile this time, not the dazzling show smile she puts on for the others or the wicked grin she seems to save for me. This smile shows all the flaws carefully covered by cosmetics – the lines, the too-noticeable gum line. It's a hideous sight.

Her face fades back into practised calm. 'I'm willing to give you another chance. I'm not usually so forgiving.'

I picture the other girls, killed for less. Had they wasted away in cells or been ripped out and destroyed?

'What happens?' I ask, thinking of the shimmering threads hanging off the hook.

'What happens when what?'

'When you remove strands. Where do they go?'

She smiles again, but it is one of polished venom, not actual mirth. 'Perhaps you can go to your training classes and find out, instead of wasting away in a cell.'

She leaves me here to ponder this, but deep down I know that they aren't going to answer the kinds of questions I want to ask. Enora had genuinely not known the answer when I asked her the same question during our first meeting. But why hide what really happens if ripping is such an integral part of our jobs?

Unless the ripped could be saved.

7

I taste iron and my lip stings from where it split open against my teeth. So much for a low profile – not with Pryana in my training group. Maela officially released me a few days ago, shortly after our little chat, and even though I spent considerable time thinking of the right way to approach going back to training, I was still at square one. I'd planned to apologise, but the words never came. The other Eligibles seemed as cold as Pryana, clearly not impressed by my showdown with Maela. The looks they were giving me were pretty easy to read. In fact, they reminded me a lot of how the girls at testing had treated me. They thought I was awkward and incapable. And maybe they were right. Regardless, I found myself shuffling into the studio for our loom instructions without saying a word to Pryana. It probably wouldn't have mattered anyway. It was obvious that she laid the blame for her sister's death at my

feet. I was a much easier target than Maela – and a much less dangerous one.

We were finally working on real looms again. After that first disastrous experience, we'd each been given three days of practice with an artificial weave before they allowed us to work on a real piece. The fake weave had felt lifeless under my fingers, but it was easy enough to work with. By the end of the first practice session I had proved my ability to alter easily enough. But, as if I needed another way to alienate myself, most of the other girls hadn't. They were passable as Spinsters, but their work was sloppy or they took too long or they lacked the confidence to really dig into their tasks. By the end of the practice days, we all were cleared to try simple tasks like food weaving, but Pryana and I found ourselves singled out. We were both working on weather instead of food. I'd hoped this would give me a chance to talk with her.

I knew she'd be upset but I hadn't expected her to come right out and hit me. I'm weak after several days in the cell and very little edible food and water, so Pryana's blow knocks me on my butt. I'd like to think it's because I was caught off guard, but I've never had an occasion to test my fighting skills. I can't blame her for being angry. I wish I could slug someone for what the Guild did to my family.

'I promise you,' Pryana says, leaning over so her breath is hot on my face, 'your life will be torture as long as I'm around.'

'Fair enough,' I splutter against the blood pooling along my gums.

She doesn't like my answer. I can tell because her eyes

narrow into slits. The whole situation is ridiculous. A feud entirely of Maela's making. I meant well when I stepped forward to take Pryana's place at the testing, and there was no way for me to know it was a piece containing her sister's strand.

This won't stop her from hating me.

Pryana settles back onto her stool and resumes her work, weaving furiously. It should make me mad, or at least indignant, but I think of Amie and how her fine blonde hair waves around her ears. It's my fault what happened to them – to both our sisters. I started it all.

Our instructor, an over-eager older Spinster who should not be wearing so many cosmetics, doesn't notice any of this. She's busy flitting from Eligible to Eligible, guiding their work and offering encouragement. She's an excellent teacher. I feel a pang and wonder how many teachers were named on assignment day in Romen. Not me. I return to the task of weaving a short rainfall over the north-eastern region of our sector.

My loom is larger than the other girls' and its gears and tubes take up an entire corner in the room. It's a much newer loom, usually reserved for the instructor to demonstrate on while the rest of the class practises. The other looms in the room are small, some even rusted, but all in working order. They are pressed so close together the other Eligibles can hardly move to work. Pryana works on one of them. Add that to her list of reasons to hate me. I sigh, thinking how long that list is getting, and how impossible it will be to get back in her good graces. But I can't let myself get distracted when I'm doing something that requires this much of my attention.

Weather is trickier than food, because the strands that compose rain or snow have to be knitted into the ones that make up clouds, which are in the sky strands.

Rations are a simple alteration task. The raw material is available and woven into the supply chain to the farmers and store owners. Livestock and plants can be raised and tended by men, providing valuable roles for citizens, so all we have to do is weave the raw material onto new farms and then remove the crops for even distribution throughout the rest of Arras. It's basic weaving – take a strand out, re-locate it in a new piece, weave a new strand into the old piece to grow. Thus crops are farmed and food gets from farm to market. But it's mind-numbingly boring work. Apparently over one thousand Spinsters in Arras's four coventries do this day and night. Two hundred are stationed here, and I hope I don't get assigned to the task. I bet Maela would love to stick me at a station doing simple addition and location for hours every day.

At least the weather gives me room to experiment. Our raw materials come from sources gathered and managed in the various sectors, a process they haven't really explained to us except to flash some pictures of mammoth drills and large factories that separate and organise the strands. I take the material – slate fibres for the rain clouds, brilliant gold lightning thread – and weave them together. Then I insert them into the designated locations called up on my loom. It's a gradual process, carefully adding the elements so that the storm arrives at the predetermined time, when citizens expect it. The teacher warned me how angry people can get if they are caught in a storm moving

in too quickly or slowly. Too many mistakes and you're demoted to something like the food-supply chain. The bands of time, which never stop moving across the loom, slowly eat away the threads we add. I use stock matter to replace them as quickly and precisely as I can. Otherwise there'll be a dark-out in the area I'm working on. This happened once when I was younger, and my parents dragged us to the cellar to wait it out. It wasn't dangerous, but when you're seven, seeing the sky disappear is pretty scary. I had nightmares for weeks.

I love the feeling of the weather threads in my hands, and being able to work with a loom is much less tiring than weaving with my hands. No one else here seems to have the skill to work without a loom, and I'm more than happy to keep using the machine. The rain clouds swell against my fingers as I add them into the skyline, and the lightning bolts tingle across the tips. Somewhere in the north-east, it's flashing across the horizon, warning of the impending downpour in case anyone missed the Stream weather schedule. I want to hate the work, but creating the rain is relaxing, fulfilling even. The tapestry is beautiful — a shimmering, shifting web of light and colour.

'Adelice.' My instructor beckons me to join her in a far corner. A few of my classmates notice but quickly return to their assigned tests. No doubt they expect I'm in trouble again.

But it isn't just her waiting in the corner. Pryana is with her, and she's not happy to see me.

'I've been asked to send you two with the gentleman in the hallway,' the instructor tells us in a lowered voice, so the others won't hear.

Pryana casts a terrified glance at me, and I know we're thinking the same thing: Are we in trouble for fighting? Well, more her hitting me and me standing there taking it, but same principle.

'You aren't in trouble,' the instructor assures us. She must see the fear on both our faces. 'You're moving on: you are Spinsters now.'

To my surprise, this news brings a feeling of relief. I'm eager to learn more about what happens here at the Coventry. Of course, the drawback is that I'm moving on with Pryana. Regardless of what Jost believes about Maela's desire to keep me alive, I know both she and Pryana will be hoping to watch me fail.

Outside the training room, Erik is waiting. Today he's dressed in a dark blue suit with subtle stripes intricately woven into the wool. It's amazing how less than a week of experience with weaving draws my attention to things I never noticed before. How fine the cloth is and how expertly it hugs his body, tailored to fit him precisely. He clears his throat, and I shift my eyes quickly to the floor.

'I have the honour of escorting you both to your evaluation. You will be assigned to a novice studio from there, and you will meet with your mentors to discuss what changes to expect.' His tone is clipped and impersonal. He's given this speech before, probably dozens of times. So when Maela is busy, I can count on Erik being around.

'Pryana, your personal belongings are being taken to your new quarters in the lower tower.'

'Personal belongings?' I blurt out before I can stop myself.

They both turn and look at me. Pryana understands first, and her face twists into a look of malicious amusement.

'Of course,' she simpers. 'We could bring items that mean something to us. Clothing, pictures of our families.'

Her delight goes flat at the last word and pain flits across her face. I wonder if anyone from the Coventry bothered to find out if her sister died, but I'm pretty sure the answer is yes.

'You don't get personal items when you run,' she continues, eyes flashing.

'I guess not.' I step closer to Erik and further from her.

'It's like you never even existed.'

'At least I'm not caught up blaming the wrong person,' I say, the words slipping out of my mouth before I can swallow them down.

Her nostrils flare, but she composes herself quickly. 'What? You think because I didn't rip that day I'm inferior to you?'

'I think you didn't rip because you're scared and you're taking out your anger at yourself and the Guild on me.'

'That's where you're wrong,' Pryana growls. 'We were only there because of you. Don't try to deny it. You can believe anything you want, but the truth is that the whole thing was your fault. Maela was testing you. You failed.'

She's got me there, and I can't think of a thing to say in response.

'Adelice.' Erik steps in like he's missed the entire argument. 'You'll stay in your previously assigned quarters.'

I focus on the fact that I don't have to leave my comfortable new room. Screw Pryana and her personal belongings.

'Since we'll be seeing much more of each other,' he continues, taking Pryana's hand, 'please call me Erik.'

'More of each other?' Something about this news sends a tingle down my neck.

He looks equally pleased with this announcement. 'Although you are being moved into the Spinsters' quarters, you're still under observation. During the next few months, you'll be evaluated and assigned a more permanent position.'

'Will the others be joining us?' Pryana jumps in, asking exactly what I'm thinking. I'm reminded of the one afternoon we were friends.

'We will keep the others under evaluation until we're certain there are no more Spinsters in the group. Some might end up doing the basic food weaving, but they'll probably never get any further.'

No more Spinsters? I can't believe that they can weed us out so quickly. Will the others be sent to make clothing or work in the kitchen? I'm glad I won't be there when the perpetual excitement drains from their faces. They left home expecting a glamorous life, not a life of tailoring and cleaning. And yet I'm grateful they weren't chosen. Anyone who would treat joining the Coventry with as much passion as those girls doesn't need to be part of the Guild. Eager girls want to please people like Maela.

'You know, Erik,' Pryana purrs, crushing against him, 'we've all been wondering why Adelice has a room in the high tower.'

His response is so well rehearsed, I can almost see the time stand still. 'Maela has a reason for her actions.'

He must say that a lot. It seems to appease Pryana. Or maybe she's smart enough to stop asking questions.

'Pryana, you will be meeting your mentor here.' Erik opens a large metal door and quickly withdraws her arm from his. Too quickly. Pryana notices and skulks inside.

'We aren't training together?' I ask as innocently as possible, as Erik shuts the door.

'No.' He grins. 'You're off the hook for once.'

I try to keep up my wide-eyed act, but it crumbles easily. 'Thank Arras.'

'I'll pretend I didn't hear that.' Erik laughs and offers his arm.

I slide my own through, feeling a little awkward. I've never walked with a man like this. 'So, can I ask you something?' I try to sound nonchalant, but it comes out too rushed.

'Of course,' he says airily, and I'm struck by how casual he is when he's away from Maela.

'How did you wind up here?'

'That's a long story.' He sighs.

'I'm betting most of us have long stories.'

'You'd be right,' he agrees. 'I sort of ran away from home, and now there's nothing to go back to. I was only fifteen at the time, but the Guild took me in when it became evident I possessed certain necessary qualifications that Maela needed in an assistant.'

'Necessary qualifications?'

'I have what can best be described as flexible morals.' He turns the full force of his crooked smile on and slows his pace.

'Did your parents die?'

A shadow of a frown flits over his face and he nods. Although he quickly changes the topic. 'Did Josten take good care of you the other day?'

For a moment the question paralyses me, but then I remember that Erik had sent him to check in on me, so I say yes.

'I'm sorry I couldn't return but I had some pressing duties. Maela can have quite a temper, especially when she's been challenged.'

'I noticed.'

'I don't want to throw you back in the cell again, Adelice, so if you could be a little more . . .'

'Amiable?' I offer.

'Obedient,' he corrects, and I wince at the term.

'I know as well as anybody how unfair she can be, but she's running the show, so take my advice.' There's a plea in his voice, and it runs all the way up to his sparkling eyes.

Enora is waiting for me in a large, airy room. On one side windows overlook the enclosed courtyard. I think they're actually real, and I long to reach through and feel the air. The others look out onto the sea. It's calm today, a perfect mirror of the cloudless sky. These screens were probably programmed to make me feel tranquil, and perhaps less defensive. Against the wall screens overlooking the sea, a small steel loom sits.

'How are you feeling today?' she asks as we enter. I smile. I suspect that my mentor may only be a few years older than myself, but she clucks over me like a mother hen.

'Great,' I respond simply, wondering if she sees the fat lip Pryana gave me.

'Enora, can you take her back to her quarters when you're finished? Or would you like me to return?' Erik asks from the doorway.

'I can manage it,' Enora says graciously. 'Thank you for your assistance.'

Despite how much I like her, I feel disappointed that I won't be seeing him again today. 'Yes, thank you, Erik.'

'It was my distinct pleasure.' He bows his head slightly and then he's gone.

'He's a bit of a charmer,' Enora warns.

I roll my eyes. 'I couldn't tell.'

'It's none of my business, but . . . Oh, never mind.' She leans in and tugs at my fitted jacket. 'We have more important things to worry about.'

'Have we run out of mascara?' I ask in mock horror.

'As much as I love your particular brand of sarcasm, I'm going to need you to bite your tongue. You've been invited to a special council meeting.'

'What council?' I rack my brain trying to remember all the names and departments they've been throwing at us this week, but I can't remember any councils.

'It's a meeting between the chair of the training panel and the Guild's official Coventry Ambassador.'

'Cormac?' I ask apprehensively.

'The one and only,' she confirms, leading me back into the hallway.

'So Cormac is the entire council?'

'No, Maela sits on it, but she won't be attending.'

'Cormac and Maela comprise a council that oversees things here? That explains a lot,' I mutter. I can't help thinking of our last meeting, when he made me eat at Nilus Station. He must have known they were going to lock me up without food. I don't know if this makes me like him or hate him.

'Is this because of the thing with Maela?' I ask, dropping my voice so the security monitors won't hear me clearly.

'Officially, no,' she whispers. 'But of course it is.'

'Great,' I mutter, wondering what my punishment will be this time, and then one thought stops me in my tracks.

Amie.

My last meeting with Cormac is a bit hazy from the Valpron injection, but if they still have her it might not be me that they punish.

'Adelice.' Enora tugs at my arm.

I don't move.

'You aren't in trouble,' she tells me quietly.

'I'm not?' Considering how much time I've spent in the cell, I find this hard to believe.

'Come on.' She pulls again and I allow her to drag me along.

'If I'm not—'

'Maela,' she confirms under her breath.

'For what she did to that academy?'

'For a lot of things.' She frowns at me. 'Maela has been overstepping her bounds in the Western Coventry. She wouldn't even let me down there to see you, and that's not within her power.'

Then why didn't you come?

'I thought she was in charge,' I point out.

'You have a lot to learn,' Enora says with an empty laugh. 'Now that you are an invited Spinster, you'll dine with the others and get to know the system here. Believe me, Maela is nowhere near the top of the Guild hierarchy.'

I raise my eyebrows. 'Care to explain the Guild then? It seems like things run a bit differently from what they taught us in academy.'

'That's the truth,' Enora says. 'The Guild is comprised mainly of men, as you know, but they use women for a lot of tasks within the government. Spinsters, for instance. But there are other positions – secretaries, nurses, assistants—'

'Like everywhere else in Arras?' I clarify. This information isn't all that surprising *or* interesting.

'Yes, but they try to keep as much information about what each coventry does a secret. The Guild oversees our work here, places work orders, and steps in to discipline when necessary. Sometimes I think Maela hopes to advance into the Guild ranks, so she can travel around the four sectors, from coventry to coventry.'

'Is that even possible?' I ask.

'I doubt it,' Enora says. 'I don't think the Guild is going to allow a woman into a position of political power. That won't stop her though, and if I had to lay money on a woman who could rise from under the Guild's thumb and out of the Coventry, it would be her.'

'Not that I'm a fan of Maela's ego getting any bigger, but don't we already have a pretty powerful position?'

'That's where someone like Cormac comes in,' Enora explains, her soft voice rushing through the information

as we walk. We must be getting close to our destination. 'Officially, he's a spokesman who keeps the public apprised of what goes on in the coventries and the work we are doing. People think he's a friendly goodwill ambassador between the Spinsters and the people.'

'Unofficially?'

'He keeps us in our place. He may not be head minister, but he's just as powerful. Don't let him fool you. That's why he's here.'

'As thrilling as that information is, why am I being dragged into this?' I ask.

'Good question.' Enora sighs, and I'd bet she's wondering how she got stuck mentoring the new troublemaker.

'Don't they tell you anything?' I didn't mean for this to be an insult, but Enora bites her lip as if it were.

'No, they don't, Adelice.'

'They don't tell any of us anything,' I note. 'So it's probably stupid to ask, but did you find out about my sister Amie or my mother?' Asking sends a thrill of dread through my stomach.

'I'm sorry,' Enora says, shaking her head. 'The one person who might have information has been travelling.'

'Travelling?' I ask in surprise. 'Is it a politician?'

'No, she's one of us,' she says quietly, but I can tell she can't say any more.

I stop asking questions even though my mind is heavy with them, and she leads me to a large red-lacquered door and knocks timidly. The door flies open.

'Yes?' an officer dressed in the jet-black uniform of the Guild Special Service asks without meeting our eyes.

'It's fine,' a familiar voice calls from inside the room. 'They're my guests.'

The officer moves to the side, and we step into the lounge. It's more dimly lit than most of the rooms in the compound. Probably due to the heavy velvet curtains that drape the oversized windows. Enough light streams in that I can make out the plush sofas and slick leather chairs strategically placed around the room, but the lack of natural light leaches the colour from the furniture. Cormac sits by a marble hearth, cigar in one hand and cocktail in the other. He's clad as always in his double-breasted tux, although his bow tie hangs loosely around his unbuttoned collar.

'Miss me?' he asks.

'It hasn't been that long,' I remind him.

'I'm sure it's felt like a lifetime,' he says, running his eyes down me. 'Adelice, you are looking . . . malnourished.'

'Cormac, you're looking overdressed.'

'Good,' he sneers. 'Now the hair matches the attitude.'

Beside me Enora fidgets.

'And who are you?' he asks, turning to her and squinting in the dark.

'Enora,' she says quietly. 'I'm Adelice's mentor.'

To her credit she sounds calm.

'Nice to meet you, Enora,' he says, taking a swig from his glass. 'I'll have Adelice escorted back to her quarters when we're through.'

'I'm happy to stay,' she tells him.

Cormac chuckles like this is a bold suggestion and shakes his head. 'That won't be necessary.'

With one worried look, Enora steps back through the door, and I'm left alone in the room with the Guild's official Coventry Ambassador.

'Sit,' he commands. 'Cocktail?'

I shake my head.

'Whatever.' He sets down his glass and moments later, someone steps from the shadows to refill it.

I feel my breath catch and turn away, hoping Cormac didn't notice my reaction.

'Will you be requiring anything else?' Jost asks him, and I feel heat creeping into my cheeks. I'm suddenly thankful for the heavy curtains.

'Not at the moment, but stay close just in case,' Cormac says in a dismissive tone.

'Happily,' Jost murmurs, but our eyes meet as he turns and I can see he's anything but happy. A moment later he's faded back out of sight.

'So you've been causing trouble,' Cormac informs me as he swirls his whisky.

I focus on the soft clink of ice against the glass, and say nothing.

'Maela has overstepped her bounds as usual,' he continues. 'Technically, she's your superior, you know.'

'Technically?' I ask in surprise.

'Do you think we usually let girls who try to tunnel out of their houses live?'

'So why me?'

'Your skills assessment at your testing was off the charts,' he admits, setting his glass down and leaning forward.

'Why are you the only person who tells me anything?' I

ask, shifting back in my chair.

'Well, I know more than anyone else.'

'But they know more than they let on,' I press. His cologne's heavy musk is making my head swim, and I can't hold back the thoughts I've locked in since my arrival.

'They do,' he admits, 'but I have so much more power. It's easier to share little secrets when you're in charge.'

'And you are?' I ask him pointedly. 'Then why tell me? You have no more reason to trust me than they do.'

'No, I don't,' he says, 'but unlike them, I can have you killed.'

'And I thought we were finally becoming friends.'

Cormac laughs a deep, barking cackle. 'You are delightful. I do hope I don't have to kill you.'

'Finally, something we can agree on.'

He reaches out and places his warm hand on my knee. 'You could be the most powerful girl here if you start playing your cards right.'

I shift my leg away and cross it over the other.

'I'm here to make sure Maela doesn't kill you,' he says, straightening back up in his chair, 'and you aren't making that job easy.'

'And if she kills me?'

'We'll rip her.' There's not a hint of sadness in his voice.

'Does she know that?'

'I've spoken with her,' he assures me. 'Of course, it makes her hate you more.'

'Fabulous.'

'You'd be wise to stop trying to piss everyone off and start worrying about yourself.' The amusement is gone

from his voice. 'I can keep her from killing you, but until you move out of her control, you're still at her mercy.'

'And how do I do that?'

'First, you start doing your job. Then you start making allies.'

'Enora already told me to make friends.'

'You're going to need more than friends,' he says. 'Your only chance is to move past Maela's grasp, and to do that you'll need someone with real power here.'

'Any suggestions?'

'I have someone in mind.'

I feel his eyes travel back to my legs, and I straighten in my chair. Out of the corner of my eye, I see Jost stiffen in the shadows.

'Adelice, you'll be accompanying me on a public-relations tour of Arras this weekend. Your aesthetician and stylist are fully prepped on expectations, and I assume your mentor—'

'Enora,' I remind him.

'Yes, her,' he says. 'She'll inform you of protocol measures.'

I swallow hard and nod.

'See? It's easy.'

'May I ask you something?'

'More polite every day.' He raises one eyebrow, which I assume is a yes.

'Did you find my mother?' With the death threat hanging fresh in the air, now seems like a good time to ask.

'Hold on.' Cocking his head to the side to use his compliant, he voice-dials a woman named Penny.

'Can you pull the binaries on Lewys Subject Two?'

My eyes drift to Jost again, who's stepped forward into a slant of light. He gives me a tight-lipped smile. I think he's trying to be supportive.

'No, I don't have the personal identifying sequence. It was the mother.'

Subject. It. It pains me to hear my mother described this way.

'Thanks, doll.' Cormac turns his gaze back to me. 'She was found during the cleaning of Romen and removed.'

'You ripped her?' The words are thick on my tongue, and I barely push them out.

'Standard procedure and much more humane than how I usually deal with traitors.'

I can still feel the sticky warm blood on my dining-room floor. I know exactly how he – and the Guild – usually deals with them.

'You,' he calls to Jost. 'Have Maela's assistant pick her up.'

Jost grunts from the corner and taps the order into the small companel.

'Adelice, one more thing.'

I stare at him, blinking hard against the tears burning up my throat.

'These are Stream events, which I'm sure you know.'

I nod once. Guild events are required viewing in every home. They usually consist of a lot of back-patting and flashes to the beautiful, important visiting politicians. Since the Streams come in automatically, my parents usually let them play while we continued our nightly chores and activ-

ities. When we were very young, Amie and I would squeal over the lush satin dresses and sparkling jewels worn by the visiting Spinsters. Now that would be me.

'Remember the deal we made when we first met?'

I tilt my head at Cormac curiously and sift through my recollection of that night. I hate the fuzzy final memories I have of my retrieval and the last time I saw my parents, and if I could remember more from that night, I wouldn't want it to be memories of Cormac.

'Stupid Valpron.' He tilts his head again and barks: 'Penny, the head medic for the Lewys retrieval. Put in a removal request.'

I gasp, and in the corner Jost whips toward us but doesn't come forward.

'So incompetent,' Cormac tells me, but there's no anger in his voice. He's already moved on. His poor secretary probably hates her job.

'I told you I had someone you loved very much and you put on a dazzling show,' he continues.

'Too bad you ripped her,' I say with only the slightest break in my voice.

'No, not your mother,' he says. 'Your sister, what was her name?'

'Amie,' I tell him in a small voice.

'She's been rewoven, and I'm told she is safe and happy.'

'Happy?' I ask doubtfully.

'We did some modifications on her.'

'So you turned her into someone else?'

'She's in essence the same,' he assures me.

'But you took away her memories of my family. Of me.'

I can feel the tears drying up as I struggle with this new information.

'One of our very best Spinsters in the Northern Coventry cleaned her thread,' he says with a patronising tone.

'What does that even mean?' I explode. 'First you alter my town, and now you *cleaned* her thread?'

'It's a process we've been using on deviants for years. If a child shows a predisposition to violence or mischief, we go in and map his or her brain. The method allows us to follow how the individual's brain processes information, and then we isolate the problem areas and map where the issues occur in the individual strands.'

'So you can see how their minds function and store memories, but how does that change anything?' I ask, looking past him, afraid to meet his eyes.

'We can often replace parts of the thread with artificial or donated thread material. It's a science we're still perfecting,' he tells me. 'But it's usually very successful. It's a lot like the renewal patching that strengthens and refines an individual's threads. Someday, we'll be able to completely control both techniques, eradicating behavioural issues and larger problems like ageing.'

I shudder at the thought, but I'm not surprised someone like Cormac wants to control ageing.

'If Amie's a completely different person, I'm not sure we have a deal any more,' I hedge, hoping he'll reveal more about where she is or what's happened to her.

'Screen,' he orders, and a burst of colour illuminates the swirling marble mantel. 'Location service.'

'Clearance?' a pleasant voice prompts from somewhere in the ceiling.

'Cormac Patton.'

'Subject?'

'Lewys Subject Four. Amie?' He looks to me for confirmation, and I nod.

The abstract pattern draws together and blurs, slowly forming the shape of a young girl. Her back is to us as she walks with another girl along a shady, tree-lined lane.

'Visual realign. Face recognition,' Cormac orders.

It's not necessary. The girl's hair is pulled up loosely and it curls into soft, golden tendrils at the backs of her ears. I turn from the screen as it flashes an image of Amie, laughing, with her new friend. Happy. My heart cracks along its barely healed lines and falls back to pieces.

'No harm done,' he confirms. 'Do I have a date?'

'Do I have a choice?' I manage to ask.

'Of course,' he says. 'Although, choose wisely.'

'I'll see you tomorrow,' I tell him quietly, holding back the tears in my throat. There's no way he heard me, but he doesn't ask again. I'm grateful for a knock at the door. I couldn't handle being with Cormac much longer. Erik ducks into the room and strides over to him.

'You're Maela's assistant?' Cormac asks smugly, staring at his wild blond hair.

Erik, to his credit, smiles and extends his hand. 'Erik, sir.'

Cormac stands and shakes his hand. Clapping a hand over his shoulder, he turns Erik to face me. 'Escort Miss Lewys to her quarters. Oh, and Erik?'

'Yes, sir?'

'Keep your hands to yourself.'

'Of course,' he agrees, without missing a beat.

Letting go of Erik's shoulder, Cormac turns back to the corner.

'Bring my meal here and order my motocarriage for pick-up in an hour,' he orders Jost.

'Sir.' Jost bows and moves across the room to exit. As he passes, he dares a glance at me. Beside me Erik bristles at Jost's appearance. I hadn't pegged him for an elitist.

'Miss Lewys?' Erik offers me his arm after Jost has passed.

I make it to the hallway before the tears start.

'Yeah.' Erik pats my hand. 'Ambassador Patton has that effect on me too.'

'Sorry,' I whisper, and offer him the smallest smile I can muster.

'Don't be,' he says. 'It's nice to be around someone who has more than two emotions, and if I have to suffer Maela's wrath later, I might as well enjoy your company.'

'She's going to be mad?' I ask between sobs.

'Patton's a jerk. He sent for me to put Maela in her place – remind her who's in control. I mean, I've met him at least ten times before today.'

'But you were so polite when he forgot your name.'

'Being rude won't get you anywhere,' Erik says. His tone is conversational, but I'm sure it's a warning.

He lets me cry for most of our walk back through the halls, and in the brass lift he hands me a soft linen handkerchief.

'Thanks.'

He nods.

At my door, I offer it back to him.

'Keep it.' He pushes it into my hands. 'I have a feeling you're going to need it more than I am.'

I wish I could tell him he's wrong.

8

As a child I sat rapt on the bathroom floor and watched my mother line her eyes with a fine pen and then smooth pink rouge on her cheeks. She was the perfect Western woman – attractive, groomed and obedient – but she was made more beautiful by her laugh-lines and the faint crow's-feet that crinkled as she smiled. Day by day, I am remade, into someone else, and I wonder if age will ever leave her tracks on my face. I'm sixteen now, and I will be almost flawless forever. That thought helps me fall asleep at night, secure in my place here, but it also wakes me up trembling with nightmares.

Stockings are the biggest sartorial change in my life. The first time I wore the flimsy hose I loved how the silk caressed my bare legs, but I soon realised that they leave a film of sweat on my skin. The seam is always running crooked up the backs of my legs, and the stockings con-

stantly slip down. Keeping up my proper appearance has ceased being glamorous, and now that I'm expected to travel with Cormac Patton, it's even worse.

I've spent little to no time at a weaving station since his visit. Instead I've been fitted and measured and trained in etiquette. While it's saving me from actually using my weaving ability, it's also leaving me plenty of time to dwell on the fate of my mother and sister. The image of my father in a body bag is inexorably burned in my mind and while I see it when I close my eyes to sleep, at least his death is real to me. But my sister's fair hair and my mother's flawless face feature endlessly in my dreams. I obsess over Amie's new life while they pin and tack my new gowns. She would love this – being fitted for fancy dresses. At least *my* Amie would. The idea that she's alive but a completely new person makes me ache like I've been hollowed out and left to stand too long without a core. It's too much to process, so instead I count the dresses I'll need. Dresses for rebounding, dresses for interviews, dresses for pictures. Judging by the amount of silk and tulle filtering into my quarters, I'm not looking forward to wearing any of them.

Enora might as well move into my quarters. I'm expected to know every Guild official, the name of his wife, where he resides, and his sector's primary exports. Arras has a prime minister, and then each sector has a governing minister; every metro has one as well. The roles are granted through bloodlines as long as each man has a male heir. A Guild office can never pass to a woman. It's more information than I learned in ten years at academy, and I can't imagine how I'll ever use it. I'm not much for small talk.

'Will there be a test?' I ask Enora after the third hour of quizzing she's given me on the Eastern Sector.

'Why don't you call and ask Cormac?' she snaps, clearly as tired of this as I am, but too worried to send me off unprepared.

'So how do I address these officials?'

'Address?'

'Yes, what do I call them? Are they considered ministers?' I recall how many of his officers refer to Cormac as Minister Patton instead of Ambassador.

'You shouldn't address them at all.' She looks at me like I've lost my mind.

I don't bother to hide my annoyance. 'Then why am I learning this?'

She lets out a long, motherly sort of sigh before responding. 'As Ambassador Patton's escort, you will be expected to remind him of important names and information.'

'Wait a minute.' I tug out of the grip of the seamstress who is quietly sewing at my feet and turn to Enora. 'Are you telling me I'm learning this so Cormac won't have to?'

'Of course.'

'But I shouldn't talk to these people?'

'Only if they address you and only to make very casual conversation.'

'Unbelievable.' I'm not sure if I'm referring to the expectations or to Enora thinking this is normal.

'That's another thing.' Enora hesitates. 'You're a bit too comfortable with him. Has Ambassador Patton asked you to call him by his first name?'

'I can't remember. He doesn't seem to mind.'

'Adelice,' Enora says quietly. 'He usually visits us once or twice a year, and he's informed our head valet that he'll be here at least once a week for the next month. Because right now he's enamoured with you.'

'Enamoured? Yuck, I just ate.' I don't care if half of Arras's female population would run naked into his bed, he's way too old for me. And I still don't trust him.

'You amuse him,' she continues, ignoring my comment. 'Just remember he's the one who can sign the execution decree.'

So she knows. I hadn't bothered to fill her in on the particulars of my meeting with him, and I'd purposefully forgotten to mention his remark about killing me. She worries enough.

'Until he tells you otherwise, call him Ambassador Patton.'

'Fine,' I agree, stepping back onto the stool to allow the seamstress to continue working on my hem.

Enora pauses and draws in a breath, watching my fitting for a moment. 'Maela has asked to go over your itinerary with you.'

'That'll be fun.'

'Behave yourself,' Enora orders me in a disapproving whisper.

A few minutes later, Maela enters my bathroom and gives the gown I'm wearing a critical look. 'Interesting choice.'

I pretend I can't hear her.

'Ambassador Patton's office has telebounded your official itinerary to me.'

'I'd be happy to go over it with her,' Enora offers.

Maela's eyes burn, but she laughs at the suggestion. 'I think it would be better if someone who has attended an official Guild event outside the compound briefs her. Why don't you run up to the depository and retrieve suitable adornments for her?'

Enora gives me a sympathetic smile and leaves. Having succeeded in getting rid of Enora, Maela knows I'm at her mercy.

'You've been to one of these before?' I ask her.

'You don't think you're the first Spinster to catch Cormac's eye, do you?' Maela asks.

So that's her hang-up. 'I haven't given it much thought actually.'

Maela turns her attention to her personal digifile. 'You will leave here tomorrow at seven in the morning and rebound to the Nilus Station, where you will have an image shoot with the local Stream crew.'

'I came here through Nilus,' I tell her, but she ignores me.

'From there, you will rebound to the Allia Station in the Eastern Sector, followed by the Herot Station in the Southern Sector and the Ostia Station in the Northern Sector.'

'That seems like a lot of work,' I say, grimacing for emphasis. If I thought this would break the ice between us, I was wrong.

Instead Maela whips around to me and glares. 'You don't deserve this. There are dozens of girls here who'd give anything to escort Cormac without acting like some entitled brat.'

I'm guessing she's one of them.

Just as quickly as her rage appeared, it evaporates. 'At each stop you will participate in an image shoot,' she continues. 'You will be given a set of appropriate responses to the Stream crew's questions and only speak when you are asked a question directly. Do you understand?'

'Yes.' I nod. 'See! I did it!' I add with mock enthusiasm.

This time she ignores my jibes. 'You will visit Guild officials at each stop. I assume Enora has gone over expectations.'

'Yep.' I smile brightly. 'Shut up and look pretty.'

Maela's head snaps up, her face ripe with disapproval, but she doesn't lecture me again. 'The following morning Ambassador Patton will escort you to several image shoots and various scheduled appearances. Your aesthetician crew will rebound behind you.'

'All of them?'

'Yes.' Maela's face contorts in impatience, showing her age. 'As will your personal guard.'

'But I don't have a personal guard,' I point out.

'Ambassador Patton has reassigned Erik to escort you,' she says calmly.

I am acutely aware of the number of scissors scattered around the room.

Maela keeps her eyes on her digifile, probably trying not to stab me. Apparently Erik was right about Cormac wanting to get under her skin.

'Valery will be attending you, of course, and she is bringing an assistant. Cormac has also ordered that Josten Bell serve as his valet.'

'Josten Bell?' I keep my face turned down to the seamstress working at my feet.

'He attended you in the cells,' she tells me, studying my face. 'Don't you remember him? He's our head valet. I thought he'd taken an interest in you.'

'The rude one?' I ask.

'That's him.'

'Why?' It feels like a trap to send me travelling with two young men, or maybe Cormac's just really stupid.

'He attends Cormac – excuse me, Ambassador Patton – when he calls on the Western Coventry,' she says, checking her digifile screen. 'The ambassador has a fondness for him, or rather for his cocktail-mixing skills, and since his usual valet is unavailable, he took ours. It seems he doesn't care about our ability to function while you two are travelling.'

'I guess I didn't think he was anybody important.' I try to keep my tone dismissive and casual, but I'm aware of how fast my heart is beating. Not only has Maela noticed Jost's attention to me, now he's being dragged into this mess.

'He's not,' Maela assures me as she disappears back into my bedroom.

'That's what I thought,' I murmur to no one in particular.

Enora comes to help me pack, and my primary aesthetician, Valery, trails behind her. I'm grateful for the company. I know I'll never sleep, like the night before Winter Solstice, when all you can think about is presents. But this time it's fear, not excitement, that's keeping me awake.

Valery whispers something into Enora's ear and she

squeezes her forearm in response. 'Ready for tomorrow?' she asks me, leaning against Enora.

I bite my lip and screw my face into one of panic. Valery laughs, but Enora shakes her head in amused disapproval.

'I've been prepping her all day,' Enora says to Valery, but her eyes are on me. 'She'd better be ready.'

'If you prepped her, I'm not worried,' Valery says, giving my mentor's arm a friendly pat. 'But I'd better be ready to do my part.' My aesthetician grins at me and slips into the bathroom. She'll be sure to have all her tools ready for this trip: the thought sends me spiralling back into dread.

Most of my belongings are being sent along with the crews following me through the rebound stations, but Enora hands me a small red box tied with a satiny white bow. It reminds me of the presents my parents brought into my room on my birthday each year. I never got a chance to enjoy the perfume they bought me on my last one, a gift to celebrate turning sixteen and the promise of my long-awaited dismissal. I ooh and aah as I open Enora's gift, but I have to fight the hollow ache it prompts in my chest.

It's a personal digifile.

'For your rebounds,' she tells me as she shows me how it powers on. 'I know they can make you sick, so I thought this might distract you. It has all the information you need.'

I gently touch the screen and it offers me a variety of entertainment options: cosmetic and clothing catalogues, Stream vlips, and the latest Guild *Bulletin*.

'Thank you,' I say, genuinely pleased with the gift. Although I've seen some people like Maela using them, in Romen only highly ranked businessmen could afford digi-

files, and I've never seen a woman use one outside the Coventry. It makes me feel important to have one of my own.

'It will also allow you to communicate directly with Ambassador Patton,' Enora says, sliding her finger to select complant compatibility. 'He wanted us to fit you with a complant, but Maela threw a fit.'

For the first time I'm grateful for Maela's jealousy. 'He wanted me to have a complant?'

'He's been pushing for Spinsters to be fitted for years,' she tells me. 'He claims it will allow for quicker response to imminent threats to Arras.'

'Is he right?'

'No, we're prepared with Spinsters on emergency duty at all hours. He's more interested in keeping tabs on us.'

I try to hide my surprise at her openness. Despite her kindness, Enora rarely speaks so directly with me.

'Why did Maela say no?'

'Don't worry,' she says, and laughs. 'She's not reconsidering your relationship. She couldn't get approval from Loricel, so I suggested this.'

'Loricel?' I ask, scanning through the files.

'She's the only person around here who says no to Cormac.'

I set the digifile down and pay closer attention. 'Who is she?'

'She's the Creweler.'

'Like you?' I ask, recalling Enora's various duties.

'No, I'm nothing like her,' she admits. 'I merely assist her on certain projects.'

'But there's more than one, right?'

'Not really,' she says, lounging back on a floor cushion. 'True Crewelers are very rare. Loricel is the only Creweler in Arras.'

'The only one?' I stop pacing and sit down next to her.

'Crewel work is an act of pure creation. Crewelers do more than weave the fabric of Arras. They can capture the materials to create the weave. Only they can see the weave of the raw materials.' She looks at me pointedly. 'It is only through Loricel that Arras survives. The Spinsters wouldn't have any matter to weave if it weren't for her special gift.'

'How old is she?' I ask, my stomach dropping. All the years of hiding and lying about my ability to touch the weave without a loom, even here at Enora's request, make sense now.

'It's hard to say, with renewal patches and medication,' Enora says lightly. 'But she's been in service for over sixty years.'

She must be ancient. 'What happens when she dies?'

'They'll find a new Creweler.' Enora's gaze is steady on mine. 'But so far there haven't been any real contenders.'

'And if we can't find one?' I whisper.

'Arras will fade away.'

I search her face for a sign of sadness or fear but it's not there. If the possibility of Loricel's death frightens her, she doesn't show it. But the image of Amie laughing with her friend floats to my mind, followed by how Jost's eyes crinkle when he smiles. Without a Creweler, they'll fade away too. It's a possibility I can't even consider.

'Cormac showed me Amie, you know,' I say in a quiet voice.

'Your sister?' Enora confirms, and I nod my head.

I haven't spoken of her often since I've been here. My life feels split in two: before and after. Everything that preceded my retrieval is a secret. A past life that has no place here, and although Amie is alive, for me she exists only in that time. I keep her there in my private thoughts, but something about the memories parading through my head as they prep me for travel longs to break free and be acknowledged.

'She was happy,' I say, and I hear how my voice almost echoes from the pain. I don't tell Enora that Amie's different now or what's been done to her. Or that my thoughts have turned from memories to plans, and that the real reason I'm going along with this tour is to get out from behind the Coventry walls to the world of before, where Amie still exists, even if she's changed.

'I think rebounding will be much more comfortable for you this time,' she says, pushing the digifile into my hands and forcing my mind back to the present moment.

The shackles from my first trip flash through my thoughts and set my hands trembling. 'I won't be—'

'No,' she says in a rush, reading my thoughts. 'You will be travelling in first-class rebounding chambers. Ambassador Patton wants you kept happy.'

'I'm still not sure what I did to deserve this,' I admit.

Enora smiles sadly. We're not stupid enough to believe the top-notch privileges I've been receiving have anything to do with me deserving them. 'I guess we'll have to wait and see.'

In the morning, I ride by motocarriage to my rebounding appointment. Erik and Jost come with me, but the rest of my crew follows behind. Erik keeps up a steady stream of chatter, but Jost sits quietly to the side. I laugh with Erik, but I feel the thickness of the air in the back of the carriage – Jost isn't happy about being sent all over Arras. And he doesn't seem thrilled about me chattering away with Erik either.

My scruffy friend has been cleaned up for the event. Jost's face is closely shaved, and his hair is combed and tucked behind his ears. It brushes the collar of his grey wool jacket.

'How do you two know each other?' I ask Erik, pointing at Jost.

Jost startles out of his malaise and stares at me.

'You said he sent you . . .' I trail off, not wanting to talk too much about what Jost told me in the cell in case the Guild has installed audio transmitters in our motocarriage.

'Jost is the head valet,' Erik informs me. 'When I couldn't come to your cell, I asked him to attend to you.'

'Okay.' I nod, not sure I believe it's as simple as that. Jost spoke as though he knew Erik. As if they had a history of some sort, and not a pleasant one.

'Are you nervous about rebounding?' Erik asks, changing topics.

Out of the corner of my eye I spy Jost settling back against his seat, but his eyes remain on me.

'Yes,' I admit, trying to ignore the steady gaze of Jost's blue eyes. 'My first experience wasn't very pleasant.'

'Well, that was not a typical experience,' Erik tells me.

'I forgot. You were there,' I remember out loud.

He nods. If he's sorry about ordering the medic to dose me, he doesn't show it.

'Enora gave me this,' I tell him, producing my digifile from my handbag.

Erik lets out a low whistle. 'Fancy gift.'

'Really?' I ask, flushing. 'I assumed most Spinsters got one.'

'Nah, Maela has one, but only because she sits on the training panel. Enora pulled some strings for that,' Erik says.

'I had no idea,' I admit.

For a brief second Erik's eyes flash to Jost's, but whatever prompted the look, neither speaks. The conversation trails off again and I'm grateful the ride is short, because my stomach is doing cartwheels.

The rebound station that sits outside the compound walls is small and unassuming. Erik escorts me through the double brass doors into a small lobby with one brushed-velvet chair, which I'm forced to sit in. Behind us, my team, along with my gowns, bags and carts, filters in, packing the tiny room. A polished woman in a sky-blue suit appears from the hallway and speaks briefly with Erik. I watch as he nods and gestures to the group. A moment later, she strides over and beckons for me to follow her. I walk by her side. Behind us I hear Erik smoothly directing the rest of the group into an ordered line.

'You're rebounding into Nilus?' the woman asks me evenly, and I manage a nod. She's older, with her hair neatly kept in a simple bun, and she guides me with the expertise

of someone who's done this her whole life.

'Your rebound will take about an hour,' she continues, leading me into a softly lit room and directing me to sit in an overlarge leather seat in the dead centre of the chamber. She reaches towards a panel beside me, and I hear the click of a button as she pushes it. I tense, waiting for the metal helmet to lower onto my head, but instead a small oak tray table glides over my lap. I exhale as she fastens a long, thick belt diagonally across me.

'Have you rebounded before?' she asks curiously.

'Yes.'

'I'm sorry to ask,' she says. 'You seem nervous. Most people aren't as scared the second time around.'

I shrug weakly, not wanting to tell her I was chained to the chair during my last rebound.

'You'll be fine,' she tells me sweetly. 'I'll bring you some tea.'

She disappears out the door, and Erik's head appears in the doorway. 'I'll see you at Nilus.'

'See you there,' I manage.

He continues past my door and Jost follows him. Our eyes meet for only a moment, but I can't think of anything to say to him. As soon as he's out of my sight, the steward-ess reappears with a glass of iced tea.

'Best not to drink anything hot until you're more accus-tomed to rebounding,' she advises, setting it neatly on a square white napkin in front of me.

'Thank you,' I tell her sincerely, and she pats my arm as she exits. I feel my chest constrict, the memory of my last stewardess tugging at my mind.

After the door is shut, the room begins to shimmer, fading in and out around me. This time without the helmet blocking my vision, I'm struck by how beautiful it is. Strands of golden light wind around me, and the rebound chamber gradually dissolves. I relish the few moments when everything is pure time, knitted with raw material, as it is seconds before the weave binds together into the new room. I forget about the tea and the digifile I'm clutching in my sweaty palm as the room flickers in and out of my vision and another slowly and gracefully replaces it. I relax back into the chair as the hour passes, noting how each piece of the room is carefully rewoven until I'm in a bright red space decorated with a vibrant pattern painted in gold along its walls. As the last bit of the chamber settles into place, a pretty young girl bounces into the room.

'Welcome to Nilus Station, Miss Lewys,' she bubbles, pushing my tray back and undoing my restraint. 'The rest of your party will be here shortly. Please rise carefully.'

As soon as I start to rise I understand her warning. My legs wobble and shake as though I've been sitting for hours. Clutching the arm of the chair, I force myself upright and take a deep breath.

'It takes a long time to get used to it,' she says. 'At least that's what most people tell me.'

I survey the girl more closely. She can't be much older than me. She was probably assigned here shortly after my retrieval. This could have been my assignment.

'Have you ever rebounded?' I ask her.

'Oh, no.' She flushes. Dropping her voice as she helps me off the small platform, she confesses, 'My boss told me

he's going to rebound me to Allia. The station manager there owes him a favour.'

'Well,' I say, trying to sound enthusiastic, 'the first trip is the hardest.'

'I know!' she squeaks. 'I'm nervous, but it's a once-in-a-lifetime chance.'

Jost is waiting for me in the hall and the young steward-ess flashes me a grin as she disappears around the corner. 'Nice to see some enthusiasm,' he says drily. 'Erik is check-ing to make sure everything is in order.'

'Great.'

I can't think of anything to say to him, so I press my lips together apologetically. I hate having to pretend he's beneath me, but I don't want anyone questioning our familiarity with each other.

'I know,' he whispers.

'I'm sorry.' The understanding look he's giving me makes me feel worse.

'Hey, I told you to play dumb.'

I nod and vertigo from the rebound sends me reeling forward. Jost catches me easily, and my arms tingle where he touches my bare skin. The sensation travels up my arms and settles in the nape of my neck. I know I should pull away, but before I can, the click of shoes in the hall behind us startles us apart. Jost casually steps back as Erik comes into view.

'Cormac won't be joining us until Allia,' he tells us. 'Something's come up in the Eastern Sector. Adelice, do you need to use the powder room?'

I shake my head, anxiety twisting my stomach into knots

again. I've never spoken in public before.

'Don't worry,' he says, extending the crook of his arm. 'The reporters are limited to fifteen minutes. You remember your answers?'

'Yes.'

'You'll be fine.' His tone is reassuring, but it does nothing to steady my nerves. Erik strikes me as the type who doesn't ever get nervous.

We exit through the rebound company's lounge into the station lobby. It's empty except for strategically placed guards.

'No travel allowed between stations today, except for invited dignitaries, and we'll have Special Service guards at every stop,' Erik says.

'I'm a dignitary,' I say, willing myself to believe it.

'Hard to believe, right?' he teases, which makes me smile a little.

Jost ambles up beside me, and I realise the two are now flanking me like I've seen Erik and Maela's guard do with Maela. Standing between them, I shift uncomfortably while we wait for the guard at the main entrance to clear us. After a few minutes, the guard motions for us to continue.

Without the usual foot traffic of businessmen, the grand marble hall of the station is quiet, the only noise coming from a small group of Stream reporters. As soon as they spot us, they snap to life and swarm around. The guards keep them at a safe distance, and I'm glad to have Erik and Jost standing by me, but when Erik steps forward to speak, the guards are the only buffer between me and the vlip recorders.

'I've been assured you've received your assigned interview questions and placements. You have fifteen minutes to get your footage before Miss Lewys's next rebound.'

The group organises itself quickly and I'm met with the questions Enora prepped me for yesterday.

'Miss Lewys, what is your favourite privilege as the newest invited Spinster?' a boyish reporter asks me in a clipped, businesslike tone as a vlip operator looms over his shoulder.

'The clothing,' I respond automatically. I try to sound casual, but I know my words are being broadcast on live feed across Arras as part of the promotional tour. 'It's so nice to have pretty things to wear every day.'

'Bit of a change from the old purity standards?' another rosy-cheeked reporter breaks in jovially, and a few others laugh, but a guard pushes him back and the group returns to the business at hand. It's enough to loosen me up though.

They ask about the food, my work, the other Eligibles, and I recite my answers as naturally as possible, like a good machine.

'Last one,' Erik whispers to me as a middle-aged man steps forward with his vlip recorder thrust in front of him to catch my response. He's dressed in an unremarkable navy-blue suit and he looks as bored as I'm starting to feel. I sift through my prepared responses for the answer to the only question left unasked and wait to answer, ready to retreat back to the comfortable chair in my rebound chamber.

'Miss Lewys,' he begins smoothly. 'Can you tell us what happened to your parents, Benn and Meria Lewys?'

9

Erik's response to the question is so expertly choreographed that I can see him rising above personal assistant soon. If the other Stream reporters felt any allegiance to this man, they don't show it. Instead, several back away from him. Jost gently takes my arm and pulls me into the rebound company's lounge, but I can see the vlip operators and reporters part for the guards. The man who asked about my parents doesn't put up a fight, but he keeps his eyes on me as they lead him away.

'Sorry about that,' Erik says, moving to block my view of the activity in the station hall.

Play dumb. I can see it in Jost's eyes.

I shake my head. 'Guess he didn't get his question memo in time.'

'Probably not.' Erik smiles. 'We still need to do the image shoot. I think everything is reorganised and ready for you.'

I follow him back into the silent hall. The Stream crew gathers around us mechanically, but no one speaks. The flash of cameras and hurried instructions from my aestheticians do little to distract from the sombre atmosphere in the echoing hall. I turn to see the rosy-cheeked reporter who'd joked during the interview standing at my side. I meet his eyes and smile, but he looks away. These reporters may not have stopped the guards from taking the other man away, but obviously they feel the sting of it.

I'm too distracted to enjoy my next rebound, but this time when the stewardess helps me from my seat I'm not dizzy, which is good because Cormac is waiting in the doorway, and I don't want him to see me stumbling around. He immediately drags me into a small bar next to the lounge. The place is empty. Not even a bartender is here, thanks to the travel restrictions security has arranged. I perch on a tall mahogany stool and rest my arm on the cool wooden counter, feeling a bit out of place.

'I hear you had some excitement,' he says, straightening his black bowtie as he surreptitiously looks me over.

'I guess so.' I shrug like I hadn't noticed.

'It was nothing,' Erik says as he strides over to him. 'Adelice handled it like a pro.'

'I bet she did,' Cormac responds. 'Where's my valet?'

'I'm here,' Jost calls from the door.

'Good, make me a highball,' Cormac orders. Turning back to me, he says, 'It's really incredible. I can have him make you one. I'm strongly considering reassigning Jost to a permanent position. He's the only valet who knows his place.'

I stare blankly at this suggestion, but manage to shake my head at the drink offer. I don't like the idea of him taking Jost away from the Coventry, and I bet Jost wouldn't either.

'Probably best. Wouldn't want you drunk for the Stream crews.'

I quickly learn that Cormac's idea of keeping on time is different from the rest of the group's. His schedule apparently calls for a quick cocktail followed by syrupy banter with the long-legged stewardess who made the mistake of coming to check on us.

It's Erik who finally says something. 'Sir, we need to hurry or we'll have to cut the image shoot.'

'The image shoot? Didn't they get enough poses at Nilus?'

'Yes,' I break in, forcing myself to sound sweet, 'but not with you.' Even I'm grossed out by how saccharine my words sound.

'I guess you're right. They'll want photos of me with my escort,' he says, looking away from the girl and downing the remnants of his drink.

'Of course,' I continue in the sugary voice, 'and we don't want you drunk for the Stream crews either.'

So much for sweet.

Cormac's grin slips from his face, and he elbows past us to the bar's door.

'Adelice,' he says with his back to me, 'try to keep a lid on it.'

'Of course, Cormac,' I reply. I know better than to provoke him this way, but I hate the way the rest of his team kowtows to him. I can only imagine the panic attack Enora would be having at this point.

'You seem to have quite an effect on him,' Erik mur-murs, coming up beside me.

'Cormac and I have an understanding.'

Erik raises an eyebrow. Clearly he's got the wrong idea.

'Don't worry. It's a death-threat thing.'

'Oh,' Erik says, 'just that.'

The crews here are on their best behaviour, and I won-der if they've been prepped on the situation in Nilus. There's no good-natured ribbing or unapproved questions. The interview runs as precisely as loom-work, and al-though the image shoot with Cormac is less than comfort-able, it's over quickly. He slides an arm around my waist, signalling me to cosy up to him. Standing this close togeth-er, I notice an antiseptic smell that hangs on him, covering up his cologne. It burns my eyes.

'For the love of Arras, smile, sister,' a broad-faced pho-tographer calls from behind the snapping cameras, but he shuts up when a guard edges his way.

'I'd appreciate it if you made this look natural,' Cormac hisses through his perfect rows of blinding teeth.

'I'm trying,' I force through my wide-mouthed smile.

'They've got it, sir,' Erik informs him from the side, and Cormac drops his arm and strides back to the private lounge.

We don't speak again except when he barks at me to look happy at the next station. By the last rebound of the day, I'm getting bored. Eating while rebounding is harder than I imagined. It's difficult to balance the food on my fork while the room shifts and shimmers around me. By the time we arrive in Cypress, where we'll stay overnight,

I'm hungry and cranky. I answer the interview questions mechanically and smile brightly for the camera, but I'm looking forward to spending some time alone in my hotel room before my aestheticians arrive to dress me for to-night's scheduled appearance.

I've been in my room for about twenty minutes, waiting for room service, when my prep crew flies in.

'I hope you had something to eat,' Valery trills as she lays out my long satin gown on the bed.

'I'm supposed to have private time,' I snap back. 'I'm still waiting for my food.'

'You can eat while we work,' she assures me, not meet-ing my eyes. 'As long as it's not messy. Enora wants you ready to go half an hour before the event.'

'Even from afar she tortures me,' I say with a groan.

Valery shoots me a disapproving look. 'Enora is only looking out for you—' she begins, but she doesn't finish the thought, because my food arrives.

My dinner of roast goose and sweet potato curry looks delicious, but as the girls work on me I only find time to snatch a handful of bites. There's always someone powder-ing me or doing my nails.

'May I enter?' Jost asks from the sliding door to my room.

'Yes,' I croak out against Valery's hand, which is firmly holding my jaw as she plucks my eyebrows.

'You look lovely.' Jost laughs as he comes into the room.

'Oh, shut up.'

Valery sighs and lets go of my face. She gives him a scath-ing look as she squeezes past him to pull my adornments from the trunks the crew brought with them.

'That looks good,' he says, pointing to the goose. 'I had the duck.'

My stomach rumbles as he draws my attention back to the food, and I tilt my head towards the girl carefully painting my fingernails to indicate why I haven't been able to eat.

'Here,' Jost offers, picking up the plate and gathering a forkful of the potatoes.

I take the bite gratefully. The dish has grown cold but the curry still pops along my tongue.

'Thank you,' I mumble with my mouth half full.

'It's my pleasure.'

Jost stands next to me and carefully sneaks me a few more bites as the girls continue with their prep. Soon the gnawing hunger evaporates, and I find myself enjoying the light touch of my aestheticians expertly curling my hair and massaging cream onto my legs. With a full belly, I don't even notice I'm tired until Valery's irritated cough rouses me from an impromptu nap.

'We're ready to dress you,' she says.

I nod and look around the room for Jost, but he must have left when I fell asleep.

'He's not here,' Valery tells me as she helps me step into the cool satin gown.

'I'm sorry?' I ask.

'Jost,' she says, and it's clear from her voice that she doesn't buy my innocent act. 'A valet? When you could have someone like Erik?'

'Or Cormac?' her assistant offers as she zips me up.

'I really don't know what you're talking about,' I say, but I can feel my cheeks growing hot.

'Oh stop it or you'll ruin your cosmetics.' Valery laughs. 'Don't get the wrong idea. He's very good-looking for a valet. His eyes are as blue as Erik's, but he's . . .'

I give her a drop-it look, and she holds out a bracelet, which I cuff onto my wrist.

'It's probably for the best,' her assistant continues. 'Cormac goes through the ladies pretty quickly, and Erik . . .'

I can't help but turn to listen to what she has to say about him.

'He's Maela's.' Valery finishes the thought.

'Good thing I'm not interested in any of them,' I say, but I keep my eyes on the mirror.

In the reflection, I spy Valery and the girl exchange meaningful looks.

'Sure, honey.' But when her assistant goes to retrieve more of my adornments, Valery drops her lips to my ear and whispers, 'Take the happiness you can, even if it's only a little.'

Valery straightens up as soon as the girl re-enters with my necklace, but her words lodge themselves in my head. Watching her movements in the mirror, lithe and purposeful without a trace of resentment for her assignment, I hope she's happy and wish I could be.

'So exactly what's on the agenda tonight?' I ask Erik when he meets me at the door.

'Well, you looking beautiful for one thing,' he says, and I have to hold myself back from laughing.

'Does that stuff work with the other girls?' I ask, barely containing my amusement.

'Yeah,' he says, grinning widely. 'How are you so immune to my charms?'

'Years of segregation,' I say, letting myself smile a little.

'That usually works in my favour,' he admits in a whisper as Cormac exits his room to meet us.

It's not that I don't like Erik. I even think he's charming. Maybe it's my years of inexperience with boys that make his flirtations more awkward than endearing.

'You look lovely, Adelice,' Cormac says, taking my hand. He ushers me out to the waiting motocarriage. I wobble on my high pinpoint heels as I step out of the hotel, but Erik's hand shoots out to steady me. Before I can thank him, he's faded back behind me. Stream crews call out questions, but I can't see past the perpetual flashes of light from their cameras. I press closer to Cormac for safety despite his stinging smell. Part of me wishes I had a few doses of Valpron right now to make the whole thing easier, but I suppose it's for the best that I don't. I'm going to need to keep my wits about me if I'm going to get through the evening without making a serious social blunder.

Cormac beams and calls many of the crewmen by name. He answers questions, keeping his arm tightly around my waist the whole time. Once we're safely inside the motocarriage, I pull out of his grasp and run my hand along my dress to smooth out the wrinkles where he held me.

'Can't wait to get away from me?' he asks, his dark eyes gone hard.

'I'm overwhelmed,' I admit.

'Don't worry about it,' he reassures me, lighting a cigar. 'We're doing a simple ribbon-cutting ceremony, a few pictures, and then back to the hotel.'

No more dinners or meetings or interviews after this. It's such a relief.

'I can cut a ribbon,' I tell him confidently.

'Arras, I hope so. You're a Spinster after all.' He keeps the condescending grin on his face as he puffs smoke rings.

I'm not sure what to make of Cormac. I hate him, but increasingly, I'm not sure I'm justified in that. Sure, he's creepy and arrogant, but of the people I've met since my retrieval, strangely, he's shown me the most respect. If you call brutal honesty respect, that is.

The motocarriage pulls up to a large crowd. Most of the neighbourhood must be here. Seeing that many people makes my hands shake, which is going to be problematic if I have to cut a ribbon. Cormac opens my door and helps me out. There are Stream crews and dozens of people. But something about the crowd is strange. On each of our stops, the people have been frenzied, trying to touch us or calling our names, but the citizens here are fairly calm. Some even look bored, as though they were forced to come. They probably were, but that's nothing new.

'So why are we cutting a ribbon here?' I ask Cormac as he escorts me to a large brick building. I look for the tell-tale sign that will indicate what its purpose is, but I can't find it due to the audience surrounding the structure.

'It's their new academy,' he answers, placing one hand on my elbow and guiding me firmly to the front door.

If it wasn't for his arm propelling me forward, I would have stopped on the spot.

'I'm cutting a ribbon at an academy,' I say, turning to him, 'in Cypress.'

Cormac keeps his gaze on the path in front of us and doesn't respond. Suddenly I'm remembering why I hate

him. So that's why I'm here. As a reminder of what I've done. The threat isn't lost on me. Looking out over the crowd, I wonder why they're so placid. The Guild must have fed them a lot of lies to keep them from turning on us. Did they say it was an accident, like the story Amie told us about Mrs Swander?

Even if they did, the people here are too complacent. There's not a single person with a hint of rage or pain flashing across his or her face.

And then it hits me. They don't know what happened.

'What did you do to them?' I whisper.

'Why would I do anything to them?' Cormac asks with feigned innocence.

'What do they think happened to the academy?' I ask, unwilling to play his little game.

'That's not the point, doll,' Cormac says with a smirk. 'This isn't about them. It's about you.'

By this point, we're at the door and he hands me a pair of giant ceremonial scissors. Sadly, they're heavy and dull. All for show. But maybe if I aim just right . . .

Cormac's grin fades, and he steps back. Not in fear, but to let me know he can see what I'm thinking and that it won't work. He's saved from me trying by another man, from the looks of it an official, who strides over.

As soon as Cormac turns to speak with him, an older woman approaches, eyeing me interestedly. She's not a Cypress citizen. Her age shows in her withered skin and silver hair, but even with the marks of time all over her, I see no sign of the deep, honey skin and silky black hair the citizens of Cypress share.

'You're Cormac's escort, then?' she asks.

'Yes,' I say, trying to hold my chin up.

'Shameless,' she mutters, as I realise that she's older than anyone else I've met. Even in Romen, basic renewal patching assures everyone a relatively youthful appearance, but this woman's skin is as brittle and wrinkled as old paper, despite the layer of cosmetics she wears. She has to be here with the Guild, maybe she's even a Spinster stationed at the Northern Coventry, but she's clearly not taking advantage of the renewal patching available.

'Loricel, I see you've met my escort,' Cormac says, returning to my side.

'Yes, and I think it's shameless,' she tells him solemnly.

'Adelice,' he says, 'allow me to introduce Loricel. Keep your hands back. She bites.'

'Watch yourself,' Loricel warns, 'or I'll rip your ass right out of Arras.'

'We have a love—hate relationship,' he says to me. 'Adelice is our newest Spinster. Her aptitude tests are off the chart,' he tells her.

'So you're the one that has Cormac's attention. He hasn't been so interested in the Western Coventry in years,' she says, squinting to look more closely at me. There's a sparkle of something – respect, maybe – in her eyes now. I can't help returning her interest. This is the woman I've heard of in bits and pieces from Enora. The Creweler. I'm finally meeting the most powerful woman in Arras, and I'm not sure what to say to her.

Before I can respond, a guard dressed in full Guild regalia approaches, and Cormac leans in to talk to him. With

the chatter around us, I can't hear what he's saying, but it doesn't stop me from trying.

'So are you enjoying yourself?' Loricel asks me.

'No,' I say, distracted by my eavesdropping.

Loricel raises one eyebrow, revealing a map of wrinkles etched along her forehead, and laughs. 'Good. You're exactly what they said.'

'And that is?' I ask, trying to keep the curiosity I feel out of my voice.

'Smart and foolhardy,' she says. 'It's a great combination for making conversation, but not the best for staying alive.'

'That's what they tell me.'

'They're keeping you off the loom?'

I nod, wondering how she knows that, but then I remember what Enora said about her. As Creweler, Loricel would know everything going on in Arras.

'They're trying to win you over,' she informs me. 'They'll try appealing to your desires first. Clothes. Power. Parties.'

'And if that doesn't work?' I ask.

'Then they go after your heart.'

'Aren't they the same thing?'

She smiles and the lines on her face soften. 'How old are you?'

'Sixteen.'

'Most sixteen-year-olds,' Loricel says, 'don't know the difference between love and desire. That's how they keep Spinsters weaving, and why they test at such an early age. You're blinded by silk and wine.'

'I don't care much for wine,' I say flatly.

'What do you care for?' she asks, but before I can answer she continues. 'Because that's what they'll go after.'

My heart beats wildly, and I remember how easily Cormac pulled the surveillance of Amie walking to her new home from academy.

'My sister,' I whisper to myself.

'They'll find the others first. They'll save her for last,' Loricel says, shaking her head.

'There are no others,' I say.

'Don't be so sure of that. You might not know who they are, but the Guild does.'

'Why do you care?' I ask, not bothering to hide my curiosity. She's nothing like I expected.

'Because I once sat where you are, with a handsome, smarmy Guild official, and no one told me,' she says, and the lines on her face reappear. With a curt nod, she strides away and disappears into the crowd.

'That old witch scare you?' Cormac asks, coming back over to me.

I shake my head. 'No, she doesn't approve of me escorting you.'

'She wouldn't,' he says.

I'm forced to smile and pose for the cameras while the Cypress crowd mills about. There's nothing natural about how they're acting, and I wonder if they've been given Valpron for the evening to ensure our safety. When the ribbon flutters to the ground, I hand the scissors back to Cormac.

'Your point's been proved,' I say, my words thick. Something about the audience's lack of interest makes me feel

the shame more acutely, as though I'm hurting for them because they can't.

'Oh, not yet,' he whispers.

I don't bother to ask him what this means. I'm tired of his cryptic warnings and little jokes, so I turn back to the crowd and stare out across the sea of ebony hair. The citizens of Cypress look so similar, just like Pryana. I must look like a freak to them with my pale skin and fiery hair.

And that's when I spot her.

Pale golden hair that wisps around her ears. A spot of light in the dark. She's as bored as the rest of them. She's also one of the only girls here tonight.

Most of the others were killed.

But she's been rewoven, I think, *to a more deserving family*. And my actions placed her here, with a family that deserved a child in exchange for the one Maela's hook stole.

I don't even think. I dash towards her. This actually elicits a response from the crowd. Men jump back and mothers snatch up toddlers from the ground. I must look insane, flying through the masses, my hair whipping behind me and my ankles barely keeping me straight up in my heels. All that matters is getting to her, and no one tries to stop me. They're too surprised.

When I reach her, a woman pulls her close to her side, and I look at her more carefully. Unlike the others, this surrogate mother regards me with fear. But Amie stares at me with blank curiosity. There's no hint of recognition in her eyes. The eager greeting, the one she used to give me every day after academy, doesn't spring from her lips.

She has no idea who I am.

'Amie,' I whisper, stretching out my hand, and willing her to remember.

'Her name is Riya,' the woman informs me, her voice full of warning. 'She's my daughter.'

'Her name is Amie,' I challenge her under my breath.

'My name is Riya,' Amie repeats, mimicking the woman's warning. But there's a sadness in her tone. Not for herself, but for me – for the crazy girl whispering desperate lies in front of her.

A warm hand touches my shoulder gently.

'Come on,' Jost says gruffly. 'We need to go.'

I look at him, barely able to see him through the veil of tears I'm trying to keep from falling. He leads me back to the waiting guard. Cormac is off somewhere, saying his farewells, but I'm sure he caught my little scene. Just like I'm sure he orchestrated this whole evening.

'Are you okay?' Jost asks.

'Fine. It was a mistake,' I lie to him.

But I can tell from his face that he doesn't buy it. 'I have to check on Ambassador Patton. We'll be leaving in a few minutes.'

I try to let his words reassure me, but they don't, so I open my own door and slide into my seat to wait for Cormac to be finished with his schmoozing. I'm about to shut my eyes to escape this horrible night when Erik slides into the motocarriage next to me.

'I have to make this quick,' he says.

'Sure,' I say, the surprise distracting me for a moment.

'Cormac's sending me back to the hotel alone.'

'You're not coming with us?' I ask, alarmed.

'No.' Erik looks me straight in the eyes. 'Cormac's a powerful man, and it's stupid of me to advise it, but if he tries anything, knee him in the crotch.'

My eyes snap open and I have to press my lips shut to hold back laughter. 'You got it,' I manage, barely keeping it together. Trust Erik to make me laugh at a time like this.

'Here.' He presses a thin microdisk into my hand.

'What's this?' I ask, carefully fingering the disk before tucking it into my handbag.

'Pop it into the drive on your digifile and it will connect you to me,' he says. 'Let me know when you make it back.'

He's staring intensely at me as he says this, and I feel my breath catch in my throat. 'Do you really think . . .' I begin, but I can't finish the thought.

'I never know what to think with Cormac,' Erik says. 'That's the problem.'

Before I can stop myself my hand stretches and grabs his. He squeezes it reassuringly, then drops it, and slips back out of the motocarriage. If I go now, I could catch up with him, but I might get him in trouble. But the alternative – leaving alone with Cormac – terrifies me.

'Ready to go?' Cormac asks, getting into the seat next to me. Too late.

'Of course.' I swallow against the dread sitting raw in my throat.

'What did Erik want?'

I hesitate for a second. 'He wanted to go over tomorrow's itinerary since he's headed back to the hotel.'

Cormac regards me thoughtfully and then smiles. 'Attention to detail. I like that. He'll be advancing out of the

Coventry in no time. I want to show you something,' Cormac says. He avoids sitting too close, and I don't blame him. I'm sure he knows his plan worked.

I don't bother to say anything about what happened tonight, and neither does he. The message was clear enough without him having to spell it out for me. We only ride for a few minutes, but in the dark I can't see much through the motocarriage's tinted windows. When we finally stop, Cormac opens his own door and walks around to mine. The driver stays inside.

As he helps me out, I'm met by a near-black sky dotted with sparkling stars. We've exited only steps from the edge of a precipice. In the darkness, I can barely see the valley hundreds of feet below us. Stretching past it, lights blink and waver, marking diminutive cities scattered around the cliff.

Cormac drops my hand and steps closer to the edge. Stretching his arm over the abyss, he calls to me, 'It's yours for the taking, Adelice.'

I clasp my palms across my bare arms and shiver against the breeze.

Cormac sits silently in the seat diagonal from me on the ride back, and I wonder if, with all the posing and Cormac's eager hands on my waist earlier, I jumped to the wrong conclusion when all he wanted was to show me a vista. But after tonight's charade, I'm not sure what any of it means any more.

Between holding back tears and the crippling guilt washing over me, I can barely keep my eyes open. It's exhausting, but as I'm drifting off, Cormac's voice startles me

awake. I snap to attention, but then I realise he isn't speaking to me. His head is cocked to the side, so I close my eyes again and listen.

'You've known about the situation in Northumbria for weeks,' he says. 'It shouldn't take this long to deal with a simple taint.'

He pauses, and I wish I could hear what he's being told. Complant convos are too one-sided.

'I see.'

I peek through my lashes to see that he's frowning.

'This is getting out of hand. If we can't find the source, we're going to have to alter the entire Eastern Sector,' he says, 'and, Hannox . . .'

My heart flutters at this name, but I can't recall where I've heard it.

'Did you get anything out of that guy from Nilus? Yeah, if this thing has spread way up there . . .' He pauses in response to something Hannox is saying. 'I don't think Protocol Two is necessary at this point, but have Intelligence draw up a plan.'

I'm still watching through barely open eyelids, pretending to sleep, when he leans forward and places his head in his hands. Then he looks up at me and I almost stop breathing. He keeps his gaze on me for a minute, then pours another whisky.

10

The morning comes in streaks of purple outside my hotel window. It's the real sky, something I never see at the compound, where every view is a programmed image. This is the dawn that awakens citizens in Cypress, and for the first time since the motocarriage, I close my eyes. Opening them, I pretend I'm waking up like I might if I lived out here. It's time to prep for work. I'll tram into the metro, and perch at a desk waiting for telebounds and coffee rationing. No, I'm prepping tablets for the day's curriculum. I'll teach about the seasons. How each serves a function and is carefully timed to maximise its usefulness to food Spinsters. But the lesson fades, replaced by looms and fingers and stone walls. This room is no more real than my life there; both were created by Spinsters.

I'm not out of bed before a maid comes bustling into the room to clean up.

'I'm so sorry, miss,' she exclaims, but something in her voice isn't sorry. Her words sound rehearsed. Of course, I might be getting paranoid at this point, too.

'It's okay,' I assure her, slinging my legs out of the bed. 'I need to be getting up now anyway.' Especially if I'm going to have a minute to myself before my crew gets here to prepare me for our final rebound back to the Coventry.

'I'll get out from under your feet then,' the maid offers, but I shake my head, indicating she should stay.

There's not much packing to do, so I order up a small breakfast of scones and tea and plop down to wait in a chair. I'm so used to having someone hovering around me that it doesn't even feel awkward to have the maid here straightening. I watch her work. She's about my mother's age.

'Is there anything I can get you?' the maid asks kindly.

'I'm fine,' I say with a smile, not willing to betray the hot anger building in my head by saying more.

'Well,' she starts, but then she stops and a sheepish grin slides onto her face. 'I'm sorry. I had hoped to meet you. It was very rude of me to barge in on you this morning.'

So that's what this was about. Another person eager to see a Spinster or ask for a blessing. It's not that I mind so much as it makes the guilt bubble up and threaten to spill over. If only she knew I was responsible for the accident that claimed the local academy.

But I simply hold out my hand to her and say, 'I'm Adelice.'

'It's an honour to meet you,' she says, clutching my hand in hers and not letting go. 'I thought you might know my daughter. She was retrieved this year as well.'

'Pryana?' I ask the woman, and her face lights up. That's when I realise it's no more a coincidence that we came to Cypress for the ribbon-cutting ceremony than that we stayed in this hotel. The academy. Amie. And now Pryana's mother. Cormac wants me to see the consequences of my decisions and remind me of how powerless I am without the strength of the Guild behind me. But his plan has a weakness: now I know where Amie is.

'Oh, you do know her! Is she well?' she asks.

I do my best to muster up a warm smile, and nod. With the loss of her other daughter, even *some* news about Pryana must feel like a gift.

'I'm very sorry about what happened here,' I manage to whisper. Part of me longs to tell her the truth – that I'm the reason the academy was destroyed, but when I gather up the courage to look into her eyes, they stare blankly back at me.

'Sorry for what?' she asks, and her voice is as empty as her eyes.

'For the academy,' I tell her, pulling my hand back from hers.

'It's lovely,' she says automatically. 'I wish it had been this nice when Pryana was attending it.'

'But your daughter . . .'

'Pryana?' she asks in a confused voice.

'No,' I answer slowly, watching her closely. 'Your other daughter and the academy . . .'

'Pryana is my only daughter,' she says, but something about her tone is not reassuring. There's no surprise or amusement at my mistake, but only a mechanical, unemotional response to my apology.

'I must have been confused,' I tell her. 'I thought Pryana said she had a sister.'

'She's an only child,' her mother says, and her face brightens again. 'My pride and joy.'

'So what exactly happened to the academy?' I ask, less interested in the facts than in what she believes occurred.

'It was upgraded. We got called to a town hall meeting, well, the girl neighbourhoods,' she says, and the automatic tone returns; but for just a moment she seems to struggle with what happened at that meeting. 'Anyway, they upgraded the girls' academy. It makes sense to me. We've produced more Spinsters here than any other metro in the four sectors.'

I swallow hard and turn from her.

'Pryana mentioned that,' I say in a quiet voice, my mind no longer centred on this conversation.

'It sounds like you two are good friends,' her mother says happily, and I don't have the heart to correct her. 'Will you do something for me?'

'Anything,' I say, expecting her to give me a message for Pryana, but instead, she leans in to whisper, 'Keep an eye on her for me.'

That won't be hard.

Enora meets me at the rebound station back at the Western Coventry and drags me away before Jost or Erik can join us. I feel awful for not thanking them for watching out for me this weekend, but since Enora can barely control her shaking hands, I go along with her.

'You're wanted upon arrival,' she tells me.

'Okay.' I consider telling her about the conversation I

overheard between Cormac and Hannox but don't know where to start.

'Have you manipulated the weave again without a machine?' she asks me in a quiet voice. Her gaze is so demanding I almost believe I have. It's clear she assumes as much.

'No.' I pause and try to remember if that's right. 'No, I don't think so.'

'No or maybe?' she presses.

'No,' I repeat more confidently. 'What is this about?'

'You've been called to train,' she says in a small voice.

'With Maela?' I ask, not hiding my annoyance.

'With Loricel.'

Now I understand why Enora is shaking.

'Oh,' I say. 'I met her in Cypress.'

'You must have made quite an impression,' Enora says.

'She knew about me,' I tell her, 'and she didn't approve of me being there with Cormac.'

'She wouldn't.'

'That's what he said. And I agree. He is too old for me,' I joke, trying to lighten the mood.

But Enora isn't laughing. 'Loricel doesn't approve of his influence on the Coventry. She thinks we should be self-governed.'

'Aren't we?'

'Loricel may be, but the rest of the Spinsterhood is closely monitored by the Guild. We may be more powerful than the rest of the female citizenry, but that's not much to boast about.'

I think back to Cormac's orders, his conversation about Protocol Two, and the way he offered me Arras like it was

his. Amie's voice rings in my head: *control — Spinsters have control.* Had I believed it, too?

'Should I tell her about what I can do?' I ask under my breath.

Enora's gaze stays on me, but behind her eyes she drifts somewhere else. When she finally speaks, her voice is as hollow and distant as her eyes are. 'No. I've learned from experience that some secrets must be kept, even from someone with the best of intentions.'

I search her face for a sign that she realises she's made a value statement. She's been honest and not spoken in riddles, if only for a moment. And though I still don't confess about Cormac, or Erik's concern, or Jost feeding me dinner, it brings us closer. I can't deny the wall between us, separating us from total honesty, but I'm no longer sure which of us built it.

But one thing is bothering me. 'Speaking of secrets. Why didn't you warn me about the Cypress event?'

Enora's look says it all: because she didn't know about it.

'What about the Cypress event?' she asks quietly. 'We didn't get the Stream for that.'

'Nothing,' I mutter, and before she can question me further, we're back within the compound's walls.

Enora doesn't give me time to change out of my travelling suit. Instead she drags me to the airy room where I was assigned the first day I became a Spinster. I haven't been back here since then. The window is open and chiffon curtains swirl around it. I look at the loom — my loom — more carefully. It's polished and looks untouched. The series of gears on either side of it are still, waiting for me to will

them to life. And next to the silent machine, Loricel waits.

I'm jealous of her simple navy pantsuit. I can't remember the last time I was allowed to wear pants. I'm also struck by how powerful she looks in comparison to most Spinsters. She's not overdone like the others.

'Thank you, Enora,' she says.

Enora nods. 'Is there anything I can get you?'

'No, this will be fine,' she says, drawing up one of the studio chairs. 'The wall screens are lovely here, don't you think?'

I smile, not sure what to say.

'I want to work with Adelice alone today,' she says to Enora, and my mentor smiles. It's the first time she hasn't looked scared to leave my side.

'Access Alpha L,' Loricel says out loud when Enora's left the room.

'Access granted,' a disembodied voice sings from the panel.

'Turn off security monitors and audio surveillance,' Loricel commands.

'Monitors and surveillance will be turned off for one hour.'

'That's better,' she says to me, patting the seat next to her.

I sit and stare at her.

'How is your training going?' she asks.

I blush at the question. I barely know how to turn on the loom, never having woven on the machine unsupervised. 'It's not,' I answer honestly.

'I figured. Cormac never has the right priorities.'

'It's my fault,' I confess. 'I haven't made training me easy.'

'No Creweler ever does,' she mutters.

'Oh, I'm not a—'

'You are a Creweler. You have been since you were eight years old.'

My mouth falls open, and for the life of me, I can't shut it. I was eight the first time I accidentally caught time while playing in my yard. Mom had made me smooth it out, and then she huddled with Dad at the dinner table, talking in the hushed voices parents use when they're worried. A scene that became too familiar at supper.

'Part of my job is to find and train the next Creweler. I found you that day when you slipped.'

'So you always knew?' I ask, my voice barely a whisper.

'For a long time I've been worried about my age. I am more capable up here,' she tells me, tapping her head, 'than anyone else in this forsaken Coventry, but this body is failing. I needed to find my replacement.'

I remember the nights I spent training to fail the testing, crawling through the holes under my house, the body bag in my dining room, but it was pointless because they were always coming for me.

'I've known it was you for a long time,' she says sadly. 'But when your parents tried to teach you to fail, I hoped they would succeed.'

'Why?' I feel oddly violated by her admission. She'd watched me for years and yet not stepped in when things went very wrong on the night of my retrieval.

'I am sorry about your parents and your sister. I could

do nothing to save them.' Loricel pauses. 'I had to give you every opportunity to escape this, and that meant sacrificing them.'

Tears rise up, threatening to choke me. I try desperately to focus my anger on everyone else and not on the old woman sitting next to me.

'There are things I need to teach you that the Guild cannot know about, but things are moving more quickly than I expected,' she admits with a sigh.

I know if I open my mouth to ask her what things, I'll start sobbing, so I stare ahead instead. Rising from her chair, Loricel walks over to the wall and enters a code on the companel with surprising speed. Almost instantly the gears of the loom begin churning. They float against one another and shimmering strands of light snake around them, weaving together. The threads glide onto the surface of the loom, forming a tapestry of light.

'It's a simple piece.' She runs a finger along the weave in front of us. 'I'm assured this is a terminal patient being taken care of at home. Her daughter sent us the request.'

Ripping. She's here to finish what Maela started. And what kind of daughter puts in a removal request? I try to imagine signing a form asking the Guild to rip my mother. But even though I want to back away, I move forward to inspect the piece.

It's simply woven with long, thick strands. I can almost see it when I touch the weave: a small house in the country, unadorned by a Spinster's hand, allowed to flourish and evolve by nature's course. Unlike the last piece I was given to rip, which was intricately woven with thousands of tiny

and unique threads, these strands are rich and coarse, woven into a humble piece. The weakened thread is easy enough to find in such an austere piece, but despite its frailty the strand is long and coloured in hints of gold and copper. It's thick despite wear and even now as it slowly decays, there's a sense of vibrancy. If Loricel had imagined this would be easier than ripping one of a thousand threads in a complex weave, she's wrong. Removing this strand feels like a violation – an act against nature. It's the life force of this piece, and everything this thread touches, regardless of our attempts to repair around it, will be irrevocably damaged once it's gone.

Taking a silver hook from the small cubby at the edge of the loom, I slide the crook under the large fraying thread and gently pull it loose. It comes out quickly and the threads around the gap look homeless now that I've removed their base. The thread hanging on the end of my hook was the starting place for so many of the other threads. Its loss affects them all.

But I feel nothing. I wait for tears or vomit to burn up my throat, but there's nothing but numbness.

'Now this can be sent to Repair,' Loricel says quietly.

I nod, and Loricel enters a new code. The rest of the piece moves slowly off the loom, creeping to the Repair Department, which will bind the piece back together, closing up the hole and tidying the frayed ends caused by ripping out that one thread.

'*You* could fix it,' I say.

'Yes, I could, but that's not why I'm here. You must make the hard choice, Adelice, before you can move for-

ward. Decisions must be made. Often between life and death. It is hard to make a decision to save thousands when it compromises one.' Her voice is a hollow whisper, and ghosts echo in her eyes. 'It is easier not to be put in that position.

'As Creweler, you can create new places – oceans, lakes, buildings, fields. It can be rewarding,' she continues, and as I watch she enters a new code into the companel. A moment later, a new piece of Arras appears on the loom. It's nearly blank, a hint of green glistening against the bands of gold, and she clicks the zoom wheel to bring it into more detailed focus. It's a simple piece of land. Maybe a park or a field lying outside metro limits somewhere. There are no trees, no rocks, just a valley of lush, green grass. For the first time I notice the small bag she carries with her as she places it at the foot of the loom and gestures that I should let her sit on the stool.

'Normally, I work in my own studio, but I brought my supplies with me today,' she says with a kind smile. 'You must get a feel for your own loom. I have clearance to call up the weave on any machine. Now if I must show you destruction, I want to balance that with the beauty of what we can do.'

From the bag, she draws out spools of thin blue thread. It's hard to describe what raw material looks like. The colour of the strands is an innuendo – the possibility of colour rather than a clear shade. As though I understand it's blue only because I've seen the colour before. The thread itself is light and cool to the touch, and when she unwraps it from the spool it glimmers and sparks with energy. This is

the very raw material that is sewn into the weave by the skilled hands of Spinsters, composing all objects in Arras. I can't think about it too much, because part of my ability stems from my hands' natural desire to weave. My conscious mind plays little role in the task. I've added to Arras before, but that act adhered to a strict pattern established by more experienced Spinsters.

After carefully removing some of the green threads from the weave on the loom, Loricel takes a blue strand, and slipping it through a small thin needle, begins to add it to the spot. She works quickly but expertly, subtracting the green and adding the blue in a tight weave. When the entire section has been replaced, she takes another piece of sheer thread and embroiders along the edge. My mother cross-stitched kitchen towels when I was a child and the technique is similar, but Loricel uses no pattern and her embroidery illuminates the section. Even in its abstract state, the weave is stunning.

'This binds the new addition,' she explains as she finishes embroidering the edge. 'It's key to permanently altering the weave.' When it's done, she puts the extra raw materials back into her bag and clicks the zoom wheel on the loom. Where previously she'd shown me a simple valley, a radiant lake now resides. A source of water for the residents nearby.

'Later, the farmers can add fish, and the town can ration it as food,' she explains. 'I'm particularly fond of adding lakes. Something about water tugs at my soul.'

I am silent with awe, finally understanding her significance now. With the ripped strand from earlier resting

in my palm, I feel in even greater contrast to the woman sitting beside me. She is life. I am death.

I'm not surprised when Enora announces I'm training for Crewel work as we walk to the dining room that evening during our meal shift. At the table I sit next to her and watch as Pryana takes her spot at the end of the table – next to my empty chair. We're assigned to sit by rank of importance at the table. Now only Pryana, who is still training, sits at the end. To anyone else she would look oblivious, but I see the slight fury blazing in her cheeks when she spies me towards the front of the table. Her head stays down throughout dinner. I feel badly for her. At least I have Enora, but Pryana sits alone, isolated from the rest of the group. I'm sure she hates me even more now.

'How long have you been training, dear?' The Spinster who speaks to me draws out her words until they sound like warm, thick honey dripping slowly off her tongue. She must be from the southern stretches of Arras. We don't have much of an accent in the Western Sector.

'What day is it?' With the travelling, I've lost track of the date.

The Spinster oozes a slow chuckle. 'It's October fifth, dear.'

The still-warm air had a bite to it the day I made my fateful slip at the testing facility back home. The leaves were barely yellowing, and running home might have pinkened my cheeks, but a jacket wasn't necessary yet. That was September. Only a couple of weeks of my life have been spent in the Coventry. In many ways my life in Romen feels like a faded, long-past memory, and yet it seems that only

yesterday my mother commanded me to clean my room or I braided Amie's hair. My memories of them are vivid, but blurry at the edges as though they are slipping away.

'Less than a month,' I say out loud. I don't tell her how much of that time was spent in cells.

'A month?' Her eyes widen, and her deeply lined lids look garish and frightening. 'That must be some kind of record.'

A few of the others nod in amazed agreement. Enora, who has been busy talking to the woman next to her, notices my discomfort and jumps in. 'She scored very highly on her aptitude tests and we needed more help in the Crewel department, so we brought her up.'

She smiles warmly and everyone relaxes into other conversations, except the southern Spinster, whose eyes stay fixed on Enora in a fierce way. She looks like a caged animal, both frightened and eager. I don't like the way she stares at my mentor. Who could be threatened by Enora? I make a mental note to steer clear of this woman from now on. She's a climber.

I pretend to lose interest in everything but eating, but I feel eyes on me. I look up to discover Maela studying me. We are roughly equal in our positions at the table. She heads up the lower Spinsters, and I trail behind the trained Spinsters, apprenticed to Crewel work, so we overlap. I see the wheels turning in her mind. Eyes slightly glazed, the purse of her lips, the tightness of her jaw; she has nowhere to go, and I've only begun my own rise in this world. But she'll find a way to climb further up – her kind always does.

'Are you excited?' the southern Spinster asks sweetly.

'I'm sorry.' I blush, confused by her question. 'Should I be?'

'For the State of the Guild ball,' she says, as though it's the most obvious thing in the world. 'It's next week.'

'You're right,' I say, remembering images from the *Bulletin*. The ball was always held in the autumn months. 'I had forgotten.'

'Will Cormac be escorting you to this event, too?' The sugar is gone from her voice.

'No,' Enora says, looking directly at the other woman. 'Spinsters don't have escorts at events held within the Coventry, remember?'

'I must have forgotten,' the woman says flatly, and turns back to her other conversation.

I guess we won't be friends after all.

'Don't worry, your dress is ready,' Enora whispers from her spot a few spaces down.

'I didn't think I'd have to ward off Cormac for a while,' I mutter, not sure she can hear me.

Enora snorts. 'Think again.'

11

The whole event is over-the-top. I should have expected as much with Guild officials in attendance, but despite my being used to feeling surprised at the ridiculousness of the Coventry, this is too much.

It began with my dress. I'd felt out of place in my gown at the ribbon-cutting ceremony in Cypress, but tonight I feel naked. Even now as I idly shake hands and dance with official after official, I feel nothing like myself. At least with my usual wardrobe of dress suits I'm mostly covered. To say this dress leaves nothing to the imagination is an understatement. Made of emerald-green silk, it flows along the curves of my body. Not that I have any, but something about this gown – and the subsequent lack of underwear it necessitates – makes it look like I do. It drapes down and

rests at my tailbone, exposing my entire back, and I don't even want to think about the front. The thinness of the vibrant silk feels like nothing at all. I might as well clutch some fig leaves and hide in the corner.

The photographers go wild over nearly nude me and over Pryana, who's dressed in a strapless black velvet gown that lets one of her long amber legs slip through a thigh-high slit to reveal she's stockingless. As they click and capture, I spy a whole pig on a spit in the middle of the room, an apple shoved ceremoniously in its mouth. I know just how it feels. Pryana seems much more comfortable in front of the cameras, flashing her dazzling smile and striking spontaneous poses. I don't usually fall into the shy category, but I've never been the centre of attention like this before.

A strong hand grabs my elbow and keeps me from fading into the background of the party. 'You're at my table,' Cormac whispers in my ear.

'My dream come true,' I reply.

'I'm sorry?' he says in a voice that dares me to repeat myself.

'I said, lead the way.'

Our table is the first in a carefully ordered line near the podium, and far from the noise of the dance floor. As Cormac pulls my chair out for me, I glance at the other name cards. I recognise several of the names, and the throbbing panic I'm trying to hide pulses harder.

'Can I get you a drink?' Cormac asks.

I take one more look around the room, recognising nearly every man here from the Streams I watched as a child, and nod.

'Sooner or later everyone takes up drinking.' He laughs and makes his way over to a small bar in the corner.

I'm inspecting the silver service when the rest of our table joins us. I'm stuck with a group of politicians and their wives. I keep my head down except to take hurried sips of the wine Cormac brings me. Loricel takes a seat, and I feel relief loosen the panic in my chest, but she stares up at the podium, blowing air through her nearly closed lips. The other women ignore her – and me – giggling about so-and-so's dress and who's gone bald. The men discuss policies and people I've never heard of. I find myself intensely grateful for the drink Cormac brought me, even if I can barely handle the way it burns my throat.

Servers arrive with giant silver platters, and I marvel at their ability to carry them. Most of the waiters are typical, gaunt lower-class assignees, brought in especially for the occasion. Fewer rations means less eating, which means less muscle tone. But they balance the platters and serve each plate with precise ease. At least there's food here. I unfold my napkin in anticipation, but Cormac pulls it out of my hands and places it back on the table.

'Not until they bring your plate,' he mutters. There's a tinge of horror in his voice at my faux pas.

I keep my eyes on my plate after that. A salad of bitter greens with bits of tart fruit and a sweet dressing. Soup with shark fin and leeks. A large, leaking steak for the men, and petite slices of chicken over a bed of rice for the women. I can't help eyeing Cormac's dinner.

'Here,' he says, holding up a forkful. 'You already look like you're wasting away.'

I savour the bite of juicy meat, and the woman across from me stares as I eat it.

'Magdalena,' Cormac says in mock admonishment, and she giggles.

'I can't remember the last time I saw a woman eat beef,' she admits, and the other two wives at the table laugh in agreement.

'We eat it at the Coventry,' I say, and then flush for drawing attention to myself.

'Of course *you* do,' Magdalena says. 'You have third-gen renewal patching. Only second gen is available to us.'

'Oh.' I have no idea what she's talking about.

'I heard they're working on a fourth gen,' another wife says in a low voice as the men return to talk of politics.

'Good, they'll finally release third gen for the rest of us,' Magdalena says to the other wives. 'Of course, I can't imagine what fourth gen is.'

'I hear it's as if they put you back in the womb. You come out like a baby,' the other tells her.

Magdalena's eyes stay on me. 'I'll settle for third gen.'

I turn to see Loricel watching this exchange with the hint of an upturned lip. I wonder how old she really is. If she has this much tech at her fingertips, why is she showing her age at all? Or is it that she's actually extremely old, and only now starting to reveal it?

'Older than you think,' she mutters, and I turn away, embarrassed that she knew what I was thinking.

They're clearing our dessert plates and offering coffee when a broad-shouldered gentleman crosses to the podium. He waits as the conversation dies down. It's Prime

Minister Carma, current head of state.

'Greetings to you, keepers of Arras. This has been a momentous year. We have seen unprecedented peace and prosperity . . .'

I'm straining my neck to see him, but I wish I were at home where I could go about my night while the address streamed unobtrusively into my life. Here, next to Cormac, Stream crews are recording guest reactions, so I keep my face blank. They won't show someone as uninteresting as me. My mind wanders to Jost, and I wonder if he's stuck serving the officials. I wish he would come and feed me now like he did in Cypress. Jost knew exactly how much to scoop on the fork, and when I was ready for the next bite. I remember how his jacket was warm and soft in the cell. I want him to take care of me now. But even thinking about him is a welcome distraction from this evening's politics, until everyone at the table starts to whisper in exhilaration, drawing my attention back to the speech.

'We're confident that safe mind-mapping will be available to the general public by this time next year,' Prime Minister Carma says from the podium. 'Imagine being able to save the treasured memories of your elderly grandparents before their removal or to deal painlessly with behavioural issues in your children. Until now these minor inconveniences have been the only flaws in Arras, but soon they'll be a thing of the past.'

'Wish we had that last year,' Magdalena says quietly to the other wives. 'Korbin held on to his mother for two years before I convinced him to put in the removal request.'

The wife to my left laughs, and whispers, 'Not to men-

tion dealing with Joei. I didn't think I would get her through testing without killing her!'

My eyes meet Loricel's, but I say nothing.

The speech continues with crop predictions and reports and proposed changes to the weave, which the Guild will apparently be voting on in the coming election. Then the prime minister begins calling on various officials to stand to receive recognition for their contributions throughout the year. When Cormac's name is called, I try to smile at the vlip recorders that are trained on us.

Prime Minister Carma ends the accolades with his arm pointed to our table. 'And, as always, the Guild offers its gratitude for the continued service and skills of the head of Manipulation Services, Loricel.'

She doesn't stand. She doesn't even smile. They clap anyway.

Cormac is called away when the address is over. Loricel leaves soon after, and I wait at the table, unwilling to risk going near the dance floor, where the older Guild officials linger, dragging Spinsters out to dance. That leaves me to eavesdrop on the gaggle of wives whispering across from me.

'He may have the half the women in Arras drooling over him, including you,' Magdalena says, poking the woman next to her, 'but he'll never get the nomination.'

'Men like him, too,' the other wife protests.

'No, they're jealous. There's a difference,' Magdalena points out. 'And even if we did have a say, he still wouldn't get elected. Cormac's single, and no bachelor will ever get elected head of state.'

'You're just hoping Korbin will get the nod,' whispers the other wife.

I peek over at them and notice Magdalena flinch at this accusation. Her eyes travel to mine.

'Regardless, Cormac won't ever be prime minister if he keeps running around with little girls,' she says bitterly.

I take this as my cue to finally slip back to my apartment. I'm sure they'll turn their venom on me next. Scanning the room, I don't see anyone who will stop me from leaving, unless one of the officials tries to get his hands on me. That's something I'd like to avoid, as the men who are here alone are as undesirable as they come – dumpy, hairy, and smelly. The only girl who would go after one of them would be a girl after power.

I guess that's why Pryana's draping herself over the dumpiest, hairiest, and smelliest of the undesirables – the minister of Ambrica, a large region that contains most of the Eastern Sector. It's situated along the seaboard, and his bulging waistline is evidence that he enjoys the benefits of a rich seafood diet as well as far too many of the wines that are produced in the region. Unfortunately, he seizes my arm as I try to steal past them.

'You must be the other new hire.' He winks at me, and Pryana glares, her body still pressed against him.

'I suppose so,' I say, as bored as possible.

'You are a fine-looking pair. These days it's rare we get two ideal new Spinsters at the Western Coventry in one year,' he says, moving so close to me that the stench of garlic and whisky stings my nose. 'But you two are exquisite.'

I try to think of something clever to say without insulting

him or encouraging his perverted commentary. I can't come up with a thing.

Thankfully, Pryana, who appears to be trying to permanently adhere herself to him, steps in and bats her overlong lashes. Her body language tells me to back off, and I want to scream at her that this is the last place I want to be.

The minister grasps Pryana firmly at the waist. 'You, my dear, are like midnight.'

She smiles and leans in to whisper in the minister's ear, but he pulls away and clutches at my wrist. My skin crawls where his doughy hand rests, and I'm grateful my arm is the only thing he can reach. 'But you,' he continues in a husky tone, 'are like a pearl.'

'Funny, Cormac says the same thing.' It works. He immediately drops his hold on me.

'Pity he had to leave,' the minister slurs. 'Called to Northumbria, I hear.'

Why he left is news to me, but I nod as though I'm in on everything. 'He said something about it during dinner.'

The minister, a little too drunk, tries to straighten up as though we're talking official business, which results in Pryana falling off him — literally. Her lips tighten against her teeth and her nostrils flare, but she coolly tugs him away from me. 'Dance with me.'

'Oh yes,' the minister slobbers as she pulls him toward the vibrantly lit dance floor in the centre of the banquet room. 'It was lovely to meet you, Alice.'

Alice. Wonder what he thinks her name is.

'Was he talking to you?' a smooth, strong voice asks from behind. I turn, expecting to see Jost, whom I've seen

wandering about the hall, but find Erik.

'You look disappointed,' he notes.

I am disappointed, but I shake my head. 'No, you sounded like someone else.'

A frown passes over his pale face, but it's gone as quickly as it comes. 'If you're expecting someone else . . .'

'Oh, well, any moment I'm expecting to be mobbed and eaten alive by fat old men,' I say matter-of-factly.

'I suppose I should leave you to it then.' He pretends to turn away, and I punch him lightly on the shoulder.

'Ouch, you could have mentioned you didn't want to be mobbed by fat, old men,' he says.

'Why would you ever think I would?'

He points to Pryana hanging on the minister. 'She doesn't seem to mind.'

'Well, I'm not Pryana.'

'So does that mean you are available for this dance?' He grins at me. No amount of Crewel work or weaving could achieve such a perfectly crooked smile.

I nod, and he leads me over to the floor. Pryana flashes a scathing look in our direction, but immediately turns her attention back to her prey.

'You know, dancing naked is easier than I imagined it would be,' I say without thinking as the music slows and Erik draws me into his arms to dance.

'Naked?' he asks quietly against my ear.

'Oh, nothing.' I can't believe I said it out loud. 'I feel naked in this dress.' *Twice.*

'You look it,' he admits. 'I have to be honest, I *really* like this dress.'

195

For some reason this is hysterically funny to me, and I actually begin to giggle. 'I should have known that would be your stance.'

'So which of our lascivious ambassadors do you have in your sights?' he asks, scanning the room thoughtfully.

'I'm not sure I follow.'

'They do this every year. Host the State of the Guild here so the officials can drool over the new girls. The other coventries host similar state dinners throughout the year.'

'Gross,' I mutter.

'It is, isn't it?' he whispers, amused. 'But, really, no lucky bachelor this year?'

'I think I'll let Pryana have her pick,' I say, watching her simper and pout at the minister.

'I doubt his wife will let him bring her home,' Erik responds with a wink.

'Wife?' I pretend to gag.

'Oh, they're all married,' he informs me. 'The young ones' wives insist on coming, for obvious reasons, but by the time your husband looks like that –' he tips his head at an older man with more hair in his ears than on his head – 'you're happy to let some poor girl take care of business for you.'

I sigh. 'I should tell her. She'll break purity standards and then . . .'

'Why? She hasn't done you any favours.' He tightens his grip on my waist to keep me from pulling away to go to her.

'So? She's being used.'

'As far as I've seen, she's throwing herself at him,' he

says. 'Shamelessly, I might add.'

'You have a point. It just feels wrong.'

'She's hoping to move up,' he says. 'You all hope there's some way to rise in the ranks or to escape. The sooner she learns there isn't, the better.'

His cold response sucks the air out of me. He may have been talking about Pryana, but he knew I was thinking the same thing.

'Don't be offended.' He takes my chin in his hand and draws my face up until our eyes meet. I can see the red of my hair flaming in his deep blue eyes. 'You aren't throwing yourself at a fat, old letch.'

'But you know I would take any opportunity to escape,' I whisper.

'The difference,' he says, matching his voice to mine, 'is that you're smart enough to realise a ploy like that won't work. You'd have a plan.'

I blush and turn my face out of his hand so he can't see my embarrassment.

'In fact,' he murmurs, leaning against my hair, 'I can't wait to see what you'll try.'

'Try?' I ask innocently.

'To escape,' he clarifies, and I stiffen in his arms. 'No, don't worry. If you can get out, more power to you. No one ever has before.'

'Perhaps because they depended on men to do it?' I offer, and look up to see his mouth split into a wide grin.

'See what I mean?' He laughs and pulls me closer. 'You're already smarter than every girl here.'

'Including Maela?' I spy her out of the corner of my eye,

chatting animatedly with a gentleman at the bar. I'm glad she's otherwise engaged.

'Especially Maela,' he says, and sighs. 'She's not an intellectual. She acts on her whims.'

'She must have had a rough childhood.'

'Yes,' he says solemnly, 'there was a serious lack of puppies.'

I laugh and settle against his chest, glad I'm smart enough not to be cosied up to a drunk old man, but wondering exactly what I'm getting myself into with a charming young one.

Enora's voice hissing in my ear pulls me away from the moment. 'Come with me now.'

As she drags me away, I shoot Erik an apologetic look. Without wasting any time, Enora pulls me into the powder room.

'What are you thinking?' she demands.

'I don't—'

But she cuts me off with a finger and throws open the door to the toilet. It's vacant, so she crosses over to the main door and locks it.

'Now?' I ask.

'Yes,' she snaps.

I fold my arms over my bare chest. 'I'm not sure what you mean.' Except, of course, I am.

'Don't play dumb. It doesn't suit you.'

'I wasn't aware that I couldn't dance.'

'Of course you can dance,' she responds irritably. 'You can dance with the old officials. You can even dance with a young one if his wife will let you.'

'But Erik is off-limits because he's unmarried?'

'No, he's off-limits because he's Maela's,' she says, throwing up her hands. She's not usually so dramatic. 'And in case you missed it, she already hates you.'

'No, I caught that.' The fun I was having moments ago leaks away. 'And what do you mean "he's Maela's"?'

'Adelice, I know you aren't stupid.'

'Let's pretend I am.'

'Fine. She's in love with Erik. He was some nobody who came to work in the kitchen a few years ago, but then Maela adopted him.' Her voice shakes with panic, not rage.

'She's ten years older than him. At least.'

She shoots me another exasperated look. 'Back off before she takes even more of an interest in you.'

'I was just dancing with him,' I argue, not sure even I believe it. 'It's that or let some creepy Guild official paw me all night.'

'Ad,' she pleads, 'I sympathise, I really do, and Erik is very charming, but there are two things you need to consider. The first is how angry Maela will be if she finds out.'

'And the second?'

'That Erik's intentions aren't necessarily as honourable as he makes it seem.'

I blush. 'Look, I know we aren't allowed to get married, and I know there are limits, but I never thought . . .'

'That,' she says pointedly, 'is not what I'm talking about. You're cosying up to Maela's assistant. You don't find it suspicious that he's taken an interest in you?'

'Well, I do now.' How had this not occurred to me? Since our trip together, I'd started to trust him without even realising it.

'You're already walking a thin line – the way you ran and the attention you're drawing to yourself. Arras doesn't work this way, Adelice. Secrets—'

'Don't have a place here.' It bursts viciously out of my mouth.

But instead of being annoyed, she titters wryly. 'No, there are plenty of secrets here, believe me, but some of us realise the danger of flaunting them.'

I open my mouth to protest, but she raises her hand to stop me.

'Let me finish. I don't want to be another person trying to control you—'

'Then don't!' I yell. 'You aren't my mom.'

'I'm not trying to replace your mother. No one can do that,' she says in a quiet voice.

'No,' I retort. 'Not even the Guild.'

Enora backs away from me. She opens her mouth to speak but closes it again as if she can't find the right words. We both know there are no right words when it comes to what the Guild did to my family.

'I have to get back before they notice I'm gone.' Enora reaches out a hand as if to comfort me but thinks better of it and heads out to the party.

I take my time going back to the ball, afraid I'll cry in front of the Stream crews. When I'm sure I'm calm enough, I slip out of the bathroom, still trying to decide how to dump Erik so I can sneak to my room and rip open a pillow, when a pair of strong hands pulls me away from the busy banquet room and into the dark hall.

'I thought I'd been left to fend off drunk old men,' Erik

says, quietly, to avoid sending an echo down the empty marble hallway.

'The Guild officials are getting broad-minded,' I murmur, the ache in my chest suddenly spreading to where his hands hold my bare arms.

'Come on, I want to show you something.' He slips his fingers through mine, and against my better judgement, I follow him.

'Erik, I don't think this is a good idea.'

'Let me guess.' He laughs good-naturedly. 'Enora was warning you that Maela will put your head on a spike if she catches us together?'

Something about the casual way he says this makes me feel silly for listening to her.

'Why do you think I'm pilfering you away tonight?' he asks earnestly.

Enora's warning about his intentions echoes in my head. 'I'm not sure.'

'Because Maela is too busy to notice, and by this point everyone else is too tipsy to watch you.'

'So it's true then?' I ask breathlessly. 'I'm still being watched.'

'Of course you are,' he says. 'We all are, but on nights like this security is busy keeping Spinsters to their purity obligations, and I told them I would keep an eye on you.'

Another reason I shouldn't be here with him now.

'Where are we going anyway?' I ask as he leads me down another empty corridor.

'We're here.' He drops my hand and dramatically opens two large wooden doors directly in front of us.

The moon casts a faint silver glaze on the flowers and sparkles at us from the cobbled walkway that leads into the heart of the garden I walked through on my first day of orientation. I've rarely been outside since my arrival here, and then only under close supervision. Right now Erik is anything but a chaperone.

He offers his arm and sweeps me toward the centre of the garden. 'Care to dance away from those prying eyes?'

There's no music, but he leads me elegantly into a waltz. His blond hair glows in the dim starshine, and he looks like he belongs here in the cool night.

'You haven't asked me why I'm doing this yet,' he whispers in my ear.

I have to swallow against the frantic pulse in my throat to speak. 'Will you tell me the truth?'

'Possibly,' he says. 'Although I'm not sure you are ever supposed to tell a lady the truth.'

'You won't know until you try,' I argue.

'Okay. I like smart girls,' he tells me. 'And a smart girl who's also gorgeous – how can I resist?'

I rest my head on his shoulder so he won't see how much I like this information, even if he's probably lying.

'So is that why you're with Maela?' I ask, my face still turned from his.

He snorts at this. 'With Maela? That woman does not know when to let go.'

'You haven't . . .' I'm not sure I want a straight answer even if he'll give it.

'She never understood how it works,' he says. 'She's not as bright as you are.'

I think about Enora's warning and try to pull away from him. 'Erik, I'm already on Maela's bad side. There's no need to make it worse.'

'You have to remember she controls me too.' For a moment he sounds sincere but then the arrogance returns. 'We may never get another chance.' But underneath his sense of entitlement, there's a subtle fear hidden in his eyes, and it looks familiar. It reminds me of the way my father looked as he dragged me to the tunnel. I cling to Erik a little tighter, remembering how easily people can slip away.

'It doesn't matter. We have a little fun now and Maela finds out and does something awful to one of us, or both of us, and for what?' I force myself to pull out of Erik's grasp and look him in the eyes. 'There's no future for us.'

'Look, you can play the innocent with everyone else, but not me.' His voice is low but earnest. 'I know Maela is watching you. She thinks you're dangerous, which means you are.'

'Maela thinks she's the centre of the world. I wouldn't put too much stock in her opinions.'

'She's scared of you,' he says.

'Why? I'm not her problem any more.'

'I don't know.' Erik sighs. Clearly he'd hoped I'd open up more. 'It has to be something that happened at your testing. She's been different ever since you arrived.'

'Oh, she wasn't a psycho before?'

Erik shakes his head and the moonlight bounces off his golden hair. 'No, that's nothing new. I thought I'd have to kill you when you first got here.'

I groan. This is so unfair. 'She really hates me.'

'No,' he says, 'the Guild executes any girl who runs. Standard no-tolerance policy. When she had me sedate you, I assumed——'

'And you would have done it,' I accuse him.

'It's not that simple.'

'I wasn't really running,' I admit. 'My parents were trying to hide me.'

'Doesn't matter,' Erik says, unshaken by the confession. 'They would kill you *and* your family then.'

'Why?' The word forms on my lips but no sound comes out.

'A girl who tries to escape or run with her family after testing can never be loyal enough to trust. Runners rarely ever make it to the Coventry after they're caught, but Maela lives for gossip, so I hear about it when one does. It seems to happen frequently in the Western Sector. People whose parents hide them – whose parents try to cheat the testing process – have poisoned minds.'

'And the girls who come willingly *are* loyal?' I demand.

'Of course. The Guild controls their families, Adelice,' he says. 'Not many question it, and those who do——'

'What happens to them?'

Erik shakes his head.

'Is that why they watch us? Me?' I ask flatly. 'Because my parents are dead and my kid sister wouldn't recognise me? Because they have nothing to hold over me?'

'Maybe,' Erik admits, and I hit him hard in the chest. I hate him for telling me the truth. I hit him again and again, and he lets me. Finally my hands hurt from hitting the mass

of his solid chest, and I crumble against him. For a long time we say nothing and I pace my breathing to his; our chests rise and fall rhythmically, a promise of normality.

'Adelice,' he whispers, still holding me perfectly still. 'I wouldn't count on them both being dead.'

My breath catches and blocks all my thoughts from tumbling out.

'The Guild is too smart to kill off a Spinster's family and expect her to be of service to them, but they'll make sure that you have almost nothing left,' he warns me, speaking so quietly against my hair I barely hear him.

'They have my sister, Amie.' I force myself to face facts. 'They remapped her though.'

'Younger than you?'

'Twelve.'

He furrows his brow. 'And your parents – did you see them die?'

The body bag in the dining room flickers into my mind.

'My dad. I know he's dead,' I say in a hollow voice.

'But they only *told* you they killed your mother?'

A thousand tiny pieces of shattered hope tug together in my chest.

'Wait.' I pull back and meet his eyes. I keep my voice low but everything comes out in a rush. 'Are you saying my mother might be alive?'

'Yes, she's definitely alive.' But he barely gets the words out, because my mouth is on his. I'm kissing him out of joy or maybe panic, but soon the kiss shifts from excitement to something much more serious, and my body moulds up against his. His lips move slowly, his hand pressing against

the small of my back. I want to weave this moment out and make it last forever. The feeling of my heart racing, the slight taste of wine on his lips, how my hips lock against his.

But Maela has other plans.

12

When Erik and I break from our embrace, Maela is standing several feet away on the small stone path. The moon shines behind her, obscuring her face, but her posture – straight and rigid – tells me all I need to know. Well, almost. I need to know how long she's been there more than anything else. More than I need to know how she feels about the kiss or what she'll do to us now that we've been caught. I have a pretty good idea about that.

'Erik,' she says in a calm voice. 'I need you to escort a couple of ministers to the guest quarters. All of the valets are busy.'

Erik glances over at me, and then back to her. His hand is still on the small of my back and when he removes it, the bite of night air blows along my bare flesh, making me shiver. He casts a worried look my way, but turns to Maela. 'I'll escort Adelice to her apartment first.'

'I think you've given her enough attention this evening,' Maela murmurs, stepping forward. As she does, the shadows fade off her face, and I see that she's crying.

I never thought I'd feel sorry for her, especially if I was ever lucky enough to hurt her. But her running mascara makes me want to shrink back and hide among the vines and branches.

'Were you following me?' he demands.

'I needed you,' she says quietly.

'There are fifty other guards in there,' he says, shaking his head. 'You don't own me. I work for you.'

Her nostrils flare at the cruelty of his words, and even I feel their sting. *This is getting awkward.*

'You wouldn't be here if not for me,' she reminds him. 'You'd be stuck slaving in the kitchen or rotting on some boat trying to fish for a living. So unless you want to go back there, I expect you to see the ministers upstairs. Adelice can find her own way back.'

At the mention of his past, he's not willing to press it further, and he disappears into the wild, black silhouette of the trees without another word to her – or to me.

Maela isn't moving. I consider my options. I can try to leave, but I will have to pass her, which will put me within arm's reach, and I'm not altogether comfortable with that idea. Or I can strike up a conversation, but nothing is running through my head except the feeling of Erik's lips, and she's not going to want to discuss that. The third option is to stare her down, and since that's the least dangerous one it's what I do.

'Good night, Adelice,' Maela says, turning away from

me. 'The party is still going on, but I've had enough.' Without another word she withdraws along the path that Erik took.

When I get back to the hall, Erik is busy gathering up drunk politicians, and I try to avoid catching his attention. Things are complicated enough at the moment. Maela is nowhere to be seen and neither is Enora. Good. I don't need a night in the cells or a lecture right now. All I need is a bed.

Whether it's from the relief of having hope that my mother is alive or a bit too much wine, I slip into a deep sleep as soon as I hit the sheets, but what seems like moments later I'm shaken awake. It takes me a while to adjust to the sight of a panic-stricken Enora hovering over me.

'What time is it?' I croak against a dry, scratchy throat.

'It's four in the morning,' she says in a rush. I wonder – mostly coherently – why she's here so early.

'Okay,' I mumble, and try to roll out of her reach.

'This is serious,' she hisses. 'Maela will have someone here for you in a few minutes. I don't have much time.'

Erik. He's on his way to my room. I sit bolt upright in bed and brush the hair out of my face.

'Here.' Enora shoves a dress into my hands. 'Put this on. You won't want to be wearing that.'

I look down and realise I'm still in the silk gown from the party. I quickly yank it off. There's no time to tell her I need underwear, so I slip the new dress on, feeling awkward and vulnerable.

'Give me your hands,' she demands, grabbing them her-

self when I'm not fast enough. A moment later she brushes my fingertips with clear gloss. 'This will help, but it won't keep you from feeling it.'

'Feeling what?' I ask slowly, but before she can reply Maela's brutish guard with the shaved head walks in. I'm relieved and disappointed.

'Enora.' He tips his head to her in greeting. 'Maela needs Adelice for a special testing.'

'Wait,' I say, even though he's not speaking to me. 'I thought I was done with testing.'

They share a look that sends stomach acid into my throat.

'Occasionally,' Enora says in measured syllables, 'we are tested spontaneously. It is a chance to see how you perform under pressure.' Her expression reminds me of the one on my mother's face before she fled into the tunnel. She's lost, no matter what she does, and it drags down her eyes in sadness.

Instinctively I fling my arms around her and bury myself in her neck. Enora's arms are warm and strong, and I want them to be my mom's. 'Your soul is your own,' she whispers into my hair. 'Don't let them take that. No matter what they do.'

Words will betray me and allow the tears to come, so I smile bravely as I pull away from her and follow the burly guard without asking more questions. Turning one last time, I see the concerned look on Enora's face, but she quickly replaces it with a smile when our eyes meet. We both know this testing isn't spontaneous or an evaluation of my progress. This is a new punishment.

My fingertips are hard like rocks where Enora painted

them with the clear lacquer. I can still feel them but as I press them together, the nails bend back. But the skin is numb where she brushed the gloss.

'Word to the wise,' the guard offers in a gruff voice. 'Don't do that.'

'What?' I ask.

'That,' he says, and his eyes dart to my fingertips. 'You'll get her in trouble for helping you.'

A slow aching chill spreads out through my chest and down into my arms and legs. What have I got myself into?

'Is Erik okay?' I ask, trying to sound casual. 'He usually escorts me to these things.'

'Yeah.' The guard snorts. 'Maela has switched up assignments for the time being. He'll be sticking closer to her in the future.'

This news doesn't surprise me, but it still hurts. Erik might have been a friend, and even if his intentions weren't exactly noble, he made me laugh. And then there was the kiss. Something I don't know how to deal with.

The halls are quiet. No hint of a party lingers – even the late-nighters must be in bed. What kind of punishment takes place at four in the morning? The kind no one can know about. Enora warned me this would happen if I hung around Erik, but I didn't listen.

My new guard leads me up to two swinging doors and holds one open. 'I'm Darius, by the way,' he informs me, and as soon as I'm through the door, he's gone.

Swollen white plastic covers the walls of the stark studio. One window. One loom. One person. Maela's already there, fully dressed. And I have no underwear on. She must

keep her aesthetician locked in her bathroom. But when she turns, I see she has no cosmetics applied. Her face is softer, lacking the harsh angles rouge and liner give it. She looks average, maybe even pretty, but her eyes are the same: cold and hateful.

'On occasion,' she says, 'we are required to perform an unexpected test on a new Spinster. A few Guild officials expressed concern over your readiness to start Crewel work. As you know, this work is of the utmost importance, and it's my duty to assure them you are ready.'

'Which officials?' I ask, calling her bluff.

She smiles, unfazed. 'Don't worry about that. The important thing is that you focus on completing the task I have for you.'

'Have you spoken with Cormac?'

'I don't have to approve training activities with Cormac,' she says, staring out the window.

'Loricel?' I ask, wondering if she's approved this.

'She isn't interested in the rest of us,' Maela spits. 'And at her advanced age, she's been in bed for hours.'

I nod and mentally sort through all the comebacks I could make. In the end, I opt for silence.

'Spinning is delicate work,' she purrs, and I notice for the first time how quiet the room is without the hum of the loom. 'I know you are aware of that.'

I feel my jaw tighten. All I've ever seen is Maela mutilating Arras – and she's going to give me tips?

'You must approach your work with precision and delicacy, regardless of what is going on beyond this room,' she continues. 'We call this a stress test.'

She turns, but looks past me, and I follow her gaze. For the first time I notice a large oak loom with thick steel strands stretched across it. It's nothing like the modern automated machines I've been training on. There's a crudeness to it. The wood is warped and scratched, and the small bench that accompanies it is made of a solid piece of unfinished tree stump. This isn't going to be comfortable.

'If you are gentle, you can weave anything,' she murmurs, beckoning me to take a seat on the stump. 'How else can a Spinster weave time? It's so precious. Once we had no control over time. It slipped right through our fingers. No power over death or famine or disease. And then science gave us weaving. But if we are not careful we could lose the control we have now.'

I've had enough of this patronising charade. 'Is this because of what happened between Erik and me?'

Maela's nostrils flare and she moves away from me. 'This exercise,' she continues, bypassing my question altogether, 'will teach you delicacy and control.'

She leans toward the loom and deftly, but very softly, fingers a steel line. It pings as she releases it. Taking a thin wirelike thread, she gracefully weaves it through the steel cables on the loom. In. Out. In. Out. Until she yelps and draws her index finger up to her mouth, wincing.

I want to ask her what's wrong, but it seems bad form since we're enemies and everything, so I wait until she removes her finger. Blood blossoms from a small cut, and the nature of this test becomes clear.

'This spool,' she says, holding a large metal cylinder out to me, 'needs to be woven through by noon.'

'That's it?' I ask suspiciously, afraid to take the thread from her. Light glints off its coils.

'That's it.' She presses her lips together in a smirk. 'By noon, or you'll be reassigned.'

'I assume the ministers will need to see my work.'

Her jaw flexes under her skin, but she maintains her composure. 'Naturally.'

'Naturally,' I agree.

She leaves the room, and I gingerly touch the 'thread'. It's razor sharp. Even more carefully, I reach out to feel the steel bands that comprise the warp of the loom. They're almost totally rigid. Razor wire and a fake loom. She's out-done herself this time. I'll be lucky to have fingers at the end of this.

My first pass goes through easily and I avoid cutting my fingertips. It makes me overconfident, and the next pass slices off the tip of my left index finger. Tears sting my eyes as air hits the open flesh. This is no minor wound, but Maela is looking for any excuse to banish to me to kitchen work or worse, so I pull on the cylinder until I have enough slack to reach the hem of my skirt and use the wire to slice a few inches off it. Cutting several smaller pieces, I wrap each of my fingers, starting with my bleeding pointer. I'll have to adjust to my clumsy covered fingers, but I can't leave them exposed.

It's slow work. Occasionally the wire catches on the tops of my hands and leaves angry streaks of blood across them, but I press on, fighting against the growing pulse from the wounds. The makeshift bandages last for a while, until the one covering my bloodied finger is soaked through and the

others are in tatters. The sun is rising in the east window, and I have five hours left at most, but the spool looks untouched. Taking a deep breath, I peel off the fabric covers, except the one blocking my bleeding left index finger, and grip the wire firmly between my right index finger and thumb.

I focus on breathing, filling my lungs completely with each inhale and then slowly releasing. Bleeding welts cover my hands, but I press on, ignoring the dizzy, light-headed feeling. And between my body expecting breakfast – stupid set mealtimes – and dripping blood everywhere, my mind drops into oblivion.

The lack of noise in the room roars in my ears, or maybe it's my heartbeat. There's no clock, only the faint glow of morning light breaking in patches on my work. It reflects back off the white plastic-covered walls, heating them, so their synthetic stench fills the air in the studio, making my stomach hurt. Everything is bright, blinding in its artifice. Only my warm blood on the cold, steel lines contrasts with the harsh brilliance of the space. But despite the searing pain, I get through three-quarters of the spool before Maela returns.

She smiles at the sight of my wounded hands. 'You have two hours left, Adelice.' Leaning over my work, she continues, 'I was thinking about how rude it was for us not to give you more updates on your sister.'

I lose my careful grip on the wire and slice a fresh cut into my palm.

'It's common for us to allow a letter or to provide some information during the initial training,' she says, still hov-

ering over me. 'But we generally don't do that for traitors.'

'Yes, I'm aware of what you do for traitors,' I say.

'Then you already know we can be merciful,' she replies innocently. I want to wrap the wire around her thin, pale neck.

'Unfortunately, your parents committed treason, and of course there was the issue of the contraband found in your house,' she tells me, 'so your parents have been removed.'

'Cormac told me,' I respond. But even though I already knew, I feel the heat of tears when I blink. I have no energy to fight them.

'I see. You also know that your sister, as a minor, was rewoven. You know she's in Cypress, where many of our finest Eligibles are found each year. As she probably shares your talent, she's likely to prove useful to us in the future. We're keeping a very close eye on her.'

'Amie doesn't have any skill,' I murmur, willing it to be true. 'You're wasting your time.'

'Not at all,' Maela assures me as she lights a cigarette. 'We need to keep track of her for you. The Guild's newest prize needs to be kept happy.'

'Doesn't matter to me. I barely knew her,' I lie. 'We're not very close in age, and she was always more concerned with being popular and keeping up on the current phases.' As soon as it's out of my mouth, I want to swallow it back.

But I can tell from the way Maela's eyebrow shoots up that this info delights her. 'You two are different then. Maybe she'll have what she needs to succeed as a Spinster when her time comes, if that's what she wants.'

Wants? I hesitate. 'And her new family?' I think of the

216

paranoid look in her adoptive mother's eyes.

'You saw her new mother. They're an excellent, loyal family,' she says. 'There are an unfortunate number of couples who are childless, so orphans are often rewoven in-to other sections to those deserving people.'

The wire's buried half an inch in my thumb before I realise how hard I'm clenching it. I don't know why I'm stopping myself. No one would miss Maela.

'Thanks for the update. I have a lot left to do.' I force myself to return to the work, and I hear the soft click of the door closing behind her.

When Maela saunters into the room at noon, she prac-tically chokes on her cigarette to find me done. 'I guess I didn't give you enough thread,' she says in a low voice. 'You look like you got bored.'

'Maybe I'm as talented as you don't want me to be,' I counter, keeping my eyes level with hers and ignoring the woozy shakiness spreading through my body. If she thought her diversion would sidetrack me, she was mistaken. 'Will someone be coming to check my work?'

Maela's eyes narrow, but she speaks in a normal voice. 'Of course. Later.'

'Let me know what they think,' I say as arrogantly as I can, while bleeding profusely. My terse new escort takes me back to my quarters, and I try not to drip blood on the high tower's expensive rugs.

There's no one waiting in my room. Not even Enora, who I fully expected to descend on me as soon as I entered. So I let myself cry, my tears washing down along the blood soaking my skirt. I can't bring myself to examine my hands,

and a search of my cavernous bathroom yields no medical supplies. I finally call on the companel to ask for bandages and a doctor. Neither request is denied.

An eternity later someone raps at my door. I don't know who it could be. No one knocks here. The maid, kitchen staff, my aestheticians — all of them enter and exit at their convenience. So for the first time I discover my door has a peephole. Peering through the tiny circle of glass I'm greeted by a single electric-blue eye. For a moment, I freeze. It could be Erik or Jost, and I realise I'm not sure which one of them I want to see more, or if it's even safe to let either of them in. But finally I take a deep breath and open the door.

13

Maela wouldn't knowingly send me the one person I might be both dying to see and wanting to avoid, but it would be the evil icing on the cake to have Jost attend me. Does he know I'm being punished for kissing Erik? Or maybe he's just been thinking about me, too. The idea that he might want to see me sends my pulse racing so fast that my mutilated fingers throb. Now might not be the time to worry about this. He's seen me looking worse, so I instruct him to come in, anyway. Jost's head is turned away from the open door.

I clear my throat to get his attention. 'I'm not naked, you know.'

'I'll try to be less polite in the future,' he says.

'What are you doing here?' I ask as I gingerly wrap a clean towel around my bleeding hands.

'You sent for medical help.' He holds up a small medic bag.

'Exactly. They don't have a clinic here?' Realising my

exasperation might be misinterpreted – because I'd much rather be here with him than on an exam table – I quickly add, 'I'm glad you make house calls, but what *is* your job anyway?'

'I do the dirty work, remember? I'm trained to do basic medical patching. If you aren't dying, you get me. The clinic is reserved for other things.' His tone implies there's more to the story, but I can't handle any more information right now. I make a mental note to bring this up later when I'm not bleeding profusely.

'So your job is to clean up after me?' I ask, tilting my head to get a better look at him. Unfortunately, the small shift makes me extremely dizzy.

Jost catches me in time. 'Exactly.'

He helps me to the large floor cushions and takes my hands carefully. His own are warm and rough against my wrist as he inspects mine. His soft touch isn't doing much to help me with the light-headedness, but I couldn't care less.

'Do I want to know what happened?' he asks.

I shake my head. 'Maela has taken a shine to me.'

'What happened to a low profile?' Jost asks, with a follow-up groan to seal his disapproval.

'I'm tall.'

Despite his clear frustration, he smiles just a little. 'Let's clean these up. You know we're going to need to wash this off,' he says, taking my elbow and helping me to my feet. Apparently I'm not funny. But if I can't tease Jost, I'm not sure what to do with him.

In the bathroom he turns the tap on full blast. The rushing water echoes off the marble. 'There,' he says, and I give

him a quizzical look, but he just takes my hands. Instead of pushing them under the rushing tap, he cups some water in his left hand and pours it over my wounds, tenderly wiping away the blood. I'm used to people doing things for me by now – my hair and cosmetics, even dressing me – but Jost caring for me reminds me of my mother watching over me when I was ill. The ache spreading in my chest is anything but homesickness though.

Opening the pouch he brought, he takes out a small pot of salve. 'This is going to sting.'

'I've managed worse.' But as he applies it to the open cuts, I regret my bravado. I have to bite down on my lip to keep from yelping.

'How are you doing?' he asks kindly.

'I've been better,' I admit, sucking in a long breath to distract myself. 'So the Guild has you healing Spinsters in addition to your valet duties? Exactly why are you here?'

He leans closer to me and whispers against my ear, 'Did you think we could talk in your room? I don't need the Guild to know why I'm here.'

'I guess I didn't expect . . .' My mind no longer forms full thoughts as his breath hits my neck.

'A real answer?' He pulls back, breaking the spell.

'A controversial one,' I admit finally. 'I thought you were a regular working drudge.'

'Thanks,' he says. 'That's only mildly insulting.'

'I'm sorry. It wasn't supposed to be.'

'I know. I guess I'm better at fitting in than I thought,' he says, wrapping gauze around my cleaned hands. 'What's this?'

He trails a finger along the techprint on my wrist, and I'm not sure what to tell him. 'A relic from a past life,' I say with a sigh. 'My father printed me before . . .'

Jost tips his head ever so slightly to show he knows and I don't have to say the words, even though they echo and roar in my head: *before he died.*

'Why an hourglass?' he asks, studying the mark.

'I don't know,' I murmur, extremely conscious of his touch. 'It's supposed to remind me who I am.'

'Is it working?' he breathes, staring into my eyes.

'I suppose.' I watch him and weigh my thoughts. 'Why are you here, Jost? Serving the Coventry, I mean.'

'I don't even know how to begin to answer that,' he says, starting on my other hand.

'At the beginning?' I suggest quietly. He looks up and his usually bright eyes are hollow.

'I had a family once.' He pauses and turns his attention back to my hands. 'Now I don't.'

The space between us is shrinking, but I'm only now seeing the wide gulf that existed before. 'How did it happen?' I ask.

'I was married when I was sixteen to a girl from my town. Our metro doesn't segregate much in the pretesting years, and we made certain she'd be dismissed from eligibility.'

I blush at his confession but try to laugh off my discomfort. Something twists in my chest at this revelation. I don't like that he was married. Not one bit. Even if he isn't any more. 'Sixteen? I thought eighteen was bad.' As soon as I say it, I regret it.

'Yes, sixteen.' And to my relief, he laughs. 'I'd known her since we were children. We lived in a small village, Saxun, which straddles the Western and Southern Sectors. I come from a long line of fishermen. It's such a small town that assignments are dictated by family trade, and since my brother got a border pass out of town, I was the only one who could take over my father's boat.'

'So you weren't given a role?' The monthly assignment day was a major event in Romen town. Mostly it was for filling any needs in the metro, and occasionally someone might be sent to a neighbouring metrocentre, but once in a while the Guild would fill a position within the Coventry or various sector departments, which meant a border pass. It almost always went to a boy, but the whole town lived for the possibility of it. No one missed assignment day.

'You know, if you have a lot of money or none at all, it works differently,' he tells me wryly. 'The system doesn't apply to you in quite the same way.'

'Romen was the third largest town in the Western Sector,' I say. 'It was the kind of town where everything was average – houses, assignments, people.'

'The middle is what the Guild thrives on.'

'So, you were married before you came here?' I try to sound casual, but I'm feeling a bit out of my league, and I don't want him to hear the jealousy in my voice.

He nods and begins to dress my hands. 'Her name was Rozenn. She lived with her father and her brother. I was working to buy a new boat and . . .' He pauses as though skipping past something too painful to share, but he continues, his voice barely audible over the water. 'I should have

known something was wrong, but it never occurred to me.'

I lay a bandaged hand on his shoulder and his rigid muscles soften.

'Her brother, Parrick. He was a loner, unhappy with his assignment, uninterested in girls. Rapidly approaching eighteen. I tolerated him because he became my family when I married Rozenn, but the two were opposites. She was a day in spring. Everything about her was vital. Parrick stuck out the same way, but only because he was cold. He could suck the joy out of a conversation. People didn't like being around him. I didn't like being around him,' he admits. 'I couldn't understand why he was so distant and isolated.

'He was supposed to be apprenticing with his father, but he began taking long breaks. One day he disappeared and didn't return until nightfall. Rozenn was worried her father was losing patience with him, so she asked me to step in. She thought I could talk to Parrick. Maybe befriend him. He didn't want to talk to me, and I didn't try very hard. Instead I started following him.'

'Where was he going?' I ask in a low voice, my jealousy giving way to dread.

'He was meeting others – from our town and other metros near us. They talked about change and revolution. I thought about turning them in, but the stories stopped me.'

'Stories?' My voice is barely a whisper.

'Horrible stories. Families wiped out, towns rewoven. They were whispered tales, shared between desperate men. I was conflicted, so I did nothing.' Done with my

hands, Jost sits on the edge of the tub. His blue eyes burn like the tip of a flame, looking out past this room into the ruins left behind him.

'Did you tell your wife?' I stumble on the word, and doubt about Jost, about being here now, creeps into my throat and sits like a lump.

Jost shakes his head, but his gaze remains distant. 'No, I didn't want to worry her. I should have, but I was scared to repeat what I had heard. Turns out I was right. There are Spinsters trained to find these plots and anti-Guild groups.'

'Yes, we learned about it in training. The tapestry begins to bleed and stain. When people are loyal, their threads remain true to their original colour.'

'I bet Rozenn's was the most beautiful thread imaginable,' he says with reverence.

Hot tears prick at my eyes when he says her name.

'I wonder what Saxun looked like when they came.'

'I can't imagine. I've never seen a taint,' I admit. 'My parents trained me for eight years to fail the testing, and no one came for us. I don't know how deeply spread the staining has to be before it's identified.'

'Were your parents openly anti-Guild?'

I shake my head. Despite their actions, I can't claim them to have been rebels. 'No, they never spoke against the Guild. They were very careful about that. And besides, my mother was just a secretary and my father was a mechanic.'

'Was?'

'I wasn't the only one punished,' I say quietly. 'I assumed you knew.'

'I guessed,' he says. 'Anyway, the town of Saxun was

filled with rebels. Your parents were only two people.'

I think of the tunnels under my house. They had to lead somewhere. There's still a lot I don't know about my parents. 'I guess a little treason can be overlooked.'

'But only a little,' he murmurs.

'Yes.' My smile is ragged around the edges. 'What happened?'

'The Guild made an example of the town.' Jost's voice fades, and I lean in to hear him. 'They ripped out our sisters, our mothers, our daughters . . .'

'Your wives,' I add, and he nods.

His head drops and the distance between us is gone. When he speaks again, his words are broken. 'I saw it. You have no idea, Adelice. What it's like to see that.'

I recall being sent away from my grandmother's room. How the nurse closed the curtain and waited with her back turned as though she couldn't stand to look.

'She was on the dock, waiting with the other women for us to come in for lunch. She just slipped away. First her legs faded, and she looked so confused that I screamed for help, but there was nothing we could do. Those of us on the boats watched it happen. Her mouth disappeared next and she couldn't cry for help. The last thing to fade was her body.' He makes a choking noise and I realise he's crying. 'She was holding our daughter.'

I weep with him. For his loss and for the confusion I feel. This isn't the boy with the crooked grin who fed me sweet potatoes, and my grief isn't just because of what the Guild did to him but because of how different we are. I cry because I'm a stupid girl who can't curb the jealousy and

inferiority I feel towards Rozenn for getting him first. And for the distance that will always exist between us. He was a husband, a father, and I'm nothing and never will be. I guess the Guild assigned us our roles after all.

'It was the last time I saw either of them. She was sixteen, and my daughter was three months old.'

I have no words to comfort him so I take his hand and hold it softly in my bandaged one.

'I'm here because it's the last place they'll look,' he confides, finally answering my question.

'Look for what?' I ask, unsure I want to know the answer.

'Revolution.'

14

I dream of people I love. I am five, and my mother puts on cosmetics at the bathroom sink, but every cosmetic detracts instead of enhancing. The mascara erases her lashes, the rouge hollows her cheeks, and the lipstick removes her smile. She brushes her copper-red hair and the locks fade into air. Her decapitated body turns to me and gestures for approval, and she asks, as she did every day: 'How do I look?'

Amie is a baby and I cling to her, but the tighter I hold her, the more she disappears. I can't protect her. I see her rewoven, now a young girl with wispy blonde braids. I wave to her, and she stares through me. I am the one who's gone. I'm the ghost.

A large white cake the size of a loom rests on a simple table and under it my father melts into a pool of sticky black liquid that oozes closer and closer to my bare feet. He

calls for help, but I'm too scared of getting my shoes dirty, so I watch as he fades into nothing.

And in the background of the dreams, Jost stands frozen. Only the blink of his eyes shows that he's awake and watching, waiting for me to help him. But when I step toward him, I see her, more beautiful than me – laughing and pregnant – holding his hand, and I look away. When I turn, he shifts into Erik, whose free arms stretch out to me, beckoning for me to come to him.

I erase and rebuild the world in my sleep, and in the morning I try to remember how to rebuild myself. Every day I wonder how I can go back to the loom. Can I keep weaving now that I know? I can't erase Jost's story. I had nothing to do with it, but that doesn't change anything. I'm still a Spinster.

Jost comes daily to salve my hands with renewal cream, and they heal quickly, but no stylists come. A week has passed and even Enora is absent, and I wonder if I've gotten her in trouble, too. Food continues to arrive at meal hours. I stay in my nightdress, lounging by the fire, and living for the minutes when Jost comes to check on me. Today he brings lunch, and we eat together. The conversation sounds light, but only because we're speaking in code. Some of our stories we can share openly, but the things I really want to know can't be spoken out loud where surveillance might pick up our words. We can only spend so much time in the bathroom – where the sound of running water hides our voices – without raising alarm, but despite my attempts to steer all conversation toward his plans, he seems more interested in me.

'It wasn't a real fight.' I laugh as I continue a story about my neighbour Beth. 'She was bullying Amie, and I was tired of it. So I sort of knocked her over.'

'But you loved your kid sister, right?' Jost presses. 'It sounds like you two got into trouble a lot.'

'Amie followed the rules better than I did, so when I did anything that could get us in trouble, she freaked out,' I say. 'When I fought with Beth she worried that I'd be taken away for deviance counselling.'

'But you weren't,' he says.

'I wasn't, but Beth was.' I had forgotten that until now. It was one of those memories that stuck in your head although you tried to push it back and ignore it. Beth had gone away when we were twelve, and when she came back, she was different. Just as unfriendly, but not with me — with everyone.

'My big brother was only ten months older than me,' he says, calling back to the conversation. 'My mom called us hooligans.'

I smile at that, but then my eyes widen as I do the math. 'Ten months?'

His grin gets a little more crooked. 'Not a lot to do in a poor fishing village.'

I know more about babies and stuff than most girls my age. Well, I guess the other girls in Romen would have started marriage-preparation courses now. That's where they tell you about sex. Of course, my parents told me about the birds and the bees in excruciating and embarrassing detail years ago. Another one of their best-laid plans to make sure I understood my world. But sitting here with a guy

who makes me tingle all over, in the Coventry where the 'privileges of marriage', as my mom called them, were way off-limits, that info was pretty useless. And then there was the fact that he had first-hand experience that I would never have. It was definitely time for a change in conversation.

'So you were a hunter?' I ask, returning back to our code and carelessly scooping rice into my mouth: my bandaged hands still proving a nuisance to fine motor skills – and forks.

Jost nods, serious again. 'I was interested in large game. The kind that feeds a lot of people and brings in money.'

'What kinds of animals constitute large game?' I keep my voice casual. No companel would detect anything unusual – or even interesting – this way.

'Bears and cougars, mostly.'

'You can eat bears and cougars?' I screw up my face in mock disgust.

'Ad, you can eat anything if you're hungry enough.' Jost grins over a chicken leg.

The conversation falters, and we lapse into silence as we eat. Hunger is not an issue to discuss, even in code. It borders on treason, because the Guild claims there is no hunger. I lived on the borders of a large metro with my family and both my parents were assigned work, so although our meal rations were never exciting, we didn't want. Jost, however, worked hard for his food and many in his small village went without, save for the kindness of the fishermen, but even that was limited to what was left after they had delivered their quotas to the Guild.

But of course Jost never hunted a day in his life. He

worked fifteen-hour days to feed his family and a handful of neighbours, but at sea. I know this because during the brief distractions we can call up, we've established a few code words. It's been trial and error, with more than a few mis-understandings, but we're getting better at the double talk. The bears are ministry officials and cougars are Spinsters. Jost is looking for who is responsible for the attacks on the women of Saxun. What he's planning to do when he finds out, we haven't figured out a code for, and I'm not sure I care to know.

'Did you ever have a cougar attack a stag?' I'm trying to ask about Erik, but no matter how many ways I ask, Jost has no clue what I'm saying.

'I'm sure one did,' he says, giving me a slight shrug to let me know he's sorry he doesn't understand. If only my questions were as easy to follow as his body language.

And that's when I realise the solution to our problem. It's so simple, it never occurred to me. 'Jost, is sight or sound more important when hunting?' I ask excitedly.

'What do you mean?'

'If you were hunting, would you want to see or hear your prey?'

He understands and gives me a slight nod. 'Sight is good, but most prefer being able to hear.'

So there it is: the Coventry *listens* in private quarters but, unlike in the studios, doesn't *watch*. At least, that's what Jost thinks, and he knows a lot about how things work here. Now I know what to do if I can manage it, but it means breaking a promise.

'Well, thank you for bringing me my lunch,' I tell him,

and lead him to the door. He follows, but it's clear he doesn't understand. Most of the food is finished, but he usually stays longer. When I open the door and then shut it noisily before he can leave, he stays silent, waiting for me to make my point. I gesture towards the rug in front of the fire. He walks to it, and I follow behind him, concentrating hard on the strands in the room until they glimmer around me, revealing the room's weave. The time and matter are knitted closely together, and I have to focus on the golden bands of light until I'm sure I can pinpoint just the time threads. It's so much easier to see on the loom, but at least time always moves across, so I can find it if I look closely enough. Slowly I reach out with my wounded fingers and pull the strands and twist. The fire in the hearth roars up and crackles in the room so loudly it fills my ears. A chill dampens the air around us despite the climate control being on. I weave the tangled time into a web of golden light, and it domes us in a shimmering glow, stopping at the rug under our feet. We can still see the fire and the room through the translucent web, but we no longer hear the crackle of the logs, and the licking flames seem to slow until they are frozen, like a picture, when I connect the last bits of twisted gold.

'What did you do?' he whispers.

'I wove another moment.' I'm as surprised as he is that it worked. 'I wasn't sure I could.' This is what I'd done at testing. Slipped, and caught the weave of the actual room, not the one they'd given us on the loom, and messed it up a little. I'd smoothed it right back out, but that was all it took. I'd been studying the weave around me for years, enough to know that what I'd done would be noticed by the

proctors administering the test. But I'd never considered how I could use this skill until now.

'What does that mean?' he asks, reaching out toward the golden web, but pulling back before his hands touch it.

'I don't know,' I admit.

'Can they hear us?'

'I don't think so.' Biting my lip, I gesture for him to be silent and then carefully pull the strands separating us from the nearby fire. It roars back to life. I quickly reweave them, and it stops again.

'It's frozen,' he murmurs in disbelief. 'But how?'

'This moment exists outside of that reality. I can't really explain it.' But he's staring at me like I'm a freak. I don't blame him. It's not supposed to work this way. 'I know you are supposed to need a loom to weave, but I can see the weave without one.'

From the way he falls back in surprise, I can guess he's decided that I'm definitely a freak.

'Have you always been able to do this?' he asks.

'Not exactly like this, but I've been able to weave since I was a child.'

'Without a loom?' he asks in awe.

'Yes.'

'So you messed up the room?' I can tell he's having a hard time with this. I barely understand it myself.

'These,' I say, fingering the strands of light, 'are time. They always move across the weave. I guess it's because time flows forward.'

'Can it be moved backward?' he asks quietly, and I know what he's thinking.

I shake my head no. As much as I wish I could turn back the weave and save my parents, for the first time part of me is glad I can't. If I could take Jost back to save his family, would I? It's not a decision I want to face.

'But how do you do it without the loom?' he asks, trying to hide his disappointment. 'How can you even see it?'

'I wish I knew,' I say with a hollow chuckle. 'Maybe then I wouldn't be in this mess.'

'Do they know this?'

I pause, because I'm not sure. Cormac says they saw me do it at testing, but I've been careful not to manipulate without a loom here. I don't share all this with Jost though. 'Enora told me not to tell them.'

Jost lets out a low whistle as he paces the small dome, inspecting it as closely as he can without touching it. 'Enora is smart. What would happen if someone came into the room right now?'

'That's just it,' I explain. 'They couldn't. That moment' — I point to the room outside my woven moment — 'is frozen.'

'So we could stay here,' he says slowly, 'and no matter how much time passes here, no time would pass out there.'

'Exactly.' I pause, realising I don't know this for sure. 'I think. Actually, I have no idea.'

'Then it's true.'

I look at him, trying to understand what he's telling me.

'There are whisperings that Loricel's successor has come. Everyone has been trying to figure out which of you it is,' he explains. 'If it's you or the other one.'

'Pryana?' I ask, mildly offended.

Jost nods, too busy gawking to notice. 'I've known it was you since they threw you in the cell.'

'But how did they know?' Was one slip enough to mark me as a Creweler?

'I don't know,' he admits, 'but the way they treat you – afraid of you, but still deferential. They know it's you.'

I think of the threats made but never carried out.

'Crewelers don't come along often. They can't afford to lose you,' Jost tells me.

'But how is this Crewel work?' I finger the time woven around us. 'Loricel has only ever used a loom in my presence.'

'Crewelers don't merely embroider.' Jost sits down on the rug, and I join him, safely cocooned in my moment. 'Once a year Loricel visits the mining sites and separates the elements from time, so the machines can purify and distribute the material to the coventries to maintain Arras's weave. I serve at the meetings when the officials come to schedule the trips. Without her talent, the looms would be useless. That's why she gives them so much grief.' There's a note of appreciation in his voice.

'In academy, they told us machines discovered the elements.'

'You don't feel like a machine?' he asks. 'Oiled and maintained and made to do the will of those who control you?'

I don't answer. I have no response except to warn him, but even that sounds mechanical and automatic. 'You can't tell anyone.'

'I won't,' he promises. 'But they already know.'

'They think they know,' I argue.

'They know, Adelice.'

The dreams are more vivid, but I control them now. I repaint my mother's eyes and weave my sister back into my arms. My father, taken so violently, remains unsaved. I continue to try. Meanwhile, Jost and Erik take turns watching me, and I wake with their eyes burned into my conscious thoughts.

By the time Enora finally shows up to brief me, I'm seriously considering weaving myself right out of the compound. This time there are no pleasantries or small talk. Instead she gets right to the point.

'As you know, the Guild has made unprecedented advances in mind-mapping technology.' Her voice is as stiff as her posture. There's no spark of friendliness. I must have really got her into trouble for her to act like this.

'And they will be utilising this new capability by mapping every Spinster,' she continues.

'What?' I shout, jumping up from my bed.

Enora barely bats an eyelash at my outburst. 'Since Spinsters have unique abilities that are vital to the continued prosperity of Arras, the Guild is mandating that all Spinsters undergo this testing.'

'At the State of the Guild they said they could change people. Are they mapping us or remapping us?' I ask, studying Enora's placid demeanour. Something isn't right.

'Don't be ridiculous,' she says, but her eyes are empty. 'You can't remap something that hasn't been mapped.' There's no familiarity in her voice, and her usual maternal tone is now mocking.

'So is that why they're doing it? So they can remap us?'

'It would be foolish to remap a Spinster. All attempts to do so in the past have resulted in loss of weaving ability,' she says.

I remember Cormac telling me that they almost had the technology perfected to clean and splice an individual's strand. Either Enora doesn't know that or she's lying to me. I rub my hands together and stare at her. Why is she acting like this?

'My hands are almost better,' I say, holding them out for her to see the bandages.

'I'm relieved to hear that,' she says without even a small smile.

'Enora, did something happen?' I whisper, hoping the companels can't hear me.

'I'm fine, Adelice,' she says with a blink. 'I was sick but the Guild doctors have helped me, and now I'm fine.'

She's not though. Nothing is right about this. My Enora would be fawning over my hands and lecturing me right now. She wouldn't have stayed away the whole week. This woman is like a talking shell of Enora.

'What was wrong with you?' I ask.

'Anxiety issues. I was having strange urges, so naturally I spoke to Loricel and she got me into the clinic right away.'

This knocks the wind out of me, and my mouth falls open, but I quickly shut it. Loricel – why would she hurt Enora?

'What kinds of urges were you having?' I ask, trying to steady my breathing.

'Unnatural ones,' she says, as though this requires no further explanation.

'Have you been mapped yet?'

'Oh, yes. You and Pryana will be the last of the Spin-sterhood to be mapped. We did it by seniority,' Enora says, folding her hands in her lap and smiling.

'Even Loricel?'

'I don't know. I don't have access to the list,' she says. 'Although Loricel should have been the first to go.'

First to go. Is that why she hasn't visited me? Why she didn't step in when Maela punished me? Did a new Loricel do this to Enora?

'When am I scheduled?'

'Friday,' she says. 'It is quite painless.'

'I'm sure it is,' I say automatically.

The door to my quarters opens, and Jost appears with a silver tray.

'Enora,' he calls, 'will you be dining with Adelice?'

'No, I'm expected in the dining hall,' she tells him. 'I was leaving.'

She nods once at me, then exits. I'm still staring after her when Jost sets down the tray and clears his throat. Snapping to it, I freeze the time, creating a bubble around us, then turn to face him.

'Am I imagining it or is something different about Enora?' he asks, his eyebrows knitted in concern.

'You're definitely not imagining it.' I sigh, trying to piece together the information.

Jost gestures for my hands, and we settle down on the cushions. He removes the bandages and inspects my finger-tips. Even I have to admit the renewal cream has worked wonders.

'I think you're done with these,' he says, tossing the bandages to the side.

'Oh,' I say, trying hard to hide my disappointment. If I'm healed, there's no reason for him to keep coming to see me.

'I thought that might be the case,' he says. 'So I made a special lunch.'

'You cooked this?' I ask in amazement.

'No,' he says sheepishly. 'The food generators did most of the work, but I chose the dishes and laid them out.'

'It's perfect.'

I eat with my hands. I love the feeling of the foods — greasy, slick, rough, creamy. Jost laughs and shovels violet berries into my mouth. I wonder whether he still loves Rozenn. The shame of the thought creeps hot onto my cheeks, and he stops feeding me the berries.

'Ready to get back to work?' he asks.

'I guess I have to now.'

'You could stay in here,' he says, his eyes traveling along the perimeter of the bubble.

'And miss all the fun when Security realises why you've been visiting me every day?' I tease.

'I'd stay with you,' he says in a quiet voice.

There are a million things I want to say to Jost at this moment, but the only thing that comes out is the question that's been burning through my mind since he said the word *revolution*. 'What are you planning?'

'It's not that simple,' he says.

'Forget it. It's not my place to ask.'

'I'm sorry. It's just that . . .' Jost pauses, struggling for the word.

'You don't trust me,' I say. 'It's okay, you have no reason to.'

'I trust you, Adelice. Please know that.' He reaches over and cups my face, his palm searing my already warm cheekbone. 'I thought I would never trust anyone again.'

'You aren't alone,' I murmur, turning my head into his outstretched palm. He sighs.

'I know,' he says, but it's more a confession than a realisation. 'Ad, you aren't the only person who knows why I'm here.'

It takes a moment for this to sink in, but when it does I whip my head up to meet his eyes. 'How many people know?'

'Now? Two. You and one other,' he admits, lowering his rejected hand to rest on my leg. My nerves pulse along my thigh where he's touching me.

'Who?' I ask, trying to ignore the tingle running through my lower half.

Jost shakes his head. 'I'm sorry. That isn't my secret to share.'

'But you said I was the only one you trusted,' I press.

'I don't trust this person,' he says.

'But you're working together?'

'No, we're definitely not working together, but this person knows why I came to the Coventry.' He pauses before adding, 'It wouldn't be a good idea for us to work together.'

'But this person is a revolutionary?'

'No,' he rushes to answer.

'But they know why you're here? Will they inform on

you?' I feel confused by the vague turn this conversation has taken. I'm getting answers, but the kind that only lead to more questions.

'I'm not worried they'll tell on me.' He looks away to signal he won't say anything else.

I nod and try to think of a way to change the subject.

'So where does that leave us?'

Jost pulls his hand away, and I rush to clarify. 'I meant, what is your plan and how can I help?'

'Sorry.' He looks genuinely abashed for his reaction, and his hand twitches as though he wants to reach out again, but he doesn't. 'I don't know.'

'How's that working for you?' I ask, trying to lighten the mood.

'The truth is I never had a plan,' he confesses, his lip threatening to curl into a smile. 'I came here to avenge Rozenn, and I've never known how I would do it. I've been waiting for an opportunity and then you . . .'

'Fell into your cell?' I offer.

'Something like that. More like you mouthed off, and I dropped you.'

I grimace at the memory and rub my tailbone. 'By the way, I think you broke it.'

'Oh yes, it was me who broke it and not the days you spent sitting on a cold stone floor.'

'About that,' I interject. 'In the future, do you think you could bring a pillow or something?'

'In the future? Planning to get locked up again?'

'Some girls have a knack for trouble,' I tease, tossing my head dramatically. But before I can peel off the laugh

mounting in my throat, Jost's hand catches my face and brings it to his own. He traces my jaw lightly with his nose and his warm breath tickles along my neck, sending ripples of anticipation through every bit of me. I realise I've stopped breathing and I part my lips slightly to gasp for air. Jost responds by trailing his mouth up my neck, my jaw, and my chin until his lips are over mine.

It's a different kind of kiss from my first one with Erik, and yet it's the same wildly exciting feeling. Jost's lips crush into mine, and I reach out without thinking and pull him closer against me. My hand tangles in his hair, and the web shimmers around us. The rest of the world is perfectly still, but we are in motion, crumbling into one another.

15

We lie in the web next to each other and stare up at the sparkling light that encloses us. Our hands barely brushing. Not speaking. I could stay like this forever, remembering our first kiss.

Jost finally breaks the moment, rolling over to his side and propping himself up next to me. He leans in and kisses my nose. 'Hey, traitor, you hungry?' he asks, reaching toward the tray he brought earlier.

'I'm fine.' The spell broken, my anxiety comes rushing back. The last thing I want to do is eat.

He takes a bite of an apple. 'Suit yourself.'

It was a perfect moment, completely under my control, until I was reminded that the one thing I want power over can't be woven: my own thoughts. Closing my eyes, I wish I was home now; that Jost and I had met through a marriage profile; that Amie was trying to spy on my courtship ap-

pointment; that later I would climb into her bed and giggle about his hair or whisper about how it feels when he looks at me with those perfect blue eyes; and that afterwards I would lie in my own bed, designing my wedding dress. But when I open my eyes, I'm here under my frozen dome with Cormac's procedure looming in the future instead of a wedding. The only comfort is Jost resting beside me, but even that's complicated.

'They're going to map me,' I whisper.

'What?' He sets the apple down and stares at me.

'Enora was here to tell me that I'm going to be mapped on Friday.'

Jost swallows hard and sits up. 'What does that mean exactly?'

'Medics are going to map my brain. Enora claims it's so they can study Spinsters' abilities.'

'Or control them,' he suggests.

'I think that's what happened to Enora. They cleaned her thread, but I'm not sure why.'

'Mind-mapping couldn't do something like that,' he says. 'Even if they can control your skills—'

'The new method can,' I interrupt. 'Didn't you watch the State of the Guild?'

'No,' he says. 'I was playing cards with some other valets in the back. Altering and cleaning is too tricky to risk on a Spinster.' But even he doesn't sound convinced.

'The tech is safer now. I'm not sure how it works, but Prime Minister Carma said it can erase behavioural issues. That it can change how a person acts and thinks.' I tell him about what Cormac said about isolating problem areas

in the strand and splicing new material into an individual's thread. As I talk about it, my hands ball into fists. 'It was supposed to be a process reserved for deviants, but the Guild seems to have a pretty flexible policy on what constitutes a deviant.'

Reaching over, Jost takes my clenched hands and gently laces his fingers through mine. 'And you're going to let them do this?'

'I don't have a choice. It might be the only way to find out exactly how the process works.' *And it will get me into the research wing of the compound.* There might be useful records, but something tells me to keep that to myself.

'But you saw what it did to Enora,' he says softly.

'Let's hope I'm wrong about that,' I murmur. 'And don't worry, I'm not going in unprepared.'

The guard at the entrance to the upper studios regards me with suspicion. I've never been here before, so I'm counting on my promotion to Crewel apprentice to get me in, but it's pretty obvious I have no idea what the security procedure is. The heavy red door to the upper studios won't budge, and I'm eyeing the companel next to it when the guard clears his throat.

'You'll need to provide your proof of identity to the scanner.' He points to the companel.

I press my palm against it, silently willing it to open and wishing I didn't have an audience right now.

'Adelice Lewys. Access granted,' it chirps at me, and the door clicks unlocked.

Heaving it open, I duck inside without looking back at

the guard. I've drawn enough attention to myself already. I don't know exactly where I'm going, but I have a hunch. Since everything here is based on rank, I head toward the stairs. They spiral up endlessly, and I pass several floors of quiet studios before I reach the top, where I step into the most breathtaking room I've ever seen. It feels more like I'm standing on the roof of a tower. The screens have been woven so that it looks as if nothing stands between me and the sprawling vegetation outside the compound or the sky overhead. To the west, the belly of the ocean laps against the tower, and as I turn and look north it meets with a rocky shore that grows into large craggy mountains around the compound. It's not the same view that's programmed to run in my quarters.

In the centre of the space an ancient brass loom, far bigger and grander than any I've seen before, swirls and shimmers as tiny gears turn and click. It's intricately etched with words in a language I can neither speak nor read. A chair of ruby velvet, tossed with silk pillows in emerald and onyx and sapphire, butts against it. Although around me the ocean crashes, birds soar, and snow falls, I hear nothing but the soft whir of the loom.

'It's lovely, isn't it?' Loricel says behind me, and I turn to find her stroking a furry ginger animal. 'There are over eight hundred looms in the compound here, and they can all work on Arras's weave, but this is the oldest. It was the first loom stationed in the Western Coventry.'

'I'm sorry. I didn't mean to barge in on you.' I blush. Despite my close connection to her, I feel like a thief standing here and stealing the only beauty in her life.

'Don't fret,' Loricel reassures me. She nods down to the creature in her arms, obviously aware that I'm staring at it. 'It's a cat. I keep it as a pet.'

'I wasn't aware pets were allowed any more.' In fact, I know they aren't. Pets were banned two decades ago, according to the civil responsibilities class we had at academy. Nowadays 'pet' is a common nickname for secretaries. I smile, recalling how my mother fumed when her boss used the term.

'Citizens are not allowed to have them,' she says with a shrug. 'But it's one of the few perks I take advantage of as Creweler.'

I nod. That makes sense. If anyone could have a pet, it would be Loricel.

'Tell me, Adelice, what do you see?'

I look around the room and describe the foaming waves cresting over the jagged rocky shore and the mountains quickly being blanketed in snow. 'Your screens are amazing. I feel like I'm on the roof. I feel free.'

'Adelice, what did your home look like?' she asks, watching me closely.

I'm confused by the change in conversation, but I tell her about the tiny neighbourhood that sat outside Romen. The perfect street peppered with tiny bungalows and gardens. And as I describe Mr Figgins's apple tree across the street, it grows on the wall in front of me. With a startled gasp, I whirl to find my own home tucked back behind the loom. It's so close. As the first tear pricks the corner of my eye, I watch the image swirl and fade away into a stark, starless night.

'That's better,' Loricel says. 'They're screens like you said, but I patched in a locator program years ago. When you walk into the room, the screens display where you want to be.'

'But I saw mountains and the ocean,' I say.

'It's the default,' she explains. 'Anyone who enters will see it. You have to describe the setting for it to change. Like us, the program can't read minds. It's very similar to the tracking system the Guild uses to locate citizens.'

'Cormac used one to show me my sister once,' I tell her, but it feels like a confession somehow. As though I'm revealing a weakness rather than knowledge.

She smiles and then briefly describes a sunny, lonely beach. 'I prefer warmer climates.'

It's unnerving to stand in the centre of snowy mountains, my childhood street, and a lapping crystal ocean without moving, so I plop down onto the braided rug beside the loom to gather my thoughts.

'What's really out there?' I ask finally.

Loricel doesn't answer. She moves to the edge of the wall screen, but she doesn't change the program. Instead, she very carefully opens a seam in the illusions, and I realise that the images on the walls are also a form of weaving. I wonder if she's about to show me the image of the sea I watch from my quarters or even a blizzard like the one I witnessed moments ago, but I could never have imagined what the break reveals. In between the fibres of the weave, I see a shapeless bloom of light and colour.

What lies behind the screens on Loricel's studio walls isn't what I imagined. Even though I've been manipulating

the weave around me for years, only now is the truth clear. The weave we call up on a loom, or manipulate in the room in front of us is only a façade. Behind it lies another layer, even more brilliant than the first.

'None of it's real,' I whisper.

'It depends on your definition of real,' Loricel replies. 'I can touch this floor. I can touch you. I can eat the food at mealtime. How is that not real?'

And I can't answer her, because she's right. The tickle of water as I step into the bath, the way the pillow cocoons my head, Jost's hands stroking my face. How could these things not be real? And yet, standing here staring out at the raw matter flowing into oblivion, nothing can ever be real again.

'So that's it. This is reality,' I whisper, the words barely making a noise as they leave my mouth.

Loricel purses her lips together as though she's unsure where to begin. 'Yes and no. This is our reality, but not reality in the truest sense.'

'I don't understand,' I admit.

'The Guild doesn't mean us to, but if you are to take over here then you must understand.' She gestures to the magnificent work space.

I can't tear my eyes away from the open seam. My hands twitch; I want to touch it. Finally, Loricel closes it up and leads me over to a small couch.

'We create it all?' I ask.

'We create Arras,' she says. 'But we only create a mantle — a cover, if you will. Matter and time exist on another planet, and we merely harness them. The looms allow us

to weave and create Arras. Our reality is layered upon another world: Earth.'

'Earth?' The word sounds strange and foreign, but it plucks at some long-buried memory.

'Underneath Arras are the remains of the former world – a world that is no longer inhabited,' she tells me. 'Few are left who remember the name Earth, and it's dangerous for us to speak of it outside the safety of my studio. What you saw was the raw material that flows between our old home and Arras.' She stares at the wall where the rift had been.

'So that's it?' I ask. 'We've created our world on top of another world, but no one knows it.'

Loricel smiles. 'Oh no, there are some who know, Adelice, but they aren't sharing the secret. The truth has a way of changing to suit the purpose of those in charge. They would deny what I'm telling you. The Guild has worked hard to make sure we forget about Earth. Only the highest officials know, and even those working the mines are lied to about exactly what they're doing. I must be very careful what I say during my trips to visit them each year.'

'Why keep it a secret?'

'You would be surprised at the amount of discontent here. The number of plots the Guild quells each year. Arras is not as peaceful as they make the citizens believe. Some would want to leave Arras, and the Guild would never allow it.'

I think back to my parents, who clearly loathed the Guild and tried to protect me from it. I'd thought they were a bit paranoid until I came here, but now I wonder how much

they knew. And Jost's brother-in-law, who had mixed with rebels. Yes, there were people who knew, but I already understood why they kept it quiet.

'But you have access to someone who knows the truth,' Loricel continues.

'Who?'

'Me.'

'Then what are they? Arras? Earth?' I have a hundred more questions, but I shut my mouth to keep them from tumbling out all at once.

'My predecessor was the second Creweler and though she knew the story better than I, much of it was lost in the passing from her own teacher. Some of it makes little sense to us now because we have lost this knowledge and with it the words and reality they describe,' she explains.

'On Earth, a war was fought to end all wars. Many of the regions, once called countries, became involved in the battle. One created a weapon so fearsome that it threatened to destroy everyone. They called this science, but it was merely the creation of men aimed at controlling the world. However, while one country readied to use this weapon, another scientist stepped forward with an alternative idea. Although he had worked on this bomb himself, he was more interested in time and the very matter that made up the world. He called the building blocks of this matter "elements".'

'Elements? Like the raw materials we use to work the weave?'

She nods. 'He found a way to isolate the cellular makeup of his world – grass, trees, air, even animals – and to view it

in relationship to the time that threaded through the space it was in. He knew if he could build a machine that showed how elements and time knit together, people could manipulate the world in unnatural ways. You've seen the drills that mine the raw materials, I assume.'

I nod, trying to call the images to mind, but my memory of them is vague. They were monstrous and powerful beasts that smoked and ground, but into what? The training images didn't show that.

'They mine elements from Earth that we manipulate into the weave. The four coventries rest over four mining sites, and Arras streams from the compounds. There is a raw weave under Arras; it keeps our time and environment separate. Because we exist on the periphery of the weave, we can view it on the machines in far greater detail and manipulate it without risk to the weave. The scientist who created the machines called it Crewel work. Spinsters came after the initial mantle and protective field were created. We helped initiate people into the weave much like the Department of Origins brings babies into Arras now.'

'But how could they build Arras without Spinsters? Only women can work the looms.' I shake my head, trying to force my thoughts into a rational explanation.

'They groomed women for this duty, but I believe some men might be able to do the work,' she says, cocking her eyebrow suggestively.

'But why give such an important job to us?' I ask, my annoyance showing in the sarcastic tone of my voice. 'Why leave it to women?'

'The Guild can control women better.' Loricel sees me

start to protest and holds her hand up to stop me. 'Whether you like it or not, they do a damn good job of controlling us.'

Resentment toward the officials and Cormac and Maela and everyone who plays a part in this charade burns through me. 'Who was this scientist from Earth?'

'His name and the names of all those of Earth have passed from our collective memory. His real contribution was allowing for a peaceful resolution to the war.'

'You're telling me Arras doesn't want to celebrate the genius of the man who created it?' I ask, remembering the number of holidays reserved in honour of officials who have made much smaller contributions.

Loricel sighs, and gives me a frown. 'Don't be stupid, Adelice. You know they clean and alter. If they think information is too risky to Arras's stability, they remove it. The Guild doesn't want the citizenry to question the looms, and they especially don't want people to know about Earth. My grandmother confided to me that a long time ago she took an oath of loyalty to Arras to keep our family safe. I didn't realise until I came here and began apprenticing to the Creweler that it was really an oath of secrecy. It was the only way to survive the war they left behind – to promise to keep Arras's secret. But that wasn't enough for the Guild. I assisted in the cleaning of the information from the collective memory.'

'Why?' I demand. 'If they can't do these things without you, why do you do them?'

'Because no one else will. I can't alter all of Arras alone. Like it or not, and believe me, I *do not*, the relationship of

Crewelers and the Guild is symbiotic. We cannot do our work without the bureaucracy and aid of the Guild. I won't risk a war, not after the lengths we took to end the last one. Arras is too fragile to withstand it, and for every man like Cormac in our world, there are a hundred innocent women and children.' To her credit, there's not a trace of anger or defensiveness in her voice.

'I feel stupid,' I say, 'but how did creating Arras end the war? Didn't we just drag our problems here?' Now that I understand how Arras came to be, I'm not sure I buy the careful regulations-only-ensure-safety story any more.

'Arras was created, and its leaders came together to form the Guild of Twelve Nations. The population has been carefully monitored and the coventries established to maintain peace and prosperity. The Guild, while inefficient and often cruel, coordinates these efforts.'

'And all these men at war on Earth? They just made peace?'

Approval glints in Loricel's eyes. 'Of course not. Arras consists of the twelve nations from Earth that believed they could control and maintain the mantle while keeping the peace.'

'But there were others?'

'They were left on Earth with their bombs. They annihilated one another years ago.'

'Have you seen it then? Earth?' I ask, wondering how far Loricel's power stretches and what she sees on these trips to the mines each year.

'No!' There's the ring of amusement in her voice, but she doesn't laugh at me. 'I doubt there's anything to see.'

'But how do you know that?' I ask softly.

A tiny flash of doubt shows in her eyes, but she pushes it away, and they grow distant again. 'I guess I believed my mentor. What purpose would lying serve?'

I shrug and turn back to stare at the blank night sky. If there's one thing the Coventry has taught me, it's that lying always serves someone's purpose.

16

No cosmetics. No stockings. No elaborate hair. And no clothes. I feel naked in more ways than one. The thin cotton shift they've given me to wear for the initial mapping has poppers up the back, leaving even less to the imagination than some of the dresses I've worn recently. The room's blank white walls reflect off the polished silver instruments laid carefully on a table next to the edge of the large metal slab I've been sitting on for thirty minutes. My bum is chilled numb, but the time spent waiting is only winding up my mind.

A woman clad in a white coat and a hairnet bustles into the room and adjusts the slab so that it folds up on one end. She helps me lean back onto it and applies a digital med-cuff to my arm. I thought I'd feel relief when it started, but there's only dread. If the goal of this project is to make me lose my mind, then it's been quite successful already.

'This will monitor your heart rate and blood pressure,' the nurse tells me, eyes on the numbers.

'Is this dangerous?' I ask, looking at the table of very sharp medical tools next to me.

'Rarely. If you start to have a reaction to the procedure we'll administer Valpron to calm you down,' she says, with a pat on my arm.

A particularly long blade mesmerises me. I can see myself in it. 'Will it hurt?'

'Would you prefer Valpron now?' she offers, but I shake my head no.

'Dr Ellysen will be right in,' she says, brandishing a tiny needle. 'This will only sting for a minute.'

As the needle pricks my forearm I inhale sharply and blink against watery eyes.

'Good girl,' she says absently, while she places a bag of amber liquid on a rack next to me. It oozes slowly down a tube into my arm.

A very young doctor enters the room, eyes glued to his digifile. It's a bit unnerving that he looks no older than I do, but then, with the patches available here, he may be much older than he looks.

'Adelice, how are you feeling?' he asks.

The doctors in Romen who did our annual health assessments were always old and grumpy. Male placements are given based on skill, and bedside manner isn't one of the necessary qualifications. The youth of my new doctor doesn't make him any less intimidating.

'Fine,' I lie. The IV in my arm unnerves me.

'The procedure will last about two hours,' he says, not

looking up from his pad. 'During that time you will lie still. You can sleep if you would like, or I can have Nurse Renni administer some Valpron.'

'The patient declined,' she whispers to him.

'Very well,' he says, sliding the small pad into his pocket. 'I will be placing the mapping device over your head. It will scan various parts of your brain. During the process I will ask you questions, and it will map how your brain creates an answer.'

'I thought you said I could sleep,' I squeak.

'You can,' he assures me. 'You're being given a mental stimulant right now. It allows you to process information even in an unconscious state.'

I want to rip the needle out of my arm. There is no way I'm sleeping through a questioning.

'I will be sitting in the next room observing. You will hear me through this comcuff,' he says, hooking a small black device around my right ear. 'Nurse Renni, can we fit the mapper?'

She nods and enters a code on the companel. Above me, the ceiling splits wide, and out of the gaping hole, two spotlights burst on. Blinking against their brightness, I watch the mapper descend. It's a large dome, but as it comes closer I realise it's not solid; it's a series of connected wheels and gears so intricately bound together they appear to glide against one another. My eyes shift to the doctor ducking through the observatory door, and then to the nurse, who is checking my medcuff. As the device lowers over my head, I try to determine how it functions but a beam of green light breaks across my vision and I'm blinded.

'It's normal,' the nurse murmurs next to me, fiddling with my medcuff. 'You'll be able to see again after the procedure is over.'

I arch up from the table and try to shove the device off my head.

'Deep breaths, Adelice, or I'll have to get the Valpron,' she warns me.

This forces me to settle back into the darkness. My arms and legs tingle with the chill in the sterile room. Without my sight I feel trapped and immobile, like a fly in a spider's web.

'Adelice.' The doctor's voice sounds in my ear. 'We're beginning the test.'

I take a strangled breath and let it out slowly.

'Adelice, where were you born?'

'Romen, in the Western Sector.'

'Good. Answer specifically like that,' he says. 'What were your parents' names?'

I take another breath and answer, 'Benn and Meria Lewys.'

'Your father's occupation?'

'He was a mechanic. He worked on the Guild's moto-fleet in Romen.'

'And your mother?'

'She was a secretary.'

'What is your sister's name?'

'Amie,' I whisper. Each time I say her name, I see the wispy curls behind her ears.

'Please repeat.'

'Amie,' I say more authoritatively, pressure building in my chest.

'Are your parents living?'

I suck in a breath and exhale my answer. 'No,' I lie.

'Adelice, did you maintain purity standards before your testing?'

'What kind of question is that?' I demand, my hands clenching into fists.

'Please answer the question.'

'Yes,' I say. 'I maintained purity standards.'

As if I had a choice. Girl neighbourhoods sit on the opposite side of the metro from the boy neighbourhoods, and trips into the metro are carefully chaperoned by parents during approved movement hours. It wasn't always like that though. My grandmother whispered stories about how things had changed since she was a girl. On my fourteenth birthday, a month before her removal, I asked her about the marriage profiles in the *Bulletin*. Girls at academy brought them to hide under their desks, taking turns passing them to one another and giggling at the pictures of the boys.

'Why are there marriage profiles in the *Bulletin*?' I asked her. 'Can't girls and boys meet in person in the metro after they turn sixteen?'

My grandmother had deep brown eyes and she turned the full force of them on me, studying me before she answered. 'It's not as easy these days for girls and boys to meet. Parents don't like the chance of it, and most young people get tongue-tied when they meet the first time. 'Course –' she chuckled a bit – 'that's not so different from before segregation.'

'I never realised there was a before and after to segregation,' I said, feeling very small under her wise gaze.

'There's always a before and after to everything since before humanity began,' she said with a twist of her mouth, 'and there'll be an after to humans someday, too. But yes, when I was a girl. We lived together then – boys and girls. No separate neighbourhoods.'

'Did you know grandfather then, before . . .' My hushed voice trailed into a question. Even talking about boys seemed strange.

'He grew up next door to me,' she told me, widening her eyes in mock shock at the confession. 'I think it was easier to meet the marriage requirements then. Girls didn't marry complete strangers.'

'But purity standards . . .' I couldn't finish the thought. It was too embarrassing.

'Oh, yes, those,' she said with a wink. 'They were harder to keep.'

I didn't ask her if she kept them; it seemed too personal a question, even for grandmother, and because I was really embarrassed by her wink. 'My mom and dad were profiled though, right?'

'Yes, our children were the first segregated generation,' she said, and there was a trace of regret in her words.

'But they loved each other when they got married,' I reassured her, not understanding the sadness in her voice. 'So it's okay.'

'Yes, they love each other,' she said in a soft voice, and I felt peace settle into my chest. I didn't ask any more questions that day. Only now do I regret the answers I lost.

'What was your academy ranking?' The doctor's voice filters in over the memory, and I realise I've been answering

the mapping questions without listening. Stupid mental stimulant.

'I was ranked in the top quarter.'

'Were you disciplined often?' he asks.

'You guys have my file, you know this,' I say, fighting the urge to shove at the mapper again.

'We're studying how your brain processes each question and answer,' he reminds me.

By the time the doctor asks me about my fifth-year teacher, I'm bored and uncomfortable. My back muscles spasm from the unnatural angle I'm lying at and my eyes water against the laser. I answer quickly, trying to stay awake. I'm sure they're saving the juiciest questions for when I fall asleep.

'Adelice,' the doctor continues, 'when did you discover you could weave?'

'At the testing, when I wove on the loom.'

He pauses, and I bite my lip. How much can this thing tell them?

'You never showed talent before then?'

'I didn't have access to a loom.'

'Hmmm.' He murmurs something I can't make out.

'And your sister, Amie, did she ever show talent?'

I grip the edge of the metal slab. 'No.'

'Okay,' the doctor says, 'we're going to transition to talking about your time at the Coventry. What is your favourite dish from the food generators?'

I sigh and relax my fingers, returning to automatic-answer mode. He asks about my wardrobe, where I work, what my duties are and which ones challenge me. He

doesn't mention Maela, so I'm able to keep my blood pressure normal.

'Thank you, Adelice. Nurse Renni will be in to remove the mapper and IV,' he says in my ear.

Nurse Renni's hand adjusts the medcuff on my arm and then she withdraws the needle from my arm. I wait a few moments, but the helmet doesn't lift off my head. I refrain from screaming at her to take it off.

'Can you remove this now?' I ask through it.

'One moment,' she murmurs.

'Adelice,' the doctor says, drawing my attention back to the comcuff. 'I apologise, but I have a few extra questions.'

'Extra?' My mind races, and although I can't see or hear her, I'm sure Maela is feeding him more things to ask. She'll probably string this out another hour.

'It will only take a moment,' he assures me. 'Have you accepted any gifts from staff members or other Spinsters while here?'

I think of the tiny digifile that Enora gave me before my trip through Arras. Somehow I know this is what he's asking about. 'No, not really. Ambassador Patton sent flowers to my quarters after the State of the Guild.'

The young doctor clears his throat a little, and I sense his hesitation after I mention Cormac.

'Have you engaged in any sexual relationships since you joined the Coventry?'

'Are you serious?' I explode. 'I kissed Erik. She knows that.'

Leave it to Maela to make this about her pet.

He continues, ignoring my outburst. 'Have any of the

others made sexual advances towards you?'

'You mean the guards?' I ask.

'No, Adelice,' he says. 'I mean the other Spinsters.'

'The other Spinsters?' I ask slowly. 'I don't follow you.'

'I'll take that as a no.'

'Okay,' I say, confused. Was he asking if I was a deviant? 'Anything else?'

'Not this session,' he says, and the comcuff clicks off.

'This session?' I whimper, but the mapper is already lifting off my head. My eyes see only white. The nurse's arm snakes under my back and she gently lifts me into a sitting position. A moment later thick gel stings my eyes, and I yelp.

'Blink hard,' she commands.

Despite the burn, the room blurs into focus, and I stretch my stiff legs out in front of me, savouring the delicious ache of the movement.

'I'll move you to Observation,' Nurse Renni tells me.

'Observation?' I ask. 'When will I be done?'

'We want to make sure there are no side effects from the laser scans or the neural stimulant,' she says, helping me to my feet and guiding me out of the room.

The observation room has pale green walls and several beds topped with white sheets, but my eyes, still oozing gel, can't make out much else. The nurse holds up a soft robe and I slip it on over the thin gown and sit down on the nearest cot; the sheets crinkle up around my legs. Scooting back to the wall, I feel rough plastic under me. This isn't the soft, comfortable bed I'm used to in my quarters, but it's a huge improvement on the exam slab.

Squeezing my eyes shut, I open them and then repeat the action, trying to flush the gel from my eyes. I want to see where I am. Any area of the compound where outsiders work is territory I'd like to chart. But before I can even examine the shelf in the corner, the nurse reappears and helps Pryana onto the bed next to mine.

'I thought you girls could visit,' she says brightly.

'That was nice of you,' I say, and she beams back at me before bustling out of the room.

Pryana stares ahead, ignoring me.

'Well, that was fun,' I say conversationally.

'You're twisted,' she says, not looking at me.

'Maybe, but it was the best two hours of my life.'

'Two hours?' she asks. 'It took you that long?'

I frown. What does that mean?

'I was done in half an hour,' she says, glancing briefly in my direction.

'Oh,' I say. 'Probably less to map.'

'I probably don't need remapping,' she spits back.

'Sure, you're just what they want,' I say.

Her eyes narrow, but she picks up a catalogue and flips through it. 'Madilyne told me that unless the initial scans registered a need for remapping, the whole procedure would take less than an hour,' she says, the side of her mouth curling up.

'Who's Madilyne?' I ask.

'My mentor,' she says, as though this is obvious. 'Didn't yours tell you anything?'

'She told me enough.'

'Well,' Pryana says with a smirk, 'I'd get a new mentor.

266

Yours clearly isn't doing her job.'

'Are you volunteering?' I ask.

'Careful, Adelice, or they'll think you're coming on to me.'

As much as I loathe Pryana, I turn and look at her directly. 'Did they ask you about that?'

'About what?' she says, but then she sighs, grudgingly meeting my eyes.

'Other Spinsters, you know . . .'

'Hitting on me?' She shrugs. 'Yeah, it was weird.'

Pryana turns back to her shopping. She seems less than interested by the mapping questions. But if she's being truthful, and it is only a half-hour procedure, she doesn't have nearly as much to worry about.

Since it's probably not a good idea to snoop around with her here, I try not to be disappointed that I can't get a better look at this wing of the Coventry. It's under surveillance anyway. I flip through a catalogue but don't order anything. Meanwhile Pryana barks out order after order to the companel. If her wardrobe is half the size of mine, she doesn't need any of it. But she strikes me as a girl who's here to get her duty's worth. Finally Nurse Renni reappears with our clothing. We dress in a hurry, our backs turned to each other. A guard meets us at the door and leads us through the sterile corridor. There is nothing here to distinguish one door from another. No sign to suggest what happens in the rooms we pass. Not even the sound of medics working. So much for my brilliant plan of using the mapping to get more info.

But as the guard guides us into the main lobby, I spy

a nurse busily updating a digifile as she disappears behind a grey swinging door. It's the first medical personnel I've seen besides the doctor and Nurse Renni. Edging closer to the door, I catch glimpses as it slowly sways to a close – a long hallway, grey tile, a small security door, and on it the word 'research'. It's a good thing that monitor isn't on me now, because my heart just stopped.

'Ladies,' the guard says, waiting for us like a gentleman at the access desk. We exit the clinic, and he takes us back to the high tower. As we walk, I track the number of turns and count each step I take. If I can manage it, I want to get back there. But first I'll have to get clearance to go into the research area. Our escort deposits us at the brass lift, bowing slightly as he leaves.

'What floor?' Pryana asks.

'F-f-fifteen,' I stammer, shocked by the friendly gesture. She rolls her eyes.

'What floor are you on?' I ask.

'Four.'

I reach over to press the button for her floor, but her hand smacks mine away.

'Don't be stupid,' she hisses. 'If I have to ride in a lift with you, I'm going to see the high tower.'

'You live in the high tower,' I remind her.

She glowers at me. 'No, I live in the lower quarters and the lifts won't let me travel past the lounge floor.'

For the first time I study the buttons. There are five floors below the lounge button, including Pryana's.

'Oh, I just assumed.'

'Yeah,' she says, 'that's always your problem.'

'Look—' I say, heat flushing my cheeks, but before I can tell her where to shove it, the doors slide open to my floor.

There are two more plum-lacquered doors on this floor, but I've never seen another Spinster here, which is why I don't push Pryana into the lift and force her back to the lower quarters. There's nothing here she can't see, and it's not like she's going to come hang out with me in my room and have a pyjama party. But as soon as we step off the lift, I regret my decision. Two women are in the hall. Way to go, Adelice. Get caught showing off.

Their backs are to us, but then I realise only one of them is turned away, her blonde hair neatly rolled and pinned into a French twist. I don't understand what I'm seeing. Arms snaking around her waist and up her back. Slender olive arms with brilliant red nails.

'Oh, my Arras,' Pryana gasps, and the pair split from their embrace.

It's enough to startle me, and I shove Pryana into the waiting lift and push the button to shut the door. Twisting back to the women, I stare at Enora and Valery, who are frozen to the spot. Now I understand why the doctor asked those questions. And so does Pryana.

17

Enora snaps to, fleeing down the hall to the seldom-used stairs at the end. Valery shifts back on her heels and opens her mouth, but she doesn't say anything. We stare at each other. I can't quite wrap my head around it. Valery and Enora. It doesn't feel wrong exactly, just different. And a small part of me feels left out, like I should have known that the two people closest to me here share this secret. The unfairness of this thought makes me look away, ashamed. Who am I to judge them? I've been anything but upfront about Jost.

I'm the one to break the silence. 'Is that why she's acting strangely?'

'No,' Valery says with a slight shake of her head. 'This has nothing to do with that.'

I pause for a moment and then take a deep breath. 'Come on. Let's not stand out here. Besides I expected you to do my hair hours ago.'

If Valery is puzzled, she doesn't show it. She simply follows me to my door. As I open it, I catch her glancing at the door to the stairs. Tugging on her arm, I urge her inside my quarters.

In the bathroom, I turn the tap on, like Jost showed me weeks ago. Valery starts to gather her supplies: an apron, shampoos and hair tonics. I take them away and push her into the prep chair. Leaning against the wall, I study her. Valery. Kind, quiet Valery. She's a lot like Enora.

'You don't have to tell me anything,' I say.

'It's a long story,' she says bitterly.

'A lot of those around here. Look, I can't tell you what Pryana is going to do, but it's none of my business.'

'Oh, they already know,' Valery says. Her voice trembles, but she holds her chin up. 'That's why Enora is acting off.'

'Is she worried they're going to kick her out?'

'Nothing like that. She's just been acting differently since the mind-mapping. She's been . . . distant.'

I know exactly what she means. 'I noticed. She barely told me anything about it.'

'She went in twice.'

Twice? A tremor races up my spine.

'And you're sure the Coventry knew that you two were . . .' I don't even know what to call it.

'In a relationship?' she offers. 'Yes.'

'I'm sorry,' I say, looking past her to the bathtub. 'I've never—'

'Don't worry about it,' Valery says, but her voice is thick and angry. 'The Coventry nips these things in the bud pretty fast.'

'I thought they caught most deviants,' I say, feeling un-
sophisticated. This is what the doctor was asking about.
Pryana knew exactly what his questions meant, but I
didn't, because I had never even noticed anything between
Valery and Enora.

'Just because there are rules against it, doesn't mean it
goes away,' she says. 'There are more of us out there, but
we keep low profiles. It's harder when—'

'You're in love with a Spinster?'

'Exactly. We managed to keep it quiet for a long time,
but lately surveillance has been stricter, especially on
Enora.'

Because I came along.

'Do you think they did something to her?' she asks.

I think back to the State of the Guild, and Enora's own
words echo in my head: *Don't be ridiculous.*

'It was like she didn't know me,' Valery says in a soft
voice. 'I cornered her—'

'They remapped her.'

She shakes her head. 'But they can't remap Spinsters. It's
too dangerous. They only remap criminals and unstables!
She might not be able to weave.'

'Trust me,' I say, placing a hand gently over hers.
'There's new tech.'

'Why? Because of us?' Her voice cracks on the question,
and tears pool in her eyes. 'She's not even allowed to
marry. She's not endangering the population.'

'The Guild takes threats to Arras's balance seriously. I
know it's not comforting, but if they believed they could
fix her—'

'Fix her? Is that what you think? That we need to be fixed?' Valery's voice rises over the tap's rushing water.

I clasp her hand and speak in a low voice. 'None of us need to be fixed, but the Guild looks out for itself.'

Valery stares into my eyes for a long minute and then withdraws her hand like I've bitten her.

'They're after you.'

'I assume so,' I admit.

'They'd never test their new protocol on their prize catch,' she says. 'Enora was protecting you. She kept interfering with Maela's punishments.'

'I know.' I could try to argue that I wasn't to blame for Enora or Pryana's sister or my own parents' deaths, but I can't deny I'm the common factor.

'Then you know this is your fault.'

Valery stands, and with one last sob, wipes her eyes. Without so much as a glance at me, she exits, leaving me alone with my guilt.

She doesn't come to dress me for dinner. A gnawing ache in my stomach tells me I'll never see her again, and no matter how hard I try, I can't push the strange sensation away. At the table, where I sit with the other Spinsters, Enora's seat is empty, which only increases my dread. It's so consuming, I almost don't notice that Jost is serving tonight.

'More wine?' he offers. Our eyes meet, and his crinkle at the edges in concern.

'Water's fine.'

He returns a moment later with the water pitcher. He follows my gaze to where Enora should be.

'Valet,' I say, as he pours my drink, 'there's a problem with the auto light on my fireplace.'

'I'll check on it later,' he says, and fades back to attend to the other women.

As I glance down to the other end of the table, Pryana catches my eye and raises her wineglass. She smiles and then tips her head as though we're toasting something. I turn away, but I don't take another bite from any of the six courses they serve.

Jost is toying with the buttons on my mantel when I return from dinner. Kicking off my heels, I wander over in front of it. He presses a button and the fire roars to life.

'Seems to be fine,' he says.

'Silly me.'

'Do you need anything else?' he asks, raising his eyebrows.

That's my cue. A second later, I've woven a new moment into the room. Before I can speak, I'm in his arms. I bury my face in his chest, unsure where to start.

'I don't—'

'Shhh,' he hushes me. Taking my chin in his hand, he draws my face up to his. With his lips moving against mine, everything fades away. My pulse quickens, and I wrap my arms around his neck. I could stay here for eternity.

He pulls back first and I sigh, the shimmering dome and the frozen room resurfacing around us, along with all the problems of the real world.

'Enora,' I begin.

'She wasn't at dinner,' he says.

'She's been acting strange, and I think I know why.'

'Because she's . . .'

'In love,' I confess.

'I know.' Jost pauses. 'She's in love with another woman.'

I stare at him. Maybe Valery was right and everyone knew about them. Exactly how had I missed this?

'Not much gets past the head valet,' he says, reading my mind.

'Does everyone know?' I ask a bit too sourly.

'They probably do now. It was a rumour for a long time,' he says, pulling me down to the floor. 'Not the first time. Spinsters don't exactly fall out of trees. The Guild is willing to overlook some things if a girl has the skill.'

'So why the sudden interest?'

He pauses for a moment, not meeting my eyes. 'Honestly, more attention has been on her lately.'

'Because of me.' It stings, but I know he's right.

'And with the new remapping tech—'

'She didn't stand a chance,' I finish his thought, and just then something horrible occurs to me. 'Do you think Pryana will report Valery for what she saw?'

'I don't know,' he says, heaving a sigh. 'It's possible, and Valery doesn't have the protection afforded a Spinster.'

'Why do they even care?' I groan. 'She can't be the only one sneaking around. I mean, look at us.'

Jost laughs as though I've said something insanely funny. Is that what he thinks about us? That we're a big joke? I don't know if I should hit him or cry.

'What?' I ask, trying to look defiant and hoping my blush isn't too noticeable.

'Of course they care, Adelice. What if women married other women? Or if men married other men?'

In a split second, I transition from relief to embarrassment. Of course he meant them. But then something stirs in my chest, and I remember how Valery yelled at me. 'There's nothing wrong with that. It's not hurting anyone.'

'You've got it wrong,' Jost says. 'You asked why they care. The Guild. And I'm telling you, it scares them. A woman without a husband . . .'

'I don't have a husband,' I point out.

'You would have in a year or two if you hadn't been retrieved.'

'But Spinsters don't marry – and no one seems threatened by us.'

'Sure. You don't marry, but you're also locked up in walled compounds. And,' he adds, his voice taking a mocking tone, 'if you're lucky you get to go out and hang off some official's arm.'

My nostrils flare. Is that what he thinks of me? I'm leaning towards hitting him. I can cry later.

'Fact is, the Spinsters are far from a pure bunch. Why do you think they keep male servants around? To do the heavy lifting?' he continues, oblivious to the fact that I've pulled away from him.

'You have a lot of experience with that?' I ask, unsure if I'm mad at the other girls or myself now.

Jost's eyes narrow, and he regards me closely. 'Is this about us or Enora?'

'Enora.'

'Could have fooled me.'

'If they ignore that we're all secretly courting half the guard, why do they mind if she's in love with Valery?' I'm screaming, and I don't even care.

'Would you let me finish?' he asks. 'It threatens them — the officials — if a Spinster is loyal to someone else.'

'Valery said there were others,' I tell him, dropping the attitude a notch. 'In Arras.'

'Did you ever meet any?'

'No,' I admit.

'They keep it quiet and everyone leaves them alone or they're remapped. It's not only them, though. If a Spinster falls in love with a man, even an official, they'll put an end to it.'

'Remap her?'

'No, they've never done that before. Sometimes they remap him or rip him if he's no one important. Others, they threaten. It happens more often than you think.' Jost shakes his head. 'How do you think I became head valet? I kept my nose clean.'

A mixture of excitement and fear churns in my stomach. So there's no one else. 'And if they find out about . . .'

'About us?' he finishes quietly when I don't continue. 'I'm no one important.'

'Yes, you are,' I say. 'They won't be able to control me.'

'They have your sister.'

'They don't have my heart.'

And there it is. As close as we've come to talking about whatever it is between us.

'I can't lose you,' he says in a soft voice.

'You won't.'

'It's a risk for me even to be here,' he says, standing and beginning to pace the golden dome.

'They don't know I can do this.'

'Not yet.'

'I know.' I sigh and stand up. We're getting dangerously close to something we can't take back, and I'm not sure I can do this without him now that Enora's so different. 'We need a plan, but first we have to figure something out.'

He cocks an eyebrow.

'What's happened to Enora,' I remind him.

I don't know where her quarters are located, but Jost does, so I dismantle the dome and smooth the strands of time back into place within the room's weave. Out of the safety of the time bubble, we're pushing our luck, but he leads me out of my room and up two flights of stairs to her hall.

'They monitor the lift more than the stairs,' he tells me as we ascend. 'No one uses them.'

Enora's hall is similar to mine, but all the doors are painted violet instead of plum. Jost raps on the first one and waits, but there's no answer.

'You sure about this?' he asks.

I nod. I won't sleep tonight until I've spoken to her.

Jost holds his thumb to the scanner and the door clicks open to a quiet room. Large paintings hang in golden frames throughout the apartment. From the doorway the images look like flowers, but as I move closer to them they blur into a mash of subtle colours, losing their beauty. A small four-poster bed — its linens taut and its cushions precisely placed — sits next to the unlit hearth. The room feels abandoned.

'She's not here,' Jost says from the window.

A chill creeps up into my throat, but I push it back down. They can't have simply removed her. 'Let's check the bathroom.'

He follows me without a word. Her bathroom is smaller than my own and with the lights off I can barely make out her prep area except for the white plastic chair – exactly like mine – that glows faintly as we enter the empty room.

'I don't know where she is,' Jost says. 'I can run a locator on her from the valet station.'

'Wait,' I breathe, aware of the drip of a tap. My hand stretches in the dark, searching for the switchscan. When I run my hand along it, light floods the tiny space, and I blink.

Jost's eyes adjust more quickly. 'Damn it!'

I watch as he darts across the marble floor, but I can't bring myself to look where he's going. It's in his voice. I don't want to see what he sees. If I turn away now, I can go back to the still bedroom and out to the empty hallway and never know.

But then he's pulling her up, and it's too late.

Water sloshes over the side of the tub, trailing red down the white porcelain. She's pale in his arms, not the polished ivory achieved via the aesthetician's chair, but the blankness of untouched paper, bleached into absence. He struggles with her, heaving her body up by her underarms. The bloodied water laps against her bare breasts and trickles down her collarbone, and I can't look away. Even from here, I spy angry red gashes along her wrists.

'Stop,' I command in a flat voice.

'Help me, Adelice,' he says, still pulling against her heavy body.

'It's too late,' I tell him. The escaping water spreads across the marble, and I stare as it creeps toward the toes of my satin heels.

Jost looks at me but doesn't say anything. After a moment, he drops her arms and lets her body slide back into the water. The motion forces another wave up over the side of the tub, and the puddle of water at my feet surges over my toes. I should step back.

'Maela,' Jost accuses quietly.

'No,' I say, shaking my head. 'Enora did this.'

'She wouldn't—'

'The Enora we knew wouldn't.'

'Then it's still them,' he says. He keeps his voice hushed, but his words are defiantly clear. The audio transmitters must be monitoring us, but why has no one come?

'Of course it's them. It always is,' I say, and then turn to the door.

I crumble as soon as I'm over the threshold, but Jost is already there to catch me.

'I have to call this in,' he whispers.

Helping me to the only armchair in the room, Jost waits for me to settle back, but I lean forward on the edge of the seat, my elbows resting on my knees, and hide my face in my hands. Across the room, Jost speaks into the companel in a low voice. They'll be here in moments and then explanations will be expected. I don't know what to say. My mind has stopped forming words and keeps replaying the ripple of water against Enora's breasts.

'Let me talk,' Jost whispers, kneeling down next to me.

I turn my head and stare into his blue eyes. I wish I could sink into them and float away.

The guards arrive first, then a few maids, and finally Maela sweeps into the room.

'Where is she?' she asks like she can't hear the muffled chaos in the next chamber.

Jost answers, which is good, because I'm not sure I remember how to talk.

'You,' she says to me, 'stay here.'

I look up and glare at her. Not much of a chance I'm going anywhere.

Maela disappears into the bathroom, and I strain to listen. I think someone is crying. Probably one of the servants. Some poor girl rejected years ago.

I wait forever, and Jost stays crouched by my side. We don't speak.

'Adelice,' Maela says, coming back into the room, 'you found her?' She lights a cigarette and blows the smoke down at me.

'Yes,' I say in a clipped tone.

'And she was already dead?'

I clench my jaw and nod.

'And the last time you saw her?'

'Yesterday,' I lie.

Her eyes turn to slits and she opens her mouth, but before she can speak, Loricel enters the room.

'I've informed the medical department,' she says to Maela. 'As well as the main office. An investigator will be here soon. You are no longer needed.'

Maela turns to Loricel and lifts her chin. 'I'll decide that.'

'No,' Loricel says in a quiet voice. 'I will. Enora was in Manipulation Services. You are dismissed.'

Maela shoots me one withering look, but she slinks out of the room.

'You found her?' Loricel asks.

I sigh and squeeze my eyes shut. If Loricel was the one who sent her to be remapped, I shouldn't be so glad to see her.

'When was the last time you saw her?' Loricel asks.

I open my mouth, ready to repeat the information I told Maela. 'I saw her—'

'Tell me the truth,' Loricel interrupts. She's already washed her face and without the carefully applied cosmetics and patching, the cracks of age are more visible. Her eyes sink back and her eyelids droop.

'I saw her this morning,' I whisper. 'She was with Valery.'

'Thank you,' she says in a tired voice.

'Loricel,' I say, 'you have to protect Valery.'

She presses her lips into a thin line and looks away. I don't wait to hear her excuse. Standing, I stride to the door, away from her and Jost, but I hear her response. 'I'm afraid it's too late for that.'

Yeah, that's what I thought.

I'm down one flight of stairs before Jost catches up with me. His boots beat down the steps behind me, but I don't stop until his strong hand closes around my arm. He pulls me to his chest and I melt into him. I count the beats of his

heart, each more precious than the one before, until I'm sure my own heart will break. As soon as he's released my arm, I back away.

'Ad—'

'No.' I raise my palm to stop him from speaking. 'This has to stop now. You saw what they did to her.'

'She did that to herself.'

'Because they drove her to it. They warped her mind, Jost.'

'She was an experiment.'

'Exactly,' I whisper. 'To get to me. And anyone else in the way.'

'So we pretend nothing's happened between us?' he asks.

'It's the only choice we have.'

'I can't accept that.'

'We always knew this couldn't go anywhere,' I murmur.

Jost takes a step back and stares me down. I resist the urge to fall into his arms and instead push by him to the next set of stairs. There has to be another way. If I break his heart again . . .

'I won't live without you,' he whispers, and his eyes say it all – desperation, betrayal, grief. But even as these emotions flash across his face, he reaches out his hand. He would risk everything – his own life – for us. But I can't make that sacrifice. The Guild will kill him, too, if they find out about us. I can't lose him, so I have to let him go.

'Try,' I say, as coldly as I can, but I'm dashing down the steps before he replies.

18

I skip breakfast. And lunch. I don't leave my room. Valery doesn't come to style me, so I spend the day strung across my prep chair drinking a bottle of wine. Valery would have liked that; she was always telling me to relax while she worked on me. Here you go, Val. I have another glass for Enora. And then one for my mother, who would so not approve. As it turns out, there are a lot of people to drink to, and I do my best.

I devote the second half of the bottle to Jost, who isn't dead. Yet. I'm sure dragging him into this will be just the ticket to add him to my personal death toll. And no matter how much I drink, this thought sobers me right up. I can't let them kill Jost or Amie or even Loricel. I can't let anyone else suffer because of me. Which leaves me with two options: buck up and take one for the team or get out of here. The trouble with Arras is that the whole thing is watched

and controlled by the Guild, right down to my personal identifying sequence. Even if I got out of the compound, a tracker could use my sequence to hunt me down before I made it past the rebound station. Or maybe Cormac would skip catching me entirely and have me ripped.

By mid-afternoon I've come up with nothing. But since no one bothers to force me to work I slip into a pair of linen pants and a soft cotton tunic – the only clothing in my entire closet that doesn't require buckling, zipping, or stockings. It's the perfect outfit to lie down and waste away in. Staring out the window from my bed, I watch as waves seep onto the shore. There is no snow on the mountain today. Everything is placid, programmed to counteract last night's tragedy. The wine churns in my empty stomach as I stare out at the peaceful scene, and I feel anything but tranquil.

Behind me my door clicks open, but I don't turn around. I told Jost not to come, so he can go about whatever menial task he's concocted as an excuse to see me. Besides, I probably smell like Cormac by now. Not very romantic. But he doesn't go to the fireplace or my bathroom. I can't detect the exotic aroma of a late luncheon. Instead he walks straight to me and stands there; I keep my back to him.

'Go away.' Happily, my speech is clear.

'I can't.' It's Jost's voice, but he speaks in a firm tone – confident of his right to be here. 'I've been sent to retrieve you for a meeting with Ambassador Patton.'

The voice sounds so like him, but different, too. More professional, arrogant. Something clicks in my brain, and I flip onto my other side. Big mistake. Stars burst across my eyes, making my head swim. Maybe I am a little drunk.

'Been a while,' I say.

'I thought it was better to——' Erik begins.

'Stay away?'

'I didn't want to push things.'

'I think we crossed that line,' I say with a cold smile.

Erik's jaw tightens and then relaxes. I hold out my hand, and he helps me up. My balance is shaky, but, ever the gentleman, Erik takes my arm without a word. It's strange to touch him now. I can see my arm looped through his, my skin scrapes against his wool suit jacket, even the back of my clenched fist brushes against his bare wrist, but there's no spark. My nerves don't react to the contact. I replay the memory of our kiss in the garden. My first kiss. But now I feel like a watcher not a participant. If there was something there, Maela destroyed it, along with the tips of my fingers. Or maybe it's the numbing effects of that wine I drank.

We travel in silence, and Erik's stride is purposeful. Getting me to the meeting: that's his only objective. It'll be a relief to get rid of him. The delightful numbness has worn off by the time we reach the closed door. Erik nods to a tall, stern guard in that way that men greet each other.

Erik peels my arm back from his and guides me inside. He doesn't follow, but as he bows his farewell, I catch a simple 'I'm sorry' escape his lips.

Bit late for that.

Inside, Loricel sits at the far side of a large circular oak table and Maela perches on a leather-backed chair by the door. She straightens up and thrusts her chin forward as I enter the room. I'm pretty sure she's going for proud, but

really she just looks constipated. And my old buddy Cormac is at a small bar in the corner, pouring a drink.

'Good to see everything's back to normal,' I say.

From her seat across the room, Loricel's smile turns into a frown of disapproval.

'Adelice,' Cormac says, stirring a squat crystal glass, 'always a pleasure to see you.'

Such a politician.

'Have a seat,' Loricel says.

I take a deep breath and plop down into a chair. I start to cross my legs, but remember I'm wearing trousers, so I lean forward, legs wide, and give Maela a baiting grin. Her face stays serene, but her knuckles go white.

'I was shocked to hear of the unfortunate incident with your mentor,' Cormac says, taking a chair next to me.

'Were you?' I ask with wide eyes.

'I was,' he repeats in a tone that dares me to ask again. 'Sometimes the demands of a Spinster can be overwhelming, and with the important work we do here we can forget to look after our own.'

'I've felt very looked after,' I assure him.

Maela clears her throat beside me. 'Enora struggled with—'

'Save it,' I snap at her. 'We know what Enora struggled with.'

'Remember your place—'

'Enough,' Loricel says in a quiet voice. 'Adelice knows her place, and you would do well to learn your own, Maela.'

'She's barely even been on a loom,' Maela says.

287

'She's got more talent in her left pinky than you have in your whole body,' Loricel responds.

I have to bite back a smile.

'Don't be arrogant,' Loricel says, turning on me. 'She's right. With this political nonsense, you've had no real training.'

'The Coventry needs to maintain a face of power,' Cormac says, sipping his drink. 'Adelice is key to that.'

'Cormac, you worry about the political and I'll keep this world working,' Loricel says, slamming her hands down on the table. 'If you plan to move her into my position, she needs to be prepared, not indoctrinated.'

'Do I even need to be here for this?' I ask.

'Watch your mouth, girl,' he growls.

'I'd play nicer with your future Creweler, Cormac,' Loricel says to him. 'She may not be as forgiving as I am.'

'The point is, she's not ready,' Maela reminds them, and they both glare at her.

'I'm ready enough.'

'You understand the fundamentals,' Loricel says, 'but you have a lot to learn before you can assume my position.'

'What if I don't want it?'

'I wouldn't worry about that,' Cormac says, shaking his head. 'You're under stress with the loss of your mentor, but we've arranged for you to receive some evaluation and counselling. Enora's death — it reminds us how demanding this work can be.'

'Guess it's not all fancy dinners and dresses,' I say coldly.

'No, it's not,' he says. 'We'll need you here more than ever now.'

'Loricel planning a vacation?'

Cormac's eyes flicker to Maela's, and he shakes his head.

'Loricel has opted to forgo further renewal treatments.'

I look from him to her, but her eyes are vacant. 'What does that mean?'

'It means I'm going to die,' Loricel says softly.

I suck in a breath and let it out slowly. Cormac watches me from the next chair, and I work to keep fear off my face. Without Loricel . . .Well, I don't even want to consider what this place will be like then. Does she think I can stand up to him?

'So you need a new Creweler?' I ask after a long moment.

'We need you,' Cormac says.

I don't answer him.

'You'll be studying under Loricel all working hours until . . .'

'She dies.' I finish his thought.

'Yes, and it's imperative that you're prepared to assume responsibility when she passes.'

'Especially since you're already short a Creweler's assistant.'

Cormac's eyes narrow. 'She wasn't half the Spinster you are, Adelice.'

'I'm half the person she was,' I say with a shrug, barely keeping my voice steady. 'So I guess it evens out.'

'There are other Spinsters,' Maela breaks in, but Cormac shoots her a look that shuts her up.

'You needn't worry yourself about Adelice,' he says to her. 'You've wasted enough time.'

'That girl would have no training if it weren't for me,' she says, stabbing at the air in my direction.

'That girl,' Cormac says quietly, 'would be dead if it were up to you. You are in danger of overstepping your bounds.'

'And we know what happens to girls who overstep their bounds,' I add.

No one laughs.

'Adelice, you'll report to Loricel's studio in the morning. I'll let her know when your evaluation is scheduled,' Cormac says, rising from his seat and buttoning his tuxedo.

'Cormac,' Loricel says. 'A word.'

She gestures for him to follow her, and soon I'm alone at the table with Maela.

'I'm sorry for your loss,' she says.

I stare at her. She can't be serious.

'No, really,' Maela says. 'We've had our differences—'

'That's one way to put it.'

'But,' she continues, ignoring me, 'Enora was a good Spinster.'

'Did Pryana tell you?'

Maela purses her lips. 'Tell me what?'

'About Enora.'

'I was called as part of the emergency response.'

'No, about Enora and Valery. In the hallway.'

'No, she didn't tell me, but there's something you need to understand,' she says. 'If you think Pryana is a puppet of mine, you're in for an unpleasant surprise. She is a force all her own.'

'Which you created—'

'Which I propelled,' she corrects. 'I won't lie, Adelice. I wanted you to be enemies, but Pryana was never going to be your friend.'

'I don't know,' I say. 'We were hitting it off.'

'Pryana would stab her own sister in the back if it suited her.'

'She seemed pretty upset when you ripped her sister.'

'Listen,' Maela says, standing and staring down at me. 'I'd watch who you tell about your own little sister. Pryana's not the forgiving type. Believe me, I did you a favour.'

'Feel free to keep your favours to yourself in the future,' I say.

Maela tosses a bored expression my way and exits. There's no way I'm about to believe her fake sympathy or her sudden interest in me. Since I'm going to be the next Creweler, she's just doing some repair work on the damage she's inflicted.

'Done?' Erik asks, poking his head through the doorway.

'Do I get an escort again?'

'Cormac wants assurance that you're safe at all times.'

'Oh good,' I say with a sigh. 'Will you be camping out on my floor?'

'Outside your door, as a matter of fact.'

I screw my face up. I guess I won't be sneaking out to investigate the clinic tonight.

'Don't look so annoyed,' he says, taking my arm. 'This way you get to wake up and go to sleep to me.'

Despite my resentment for how he acted after our kiss, I laugh. He's just so self-assured.

'Every girl's dream,' I say, tipping my head to the side.

'I am sorry,' he says through gritted teeth.

'Sure. It's nothing.'

'I know what she did to you.'

'Drop it, Erik.'

'You have to know that it would have been worse if I'd come to see you.'

'Yeah, you're probably right,' I say, 'but I guess we'll never know.'

'So that's it, then?'

I sigh and pull my arm out from his. He's not making this easy. 'Erik, we kissed. I was a little drunk. I'm over it.'

'And what if I'm not?' he says, slowing his pace.

I walk faster, pulling him along with me. 'It doesn't matter how powerful I am — or will be after this promotion — it's not going to happen.'

'Promotion?' he repeats.

'I'm training to replace Loricel,' I say with a shrug. 'I assumed you knew.'

'No, but I guess that explains Maela's change of heart.'

'Oh, you mean how we're best friends now?'

He gives me a crooked grin. 'I wouldn't go that far, but she's definitely trying to get on your good side.'

'At least she's not trying to kill me.'

'Again, I wouldn't go that far,' he says.

'The more things change,' I mutter.

'Just forgive me?' he says, and I groan at the circularity of his thoughts. He's like a puppy chasing his tail, except it's mine he's after.

'I forgive you,' I say. 'But it doesn't change anything.'

'I can wait.'

'Erik,' I say, struggling with how much I want to share. 'It's not only that. I'm not the same as I was a few weeks ago. Things have changed, and it would be a waste of your time to wait around for me.'

He looks down at me as though he's watching my neurons firing, and I shrink back from his penetrating gaze. 'I should have known,' he says, a hint of a smile playing on his lips before fading away.

I bite down on the inside of my cheek and keep my eyes on the floor. Something in his voice is giving me goose-bumps, but he can't actually know . . .

'Look,' he says, 'I get it. But there's something you need to consider. I have more resources at my disposal and a certain value to the Guild. He doesn't. You'll get him killed.'

I swallow hard and glance up to his watching eyes. 'Is that the best you've got?'

'I'm not trying to steal you,' he says, lowering his voice. 'I know Jost better than you think. I don't want to see anybody get hurt.'

'That's thoughtful of you,' I murmur.

'Think what you want,' he says. We're at the door to the brass lift. Reaching forward, he presses the Up button and holds the door when it opens. We step in. When the lift door slides closed, he leans down. I can feel his breath warm against the back of my ear.

'Remember what I said to you that night at the ball?'

His words tingle in my ear and down my neck, but I manage a nod.

'You know that plan we discussed. If you finally have one, now's the time to use it.'

The tingle turns into an electric charge and my pulse builds frenetically in my chest, wrists, ears. 'Well, I don't,' I whisper.

'Then think of one,' he says into my hair.

He lingers there for a moment, and I close my eyes, wondering if that kiss really meant nothing to me. The *ding* of the lift door snaps them back open. Beside me, Erik straightens and extends his arm to hold the sliding door – protecting me – as I cross the threshold.

19

The strands of light wrapping one another in the void mesmerise me. I've found the seam in Loricel's illusion and opened it. I clutch my right arm against my body; my fingers ache to reach out, to discover what the thick rough weave feels like. I force myself to keep my hands back away from the breach now. This room, here in the distant tower, where we can call any place in Arras before us, is the only place that feels real.

'You could waste away there,' Loricel says behind me.

The studio was empty when I arrived, but I knew she'd be back soon. Now that she's here, I wish I had more time alone to study the rift. If I'd been here much longer, I might have crossed the line and touched the rough, raw material that billows out between Earth and Arras.

Loricel moves to stand beside me. 'It's hard to fathom, isn't it?'

'I see it,' I say, 'but it feels like another illusion . . . I want to touch it.'

'Like your hands are physically being drawn to it,' she says.

'You too?'

'Yes.'

'Have you?'

'No.' There's the firmness of resignation to her voice. 'I guess I don't want to know. There's so much possibility until I touch it. Perhaps its powers outweigh my own, or perhaps I could manipulate the raw material as I manipulate the fabric of Arras. I don't know which I prefer, so I keep my fingers back.'

'When did you see it the first time?' I ask.

'Kinsey, my predecessor, showed me,' she says, tilting her head and regarding me with half-open eyes.

'And all these years? You've never—'

'Perhaps I'm a coward.'

'No.' I shake my head. 'I think it's harder not to touch it. I want to so badly. It's a compulsion. I admire your ability to deny it this long.'

Loricel snorts. 'Maybe I'll do it before I die.'

I sigh deeply and turn to close the spot. My fingertips burn when they skim the raw material as I repair the hole; it's the most feeling I've had in them for weeks.

'You can feel it?' she asks.

'It's pulsing. Alive,' I say quietly.

'Because it is full of life,' she says. 'I know this is hard for you to accept.'

'How do you close opened eyes?' I ask her, desperate to know how she's restrained herself through the years.

'Like you do at night,' she instructs me. 'You work the loom until you're too tired to go on, and then your eyes close naturally.'

'Is that why you're refusing renewal?'

'Yes, I know it must feel horribly unfair. My leaving you here to take over, but—'

'You don't have to explain yourself,' I stop her. Even now I feel the burden of the raw weave pressing down on me. I can't imagine what it's like for her.

'I couldn't leave it,' she says. 'Not without a true Creweler in place to carry on my work. Adelice, you must know how I feel about the Guild. About Cormac, Maela, and their puppets. But that pulse you feel, that electricity, that's not them.'

My fingers sting as she speaks, reminding me how they want to touch the raw material, but I do my best to push the feeling down deep inside me. 'We don't do it for them.'

'No,' she agrees. 'We do it in spite of them.'

'Will they keep watching me?' I ask.

'They didn't stop watching me until I was seventy,' she says. 'Cormac is many things, but he was the first to realise I wasn't a threat to Arras.'

'I guess I have a while to wait.'

Fifty-four years.

Loricel opens her mouth and then presses her withered lips back together.

'What?' I ask, scanning the room. 'They're watching us now?'

'The illusions in this room are too complex to track.'

Now I understand that she's not sure she wants me to

know the truth, because it might be too much for me to live with. Loricel needs to make sure Arras has a Creweler after her death, and if I leave, it won't.

'You have to understand my dilemma,' she says finally. 'My whole life is this world. I have given everything to it.'

'I think I understand,' I say.

'I wish you could. But until you've devoted your life, fought human nature, harnessed matter itself, and contained it for decades, you can't. It's a lot to ask of anyone.' The lines on her face deepen as she speaks, as though the weight of years is dragging down her very skin.

'But if I don't—'

'Then it will fade away.'

My eyes find the floor, and I inhale for strength. 'So you won't stay, even if I leave?'

'No,' she confirms. 'My age has passed. It is up to you. Of course, I hope you will stay. I believe that you feel the pulse and understand its importance.'

'How long will it survive without a Creweler?'

'They have enough material stocked to last a decade. Maybe,' she answers. 'But it will be chaos – an extended apocalypse. And Cormac will be in charge by then.'

'Of the Coventry?' I ask. 'He acts like he already he is.'

'He oversees us now, but soon he'll be elected prime minister of Arras.'

'He'll have control over everything,' I whisper.

'Except you. If you stay.'

I take a seat on a velvet divan, working through this revelation. 'Well, you don't have to worry. My sister is here. I won't leave her.'

'That's the problem,' Loricel says. 'I want you to make an educated decision. You know about the new remapping tech?'

'They talked about it at the State of the Guild. They mapped me the other day,' I tell her.

'Cormac has mapped each of us—'

'Even you?'

She nods. 'He claims that they are trying to understand why some girls have the ability to see and touch the weave and others don't. He's particularly interested in why most men can't see it.'

'Most?' I recall her saying she believed some men could weave.

'Most can't. There are rumours of departments where men work with the weave, but the Guild always denies it.'

'Do you think they exist?' I ask, realising I'm finally getting more of the story.

'Definitely. The Coventry is just the face of the Guild. What we do is important, but many more than us are at work.'

I have a hard time imagining someone more powerful than Loricel. 'More important than you?'

'My – our – skill,' she corrects herself, 'is necessary to harness the actual raw materials. Without that Arras would decay and crumble from within. Then they need Spinsters to add and maintain, but our value stops there.'

'But they still need us.' The Western Coventry alone houses a hundred girls and women who work shifts around the clock. There's no way Arras could survive without Spinsters.

'Yes, but if they could simulate our skill, they would not.'

'That's why they're mapping me,' I whisper.

'They haven't figured it out yet,' she says. 'But the rate at which they are producing manipulation technology worries me. It will not be long.'

'I can't let them map me again,' I say, balling up my fist in my lap.

'They won't ask your permission,' she says with a wry smile. 'Besides, they already have you scheduled for it.'

'Is Cormac communicating through you now?'

'No, it's my job to lie to you. Cormac assumes I won't tell you the truth, because he believes I'll put Arras above you.' She stops and studies my face for a moment. 'Because I always have in the past.'

'Always?' I ask.

'It's not my place to make a decision for you, especially considering what they have planned.' Loricel's eyes drift to the floor and when she looks back up, they wander between myself and the walls of her studio.

'You don't have to tell me what they have planned for me,' I say. 'I'm smarter than I look.'

She laughs, but no trace of amusement stays on her face. 'They are going to map you again when you go in for evaluation.' Her words burst forth as though they've only barely managed to escape.

'I see,' I murmur.

'No, you don't,' she says in a rush. 'Then they plan to remap you.'

I think of the petty housewives at the State of the Guild

thrilling at remapping their children; they were excited to make them more obedient. I push down the scream of anger threatening to spill out of my mouth, which will surely bring the guard up. *How dare they?*

'They can study me all they want,' I say.

'Eventually they will find their answer—'

'And then they can finally kill me.' My heart no longer leaps when I speak of my death. Its inevitability is another fact of my new life here. I guess I'm transitioning well to the idea.

'Maybe, but they'll have to remap you first, to succeed in making you docile.'

'I don't think they could go far enough to make me *docile*,' I say, the last word oozing with rage.

'You saw how far he was willing to go with Enora,' Loricel says.

'Why do you think they tested the remap on Enora first? Because of her affair with Valery?' I guess.

'Criticism of the relationship was a ruse,' Loricel says. 'It provided an easy excuse to test it on her.'

'Did she know? What they planned to do to her?' I ask.

'I don't know. They took her away in the night. I wasn't notified.'

They always come in the night.

Even if most of what Loricel is telling me is pure theory, there's the bitter edge of truth to some of it. Better to be prepared. 'How long do I have?'

'They're still running tests,' she says. 'To be honest, Enora's suicide rattled them. Cormac is afraid you will become unstable, too.'

'How long?'

'A week,' she says, 'at the most.'

I stand and walk to the wall, trailing my fingers along the peaceful image of the calm ocean; it ripples where I touch it, distorting and coming back together. It's still the same image, but now it bears a shadow where my hand disrupted it.

'There's nowhere to run,' I say.

'I know.'

'Enora knew that.' I turn back to face her. 'It's why she killed herself.'

Loricel heaves a sigh. 'She was confused, Adelice.'

'Because they screwed with her,' I say, shaking my head. 'She was lost. I could see it the last time we spoke, but I didn't know what they'd done to her.'

'You couldn't have prevented it,' Loricel tells me.

'I could have. I've been fighting them since the moment they arrived at my house. If I'd come along willingly, my parents would be alive and Amie would be safe. Enora and Valery's secret would be safe. She and Valery—'

'Would be living half a life,' Loricel stops me. 'Don't overestimate your culpability. Death is the only escape for us.'

'But that's what I don't get,' I admit. 'Maela told me there was no escape, even in death.'

Loricel presses her lips together. 'I'm not sure exactly what Maela means. Her ambition makes her a powerful woman in her own right. Because of it, she knows much more about the Guild's inner operations than the rest of us.'

'What happens to people when they die before their thread is ripped?'

'It happens so rarely—'

'But it does happen,' I press.

'Occasionally. And when it does, we remove the remains of the thread,' she says.

'Remains?' I recall the intricate strings that bind tightly together to make up a single whole thread.

'When someone dies before a removal request is completed, part of their strand . . .' Loricel pauses and meets my eyes. 'Disappears.'

A chill runs through my entire body. 'Where does it go?'

'They aren't sure. That's why they're so careful to remove weakened strands themselves. It's why they capture enemies first or rip them directly. The Guild wants control over removed threads.'

A thousand questions are racing through my head, threatening to spill out at once. It's a lot to consider – plots and remapping. I take a deep breath and decide on one to ask first, before the others. 'Why do they care what happens to the removed threads?'

Loricel shrugs. 'I don't know.'

'Then who cares what happens to the parts that disappear?'

'When I first began at the Coventry, we didn't do preemptive removals. We simply patched and removed the remains. About fifty years ago, that changed,' she explains.

'What do you think happens?' I ask. Even if I'm not sure I believe everything she's told me about Earth and the origin of Arras, she still knows more than anyone else.

'I think the part of the thread that disappears goes back into Arras.'

'Into the weave? But wouldn't that provide new raw material?' I ask.

'Theoretically.' A note of distrust rings in her voice. 'It could strengthen Arras.'

'Then why rip them pre-emptively? Why not utilise them?'

'The Guild doesn't trust what it can't understand. Letting those people go is an act of faith they're incapable of.'

I know she's right, but I still don't fully understand the Guild's motives for the pre-emptive removals, and I don't think Loricel does either. This is about more than control.

'I don't understand why they don't tell us about Earth or remnants. There has to be a reason they don't want us to know about them. Even you think it's important enough to tell me,' I point out.

'Some things shouldn't be forgotten.'

'Remembrance is never useless,' I say, recalling my mother's wise, quiet smile whenever she spoke those words to me as a child. My fingers twist to the techprint on my wrist.

'It's important that you understand where we come from, Adelice. Especially if you will be assisting in the mining operations,' she continues. 'Earth's resources can't last forever, not if the Guild tries to mine without the support of a Creweler. They won't have anyone who can see the raw materials, but that won't stop them from trying.'

'Wait, if we're pulling the material from the surface,' I say, my eyes growing wide, 'then Earth is frozen!'

Loricel cocks her head to the side and regards me thoughtfully. 'So you've discovered warping.'

Warping — that's the perfect word for it. The moments I made in my quarters weren't frozen, they were warped. I take a deep breath and admit my secret to her. How I can touch time without a loom. I even tell her about the separate moments I've woven, but I leave Jost out of my stories.

'Yes,' she says. 'I knew you could do it, but I had no idea *you* knew.'

'It was a happy accident,' I say. I'm instantly drawn back to the stolen moments spent with Jost in my room. I look away so she won't see me blush.

'Are you leading with your left hand?' she asks.

I pause and consider the question. 'I don't honestly know. We were taught to lead with our right on the loom, so I don't think so. Does it make a difference?'

'You're left-handed,' she says. 'Crewelers always are. It allows us not to be constrained by the forward motion of time. That's what helps us catch it.'

'Should I always use my left hand?' I ask, flexing my left hand's fingers now and staring at them in wonder.

'No.' Loricel shakes her head. 'It's very powerful. If you can warp with your right hand, or using both hands at the same time, it's much safer until you've truly honed your ability. The fact that you can warp without starting with the left is impressive. But be careful.'

'Okay,' I say, inhaling deeply.

'There's something else you have to understand about warping,' she explains, holding out a hand in warning. 'Yes, it pauses the moment around you. But it also puts you on a

different time line. Within the warp, you can live a whole life.'

'Can I die there?' I ask. Would wasting away slowly with Jost be better than a quick, painless remap? I'd be dead either way.

'Yes.'

'And I would be dead everywhere – in the warp *and* in the real world?'

'Yes,' she says emphatically.

'But the world outside,' I say, biting my lip slightly in concentration, 'is locked in that moment.'

'That's what you have to understand,' Loricel says, leaning toward me. 'Only the moment where you've caught the time is frozen. Essentially you've created a field of safety. The time and matter around it is frozen and no one can enter it. But merely in the immediate area where you've warped the weave.'

'Outside that, time continues?'

'Yes. And eventually the Guild would be able to break through your warp, but it would take a while.'

It's a warning not to put too much faith in my happy little bubble. It can only keep me safe for so long and certainly not long enough to make much difference.

'Can you move backwards along the time line of the warp?' I ask, my voice filled with hope.

'You already know the answer to that,' she says, shaking her head sadly. 'You can't turn back time. We can harvest it, and stop it in the mining fields, but the time lines always move forward.'

'Then Earth?' I prompt.

She sits back in her seat and clasps her hands in her lap. 'There are dead spots in the mining locations where the coventries rest. These are where we capture the time and elements for Arras. The drills create warps in those locations that freeze the Earth around them.'

'But outside the warped areas, the rest of it is untouched? There could be people there still!'

'I doubt that,' she says with a hint of sadness. 'The only people left on Earth were bent on its destruction.'

I frown, watching Arras spread around me through the wall illusion. What lay beneath it?

'You know, I promised Enora I would never tell anyone I could weave without a loom,' I confide.

Loricel gives me a sad smile. 'She was protecting you. She knew it would mark you as a Creweler, but you must have known the Guild was aware of your talent.'

'I didn't want to worry her,' I admit. 'And I thought maybe if I pretended not to know they would think they had made a mistake.'

'Your mentor did the best she could in the situation, as did you.'

Kind, protective Enora. Only one thing I've learned today comforts me. 'So Enora,' I say slowly, 'was reabsorbed.'

'Part of her was,' Loricel says.

Some part of her escaped. This makes me smile.

'Adelice,' Loricel says, breaking into my thoughts, 'did she say anything to you before she . . .'

'No.' I focus on the memory of our last meeting, combing through the conversation in my head. 'She was acting strangely though. I knew something was different.'

'Cormac is obsessed with why she did it,' Loricel confides. 'He cannot confirm whether her suicide was prompted by the procedure or by her guilt over her relationship with Valery.'

'Is that why Valery was ripped?'

'He was angry,' she says. 'The remap should have reprogrammed Enora, but Valery reached out to her. He blamed her for Enora's confusion, but he can't be sure what caused Enora to act.'

'Then Pryana tattled.' It's the only way Cormac could have known that Valery had approached Enora after her remap. I should have known from the smug look on her face at dinner. 'I guess a vendetta outweighs someone's life.'

'Do not discount the power of paranoia either. If this girl was raised to be an ideal Eligible, she probably bought into all the nonsense the Guild sells its citizens,' Loricel advises.

'It doesn't matter,' I say. 'Pryana, Valery – they were just pawns in Cormac's and Maela's games. They did this to Enora.' *And they're going to pay*, I add silently.

Loricel leans forward and takes my hand. 'There's no way to know for sure what happened, because we haven't found any evidence. No note. No diary. Not a thing.'

'Are you saying someone else—'

'No,' she says. 'Enora took her own life, but her initial map showed she was conflicted. Her thoughts were unbalanced, but none of her answers indicated that she was suicidal.'

'Of course,' I say, dropping Loricel's hand. 'She was living a lie.'

'Perhaps, but, unfortunately, she left nothing behind. We cannot question Valery. If she said nothing to you –' Loricel pauses meaningfully, as though she's waiting for me to contradict this – 'then we will never know.'

Even though I'm telling her the truth, Loricel's gaze is so penetrating that I start to feel guilty. Shifting back on the divan, I press my lips together, trying to think of a way to change topics. 'So are you going to train me?' I ask.

'You do not need training,' she says.

'But you said—'

'I am buying you time.' Her piercing look gives way to one of exasperation.

It only makes me feel worse. Loricel's given everything for Arras, but I'm so selfish that she doesn't expect me to sacrifice myself. All I can think to say is thank you.

'Now go use it,' she says, shooing me out of the studio.

I slip out of the tower and past the guard. He looks at me closely, the way men regard a weakling. The last thing I need is for him to send for an escort.

'Loricel sent me for something in the lower studios,' I lie.

I'm certain he doesn't believe me from the way his eyes squint together, but he lets me go.

I rush back toward my quarters before anyone can reach me. Loricel might not believe Cormac is responsible for Enora's death, but I saw what he did to her. Even if she felt trapped here, she wasn't desperate. She seemed happy obsessively picking each outfit I wore, right down to the shoes. And she was so protective of me. She cared too much about me to just abandon me. She'd even gone to

309

all the trouble of getting me a digifile when I had to travel around Arras, and she had warned me about Erik.

The digifile!

Suddenly the lift seems to slow down and the buttons light up for each floor in slow motion. Five more left. Four. I hate living so high up! As soon as the doors open I dash out. The digifile is resting safely under my pillow, and I snatch it up.

Sliding my fingers across the screen, I frantically open folders and programs. There are games. Catalogues. An application that patches me into the daily weather programming for each sector. Nothing. It was only a gift. It's stupid to be so disappointed. Loricel's pushing had me believing Enora cared enough to – I don't know – tell me why, or at least say goodbye or something.

'It can't be,' I mutter. Erik and Jost were so surprised to see me carrying the device on that trip – it must mean something. I wish I could go to Jost now and ask why they acted that way, but that would draw attention to him.

I pick the digifile back up and start combing through the programs more slowly. *A weather program.* I think back to the first time I met Enora, when she caught me weaving a thunderstorm. Scanning through the weather application, I find a file labelled *Precipitation.* The rest of the program is organised by date and month. I press down on the file and wait for it to load, my heart pounding at the possibility of answers or information. Even a simple farewell.

Inside there's another file, marked *Thunder.* I open it and a dozen smaller files appear. The first reads, *To Adelice.*

20

I pull out every tailored suit in my wardrobe and hang them on my bathroom door. The digifile slips into most of the tiny pockets on each jacket, but I have to rip the basting stitches out of some. No matter what, I'm keeping the small pad with me from now on. I've renamed Enora's note for added safety. At least now I know where to start, even if not much else is clear.

The digifile contains information that I'm pretty sure could get me killed. Maps. Tracking systems. But it's Enora's note that burns in my brain. I think I could stand to have them find everything in those folders but that. It's too personal. But even though I've read it so many times I have it memorised, I can't bring myself to erase it. It plays on repeat in my head, spoken in Enora's soft voice. Her written words sound so much like her that reading them makes me hurt like I'll break into pieces.

Dear Adelice,

If you found this by accident, close this file. Nothing in here will do you any good, and you know I won't like it if you get into trouble!

But if you came looking for it that means you're ready for answers. I assume you'd come to me in person. So first of all, I'm sorry for leaving you. I wish I could prove to you that I fought to stay. I suppose it doesn't matter anyway, but now that I'm gone the only person you can trust is Loricel. Please believe that she will help you when you need it.

That said, there are answers you have been searching for, and you should find them on your own. I've given you everything I can to help you do this, but protect these files or I'm afraid they'll come after you.

And finally, Adelice, don't be sad for me. I'm free, and it is my sincerest wish that you will be as well. That's why I've fought to protect you, and it's why I'm giving this to you now. You're a smart girl. Keep your wits and trust your instincts, and you'll be fine. And don't ever forget who you are.

With love,

Enora

Her words offer small comfort, but they do give me hope. I choose a lavender suit to wear to dinner, and I'm sliding on the clingy skirt when there's a knock at the door. Shim-

mying into the jacket, I stash the digifile in my left pocket, right below my heart.

Cormac's at the door. This can't be good.

'Come in,' I say, trying to keep the tremble out of my voice and failing. I giggle a little, hoping I look like the nervous, awestruck girls that made up my cohort. Although it may be a little late to go fanatic on him.

He enters without a word and wanders around the perimeter of my room, stopping to finger the suits hung over my door. 'Packing?'

'No,' I say, grabbing the clothing to shove back into my closet. 'I like to plan my wardrobe for the week.'

'On Wednesday?' he asks, calling my bluff.

I stuff the suits in with my other dresses and slam the doors to the wardrobe closed. Taking a deep breath, I whirl around to face him. 'Can I help you with something?'

'No,' he says with a shrug. 'It occurred to me I've never seen your quarters.'

'Here they are.'

'Amazing what technology can do,' he murmurs. 'Did you know that each room in the high tower is woven to appeal to the Spinster assigned to it? It's very time-consuming to do so, but we want you to be happy here.'

'I love my room,' I tell him, and it's the truth. The cosy room with plush, oversized cushions is my home. It's the first place that has ever belonged only to me. But I would trade it for the cramped bedroom I shared with Amie in a heartbeat.

'It's nice,' he says, glancing around him. 'Not my taste exactly. I tend towards a more modern look.'

He drifts over to sit on the edge of my bed, and I make a mental note to send for fresh linens as soon as he's left.

'Can I order something for you?' I ask.

'Martini. Neat.'

I repeat this to the companel – having no idea what a neat Martini is – and make sure the kitchen staff knows it's for Cormac. Then I wait by the door for it to arrive. It comes with the customary speed of anything meant for an official, and I let the valet bring it to Cormac.

Taking a seat in a chair by the hearth, I start counting each breath I take and release. I get to twenty before he speaks.

'No doubt Loricel warned you about the remap,' Cormac says, but he doesn't wait for me to confirm this. 'I want you to know there are other options.'

'And the price?' I ask, keeping my eyes level with his.

'See that's what I like about you – all business.'

Something in the way he says 'like' sends me recoiling back into my chair, but I keep my mouth shut.

'The Guild needs to know that you can be counted on to serve the people of Arras,' he says, setting his drink on the tray. 'Right now your loyalty is debatable.'

'I haven't done anything to make them question me,' I say in a voice that dares him to deny it.

'You ran,' he reminds me.

'My parents forced me to run, and I was scared enough to listen to them.'

'So otherwise you would have come here and been a good girl?' he asks with a smirk.

'I guess we'll never know.' It's true I didn't immediately

314

go to the door when they came, because I expected my father to. I thought they'd cry, and I'd look scared, but I was planning to leave with the retrieval squad. There was no other option in my head until I was pushed into that tunnel.

'You were never meant to fall in line,' Cormac says, standing and walking to the fireplace, which is steps from my seat. Leaning on the mantel, he hovers over me, and I shrink further into my chair.

'So how do I prove myself?' I ask. Or at least buy myself some time?

'Do you know yet why a Creweler is so integral to the continuation of Arras?' he asks.

I'm confused by the sudden shift in conversation, but I regurgitate what I've learned from Enora and Loricel.

He puts up a hand to halt my description. 'Yes, that's what a Creweler does, but why we need her is something else entirely.'

'To protect the innocent,' I murmur.

'Yes, but such a concept is vague to someone too young to know true tragedy,' he says.

My parents. Enora. My sister rewoven into a stranger. How can he suggest I don't know about tragedy?

He watches my reaction to this proclamation, but when I don't respond, he wets his lips with his tongue before he continues. 'You think you know loss, but before Arras and the Guild of Twelve, wars spilled blood all over the Earth. Entire generations of young men died so that other men could gain more power.'

I bite my tongue and stare back at him. Loricel has already told me all of this, but to my astonishment, I realise

that he believes what he's saying. As though he's different from those evil men.

'Dictators murdered women and children for having different skin colours or holding different beliefs.' He pauses and moves a step closer to my chair. 'Because we didn't have the capacity to control peace.'

Control – the word that haunts me. That's the true difference between Earth and Arras. Men like Cormac can remove taints and troublemakers and differences much more efficiently than our ancestors on Earth.

'And are your choices better than theirs?' I ask, gripping the arms of my chair firmly.

'I make choices for the good of the many,' Cormac says, but his eyes flash and he switches tactics. 'In Arras, we ensure food is administered and available to everyone. There's no risk of famine. We control the weather and avoid the dangers of too little water as well as the hazards of unregulated weather conditions. In the past, humanity was at the whim of nature, but now nature serves us.'

'Perhaps there was a purpose to the natural order of things,' I say in a soft voice, but he ignores me.

'Families don't watch their loved ones decline and individuals are free from the fear of unexpected death,' he continues. 'We've cured most serious illnesses with renewal technology—'

'And the ones you haven't?'

'Our citizens are relieved from their pain,' he says without missing a beat.

'You mean you kill them,' I accuse.

'We remove them from a conscious state where they

would exist in pain. We've streamlined the burdens of old age.'

My hand aches where my grandmother's fierce grip clasped it, and I shake my head at his lies. There's no way he's younger than she was. The Guild's interest lies in removing the unnecessary matter in the weave. 'Have you ever lost anyone?' I ask.

'Not the same way you have,' he admits, 'but you should know better than anyone the pain of unexpected death.'

'Unexpected death' is such a political way to put it. 'No, have you ever lost anyone to removal?' I clarify.

'We don't lose in removal. We control,' he says, his jaw muscles twitching. He's a bit too fond of that word. 'And yes, I had both my parents and my wife removed.'

'Wife?' I gasp. Cormac Patton: the ultimate bachelor. The idea of him settled down with one woman is incomprehensible.

'I was married when I was very young,' he says in a casual tone. 'As you know, it's expected that citizens form domestic units by age eighteen. I was no exception.'

Except that he's always been the exception. The man flashes across the Stream with a fresh new girl at every Guild event. He's the guy my father half-jokingly referred to as a lucky bastard every time we tuned in.

I try to picture the type of woman he'd marry. In my head, she's a cross between Maela and one of the vapid rebound stewardesses. Insipid and evil — Cormac's perfect cocktail. 'What happened to her?' I ask him.

'She fell ill before renewal technology caught up with certain psychological ailments. I chose not to prolong her

317

suffering.' His tone is detached; he's stating facts, but the muscles in his jaw tense and the veins from there to his shoulders go taut. This isn't something he wants to talk about, which makes it the number one thing I want to discuss.

'But she wasn't dying,' I say, my lip trembling.

'No,' he says, 'but she was not a functioning member of Arras, and her condition prevented me from serving the Guild to my full capacity.'

I turn my head, afraid my eyes will give away my burning disgust. He got rid of her so he could advance politically and enjoy the benefits of being a widowed bachelor. 'I guess that's why you enjoy casual relationships with so many women,' I say in a cold voice.

'That's the thing, Adelice. The time has come for the family unit to be promoted again in Arras,' he says, switching on his politician's smile.

'I wasn't aware it had stopped being promoted,' I say, thinking of the marriage profiles advertised in the daily *Bulletin*. By now I would be attending courting appointments and searching for a compatible match. The thought sends a tremor through my chest as I imagine the life I never had.

My jibe only launches him into more rhetoric. 'Our laws help us maintain the family, but there are an increasing number of unnatural threats to the traditional family dynamic.'

Like Enora.

'We contain these dangerous proclivities as best we can, but the fact is that a number of dismissed women have refused to marry according to age regulations. In the Eastern

Sector, this trend is spreading, and now young men aren't even advertising marriage profiles,' he tells me.

'And you let them?' I say, not hiding my surprise. 'When the Guild has such persuasive methods at its disposal?' Is this the taint I heard him discussing, or just a symptom of a larger sense of discontent?

'Frankly, after Enora's stunt, I'm concerned about the safety of our current methods. The process may have damaged her. The remains of her thread barely held together when we removed them from the weave. It might surprise you to learn we don't want to remap the entire female population.'

'But *you* would, though,' I accuse, my blood boiling.

'Of course, there's nothing I wouldn't do for the good of Arras,' he says, dropping his gaze to meet mine. 'Someday you'll understand this. Right now you can't see past yourself. If girls stop marrying – if, Arras forbid, they live on their own – we can't protect them.'

'So you're doing it to keep women safe?' I ask.

'Yes. When expectations are clear, they are easily met, but when we begin to bend the rules, we invite discord.'

I actually think Cormac believes what he's saying, but I've seen the effects of these stringent rules. My mother being refused more children, our carefully segregated neighbourhoods, Enora trying to live a lie. Was quiet desperation the price of surface happiness? 'Maybe they aren't ready to get married,' I say. 'I wouldn't have been.'

Cormac presses his lips together and watches me for a moment before responding. 'I'm sorry to hear that, Adelice, because the Guild has decided the best way to ad-

dress this concern is to provide an example to these young women.'

'What kind of example?' I ask. I keep my voice steady.

'The Guild has enjoyed success with most Eligibles through the elite treatment and privilege afforded Spinsters,' he continues. 'They're excited to be taken to the Coventry.'

My pulse pounds in my ears, drowning out all the ambient noise. Only Cormac's practised, smooth voice funnels through, like a mandatory Stream broadcast. 'So it makes sense to give young women an example of perfect domestic tranquillity. We'll market it the same way we do coming to the Coventry – that being married is a life of privilege. And we'll use someone from the Coventry as an example.'

'But Spinsters can't . . .' I'm too embarrassed to say it out loud.

'Consummate the relationship?' he asks, a smirk playing at his lips.

I give a small nod, but keep my eyes on my feet.

'You're not stupid,' he says with a trace of annoyance. 'You can't possibly believe the whole purity-standards bit.'

'Then why tell us that?' More blood rushes to my face and settles on my cheeks. Generally, I don't consider myself dumb, but I had, in fact, always believed the 'whole purity-standards bit'.

'Family, Adelice. We can't have young women running around town. We need them at home, having babies, and serving Arras. And I'm sure you know women here—'

'But it takes away our skills.'

'You've seen some action since you've been here,' he accuses, 'and you're still weaving.'

The flush of my cheeks deepens. So much for being discreet. 'I never crossed any lines.'

'Maybe so,' he says, but he shrugs as though he's unconvinced.

'So you're going to allow Spinsters to marry?' I ask, feeling a bit dizzy.

'No,' he assures me. 'We need Spinsters to remain dedicated to their work, and our philosophy that a wife's first duty is to her husband would be undermined by such a policy change.'

I exhale in relief. The thought of being forced into a marriage, of making Jost live through that . . . I can't imagine a worse torture.

'But a Creweler can be afforded special privileges,' he says, and my heart jumps back into my throat.

'You . . . want . . . me . . . to . . . marry?'

'Consider it an order,' he says with a smile.

'Or you'll remap me,' I whisper. 'Do I get to choose?' I struggle to hang on to the faint flicker of hope this thought offers me. No one could object to Jost. He might not like the constant grooming. But as much as I try to believe it's possible, even if it were, I'd be putting him directly under the Guild's thumb. No matter how much it may hurt him, it would be better if I were married to someone else.

'I don't think that's a good idea, do you?' he asks with a cocked eyebrow. 'Your choices aren't as well conceived as the Guild would like.'

'So you'll choose for me?' I ask slowly. No doubt it will be a political match.

'We already have.' He flashes a blinding smile. 'Me.'

The blood rushing in my head drains out, and I grip the arms of my chair to stay upright.

Marry Cormac?

'I'm only sixteen,' I whisper.

'We'll wait for you to turn seventeen as custom dictates in the larger metros,' he says in a casual voice.

I struggle to make sense of what he's telling me. I stand to look out of the window. 'But how old are you?'

Cormac scowls. 'Renewal tech makes that a non-issue,' he says through clenched teeth.

'Not for me.'

'What? You think you can go out and marry some young pretty boy?' he asks, his voice rising steadily. 'Let me make this clear: it has been decided. The Guild wants assurance that you're being tightly monitored.'

'And you're just the man to do that,' I say, narrowing my eyes.

'You'll enjoy the same privileges and get to have children.'

I choke back the stomach acid this statement sends shooting up my throat. 'You can have kids?'

'Of course,' he says, straightening his tux jacket. 'My genetic materials have been safely stored since I was a younger man.'

Much younger. Of all the possibilities I mourned when I was brought to the Coventry, having babies was not on that list.

'So I'll be' — I search for the word, my thoughts moving too fast for me to latch onto them — 'impregnated.' My only solace is that if I can't escape, traditional methods of

procreation won't be necessary. Although lying back on a medic table and letting some . . .

'Our biogenetics team has created a patch that will ensure I can procreate much the same as any young father.' His black eyes gleam as he speaks.

I back slowly away from him. The thought of his body bearing down on my own – his aseptic stench smothering me – steals my breath, and I gasp.

'And if I refuse?' I ask, barely containing the hysteria I feel building in my chest.

'We remap you,' he says with an edge in his voice, 'and then you marry me.'

I cross my arms over my chest, clutching my shoulders, and shake my head. 'I'll do anything you want except that,' I beg, hot tears spilling down my cheeks. 'I'll be Creweler. I'll be good.'

'I'd hoped you would see reason,' he snarls, moving toward me. 'I would have preferred a wife with some spirit, but I'll remap you and marry you next week if I choose to.'

He's shaking me now, but I can only sob. 'Please. Please. Please.'

My pleas are breathless, lost in his gruff attack.

'Did you think,' he says, his voice full of disdain, 'we would let you run wild, screwing around with the servants and playing dress-up? Arras demands your service, Adelice.'

I wrench my arms free and fly from the room. Cormac doesn't follow me. He'll find me eventually; he knows there's no need to exert extra effort now. Scrambling into the stairwell, where I'm protected from the view of secur-

ity monitors, I tear at time and weave myself into safety. When I'm sure the moment is secure, I collapse onto the cold, hard landing and stare at the hourglass my father burned onto my wrist. How can I remember who I am if they're determined to take it from me?

I'm out of time. Even if I can break out of the compound, Cormac will hunt me down. I think of Loricel's resignation to her impending death, and for the first time I truly understand the relief she must feel. I wish I were dead.

I stay there, trapped in my own web, unable to move. There's only one person powerful enough to help me now, but even she has nowhere to run.

I go to her anyway.

21

The Creweler's studio walls are blank, and the loom sits empty. Loricel must be at dinner with the others. Maybe they'll assume I'm with Cormac and not come looking for me. The screens in the room reflect the default program, and I take a deep breath and consider where I should look first. I only have to tell the walls where I want to be and the tracking program will display that place. These walls can show me anywhere in Arras, but I'm not sure how long I have with them, so I better make my time count.

'I am in the great hall at dinner,' I command, feeling a little silly.

The walls shimmer and the great hall weaves itself across the space. I stand in the dead centre, the table stretching out around me. At the far end Loricel sits, speaking to no one. Meanwhile the other Spinsters make lively conversation that I can't hear. Each woman's skin is a pale version

of its natural colour – chalk white or dusted chocolate or muted honey. I watch as one girl throws her head back, and in my own I hear a maniacal cackle as others clap and wave their hands in exaggerated gesticulations. This is how they close their day: at a long table filled with puddings and roast meat and delicate breads filled with sweet cream. A few gulp down thin red wine. One snaps her fingers and a young man appears to refill it. His face is blank, except for the dullest hint of disgust in his electric-blue eyes.

I stare at him. Dressed in his evening suit, he bears little resemblance to the scruffy boy who carried me across that stone cell, but his eyes are the same as the day we met, the day he bandaged my hands, the day we kissed. I have to turn away or I'll rip right through the wall to get into his arms.

All around, eyes fix on me. I feel exposed, but then I realise I'm standing in the spot where the main dish will be placed, a large ham or turkey or duck. One by one, the Spinsters seated near this spot begin reaching out towards me, their hands returning with knives and forks full of steaming, white meat. *I'm being eaten alive.*

I bite my lip to keep from laughing and focus on what I now know. I have located both Jost and Loricel. I want to follow Jost, but this is my only chance to find the information I need to get to Amie if I want to pull her location up on the loom.

'Show me the offices,' I command, and the scene shifts to a busy building where smartly dressed men and women bustle about with stacks of papers. It's a scene outside the Coventry. My command must have been too vague.

'Show me the offices inside the Coventry,' I try, and the image flickers to nothing.

Pulling the digifile from my pocket, I slide open the secret file and am delighted to discover that Enora included a map of the compound. I shift the image, searching until I find what I'm looking for: the research laboratories. Next to them I spot a single room twice their size. It's marked 'repository'. They're both located near the clinic where I was mapped. Calling up the labs on the wall, I see a few men clad in white jumpsuits busily working with tubes and looms. Their workday must not end at the traditional time. I close my eyes and mutter, 'Repository.'

I can't look. Something about the large block on the map raises the hair on my neck. Slowly I open my eyes. Large steel shelves rise up in neat, symmetrical rows, lined with thousands of tiny metal boxes. Moving closer, I examine them to find each is labelled with a sequence of fourteen numbers and letters. It takes me a moment to realise I've stopped breathing.

Fourteen.

03212144 WR LM LA

The sequence drilled into my head as a child.

'It's how we'll find you if you're ever lost,' my mother said.

It's how they find each of us.

Date of birth. Sector. Metro. Mother's initials. Child's initials.

I stare at the box in front of me. Whose sequence is this?

My hand reaches out to open it, but my fingers hit the wall screen.

'It's an illusion,' I remind myself. The screens look so vivid that for a moment I thought I could reach out and riffle through the boxes.

I nearly drop the digifile from my sweaty hands, trying to find the information on the map, but thankfully it's there: a list of coordinates that will call up the Coventry's weave on the machine. Sitting at the loom, I punch in the codes and watch as the Coventry's weave spins across it. Next to me the command panel blinks red, flashing a reminder: partial within boundary diameter. It means I'm looking at a piece of the weave that contains the very location I'm in. Maela showed us this piece before, but I wonder now, as the warning light flashes at me, if I'm risking its stability to manipulate the compound from within the compound itself. But I can't think of a better – or safer – idea. And, I argue to myself, why would Enora have given me this info if I wasn't meant to use it? But . . . if I'm being honest, this is possibly the stupidest plan ever. I'm not sure if it's possible to remove a piece from the loom's weave and place it into the room's actual weave. Probably because no one has ever been desperate enough to try it. Except me.

I run my hands along the top of the loom, the weave shocking the tips of my damaged fingers. Slowing them to a soft trailing motion, I adjust the view on the loom, zooming into the weave until it focuses, mirroring the map Enora left me on the digifile, and then I see the outline of the repository. Keeping my fingertip carefully on the spot, I tease a few strands of the area out, carefully, so as not to remove the entire room from the weave, which would surely draw immediate suspicion. Holding it delicately in

my left hand, I reach up into the air with my right, and concentrating until the room's weave shimmers into view, I draw apart the strands of this room, hoping my theory is correct and that I can transplant threads from the loom into the weave of Loricel's studio. If so, then I hope to create a rift between her studio and the repository that will allow me to enter the secure facility. I weave the strands from the repository into this space and cautiously peek through.

It's not a bad first try, except that I've woven it in upside down and I'm looking at the ceiling, the storage units suspended overhead. There's no way I can open those boxes this way, so I step back through to Loricel's studio and fix it.

There's a faint hum filling the other room, and I shiver as I step through. It's at least thirty degrees colder in here than any other space in the compound. I pull my jacket tighter and step up to the nearest shelf; there's only one way to find out what's in there.

The boxes latch on the right side, and I have to try twice to raise the tiny lever. In response, the front of it slides away, revealing a small crystal cube. I reach in to pull it out. A thin strand of light shimmers, suspended in the centre and woven into a delicate knot. I turn it over in my hands and the thread doesn't move. It's too thin to belong to the person with this identifying sequence. I've seen individual threads after removal, and they're comprised of several strings knitted together; I'm sure that this is only part of the ripped thread. On the bottom, I notice an etched code composed of a series of numbers and varying bars. Sliding my digifile next to it, I open a folder labelled *Tracking* and

press the small screen up to the code. A pulsing icon flashes immediately and then a new dataset appears:

NAME: Riccard Blane
PERSONAL IDENTIFYING SEQUENCE: 06022103 EN BH BR
OCCUPATION: banker
REMOVAL DATA: 10112158 EN
REQUEST CONTACT: Amolia Blane
RELATION: wife
CURRENT STATUS: active

Active?

The strand is too thin to be the banker's remains. If he was removed two years ago, why is he listed as active? I hold the cube up to the repository lights, but no new information appears. I save the dataset to the digifile to study later and place the cube back in the box.

I tiptoe down the narrow aisle, afraid even my light footfalls might attract attention in this section of the compound. As I get further from my entry point, I begin to worry. What if Loricel returns to her studio, or someone else walks into the repository? Starting to head back to investigate closer to the rift, I glimpse the shelves one row over. Squat metal rectangles, not square boxes, compose these units. I dart quickly to them. Each is labelled with an identifying sequence, but there's no storage cube inside. Instead a thin plastic card pops out of the cubby. Fumbling with the digifile, I scan the card and wait as the dataset loads.

NAME: Annelin Mayz

PERSONAL IDENTIFYING SEQUENCE: 11262158 NU MG MA

ALTERATION DATA: 12162159 NU

RELOCATION: EN

REQUEST CONTACT: Officer Jem Blythe

KIN: none / permanent removal

CURRENT STATUS: healthy

The file includes a picture of a young girl. According to her PIS, she's only two years old now. This is what I've been looking for: records of children who have been rewoven to foster families. Amie's information will be in here, too. I push Annelin's card back into the cubby and bump the latch on the next file. The small door slides open, and before I can close the lever, the next card ejects all the way out. Reaching down I pick up the card and scan it. Maybe there's a pattern to the alterations. The first line of the dataset stops me in my tracks. Although it's not Amie.

It's Sebrina Bell.

Bell.

I jam the buttons linked to the attached image files. The girl in this image is an infant, her cheeks both dimpled and a wisp of dark curls falling across her forehead. She seems too little to smile, but she is grinning like she's staring at someone she adores. Someone like her father. Her eyes are a sparkling, deep blue. I know those eyes instantly. They must run in the family.

It's Jost's daughter — the one who disappeared right before his eyes. I choke back a sob. Clutching the card to my chest, I scan through the data on the digifile:

NAME: Sebrina Bell

PERSONAL IDENTIFYING SEQUENCE: 02262158 ES BR BS

ALTERATION DATA: 05282158 ES

RELOCATION: EN

REQUEST CONTACT: Ambassador Cormac Patton

KIN: father/abandoned mother / permanent removal /
  deceased

CURRENT STATUS: healthy

NOTES: New personal identifying sequence to be assigned
  due to collateral removal.

All the resentment I've felt toward Cormac bubbles up and mixes with this information. I slip the card into my pocket and lean against the shelf trying to slow my ragged breathing. I'll save the file in a minute; I still have to find Amie.

July 24th. Her sequence begins with 0724. The other girls' information was filed according to the sector of relocation. I scan each row of files until I find the cubes for the Northern Sector. Rushing down the row, I scan the tiny compartments, watching the numbers build in size. I've reached 0618 when I hear a door click to the north of me. I hold my breath as the tap of dress heels echoes in the silent room.

Creeping to the edge of this unit, I peer around the corner. No one. Snaking along the side, I steadily move back to the opening I've left between the repository and Loricel's studio.

The door clicks open again. I wait, praying the intruder is gone, but instead I hear another person call out and the

first person heads back toward the door. I press against the side of a shelf, not daring to move forward. Two male voices echo through the room, but I don't pay attention to what they're saying. I hear their footsteps coming nearer to my hiding spot. I slip to the next set of shelves and wait breathlessly, gauging how close they are to me now. Then to the next. And the next.

I've reached the rift when one of them shouts. My hand grips the card in my pocket; I forgot to shut the door to its cubby. I throw myself through the rift as the repository lights brighten; they're looking for me. Pulling the repository's threads from the spot where I wove it into the fabric of Loricel's room, I clutch the strands against my chest. As soon as I've put the strands back in their place, completing the repository in the compound's weave, the loom whirs to life and dismisses the piece. I drop to the chair and listen for approaching guards. No one knows I can do this except Loricel, but how long before someone becomes suspicious? And even if they aren't looking for me, this is the first place they'll come to find out who's responsible.

But when no one appears, I relax. It's only then I notice her lounging on her sedan, stroking a fluffy ginger cat. 'Loricel,' I gasp. It comes out in a gurgle of apology and surprise.

'Go.'

Her eyes won't meet mine.

'Loricel, I—'

'Leave me alone, Adelice. I need to think.'

I start to ask what she means, but she answers the question before I speak. 'I have to figure out how to cover this up.'

'I'm sorry,' I say, lifting my eyes from the floor to meet hers.

She keeps her gaze on the cat and continues to pet it. After a moment, she asks, 'Did you find what you were looking for?'

The tiny plastic card feels like a piece of lead in my pocket, but I shake my head.

'You endanger your sister by drawing attention to her,' she warns, looking at me for the first time.

'I need to know where she is,' I say.

'Cormac showed you your sister, alive and well,' Loricel says. 'It's best to leave it at that, unless . . .'

'I'm not going after her.' Not yet.

'If he perceives her as a threat, Cormac will remove her.' Loricel pushes the cat off her lap and stands.

It takes me a moment to realise she's reading the coordinates I've left on the companel. 'Ingenious plan,' she says, 'but I wonder how you found the coordinates to pull the repository's weave up on my loom.'

I bite my lip and clutch my arm around my waist, hoping she can't make out the digifile's silhouette in my pocket.

'I'm not going to tell on you, Adelice,' she says, turning to stare at the false wall. 'I told you this was your choice, and I meant it. But you're playing a dangerous game.'

My mouth is dry. 'I'm not playing a game,' I say.

'All the same, be more careful.'

She says nothing else, so I exit the room, arms still wrapped around my waist, guarding my secrets: the truth about Jost's daughter, and a small patch of the weave from the studio's screen.

22

I manage to sneak past the guard, who's busy smoking a few metres from the door to the upper studios, but I don't return to my quarters. As soon as I'm out of his sight, I shift into a confident stride, lowering my arms to my sides and straightening my back. There's surveillance on me, and I don't want to raise any suspicion. With trembling fingers, I remove the piece of the screen from Loricel's wall from my pocket and hide it in my palm. It's only a few inches wide and featherlight, but it reflects a bit of the default scenery of the studio walls.

I say only one word: 'Jost.'

An image flickers in my hand and I take quick glances at it. Long steel tables run the length of the room and girls in short, fitted dresses carry trays of dishes to deep metal basins at the wall. Standing in a far corner, Jost directs a group of boys. As soon as they disappear from the scene,

Jost closes his eyes and pinches the bridge of his nose. He looks tired as he leans against the far wall and I'm about to add to his stress. But if I don't tell him now, I may not ever have the strength. With my free hand I draw out the digifile and consult the map. I'm right above the kitchen. For one moment, I consider turning around. I've already ruined everything between us, and nothing will be the same once he knows about Sebrina. But I think of Amie, and although it's not the same, I know I can't keep this from him. Moving to the right, I duck into the nearest stairwell. I don't even have time to think of what I'll say before the stairs deposit me near the doorway.

The maid nearest me whips her head around and stares at me, her mouth hanging open. Several others stop their dishwashing, but only one wipes her soapy hands on her apron and comes over to me.

'Miss?' she says, running her eyes over me doubtfully. 'Can I help you?'

'I need to speak with the head valet,' I say, raising my chin as regally as I can muster.

She purses her lips and squints meaningfully at me. 'Jost?'

'If that's his name,' I say, waving her off dismissively. I feel like a total bitch, but the more I act like a Spinster, the less curious they're going to get.

The maid curtsies once and heads back towards the food gens, but I catch her rolling her eyes at another girl, who giggles. One look at my face and the smile drops from hers, and she rushes back to work. They must hate me.

Jost peeks around a door in the back and his eyes widen a

bit, but he keeps his expression blank. He exchanges some words with the maid I sent and then walks towards me.

'Can I help you?' he asks. There's not even a hint of friendliness in his voice.

'Yes, I need your services,' I say, gesturing to indicate that he should follow.

'I can send one of my men with you,' he offers, his eyes flat. 'I have other responsibilities. I'm not here for your amusement.'

'I was specifically told to get you,' I repeat.

A few of the girls around us slow their work to eavesdrop on our exchange.

'In the future, you can use a companel to send for assistance,' Jost says, turning to leave me.

'I don't think I'll be needing assistance in the future.'

This stops him. To the others I'm sure my angry words sound spoiled and petty, but Jost knows me too well to dismiss them – even if he wants to.

'Lead the way,' he says with a sigh.

In the stairwell, I stop him. 'We need to talk.'

'I'm listening,' he says, crossing his arms against his chest.

'Somewhere private,' I whisper.

Jost unfolds his arms and takes a deep breath. A muscle twitches in his neck, but he nods and takes me down to the basement. As we duck through a second door, I recognise the cold paving stones.

'It's been too long,' I murmur, trailing my hand along the moist rock wall that makes up the cell area.

Jost leads me into a cell and pulls out a small handlight.

It casts a harsh glow in the room. He leans against a wall and raises one eyebrow.

'I know I hurt you—'

'No,' he says. 'I can tell by the way you say it. You don't know, Adelice.'

'I was protecting you.' I move closer to him.

'I don't need you to protect me.'

'You're such a man. Can't trust a girl do anything.'

I try to turn away, but he catches my wrist.

'I don't need you to protect me,' he repeats softly. 'I need you to trust me.'

'I do trust you, idiot,' I snap.

'Then let me in,' he says, pulling me closer.

'There's more going on here than you and me,' I say, inhaling the smell of him – smoke and sweat, something sweet like honeysuckle. I want to pull the strands around us and trap us like this forever. Safe and content, if not happy. I'm not sure happiness is possible for us any more.

'Maybe,' he whispers into my hair. 'But that's their problem. We need to worry about you and me.'

'There can't be a you and me here,' I say. My whole body is cocooned in his arms, and I press my head to his chest and listen to his steady heartbeat.

'Here is all we have,' he says, drawing my face up to meet his eyes. The electricity is back, and it threatens to overwhelm in its intensity.

Jost leans down to kiss me, but I pull away.

'We won't even have that for long,' I say in a soft voice.

His arms drop from around me, and I straighten up, fighting the urge to burrow into his chest.

'Why are you here?' he asks, barely controlling the rage in his voice.

I tell him what I've learned about Enora and how they plan to remap me. About what I've learned from Loricel about Earth and the mantle of Arras. As I speak, the coldness fades from his face, and by the time I tell him about Cormac's last visit, his hand has found mine again.

'I'm sorry,' he says, interrupting my tale. 'I've been unfair.'

I shake my head. 'I deserved it.'

'You were doing what you thought was best and I—'

'Jost,' I butt in, sensing the guilt building in his voice. 'It's in the past.'

It's tender and sincere, and maybe it's not everything I want to say about how confused but hopeful I feel. It's not the questions I want to ask or even the one thing I think I want to tell him, but it's enough.

He breaks into a wide smile and wraps his arms around me.

'You're right.'

This time I let him kiss me. It starts slowly, but I press closer to him and clutch his shoulders. He holds my waist, and then his hands, warm and strong, move slowly up my back. Everywhere they touch, my body sings out for more. His lips are soft, but I demand more, sliding my arms tight against his neck and pulling him closer. He responds, his mouth opening against mine, and I feel a tremor run through my body. Finally he pulls back, our foreheads still touching, and we breathe in quick pants against one another. His breath is hot on my face, and I struggle to remember what I came to tell him.

'We have to leave.' I force the words out before I give in to the ache building up in my chest that begs for the touch of his lips again.

'Where can we go?' he asks, straightening up but leaving his hands on my back.

'I'm still working on that.'

'But you only have a few days,' Jost says, kissing the top of my head.

'I could weave a moment,' I say, still pressed up against his neck.

'And never leave?'

'Something like that.'

'Do I need to tell you why that won't work?'

I pull out of his arms and sigh. 'That's what the Guild did, and here we are,' I point out.

'On a much larger scale,' he says, 'and it's not going too well.'

'I know. I can't leave without finding Amie anyway.'

'Amie's safe,' he says, weaving his hand through mine.

I want to believe him as much as I long to run away with him and forget everything I know about the Guild. But I can't leave Amie in Cypress, and I know he only suggests it because he doesn't have anything else to lose, except me. That's about to change though. 'Would you leave someone you loved?' I ask, fingering the digifile in my pocket with my free hand. 'If I leave, the Guild might . . .'

It's too terrible to even consider.

'Why? Out of petty revenge? They have no reason to hurt her.'

'Cormac said something once,' I confide. 'He thinks she

340

might be useful. They're hoping she has my abilities.'

'But they've never proved weaving is genetic.'

'I know that, but it won't stop them from taking her. I'm not saying I have to get to her right now, but I have to keep track of her until I know what to do.' Without realising it, I've grabbed a handful of Jost's shirt, and I'm tugging on it. He loosens my hand gently and takes it in his own.

'There's nowhere for us to go,' he reminds me. 'They'll just pull our sequences, and even if you could weave out a moment, how long before they break through that?'

'I don't know,' I say. Loricel said it was inevitable, but it's the only plan I can come up with.

'We need more time,' he grumbles.

'Good thing you're with a Creweler,' I say, giving him a half-smile.

'How will you find Amie anyway? It could take you decades to comb the weave looking for her.'

'I know her sequence, but the geographic locators will be different. They change that information when they perform an alteration,' I explain.

'But even if you had her information, you don't have the clearance to pull by personal identifying sequence, do you?' he asks.

'No, but Loricel does,' I say.

'And you think she'll let you do that?' His tone is doubtful.

'I wasn't going to ask. How do you think I got this information?'

'We need a better plan than this,' he mutters. He drops my hands and runs his through his tangled brown hair.

'I haven't told you everything,' I admit, but as much as I want to blurt out what I've found, I find myself holding back. I could ignore his past, because time separated us from it, but now that distance would be removed.

He narrows his eyes and takes a breath. 'Let me have it.'

'I know how to find Amie.' My hand closes around the digifile, and I pull it out of my pocket.

'Didn't Enora give you that?'

'Yes, and she left me some other useful information.' I slide open the weather files and show him the map.

He stares at the digital image, studying it. 'Is that the compound?'

I answer with a nod. 'Complete with coordinates. And I've already broken into the repository.'

Jost's head snaps up from the screen. 'You did what?'

'I got into the repository,' I say, trying to act like this is no big deal, because he's giving me a look that says, *Have you lost your mind?* 'I can find her.'

'What's in the room?' he asks, keeping his eyes on me.

'Datasets. Info on removals and alterations.' I don't tell him about the thin strands in the cubes or the chills they send through me. It sounds too crazy.

'And you've seen them?' he presses.

I nod and slip my hand back into my pocket. The card is still there, but I can't bring myself to give it to him.

'What did they say?'

'Basic info: ID, removal dates.' I open the first file to show him Riccard Blane's info. 'There's a tracking program on here that reads the datasets.'

'How do you think Enora got this program?' he asks, pa-

cing the small cell.

I shrug. 'She must have had help.'

'I wonder—' he begins.

'There's something else I have to tell you,' I say, jumping in before I lose my nerve.

He stops and waits.

I stare at him for a moment before speaking. I'm not sure I'll know the Jost who comes out on the other side of this information. 'Here,' I say finally, thrusting the card at him.

Taking it, he looks up at me and frowns. 'What's this?'

'Scan it.' I offer him the digifile.

I hold my breath as the dataset loads, but I know as soon as it has. His brow relaxes and his mouth opens, but he doesn't say anything. Instead, he simply drops to the ground and stares at the small pad.

'She's alive,' I say in a soft voice, because he can't find the words.

Most of the time Jost looks like a boy. Even when he hasn't shaved or is dressed in a tailored suit, the curves of his face are soft and his smile quick. But here in the sharp relief of the handlight, his jaw is angular and the slightest of lines form as he squints, studying the screen. A moment later, when a smile creeps onto his face, it's not the boyish grin I love, but something that bursts from a deeper part of him. He looks like a man.

'You found her,' he whispers, and when he looks up that unfathomable smile extends out to me.

'She's safe.' For now, I add to myself.

'She's alive,' he breathes, as though repeating the words will make them more real. 'My daughter is alive.'

343

'Amie's in there, too,' I say.

'Can we get back in?' he asks, unable to tear his eyes from the image.

'I think so,' I say. 'But I'll need your help.'

'Anything,' he promises.

'Jost,' I say, kneeling down to him, 'I don't know if we can get to her.'

He cups my face and kisses me once. A new energy pulses from his lips. His touch leaves traces of fire along my body as though he's transferred this new vitality to me. I never knew how damaged he was by his loss until now.

'We'll find a way,' he says. 'We'll find them both.'

I nod and gently pull the digifile from his hand. Without it, he snaps back into action, inviting me to share my plan. I explain that I'll need his help getting back into the upper studios, but from there I can break through to the repository and find more information.

'And then?' he asks.

'Then we'll figure out what to do next,' I say. It's a horrible plan, but it's the only one we have.

Jost pretends to escort me through the compound. It's perfectly common for the head valet to chaperon a Spinster, but with Cormac on the prowl, I feel a thin veil of sweat forming across my forehead and on my palms. I do my best to look bored, but my pulse is racing and I can feel heat on my cheeks.

When we reach the security door to the upper studios, the guard runs his eyes over us. 'Does he have clearance?'

'Cormac's ordered me to have an escort at all times,' I say, willing my voice not to quaver.

'I should clear it—'

'Look, man,' Jost says with a groan, pulling away from me. 'I'd like to get to bed, so the sooner we can get Her Majesty upstairs the better.'

The guard grins; he must be used to the night shift himself.

'*She's* clear, so keep close to her,' he orders him.

Jost nods and rolls his eyes a little to seal their camaraderie.

Once we're through the door, I elbow him. 'You can go to bed any time.'

'Surest way to get around in here,' he says with a wink. 'Act annoyed with a Spinster.'

I feign a wounded expression, and his hand tightens around mine.

'You are the least annoying Spinster I've met,' he says in mock solemnity.

'Watch yourself, Josten Bell,' I warn him.

He follows me up the spiral staircase, but he keeps looking over his shoulder and nearly tripping into me.

'We'll never get anywhere if you don't hurry up,' I hiss at him.

'Sorry, Your Majesty,' he says, grinning.

When we reach the top, I duck into the studio, half expecting Loricel to be sitting there, but it's empty. Motioning for Jost to join me, I move to the loom and pull out the digifile.

'What are you doing?' he asks, watching over my shoulder.

'I learned a new trick,' I tell him.

The piece of the compound flows gracefully onto the loom, and I turn to Jost to gauge his reaction. 'Isn't it beautiful?'

'What?' he asks, frowning.

'The mantle,' I say, running my finger along the weave.

'I can't see anything,' he admits sheepishly.

'I'm sorry, I didn't mean to——'

'Don't worry about it,' he stops me. 'This is your area of expertise.'

I turn my attention to the section on the loom and carefully pull out some of the strands of the repository again. Jost stands behind me quietly, but he moves closer to me when I stand to make the rift between rooms.

With Jost here, I have to focus harder on the room's weave before it comes into focus, but when it does I slip the strands in my hand into it, creating the opening. The repository, silent and dark, stretches out before us.

'How . . .' Jost asks behind me.

'Good trick, huh?' I can't help enjoying his shock a little. 'I took a piece of weave from the loom and inserted it into the weave of the room. I transplanted it to create a passage. It's like when we rebound and a Spinster moves our weave from one spot to another, except I did that with a room.'

'Okay, I think I get it,' he says. 'So we go in there and look?'

I bite my lip and then shake my head. 'I want you to stay here and keep guard. If anyone comes, warn me.'

And if I get caught, run, I add to myself, hoping he will if the moment arises.

'We should stick together,' he says in a firm voice.

'I know how it's organised in there,' I tell him. 'It will only take me a moment, and I'm quieter than you.'

'Not in those,' he says, pointing to my feet.

I grimace and slip my heels off my feet. I take a few hops in my stockings to prove my light-footedness, and he squares his shoulders and gives a reluctant nod. Handing him my shoes, I kiss his cheek lightly and slip through the opening.

The room is silent without the hum of lamps, and I hold the digifile in front of me for light. Just in time, because I almost run into the first unit. Skidding past it, I'm suddenly thankful for the slippery stockings. I make my way to the front of the shelves where I found Sebrina's file and begin searching for Amie. The individual units are organised by date according to geographic location. I have to find the Cypress files.

I comb swiftly through this aisle and move on to the next until I find the sequences that include *E*, for the Eastern Sector, and start searching for Cypress. I'm hoping it's not more than that when my finger drifts onto a unit with her date. The rest of the data, including my mother's initials, matches, and I pull out the card and scan the code. I hold my breath while the loading image blinks. And there she is: Amie Lewys.

I can't bear to look at the information pertaining to why she was rewoven, even if I know it's mostly lies. I save her dataset to the digifile and carefully slide the card back into storage. I wonder for a moment if taking the files would slow the Coventry down if they went after Sebrina or Amie, but if they have backup files it would be a red

flag. I remove Sebrina's card and tread noiselessly back to where I found it. I have to check the card twice to recall her sequence, since my first discovery was a complete accident. I'm slipping the card back into the cubby when I hear boot steps approaching. The steady clip of the approaching footfall sounds like Jost. I've been gone long enough that he might worry, but I'm not about to wait around and find out. Stealing to the side of the unit, I press against it and peek around the corner.

Clear.

I take a deep breath and move to the next set of shelves. The steps have faded away and after checking the next aisle I dart quickly back toward the rift. I'm only a few shelves from it when I see it shimmering and fading. I barely glimpse Jost on the other side as hands reach out from the other side and pull on the tear. I abandon my cautious pace and run towards the opening. It's closing rapidly, but I think I can make it. I'm nearly there when a hand catches my wrist. I scream, struggling against my captor, but he holds me back and covers my mouth with his hand. Then he pulls me into the dark, still room, away from my escape.

23

I kick hard against the man holding me in the dark repository, and he falls back with a groan, dropping his hold on me. Without missing a beat, I dash to where the rift has closed and tug frantically at the air, hoping to find a remnant of the studio. Meanwhile I hear my abductor racing in my direction.

I abandon my search and flee to a nearby shelf. It's hard to see in the dark, so I press against the shelf and creep along it. The man's footsteps slow to a walking pace. He's searching for me now. My only hope is the door to the repository. I could weave myself out of this moment and freeze the repository, but that won't protect Jost, and I have to get back to him.

Snaking from row to row, I stay close to the shelves, afraid to step too far out and reveal myself. At the last row, I spy the door. I wish I'd studied the map more closely so

that I'd know where it led. This room is connected to the research labs somehow, so it's possible I could walk right into a room of scientists. My only hope is that they've gone home for the evening, but I can't count on that. And to get to the door, I'll have to move directly into the centre aisle and make myself vulnerable to my attacker, who will definitely alert anyone in the area. It's a no-win situation, but waiting around will drive me crazy. So taking a deep breath, I bolt for the door.

I'm not fast enough. The man steps from the shadows at the end of the adjacent shelving unit and catches me around the waist. Clasping his hand over my mouth, he hisses into my ear: 'Stop fighting me, Adelice.'

I go limp in his arms, and he drops his hold. Whirling on him, I shove him hard in the chest. He stumbles, and I barely make out the annoyance flashing on his face in the dark.

'Remind me not to save your ass in the future,' Erik says, regaining his footing.

'What are you doing here?' I demand in a low voice.

'Rescuing you,' he says, rubbing his chest.

'Who closed it?'

'What?' he asks, confused.

'The opening back to the upper studios,' I whisper.

'Is that how you got in here?' he asks, matching his volume to mine.

I nod, and begin moving back to the spot where I opened the rift. Erik follows behind me, but there's nothing left of the gap. I have no idea what to do to save Jost, but every second I waste here leaves him in their clutches.

'So is this your big plan?' he asks.

'It was,' I say with a sigh. 'But I guess it's time to move on to Plan B.'

'Which is?'

'There is no Plan B yet,' I admit.

'What exactly was Plan A?' he asks.

'Get information,' I answer.

'That's all?'

'Yes.'

He grimaces. 'You need help with your plans.'

'But we have to get back. I left Jost on the other side.'

Erik stiffens as I say his name, and I'm reminded of the rigid distance the two boys usually keep from each other. 'Well, it won't take them long to figure out you're here,' he says, tugging me back toward the repository's door. 'And you wasted a lot of time hiding from me.'

'You could've called out to me,' I say in an aggravated voice.

'I'm trying to keep a low profile.' Erik glares at me, anger burning through his eyes, but his swift pace shifts to a sprint. 'Come on.'

'We've got to get to Loricel's studio,' I tell him as we run.

'I know.' His hand is on my arm, urging me along.

At the door, he stops me and straightens a loose strand of hair. Looking at my feet he frowns. 'Okay,' he says, 'this is how we're playing it. I found you in here, and I'm taking you to Cormac.'

'So I'm a prisoner?' I ask.

'Yes, so look scared.'

'That shouldn't be hard,' I mutter.

Erik opens the door and grabs my arm roughly, forcing me through. I find myself in a brightly lit hallway. Up at the other end, two guards snap to attention and head our way.

'I caught her,' Erik calls to them. 'I'm taking her to Cormac now.'

The older of the two men glances at his companion. Both of them must be ten years his senior at least.

'I have level-eighteen clearance,' he says, flashing a card from his hip pocket.

'Yes, sir,' both shout, but the eldest's voice trips on 'sir'.

I shift my eyes to the floor and drop my shoulders as Erik leads me away. Once we're around the corner, he loosens his grip on me but doesn't remove his hand.

'How did you find me?' I whisper.

'Cormac's going crazy,' he says under his breath. 'We're on level-three alert.'

'But how did you know I was here?'

'When I escorted you on the goodwill tour,' he says, glancing back at me, 'Cormac had you fitted with a tracking device—'

'No, he didn't.' I remember Enora telling me how he wanted to insert a complant, but couldn't.

'Yeah, he did,' Erik assures me. 'They put it in your food. It's programmed to lodge in your small intestine.'

My hand flies to my stomach, and I stare at him. 'So they've been tracking my every move for weeks?' I ask.

'No,' Erik says, lowering his voice further. 'I have. I corrupted their file. Only I have the tracking link now.'

'Then you . . .'

'I suppose this changes your ridiculous plan for her,' Maela sneers. No need to play nice if they're going to kill me.

'We'll proceed with the remap and go from there,' Cormac says in a quiet but firm voice.

'She'll be a better wife then anyway,' Maela says, but while she looks pleased by this, Pryana's eyes flash with anger. She must not have heard their whole plan until now. Can it be that she's actually jealous?

Jost, who hasn't moved since we entered the room, shifts against his captors and glares at them.

'Don't like the sound of that, huh?' Maela says in a mocking tone.

'Shut up, Maela,' Cormac orders.

Her victorious smile fades, and she steps back towards the empty wall.

Cormac turns to Erik, who's still holding me in place. 'Where was she?'

'In the research area, sir,' he says.

I'd hoped he would rat me out and, at least, confirm my suspicion about him, but Erik's answer leaves too much room for interpretation, and I still can't be sure what side he's on. I was in the research area, but why not tell them I was in the repository? Is he still buying me time?

'Enough of this,' Loricel says from across the room, and I turn to look at her. She keeps her gaze on Cormac and doesn't meet my eyes.

'We need to find out what she was doing,' Cormac says, striding to the loom. 'Pull up the corresponding piece of the weave.'

Loricel moves to the command panel and enters a code. The brilliant weave of the compound glides back onto the loom.

'Loricel was gracious enough to patch up the little hole you left,' Cormac tells me. 'But I'd like you to show me exactly what you did and where you went.'

I shake my head, reeling from the sting of her betrayal. 'Ask her,' I practically spit at them.

'Let me rephrase that,' Cormac says in a measured tone. 'Do it or I'll kill him right now, and then I'll rip your precious sister.'

One of the guards removes a thick black club and presses a button on it, sending steel spikes shooting out from the top. He holds it over Jost. My eyes meet Jost's, and he shakes his head slightly. But this isn't about us any more. We have to protect Amie and Sebrina.

The whole room must hear my heart racing now, but I speak slowly, careful to stay calm. 'Fine,' I agree.

Erik drops his grip on my arm, and I walk to the loom. Running my fingers over it, I frown. 'It's not here,' I announce, turning past Loricel to speak to Cormac.

'What do you mean?' he asks. 'Loricel, where is it?'

Loricel knits her eyebrows, and she leans in towards the loom. 'I must have put it back in the wrong spot.'

Cormac pinches the bridge of his nose and squeezes his eyes shut. 'This,' he says with a sigh, 'is why I need you, Adelice.'

He mutters something that sounds a lot like 'incompetence' under his breath and motions for Maela to join him. 'Go com Dr Ellysen—'

'Ambassador, he's already off-compound for the evening,' Pryana interrupts his order, standing at a companel. Maela glares over at her.

'Then,' Cormac snaps, 'call him in and tell him to prep the remap. I'm not putting this off an hour longer. If she won't do what's best for Arras, then she doesn't deserve a second chance.'

'Yes, sir,' Pryana says.

'Yes, let's just finish this up and have her transplanted all at once. And, Pryana,' he adds, 'tell him to prep for Adelice's remap in the morning.'

I whirl towards him. 'Who are you remapping tonight?' I demand.

'I'm going to miss your attitude,' he says.

Loricel clears her throat impatiently next to us. 'I'm not worth your trouble.'

I stare at her. He can't really mean to remap his only Creweler.

'Oh yes,' Loricel says with a nod. 'Cormac thinks it's worth his time to remap me.'

'I don't have the time to explain the complex principles of remapping to you, you old fogey—'

'Look who's talking,' she cries, straightening up. 'At least I have some dignity.'

'Take her into custody,' Cormac commands, turning his back on her.

One of the guards drops his hold on Jost and moves towards Loricel, while the other drops the club and pulls Jost up into a choke hold.

'It's too dangerous,' I remind Cormac, my voice break-

ing with desperation. 'What will you do without her?'

'I'll have you,' he says, unmoved.

'And if you lose me, are you willing to risk Arras to have your precious control?'

'We have time, and your sister will be ready before our raw materials run out,' he says, staring me down.

'She can't weave,' I say, shaking my head. 'She won't be of any use to you.'

'If you already demonstrate the ability, she might have the recessive gene. Our scientists believe they can access the dormant gene and activate it.' He pauses to let this sink in. 'I've done some checking up on her. She'll be a suitable substitute in every duty Arras demands.' Cormac's smile is mocking, twisting into something more wicked and heartless at his final threat than I've seen from him before.

It hits me like a blow to the stomach. Even if I comply with his wishes, Amie isn't safe. I look at Jost, and his eyes meet mine. Even now – bent and broken – there's strength in his gaze. He hasn't given up, so I can't either.

Maela saunters back towards the loom, and with a quick glance at Loricel, she smirks at me. She's so close her over-applied perfume makes me gag.

'The doctor is coming, and Pryana is on her way to the clinic. And I'd be happy to take care of that problem for you,' she tells Cormac, tossing her head toward Jost.

My fist flies and makes hard contact with her jaw. My knuckles sing where they crack against bone. It hurts in a very satisfying way.

'This is why I told them you weren't ready, little girl,' Maela screams, wiping the blood from her lip.

The words sizzle like spat venom. I can feel the hatred in them. I raise one eyebrow at her, and she glares in response, but Erik steps forward and seizes her arm.

'Let me go,' she says, wrenching free from him. 'You're on her side.'

'I'm keeping you from making a mistake,' he warns her in a low voice.

'Sell it somewhere else, Erik. You think I don't know that you're helping her? At first I thought, *Let him bed her. It will take care of both our problems.* I was counting on you to ruin her,' Maela says, lurching towards him and grabbing him by the collar. Under her rage, her eyes reflect the wounds caused by his betrayal.

Detaching her fingers, Erik pushes her gently away. 'Now's not the time.'

Spinning back, she glowers at me over the loom. 'You're playing a dangerous game. Do you think you can save him and yourself? Your life is over, Adelice. You've proved you could never take over here. You don't have the stomach,' she growls, 'or the smarts.'

And then she laughs, and it's like she's injected me with some type of stimulant, because the weave of the room zooms into focus in front of my eyes, and I seize the strands of it with my left hand, rending it in two at my feet. The room splits down the middle, and Maela screams at the crack in the middle. It's a terrifying sight: a black abyss broken by shimmering, interlocking light. This would panic most people. They might run. They might go pale and clutch against the wall as Maela has. To his credit, Cormac looks curious, but maintains his position. Silently, I will

him to step forward, imagining myself pushing him down to an unknown fate, but he's clever and he keeps his wits. And his life.

'I may be *dumb* –' I linger on the last word for Jost's benefit, in an effort to catch his attention; maybe if he's watching closely he can foresee my next play – 'but let's see you do that,' I chide her.

Maela lets out a low hissing noise, and I realise she's stifling hysteria. For a moment, it appears I've driven her genuinely crazy, but Loricel steps in. She's on the other side of the rift, and the guard has lost his grip on her in the chaos. I can see her eyes growing hard with determination. There is no amused sparkle or friendly warmth in them now. They are cold, set, green.

'Adelice, you have the power to stop this,' she reminds me.

'I know,' I murmur. 'I just can't think of a good reason to.'

'You know what will happen,' Loricel insists, gesturing to Jost. 'Will you leave him here to die for you? What about your sister? What about me?'

I almost laugh until I realise she's speaking in earnest.

'Let's see. I can save a man who's been revealed a traitor to the Guild. Why? So they can torture him for information? So they can keep him alive, but in agony, to try to keep me in line? You know, Loricel! You know what they're capable of!' I'm shouting, and it sends a tremor down the open tear. Maela presses herself harder against the wall.

'Tsk, tsk, Maela. Who's afraid of the bad little girl?' I gloat, making no effort to hide the mocking in my voice.

One way or another, the charade between us ends tonight. Might as well get in a few good jabs while I can.

'I'm going to need you to loosen up on him a bit,' I order the guard holding Jost, stretching my hands as if to reach out and destroy more of the frail tapestry of the room.

He glares at me for a moment, and I meet his intent gaze, unblinking, until he drops his arms. It's a surer sign of defeat than anyone else in the room has shown. I edge closer to Jost, but I don't reach out for him.

Loricel is still thinking, and I know why. She also has the power to close the rift. This raises the question of why she hasn't yet, and I have to assume she still hasn't chosen a side.

'What do they have left to hold over you?' I ask her softly. 'They're going to kill you. Worse – they're going to exploit your gift.'

She smirks in a mirthless, bitter way, curling her withering lower lip into a scowl. 'They have nothing on me.'

'I know,' I say. 'But do you?'

Her hard eyes flash with fire, for a moment losing their coldness. 'You've put us in an impossible situation.'

'Not impossible,' I say lightly. 'Just challenging. Nothing is impossible for a Creweler.'

'Except reality,' she reminds me.

'Except reality,' I echo. I'm not sure what she means, but I know it's important.

And then it hits me. Reality is impossible for us to control because we work within Arras. Our talent lies in stretching and shifting. Outside of Arras, we're nothing. We only create illusion, and the sparkling, open void re-

vealed before us is only another piece of that illusion. Beneath it lies something else, a reality only I can discover. A place where Cormac wouldn't dare follow me. Earth.

But I can't leave Jost. Or Loricel. Or my sister. Because the truth is that while I'm sure I can find my way out, I don't know if I can find my way back. All eyes are on me, waiting for a response.

'Enough of this,' Cormac demands. 'I've had enough of this drama. Adelice, like it or not, you're responsible for every life in Arras. Stop acting like a spoiled child and fix this.' He's remarkably calm, but he stays firmly planted to his spot, a good distance away from the hole.

'That's just it,' I say to him. 'You treat us like children. But I know the truth.'

'We don't need her any more, Cormac,' Maela calls out. 'We'll have Loricel's skills transplanted, and there are those of us who'd make much better wives.'

'Like you?' he asks scornfully.

She falls back at the harsh rebuke. Personally, I don't think even Maela deserves to put up with this much cruelty, but it's just what I need to get her where I want her.

'Maela,' I say slowly, baiting the trap, 'do you know how to do anything other than mutilate a piece of time?'

She glares at me, still standing firmly against the wall. Erik bristles next to her but stays silent. I need her to move if I'm going to kill two birds with one stone. Or at least knock them out.

'Remember that night in the courtyard when you caught me with Erik?' I taunt, but she stays still.

She stiffens at the recollection. I'm counting on her extreme mood swings to work in my favour for once.

'Oh c'mon. You can dish it out but you can't take it? You know, I never even gave him a moment's thought before that. He sought me out.' I can see Erik's bright eyes travelling from Maela's face to mine. I try to keep my gaze directed at her now, because I know this revelation will be painful for Jost. But not as painful as the one I've just had. I know why Erik is caught in the middle of this fight, and it's not because of me. The truth was always tugging at my mind, and I refused to see, but now it's so obvious I can't believe they don't all see it. The eyes should have been enough, but there were other clues. Both from a fishing village. The pained looks that crossed their faces when they saw each other. How they seem to hate each other.

'Well, I'm glad Erik kissed me,' I say, planting my feet a bit firmer in my spot. 'It gave me something to compare to Jost's kiss.'

I risk a glance at Jost and Erik. Jost's puzzlement gives way to a look of betrayal, but Erik is watching me, trying to work out what I'm saying.

'I never realised until now how similar your eyes are,' I tell them, and Erik's gaze widens a bit as he finally understands. 'But it's that and the way you kiss that tells me you're brothers.'

It hits the room like a bomb, ripping through the minds of everyone listening. Someday I'll tell Jost I had to do this to bait Maela and apologise, but there's no time now. Maela doesn't try to act calm. She flies at Erik for hiding the information. Considering her size, it might not have done

much. Except I've left a gaping hole open in the middle of the room, and they tumble towards it. The stunned guard doesn't move, and I dare one brief look at Loricel. Her face says it all: she won't interfere.

Snapping to, I lunge toward Jost and grab his arm as Maela sends Erik over the edge of the tear. There's no sound as he falls, although I can see his mouth open. She teeters on the edge but doesn't fall. I've lost too many moments already, and each second counts. Thankfully, Jost is too weakened from the beating he took to protest as I throw us into the hole at our feet. I have enough time to see Loricel break away and move forward to begin the repair. She's fast, and I know she'll get it done before they can stop her, but she'll pay dearly. In the end, she gave me my choice.

The golden light sparkles and cracks around us, but I don't know if it's because the rift is closing or because we're falling too quickly through the raw weave between Arras and Earth. Jost has placed his arms protectively around my waist. If he's in pain, it's the least of his worries now. He must really trust me not to be screaming in my ear; or maybe despite our closeness he can't speak here. Tumbling forwards, I latch on to a strand and wrench us faster along the rough weave, moving closer and closer to Erik, who seems too far beyond our reach.

Theoretically, we could be falling forever, but I'm not exactly eager to test this. I can't leave Erik here alone though. He's twisted his head and caught sight of us. Catching on, he propels his body around so that he is falling backwards, facing us, and watching my progress. And then

something amazing happens. Maybe it's the rough, thick texture of this weave or maybe, like me, he can actually see the strands, because he reaches out and grabs at them until his hand catches one. He's still falling, but he's slowed his progress.

Jost throws his weight against me, pushing us to accelerate until he is able to reach out with his free hand and clasp it over the outstretched hand of his brother.

It would be a real moment if we weren't stuck in some void between worlds. At least I have a plan – thanks to Loricel. Well, an idea really, and I can only hope it works. Now that Jost and Erik are both safely within my control, I let go of the strand, and we slide faster along the mantle. As we hit the strands, sparks fly and bits fray. I can only imagine the damage we're doing. It's the kind of repair work they'll need a Creweler for. Maybe I'm buying Loricel some time, though I'm not sure that's doing her a favour.

Jost's hand stays closed over Erik's, and his arm is still tight against my waist. My hands are free so I reach into the strands and rip as hard as I can, wiggling my fingers under the coarse weave under Arras, and then my hands slip into something cool. Night air. The raw weave's strands are thick and tightly woven against one another and getting one hand through is exhausting, but there's a strange sense of accomplishment when I realise I've stopped our fall.

Of course, now we're floating in an extended void, so best not to get cocky. We are outside the reality of Arras and its physical laws, but honestly, I have no idea what to expect on the surface of Earth. If Loricel is right and there's nothing left, I'll have killed us all. I'm not sure I'm ready

to face that possibility, but I like the idea of slowly wasting away as we fall through strands of time even less.

If Jost and Erik want to know what I'm doing, they don't ask. Even though I can't hear them here, I would be able to see their mouths moving, but they remain tight-lipped. Right now they seem intent on letting me continue my manipulation of the strands and ignoring each other. Whatever brotherly love might exist between them, they aren't exactly giddy at their reunion. But there's no time for distractions. I push these concerns out of my mind and work harder at opening a new rift. Once it's big enough to stick an arm through it occurs to me that it might be smart to poke my head in and get a look at what I've got myself into. I don't want to drop us into the middle of an ocean after all.

I barely make out a cry of protest from one of the boys as I wiggle my head into the misplaced strands. It's dark. A large full moon casts a faint glow on shadowy objects all around me. I'm hanging above a street edged by a row of buildings. The light bounces off the black and in the distance it fades to twinkling gold. There's a stillness to the scene that makes it feel false. Another illusion. But as if to contradict me, a soft breeze brushes my face and tosses my hair. The scene remains relatively unchanged, but as my eyes adjust, I make out the wind tossing stray debris across the road. I hear the scrape of paper on concrete.

The good news is that we are not hovering over the middle of the ocean, but the bad news is that I have no idea where we are or what to expect of this world – Earth. It's more desolate than I imagined, which seems stupid, be-

cause I know there is no one left living on this layer. But there's shelter and, if we're lucky, maybe food. I suppose I thought others might have made their way out, but how could they without a Creweler?

Without me?

Regardless, it's the best option we have. I could try to open a rift and bring us back into Arras, but that would be even more dangerous. Loricel may have helped us escape, but she won't be in a position to help us if we return. I can't be sure she's even alive, and they'll be watching for our personal identifying sequences in the weave. No, it's not safe to return, so there's no other choice. Pulling back into the open weave, I work faster, more sure of myself now that I know we'll be safe when the entrance is large enough. I don't bother to look at either Jost or Erik. I'll have to deal with that drama later. Right now I have a job to do.

Time is coarser in the raw weave and my already scarred fingers soon begin to feel the work, despite the calloused tips Maela gave me. Having two other lives here depending on me, and desperately needing to get through and figure out what to do about Sebrina and Amie, I ignore the ache in my hands. They're in danger every second we waste on the surface, and, unlike during the moments I wove within the Coventry, time will continue to move forward in both realities.

When I finally manage to carve out a wide enough gap, I nod dramatically to let my companions know we need to go through. I see Jost's mouth moving, and his eyes squint in concern. I shake my head to let him know I can't hear

him and reach out with my free hand to suggest that he should enter. His mouth forms one word that's easy enough to read: No. Fine. Sooner or later he's going to want to come through. Of course, if I let go of him, he'll return to falling and probably never find this open space again. About the time I realise I'm chewing on the inside of my cheek, Erik impatiently struggles to the open spot. His left arm is still on my waist, and he pulls me along with him, like he's swimming in the air. When his free arm slips through the hole, he releases me and catapults himself forward, disappearing entirely. I turn back to Jost and raise my eyebrows. His arm tightens around me, and he frowns, but seems to realise that anything's better than being stuck in this interspace. Moving forward more slowly than his brother, he smoothly pulls me along until we are at the mouth of the opening. Looking at me for reassurance, he takes a deep breath and drags us both through. We land in a pile of crumbling concrete; it looks like the remains of a road. Apparently my hole wasn't exactly flush with the ground of the real world, but it's not so bad. We could have fallen much further.

'I thought maybe you were dropping me off,' Erik calls to us, his usually droll voice flat. He's already on the edge of the ruins, and he doesn't stop for us.

'Dare to dream,' Jost grumbles back.

And there it is. The first words they've spoken as brothers in front of me. The exchange adds a chill to the frigid night air. Erik stalks forward until I see only his silhouette in the moonlight. We watch him make his way into the metro beyond us, and Jost puts his arm around me.

I shiver in his embrace, staring out at the abandoned remains of Earth. Here time seems to stand still, and yet all around me are signs of decay — the natural erosion of a place forsaken by men. We linger in a moment suspended on the verge of possibility and ruin. But before I can reach out to break its mysterious hold, on the horizon a bloated mass appears, a ship in the air, flying low along the skyline, and from it a sweeping light bursts forth, as though to welcome us back home.

END OF BOOK ONE

ACKNOWLEDGEMENTS

As this is the closest I will ever come to an Oscar acceptance speech, I would like you to imagine me in a beautiful gown clutching this book as you read. Now that you have the proper visual, let us proceed.

Many thanks are owed to my agent extraordinaire, Mollie Glick, whose passion never ceases to amaze. Thanks for getting on that plane. A similar debt of gratitude is due to Janine O'Malley, who understood the book from day one and is the best editor a girl could ask for. And to Beth Potter, who helped me navigate part of the editorial journey. This novel is infinitely better thanks to you three.

My sincere thanks to Simon Boughton and Jon Yaged, who made me feel right at home in my new house. I can't express how grateful I am for the team at Farrar Straus Giroux and Macmillan.

I'm proud to call Foundry Literary + Media my agency.

Thank you to Hannah Brown Gordon and Katie Hamblin for answering all my emails.

I would be a lonely girl if it weren't for my writing friends, who have been with me every step of this crazy adventure. Thank you, Bethany Hagen and Robin Lucas for laughing, crying, and screaming with me, and Kalen O'Donnell, who came late to the party, but decided to stay.

My husband informs me that my wrap-it-up music is playing and that I can't thank every English teacher I ever had, so I'll hit the highlights: Bob Brennan and Alan Hunter, who both kept me reading during the lost years, aka high school. Dr Miriam Fuller, who taught me to look at stories more closely. And Dr Devoney Looser and Dr George Justice, who somehow always knew I had it in me despite evidence to the contrary.

Most important, thank you to my family, who never laughed when I said I wanted to write books but rather cheered me from the margins. To my children, who accepted my 'job' early on and proudly proclaimed 'Mommy writes books' to strangers. And to Josh – my first reader, my first everything – thank you.

THE SPARK

Showcase your creative skills

Are you between 13 and 16 years old? Do you have an interest in creativity and reading?

The Spark, hosted on Facebook, invites you to take part in some exciting projects around acting, film-making, writing and music, each linked to and inspired by a Faber book.

Become a member of a vibrant community and meet like-minded people who love reading and creating. We want you to help spread the word and get everyone involved.

Find out more by 'liking' our Facebook page or on Twitter @thesparkfeed

CREWEL